COPPER LAKE

Book Three in the Stutter Creek series

by
ANN SWANN

5 PRINCE PUBLISHING AND BOOKS, LLC
PO Box 16507
Denver, CO 80216
www.5PrinceBooks.com

Print 13: 978-1-63112-142-5   10:1631121421
Copper Lake
Ann Swann
Copyright Ann Swann 2016
Published by 5 Prince Publishing

Front Cover Ermisenda Alvarez

First Edition/First Printing January 2016 Printed U.S.A.

5 PRINCE PUBLISHING AND BOOKS, LLC.

Acknowledgements:

Shout out to Brandi Dagwan who won the contest to have a character named after her in this book. I think she made an excellent Forensic Assistant.

Acknowledgments

Dedications:

Dedicated to my daughter, author Sara Barnard, one of the strongest women I know. And also to the members of my writing group who do not care that I am twisted and weird.

Dear Reader,

Please note that Billy the Kid did not hide out in The Drugstore Café as it exists solely in my imagination. The map coordinates mentioned in the story are real public places such as hotels. I didn't want readers attempting to follow the cartographer's trail into the forests of New Mexico.

Ann Swann

COPPER LAKE

PROLOGUE

The bones were wet and cold. The clay in the soil trapped the moisture as efficiently as a layer of mulch in a flower bed. When Edgar held the femur up to the moonlight, he was thrilled to observe how fully the dirt and mold had settled into the cuts. It created an inky labyrinthine abstract on the once-white surface. He caressed the soil around the bones, and then lifted the rest of them from their shallow bed.

"Welcome back," he whispered.

It took hours to finish his work, but he didn't think of his other girl even once. Well, not more than once, maybe twice at the most. The main thing was, he no longer felt trapped. As soon as he'd begun to free the bones, he'd begun to free himself, too. His mood lightened. His outlook improved. The world looked brighter, even beneath the moon.

He felt so light by the time he finished; it was as if his feet no longer touched the ground. Starting back down the trail, he realized he didn't want to leave.

I have my hiking gear in the car, my sleeping bag, water, an energy bar, maybe even a package of trail mix.

He grew so excited, the flesh of his scalp tingled.

I'm doing it. I'm going to spend the night with my girl.

My best girl.

Sunrise coated the bones in gold. The fleshless form now reclined on a soft bed of clover. Miniscule pink flowers cradled the skull, nature's perfect pillow. Edgar gazed upon his work. "Good morning, pretty girl. I'm sorry I kept you in the dark for so long."

He unzipped his sleeping bag and pulled out his phone. There hadn't been enough light for a photo the night before, but this morning the light was perfect. He took pictures from every angle, recalling how he'd spent the entire night right beside her, drying the bones and arranging them just so.

I'd like to post them. Show the world my best girl. Instagram, Twitter, Facebook. The front page of the local newspaper…

But he knew he wouldn't do that. He wanted recognition, not incarceration.

I'll share them this way. Anonymously.

After he'd put off leaving for as long as he possibly could, Edgar zipped his nylon backpack and rolled up his sleeping bag. He ate the energy bar and drank the rest of his water before making a final pass around the scene. He was thorough. Nothing left to chance.

Satisfied everything was perfect, Edgar took one last, long look before hiking back to his car. He stowed the gear in the trunk, then wiped his hands and face with the wet wipes he kept there. He could imagine the grave dirt caked in the creases beside the ridgeline of his nose and sure enough, when he pulled the first wipe away, the white towelette was black with grime. He went over every inch of his face, neck, hands, and wrists before placing everything into a plastic bag. He planned to dispose of the bag in a dumpster on the way home.

Edgar closed the trunk, dusted the dirt and leaves from his trousers and shoes, and then climbed into the driver's seat of his champagne-colored Toyota Camry.

He glanced into the rearview mirror to make certain his face was clean. He was almost disappointed to see his same pale blue eyes looking back at him. He'd half-expected something would have changed, that some youthful spark would have returned to his gaze. But no, his usual unpleasant countenance stared back.

He conjured up the image of the numbers he'd carved into the bones so long ago before he'd buried them. *They'll never figure it out, but they'll wonder.* He pulled his shirt sleeve down over his bony wrist to cover the faded tattoo that matched the numbers he'd carved into the femur.

Oh, how they'll wonder.

CHAPTER ONE
Million-Dollar View

Kendra Dean picked up her coffee cup and drained the cold dregs before drowning it in the soapy dishwater. It was the last dirty dish. There was nothing left to clean. She'd wiped all the countertops with disinfectant wipes and checked the fridge to see if anything needed to be thrown out. Yesterday she'd swept and vacuumed the entire house and washed all the laundry.

Unlike the last few months of her life, everything here was spotless and orderly.

The kitchen radio played classic hits from decades past. Journey's anthem to fidelity, *Faithfully*, wafted across her consciousness as she stood watching the dishwater swirl away down the dark throat of the stainless steel drain. She tried not to see the parallel between the disappearing suds and the unraveling threads of her own life.

Anger bubbled up as the soap swirled away. She'd never been one for self-pity, had no use for those who wallowed in it.

She wiped her teary face with the back of her hand just as her peripheral vision caught the movement of a car pulling into the driveway outside the kitchen window.

Kendra watched as her partner Detective Woody James climbed from the driver's seat and gazed around.

Her heart thumped in her chest. *What's he doing here?* She straightened her spine and shoved her hair out of her eyes. Thinking of her unkempt salt-n-pepper mop, Kendra suddenly wished she'd taken the time to find a salon in her new town.

She opened the door before he rang the bell. Like any good detective, Woody stood just off the wide porch looking things over.

"You lost?" She was glad to hear that her voice came out as steely as ever. She hoped he didn't know how difficult it was to make it sound that way.

His blue eyes met her brown ones. "So it's true. You've gone native."

She put her finger to her lips. "Shh, don't tell my attorney. He thinks I'm still at my desk."

Grinning, he took the porch steps by twos and enveloped her in a stiff hug. "How's it goin', boss?"

She extracted herself from his embrace and tilted her splayed fingers back and forth in the air. "Been better, been worse." Then she ushered him into the house.

"This is great if you like living off the grid." He leaned down and peered out the living room window as he spoke. "Gotta admit, though. That is *some* view."

"Copper Lake." She smiled. "At sunset you can really see where it gets the name."

Woody whistled. "Million dollar view on a Sherlock's budget? You must know where *someone's* skeletons are buried."

Kendra bent her lanky frame into the corner of the nubby brown sofa. "Nope. Just happened upon a bargain. The guy who owns the place had a stroke. He's staying with one of his kids while they decide if he can come back or not." She glanced around the cozy space. "I suppose they thought a semi-retired detective would take care of it. It's not too bad for nineteen seventies chic."

She knew her face still reflected her chronic insomnia, but she prayed it no longer reflected the devastation of that horrific bad-joke-week when her husband of over two decades told her he needed "some space" right after she'd been accused of pushing a robbery suspect in front of a UPS truck.

Woody sat across from her in the matching armchair. "So, how are you sleeping?"

Her partner knew her too well.

"Oh, about like you'd expect of someone who's on suspension and under threat of a civil suit." Her right knee bounced up and down.

"Ken—"

She ignored him. "What if the perp's wife files a suit against me? Think the county will invite me back to my desk? More likely they'll simply make my vacation permanent."

Woody cleared his throat. "C'mon. We both know the creep robbed that store and beat the owner half to death. And everyone with any sense knows you didn't push him in front of that truck. Why would you? He obviously offed himself." He grimaced. "We just have to find out why."

Kendra shook her head. "He was in my custody when he did it. Who would have dreamed he would dive in front of a truck still wearing my cuffs? I've asked myself a million times why he would do that. It wasn't as if he was looking at a murder charge. Last I heard, the poor old store owner is still on life support." She swiped her too-long bangs to one side. "I just wish I had access to the files."

"Look, we know the investigation will eventually reveal the truth. There was something else going on with that creep, of that I have no doubt."

"But what if we don't prove it? I'm stuck here, in limbo, prevented from going near the case, and I'm beginning to wonder…"

"Wonder what?"

"The old man said Rudy did it—and the perp's name isn't even Rudy."

Woody shrugged. "Yeah, but the other employees explained that the old man called the guy Rudy because he reminded him of his dead son—the war hero."

Kendra stilled her knee with her palm. "Right. One even said that the uncanny resemblance was the only reason the old guy had hired him. Said they all thought he was a lowlife from the get go."

Woody moved to the sofa beside her. "Just give me a chance to figure it out. I'm working on it. I promise."

But what if I was wrong, and there really is another Rudy out there somewhere, laughing up his sleeve? "I can't keep the what-ifs from chasing each other round and round in my head." She smiled again, but it took some effort. "I thought it would be better out here since I'm on paid leave, but it's driving me crazy. Being away from it, I'm second-guessing everything that happened."

A sparrow on the windowsill suddenly seemed to require her undivided attention. Her voice dropped to a whisper. "And sometimes it's so unbelievably quiet I want to scream just to see if I still can."

Woody stood and headed back to the door. "That's why I'm here, boss lady."

Kendra watched him through the window. Tall and fidgety, his surfer-boy blond hair curled around his ears and scratched at his eyebrows. He looked good in a suit, but he would have looked more comfortable in board shorts and a tan.

Unfortunately, they lived in the mountains, not near the beach. He always talked about getting out on the ski slopes at Angel Fire, since he could no longer surf like he did back home in California, but he never seemed to get around to it.

"What brought all this on?" Kendra asked when he returned holding a bottle of wine and a bucket of Kentucky Fried Chicken.

"Peace offering," he replied.

"For what? You haven't done anything." She directed him to the kitchen table. "Can't believe you drove all the way out here from Pine River just to bring me wine and fried chicken."

"It's only thirty miles," he replied, moving around the dining room as if he owned the place. "Where are the plates and napkins? How about glasses?"

"Woody, stop."

He kept moving.

Kendra blew out her breath impatiently. She couldn't believe he was actually here, in her new space, bringing all the old stuff with him.

"Woody."

Still no response, he simply plunged ahead, searching.

She turned up the volume. "Detective!"

That stopped him.

He turned to her, bucket and bottle in hand, questions knitting his brow. "Not hungry?" His expression reminded her of a toddler, innocent but mischievous.

"What the hell are you *really* doing here?" She tried to make her voice as harsh as possible, steely like before, that of the senior detective questioning the rookie, even though he hadn't been the rookie for years.

He set the bottle on the table with a thunk. "—worried about you." He carefully placed the cardboard chicken bucket beside the wine.

She'd caught only the last half of his reply. "Worried, why?"

He stood by the table, hands empty, back straight. "Because I wasn't there," he said, "the one time in my life I actually had the flu."

Kendra groaned, moved to the cabinet to retrieve plates and forks. "Be glad you were gone, otherwise…" She looked around the old-fashioned kitchen. "This could be you."

He didn't reply to that. They both knew she was right. If he'd been at work, he would probably be on suspension now, too. On the other hand, with two of them, the suspect would have been sandwiched between them. Maybe it all could've been avoided.

At last he said, "I don't care about all that. I just came to see you." His gaze sought hers. "How are you really doing?"

Kendra closed the cabinet harder than she intended. "Woody, please. This is difficult enough—"

"Don't let it beat you down, Ken. You're better than that."

She straightened her back, moved toward the table, plates in hand. "It's not going to beat me down. It was a good collar. I'm not hiding from that. The investigation will eventually show what really happened—I know it will. I'm just tired, Woods." She set the plates down gently. "Tired of all the crap. All the ugliness. Tired of beating my head against the wall. I mean, *damn*. I took that vicious creep off the street and look where it got me. All because he took the coward's way out."

The younger detective leaned forward, hands splayed on either side of the plate she'd set in front of him. "Yep. That's exactly right. He took the coward's way out, and now we just have to figure out why. Why *did* he off himself? What were you about to find out about him while he was in custody?" He stopped talking and waited until she looked at him. "I'll find out, don't you worry."

"Thank you," she said simply. "I know you'll do your best."

He held up his hand. "Let's change the subject. What about you and Bill? Is it over?"

Her face suddenly felt skinned. She'd hadn't bothered with makeup since she was no longer going to work. Now she imagined how naked her eyes must look in the absence of their usual black liner. "How'd you know about Bill? And for that matter, how'd you even know where to find me? I specifically kept that from everyone but Internal Affairs—and they're supposed to be discreet."

He laughed and straightened up, breaking the tension at last. "You trained me, Detective Dean. I'm guessing you already know how I found you."

She pulled out a chair and plopped down, chin in hand. "So everyone knows about Bill and me?"

Woody sat opposite her. "There's talk. Does it matter?"

"No, it doesn't matter." She spun the salt shaker on its heavy base. "Of course it matters. What are they saying? I thought since my cell phone number was the same, no one would even know I'd changed my address."

His hand lay dangerously close to hers on the tabletop. "Bill came by the station looking for you one day."

She nodded. "Ahhh. Well, I never thought of that. Wonder why he didn't just call me?"

"I thought it was strange, too. I take it you guys aren't speaking?"

Kendra pressed the pad of her index finger to the tabletop where a few grains of salt had spilled. "We were barely speaking for the last *year*. Or so it seems now. I think it was the job—I just got to where I had trouble turning it off."

Her partner nodded. "Yeah. Guess that's why I'm not in a relationship, either." He stood abruptly and crossed to the glass-front china cabinet where he removed two wine glasses. "One of the reasons anyhow." He began to rummage in the drawers in search of something.

"Third drawer from the sink," Kendra said.

He found what he was looking for and crossed back to the table holding the corkscrew in one hand and the wine glasses in the other.

She took the opener and popped the cork on the bottle he'd brought. Tipping the wine into the glasses, she set his glass back across the table. "I appreciate you coming to check on me," she avoided his gaze, "but I think it's best if we don't make it a habit. The investigation, you know. I'm not supposed to be involved. Besides, you still have to go to work every day. Wouldn't want to sully your reputation."

Woody grumbled and raised his glass. "Let's at least have a toast…"

She withheld her glass, curling it into her chest. "To?"

"Retirement?"

"How about forced pseudo-retirement and impending divorce? Double toast."

Woody touched his glass to hers. "To that, then. A double toast, suckiness and all."

Kendra laughed. "To suckiness—*that* I can drink to."

He grinned and threw his wine back in one gulp.

She reached into the chicken bucket in search of a drumstick. "You always could make me laugh. Now, where are the sides? Don't tell me you forgot the damn taters and gravy, Rookie."

He stood, poured and downed a second glass of wine, and strode back out the front door. In moments, he was back with a KFC bag. "Sides," he said, removing the small Styrofoam containers.

They ate in near silence, their old comfortable camaraderie settling down around them at last.

Afterward, they cleaned up the kitchen and retreated to the porch with the last of the wine.

"It really is nice here. Quiet."

Kendra nodded. "Very quiet. I do a lot of hiking. Some fishing, too."

Woody finished off his last splash of wine. "I'd like to try it. Fishing, I mean. Maybe on the weekend?"

"It's good to see you," Kendra began. "But just because I'm not your boss right now doesn't mean our relationship has changed." She measured her words. "I meant what I said about making this a one-time deal."

Woody chuckled softly. "Friends then," he said. "Fishing buddies *someday*."

Kendra shook her head and exhaled forcefully. "We *are* friends; we *were* co-workers. Now, we're friends and ex-coworkers. That's all. Can't be anything more. Regardless of what Bill—or anyone else—thinks." She stood, placed one foot on the porch rail, and drained her glass of wine.

Woody stood, too. He was a good two inches taller than his nearly six-foot cohort. "That's harsh, Ken. Even for you."

"I think we both know what the scuttlebutt would be if folks found out we were spending our leisure time together. Heaven knows I sometimes heard it even before I left." She cleared her throat. "Internal Affairs says I can't afford any more drama."

Woody held his hands up in a gesture of surrender and then started down the steps toward his car. "Understood. But I hope we can still talk, at least. Dirks is my new *temporary* partner. I'm going to need a sounding, board."

Kendra guffawed, a strong braying sound. "Dirks? Brad Dirks? Oh my God. I hope you can keep him out of the bar long enough to do some work."

Woody didn't laugh. Instead, he turned around just as she walked down the steps behind him. "I'll call you. I still need your input. Even though you *say* you taught me everything you know." He reached up and brushed her jaw with the back of his index finger.

"Woodrow…"

He silenced her lips with the broad pad of his thumb. "I know what you're going to say. You don't have to say it again. I know we can't be anything but friends. Even though you're not my boss anymore."

She turned her head. "C'mon, Woods. Besides all the work drama, you know damn good and well I'm almost old enough to be your mother. In fact, I just found out my eldest daughter, Carrie, is pregnant—"

He threw his head back in a laugh that matched hers. "You'll be the sexiest grandmother around."

She waved her hand dismissively. "You're downright crazy."

"Yep," he murmured. "You know that much is true."

Kendra herded him toward the car with a little shove. He had managed to catch her off guard. Not many people could do that. "Good luck with your new partner," she said. "And thanks for dinner."

He smiled crookedly. "It sucks without you there, Ken. Seriously. You *are* coming back when the investigation is over. You can't *really* take early retirement."

She looked off into the distance. "I don't know. Everything feels so different."

He opened the car door. "This silence will be your undoing. You're a woman of action. Lead detective. The best."

"Go home, Woodrow. Get some rest. You'll be doing the job for both you and your new partner, as I'm positive you already know."

"Sure you don't want a fishing buddy?" His voice was back to its normal jolly timbre. "I'm a hell of a hooker." He leered at her.

"I can bait my own hooks, thank you." She watched as he climbed into the maroon Mercury, folding his long legs carefully beneath the steering wheel. "But seriously, you didn't have to come all the way out here—I appreciate it."

"You know why I'm here." His tone was solemn. "I don't know for certain what happened with you and Bill, but you know I care about you. And all that other stuff—the investigation—that's just bullshit. It'll go away eventually. Everyone knows you're the best detective in all of New Mexico." He pulled the car door closed and slipped the gearshift into drive. "And by the way, telling the sheriff you were going to stay with your sister might hide you from most of the office, but I knew you didn't have a sister."

Kendra watched him drive away in what used to be *her* fleet car. A red rooster tail of dust followed him. After a few moments, the car was out of sight, and the forest closed in around her, sealing up her thoughts.

CHAPTER TWO

Slimebucket

Ella Webb watched her eleven-year-old son, Nick, playing with the half-grown puppy. Has to be at least *part* Great Dane, she thought. "How big you think it will get, John?"

Her friend appeared to think it over. He'd brought the dog by with her permission. Her son, Nick, was still somewhat shell-shocked by the horrific events that had taken place shortly after the two of them had moved into the house on Lilac Lane.

They'd had a terrible time at first, lights going on and off, noises in the attic, a dead raccoon in the cupboard. And then the intruder…

Everyone said they were lucky to be alive.

Now, Nick was very nervous at bedtime and often came to her room in the middle of the night, drenched and shaking from yet another bad dream.

So when John Stockton—who had quite a bit of experience with both bad guys and good dogs, and whose wife turned out to be Nicky's fifth grade teacher—had found the stray pup, he'd immediately thought of Nick.

"If not for the Stocktons and Chet Boone and his endless patience with both of us, I don't know where we'd be—" That was as far as she got with that thought before the big pup tackled Nick and began to cover his face with slurpy kisses.

Nick squealed in delight. "Can we keep him, Mom? Can we? I love him, and he loves me. Don't cha boy?" He held the massive snout between his palms and looked the dog right in the eye. When he jumped up and took off running, the long legged canine was right on his heels.

"He'll be big alright." John stroked his close, gray-blond beard. "Huge, I imagine." He looked directly at Ella. "Don't feel bad if you aren't up to it. Not everyone has what it takes to raise a pet that large."

Ella shook her head. "Look at them." Nick and the dog were rolling on the lawn. "How could I separate them now?"

The tall man grinned. "He's housebroken, at least. Used Turk's doggie door at our house, no problem."

"What if the owner shows up?" Ella asked. "Are we sure he's a stray?"

John nodded. "No microchip, no flyers posted anywhere. I ran ads in all the online pet groups and in the newspaper. Beth even taped a poster at the camp store out at the lake since he was found near there."

"Hard to believe no one is looking for him. He's such a sweetheart." She smiled as she watched Nick throw a Frisbee across the yard.

The dog headed after it as if he'd been shot from a cannon before tripping over his own big feet and tumbling comically to the ground, tongue lolling. Nick laughed and ran toward the Frisbee, but the dog lumbered to his feet and beat him to it. Once it had the toy in its mouth, the tug-o-war was on.

"Someone may have turned him out in the woods after seeing how much he ate—some idiots think dogs can just hunt and fend for themselves." John's mouth turned down.

"You're right," Ella agreed. "Some people are both cruel and stupid. I just want to make certain the pup is ours to keep before I let Nicky get attached."

John shifted his weight. "Totally understandable. It's been two months, and no one has called or responded to any of the ads. I think we're safe."

"There's only one problem…" She glanced around the large yard. "Do you think he'll be okay here alone while we're at work and school all day?"

A grin played at the edge of his lips. "Thought of that, too. Since the silly thing gets along so well with old Turk, I thought you could drop him off at our place on your way into town each day. I could even meet you if necessary."

Ella chuckled. "So you're actually offering to dog sit?" Knowing he was retired from the military made the image sort of hard to reconcile.

He rocked back and forth on his heels, embarrassed. "Well, yeah, Turk and me."

Ella matched his earlier grin. "Sounds like someone has become attached."

The big man chuckled. "You know us too well, Ms. Webb."

She watched Nick and the happy dog tussle on the grass, not a care in the world. "If you're absolutely certain, then you've got a deal." She stuck her hand out for a shake. "You guys amaze me. You and Beth and everyone in this town just took us in as if we'd always lived here."

John grabbed her hand and pulled her into a bear hug just as the Forest Department truck turned into the driveway.

Chet Boone slid from the driver's seat. "Hey, hey, *hey*. What in the world is going on here?" He didn't have time to say more because that's when Nicky charged toward him, big pup trailing along in his wake like an unexploded mine.

Chet sidestepped Nicky and caught the young dog by his collar. "Hello there," he said. "And who might you be?"

The dog immediately turned his attention to the lanky wildlife biologist, sniffing his boots and jeans in earnest.

"He likes you," Nicky cried, out of breath but still grinning.

Chet rubbed the dog's floppy ears. "Either that or he smells the raccoons I had to relocate this morning." He smiled at Nick. "This your new pal?"

Nick nodded. "Mr. Stockton brought him to me. He found him in the woods and can't find his owner, so I get to keep him and let him sleep with me and—"

"Now wait a minute," Ella began. "I don't recall any conversation about where the big lug was going to sleep."

"But Mo-o-m," Nicky wailed. "He's just a baby, he has to sleep with me so he won't be scared in the new house…" his voice trailed off pitifully.

"I've got his doggie pillow in my truck." John shot Nicky a pointed look. "He's used to sleeping on it *beside* the bed—not in it."

A worried expression crossed Ella's face. "That sounds good. I suppose we'll be getting up in the middle of the night to let him outside, though."

"Nah." John walked to the truck for the dog pillow. "Just curtail the water after supper and make sure he goes out before bedtime. That's what we do. Then we secure the doggie door, so they don't run wild at night."

She smiled at her son. "Looks like you've got yourself a dog, son." She opened her arms for the hug she knew was coming.

He almost knocked her down in his enthusiasm.

The two men laughed, and John set the large doggie bed and a sack of Large Breed Puppy Chow on the porch. "Just let me know how you want to handle the babysitting when school takes up on Monday."

"Will do," she promised. "And thanks. Tell Beth thanks, too."

John touched the bill of his cap and stuffed himself into the truck to leave.

Chet looked at the two of them as John started up his truck. "Babysitting?" he mouthed.

Laughing, Ella took him in the house and gave him a hug almost as big as the one Nicky had bestowed upon her. "Yes, babysitting. Although I guess, the proper term would be *puppy* sitting." She stood on tiptoe for a quick kiss. "Can you believe it? John and Turk are going to keep him during the day while Nick's in school and I'm at the café."

"Now I've heard everything." Chet pulled her in for a deeper kiss, and the matter was put to rest.

Nick clambered up on the porch, and Ella and Chet broke apart. Her son knew they were in a relationship, but she didn't yet feel comfortable being physical in front of him. Not much at least. A quick kiss or hug as a way of greeting was about the extent of it. Nick's biological father had never been in the picture, and his stepfather had turned out to have a violent streak. She didn't intend for Nick ever to go through that again. This time, she was taking things much more slowly.

The crazy pup raced past Nick and crashed through the house as though in search of something. "What's he doing?" Nick stared after his new pet in awe.

"Looking for water would be my guess," Chet replied. "Look at that tongue hanging out. You two had quite a romp."

Nick dashed toward the kitchen and started flinging open cupboard doors. "Where's our big bowl, Mom?"

They all heard slurping sounds coming from the bathroom.

Chet laughed as the dog padded back toward them trailing water like a sieve. "I think he already found the 'big bowl.'"

"Ewww!" Ella sounded as if she were having second thoughts about saying yes, but then she, too, laughed and shrugged. "I think I'll just call you Slimebucket." She patted the huge head and yelled for Nicky to bring a towel. The dog flopped down in the middle of the room, exhausted, tongue still lolling and dripping.

CHAPTER THREE

Earlier That Day – Edgar

The road through town was quiet. Sunday morning, most people were either at church or sleeping in. The crisp fall air gave folks a brief respite from yard work. Soon it would be time for cleaning out choked gutters and raking up enticing piles of colorful leaves, but for now, all was calm, and only a few trees released their desultory, breeze-borne treasures.

Edgar was so much more relaxed since spending the night with his best girl. He was even looking forward to going home to his wife. That hadn't happened in a while. All the new talk about making babies and expanding their family had sliced open his psyche as easily as a scalpel slicing through flesh. But now, this morning, things were so much better.

He turned off at the Lilac Lane exit.

Just a couple more miles until he reached the turn for his own rural road and the huge farmhouse he and Candy had found the first day they'd arrived.

She'd been surprised that he no longer had family members living in the area since he'd been raised just thirty miles away.

He just told her they'd all died or moved away. What he didn't tell her was that his mother had overdosed on a mixture of alcohol and prescription drugs, and that his deadbeat dad had been gone so long he had no idea if he was even alive. His parents had not been The Cleavers; that much was certain.

Did that color his take on families in general? Edgar thought it was possible, but Candy had seemed to understand. Families were simply too messy, too complicated. He'd told her all that when they first met online, but from time to time he reiterated it, in person. To make sure she didn't forget.

And she said she totally agreed. Candy said she never wanted children. She had four rowdy siblings and had always craved peace and quiet. Just being his wife would be enough for her, she said. "In fact," she told him, "I'm looking forward to throwing myself into all the Stutter Creek charity organizations and joining all the local clubs. I can't wait to be a Junior Leaguer."

And then her sister had come up pregnant.

Edgar turned off Lilac Lane onto Robin Road.

He never failed to admire the old house as he approached. The two-story farmhouse sported unquestionable curb appeal with its white clapboard exterior and climbing, still-blooming trumpet vines. No matter which direction one approached the neat home, those orange tubular blooms stood out vividly against the pristine walls and fences.

He smiled. The panoramic view of his home filled him with pride and joy. It was his *normal* mask. Up until now, the stress of the last few months had taken that simple comfort away from him. He'd been unable to enjoy anything. All he could think of was *what can I do to make things right again? To make everything the way it used to be, the way it should be?*

He'd even found himself fantasizing about the house across the way, the one on Lilac Lane. The one where Ella Webb and her son lived alone in their small lilac encased farmhouse. And that wouldn't do. NO. It would not do at all. Way too close to home. He wished he'd never met Ella Webb. But she was the owner of the most popular diner in town, the historic Drugstore Café. Everyone knew she lived alone with just her young son for company.

Edgar was very thankful when he found out the wildlife guy was there so much. It helped him keep everything in perspective when life got stressful—when his *wife* made life stressful.

He drove into his garage and unloaded the hiking and camping equipment. It took only minutes to stow it all away in plastic bins. His backpack he reloaded with bottles of water and energy bars plus his Garmin GPS unit. He had plugged it into the car charger on the way home so it would be ready the next time he needed it.

The house was silent. From somewhere down the road, he heard a car start up. He slipped off his shoes and started toward the guest bathroom to shower.

From the dim hallway, he glanced into the formal living room.

Candy sat in the wingback chair facing the window. Her head was bowed. She must be asleep, or she would've seen me drive in. Wouldn't she have seen me drive in? What is she doing?

A single wretched sob reached his ears.

For the first time in their relationship, he was uncertain how to proceed. Crying was one thing he simply did not know how to deal with. He'd never given her any reason to cry—never. Emotional outbursts terrified him. He'd spent the past year catering to her every whim in order to avoid a scene such as the one about to transpire.

"Candy? Are you crying?" He stepped toward her, but couldn't bring himself to touch her.

She twisted in the chair. "Who is she, Eddie?" Her red-rimmed eyes were sore and accusing.

He was completely taken aback. "Who is who?" He immediately pictured the bones. *Did she see him, had she followed him somehow?*

His wife stood and faced him. "You know what I mean. Who are you sleeping with? You've been gone all night—you weren't at work. There was no emergency. I checked." Her voice cracked, and she sat down again, showing him her back.

He released a tortured breath. "No, no, no. You've got it all wrong." He searched his mind for a believable excuse. *I was with someone. Just not the way you think.* "Come on sweetie," he loved calling her sweetie—her name was part of her allure for him. The morning light had waned when he crossed the few steps to kneel before his wife. He hoped he wasn't going overboard. Up until now, he'd never had any reason to apologize to her. He wasn't sure he knew how.

She wiped her nose with the balled up tissue clutched in her shaking fist. "Where were you?" The rose-colored curtains filtered the almost-noon-sun, casting Candy in a very pretty light. Tears glittered in her lashes.

For a few moments, he forgot about his best girl, the one he'd left in the forest. Something about the morning hue reminded him of why he'd married Candy even after he'd been convinced he would never have that sort of life. "I went hiking; you know that."

"But you didn't come home." Her accusatory gaze glanced off his cheek like a slap.

He shook his head. "I had a flat. That's all. My spare was flat, too. I had to sleep in the car—then the ranger came by this morning and took me to get it repaired. It's no big deal."

"Why didn't you call me?" Her voice still shook a little, as if she wanted to believe him, but was afraid to.

Finally, he reached for her hand. "I couldn't get a signal." He caressed the fingers of her left hand with his index finger. A sudden tactile memory of his fingers caressing the soil around the bones made him shudder. It was not an unpleasant sensation. "You know how the reception is up there, in the mountains."

Candy straightened her fingers. The tattered tissue fell to the floor, and he had to concentrate to keep a smile off his lips. Although it had taken years of practice, he had finally become adept at employing the appropriate facial expressions in most social situations. He knew a smile now would totally blow his fictitious alibi.

"Are you telling me the truth? Because if you've found someone else I want to know. I don't want to be made a fool of."

Edgar shook his head as he continued to caress her fingers. "I walked for miles trying to find a signal to call you." He scrunched his brow dramatically. "I had to give up when darkness fell—that's when I decided to sleep in the car and hike out this morning."

Her head came up. "I thought you said the ranger came."

He nodded emphatically. "Yes, exactly. That's why I'm home so early. He had come before I was even awake, thank goodness. I wasn't looking forward to hiking ten miles back to the ranger station." *Now* he smiled. His white, even teeth showed briefly. "I'm so sorry I worried you. I hurried home as fast as I could."

Candy pushed her fine blonde hair off her wet cheek and pulled him to her breast. "I shouldn't have doubted you." She sniffled. "I was just so worried—you've never been gone all night unless there was some emergency."

He held her gently.

She stood and straightened her demure blue dress. "You must be starving. I'll make your favorite omelet."

He held onto her fingers. "What about church? You never miss."

Candy swiped at her still-damp face with her other hand. "I didn't think I would enjoy it today. We'll have breakfast together. I'll go to the evening service tonight."

Edgar smiled. She had never put off church for him before. Maybe there was some hope after all—as long as she didn't start talking babies again. He *never* wanted kids. They terrified him, too.

He'd met Candy online at BestDates.com. She was shy, and he was a complete social pariah unable to start, much less sustain a face-to-face relationship.

For six months, they had talked and exchanged photos. She admitted to him that she'd taken so much teasing about her name over the years that she'd been on the verge of having it legally changed.

"I like it," he'd said. "It's sweet."

"Yeah," she'd typed back. "It's sweet all right. Like a stripper or something."

He'd laughed at that. It was true. More than one of the phone-sex women he'd perused over the years had been named Candy. The dichotomy of the name stacked up against her innocence and virginity gave him quite a thrill. Though he never thought he would have a *normal* relationship, he had found himself growing more and more attached to her over the months.

When she finally suggested they meet, he had shocked himself by saying yes.

Within months, they had eloped to Vegas to get married. It was the only way she would sleep with him.

For the first time in his life, Edgar felt normal. Having a wife was like having the whole normal *costume*, not just the mask.

We are so good together, he thought, remembering all the ways she'd improved his life. The two of us are a family.

We don't need anyone else. I even gave up my other girls. I did it for her. Now she can do this, for me. Just like we agreed in the beginning.

Then I will put my favorite girl back where she belongs.

CHAPTER FOUR
Sunday Afternoon

Now that the weather was cooler, the deciduous leaves fell like rain. They mounded into luscious orange and yellow drifts that were—for the next few days at least—soft and pliable. The conifers stood like evergreen sentinels resisting the coming of winter.

Halloween passed quietly. Kendra had stacked bright pumpkins on each of the four porch steps. She'd tried to liven up the landscape even more by carving a jack-o-lantern the way she and the kids had done back in the day.

But the fun had turned sour when she sliced open the webbing between her thumb and index finger. The result had been a trip to the clinic for stitches. When she got home a couple of hours later, the bright orange pumpkins shone eerily through the early evening mist coming off the water.

She admired the soft splash of color as she pulled into the driveway. She'd tried to happy-up her home. But there'd been no one around to admire her efforts. No one to appreciate the autumn display. Few families lived on this side of the lake. Most of the places belonged to retired older couples, or the homes were simply empty-and-waiting vacation homes.

The silence of the lake setting seemed to breed loneliness. The mist blanketed the water and shrouded the solitary doe peering at her through the fringe of trees. Depression seemed to hover about the old house like a stray waiting to be let in from the cold.

Kendra spent the dark holiday alone except for the deer that wandered through the yard to eat the corn she scattered there. She wasn't used to being alone. She was used to working and raising kids and trying to juggle all that with what she'd thought was a satisfying home life.

Even after the kids had grown and gone away to school, they were always coming home, bringing laundry, looking for money or advice.

This new silence was difficult to say the least.

She tested her thumb, grimacing at the pull of the stitches. The Sunday afternoon clinic had been nice, bright, and nearly empty. The receptionist had called the doctor to come in just for her. He didn't stay at the clinic, but it was a small town. He made it there in less than half an hour.

"Not too many weekend emergencies in the offseason," the receptionist had told her. "Right now we mainly get kids with colds, stuff like that. But when the snow flies and the slopes open, look out. We'll be *swamped*."

From the tone of her voice, Kendra thought the girl was looking forward to ski season. Maybe it'll be better for me, too, she'd thought. *Maybe I'll be back in Pine River by then.*

Over the next few days, Kendra did everything she could think of to pass the time. She hiked, fished, and chatted with the kids by phone. Two of them, Keith and Willa, were in college getting ready for Halloween parties. She also talked to Carrie and her husband, Rory. They were nesting in preparation for their first child.

She talked to no one else. For a fleeting moment, she thought of calling Woody James, but as her finger hovered over her contact list, good sense took hold and she clicked the phone off and poured herself a glass of wine.

All three kids, plus Carrie's husband Rory, planned to join her for Thanksgiving. She knew it was a trade-off she'd regret later when they spent Christmas with their dad, but she wouldn't think of that now. She went to the closet to pull out the rest of the things she hadn't unpacked yet.

The first box was marked Christmas decorations. *Damn. Not a good way to start.* She put that one back and took out the next one. It was marked Keepsakes. *Yes. This has to be it.* Her grandmother's tablecloth was the one item she wanted to find. She wanted to make certain it graced their turkey day table.

Kendra dragged the box into the middle of the living room floor. Her hand tingled as the anesthetic began to wear off.

She poured another glass of wine and carefully opened the box. *It has to be this one. If not, I've lost it. Or Bill got it by mistake. Be damned if I call and ask him. But it's my grandmother's tablecloth, not his.* She grimaced. *He'd probably throw it in the fireplace just for spite.*

She dug through the box carefully.

It wasn't there.

She closed that box and pulled out another. It was marked Upstairs Closet. *Had it been in that closet?* She tried to picture the linen closet in her mind—sheets, blankets, mismatched pillowcases—yes, it could've been there. Images of her home flashed through her mind. Fifteen years they'd lived in that house, raised their kids, shared family dinners, birthdays, Christmas mornings. And now…

She split the tape on the second box. A musty smell drifted out. That upstairs closet had always held castoffs and remnants. Once a thing was relegated to that closet, it was seldom seen again. The tablecloth wouldn't be there—hadn't she used it every Christmas, every Thanksgiving? Wait, last Christmas Eve there'd been that murder-suicide at the Mountain Lodge Apartments. Holiday season was always a bad time for that sort of thing. She and Woody had shared turkey subs with the crime scene crew at midnight.

Bill had cooked a beautiful ham for the kids. And she'd made certain she got home before dinner. Of course, Bill hadn't bothered with the tablecloth. It was paper plates, and Solo cups all the way. He'd said he didn't mind that she hadn't been there to put on the usual big family meal—said he understood it was only the job.

Bill was a firefighter. He'd always worked twenty-four hours on and forty-eight off. They'd agreed it was the ideal situation for the two of them, and especially for the children. *Until it wasn't.*

But she wasn't going to go there, either. Not tonight. She was determined to find that tablecloth. It became a mission.

A scrap of old movie dialog flitted through her head. "I'm on a mission. A mission from God." *Now where did that come from, The Blue Brothers movie?* She was pretty certain that was it—a silly movie, but a lot of fun. She and Bill had seen it together a million years ago.

She stowed that memory away and continued delving into the *physical* past.

The first thing she pulled from the musty box was Willa's baby blanket, the white one with the pink and blue stripes around the edges. The one she came home from the hospital in. Beneath it rested the little knit cap all babies wore in the hospital nursery. *What a strange place to put these. Guess my mind wasn't as clear as it could have been when I packed up. Could've sworn this was in the trunk in our bedroom.*

She wiped salty moisture from her cheeks as she pulled out Keith's first pair of overalls. Her mom had made them for Keith's first birthday party. Kendra caressed the softly worn denim. Her mom had appliqued a tiny blue bear on the overall pocket. She'd been such a talented seamstress, always making things for the kids. She'd doted on them terribly. Kendra felt her absence now almost as acutely as the day she'd died.

The next item in the box was Carrie's Easter dress. The one she'd thrown a fit for at Walker's department store. It had been so unlike her to throw a fit for anything—she'd been the good child, the easy one—that Kendra had broken her cardinal rule of parenting and given in. In fact, she'd been so embarrassed by the tears and begging that she'd bought the floral contraption without even making Carrie try it on.

When they got home, they discovered that the dress hung off her daughter's thin frame like a brightly colored sack. Nevertheless, she loved it. There wasn't another one in a smaller size, and she'd refused to trade it for a different style.

It seemed as if Carrie and the dress were somehow connected. It reminded Kendra of déjà vu and the way some places just seemed familiar the moment you walked in. Or how you sometimes felt as if you'd known a person all your life even when you'd just met. That's how it was with Carrie and the dress. As if it were a talisman from another life. Carrie kept insisting it had *always* been her favorite.

Down to the wire, with Easter coming the very next day, Kendra's mom had sprung into action and altered the dress, smiling at the late hour. *And then I didn't even get to see her wear it to church, Kendra recalled. A hit and run on Devonian Drive had taken me away in the early morning hours. Strange how I can remember all those things so clearly right down to the addresses. Those events occurred years ago.*

Moisture collected in what she called the old-lady lines beside her nose and mouth, clung to her lashes. She sat back on her heels as she remembered Carrie swishing around after church in her pink and purple floral dress. "I'm too big to hunt Easter eggs," she'd declared the day before when Willa and Keith had colored and decorated two dozen pastel beauties.

Trying to appear older than her years, Carrie had tried to set herself above the child's play, but at the last moment she'd flung herself into the fun and found more eggs than anyone—including her cousins.

That was one egg hunt I didn't miss. Didn't make the church service, but I did get to hunt eggs in the afternoon. Always a tradeoff. How much did I miss out on? Was I like Carrie, trying too hard, unable to do it all? Should I have let go the way she did? Kendra downed the rest of her wine and pulled out the last item—a slim, white shirt box.

Nestled inside, in a layer of tissue paper, lay her grandmother's lace tablecloth. She smoothed it gently. This one had ridden across the country in an old steamer trunk in the back of a covered wagon. The pioneers had been headed west from Arkansas to California. They'd made it as far as the territory that would later become known as New Mexico before they'd given in and settled down.

Kendra let the old lace slip through her fingers. The tiny black stitches in the webbing of her hand snagged on the lace a couple of times. *When did I last use the tablecloth? Not recently. Was it two years ago, three? How did time get away from me? In two short months, I'll be a grandmother myself.* She looked down at the hand-tatted cloth. *I'll pass this down to one of the kids, but which one. What if none of them want it? What if they don't even want to come for Thanksgiving?*

She looked around her lakeside rental. It was old fashioned. The elderly gentleman who owned the place had been fortunate to have a daughter who would take him in during his time of need.

Will mine want me when I get old and feeble? Now that I've destroyed the whole family?

She thought back to the day Bill had told her he was tired of being a single parent. That he was tired of her putting Woody and the job ahead of him and the kids. At first she'd thought it was some sort of twisted joke—she was going through hell with the allegations that she'd either pushed a suspect in front of a truck, or intentionally allowed him to commit suicide by stepping in front of it—then she'd seen Bill's ancient leather suitcases near the door.

Kendra was afraid all the kids blamed her. They had to, the way Bill told it. Had she put her job ahead of her kids? She'd never thought so, but now she wasn't so sure. But Woody? Where had that come from? He was her partner, nothing more. Everyone knew that—she'd thought Bill did, too.

Keith hadn't taken it so hard. He seemed more focused on finishing college and getting his career started, but the girls, they were a different story. They were Daddy's girls, both of them.

Unfortunately, Kendra hadn't had time to focus on Bill at that moment. On top of her problems with the civil suit, she'd also been preoccupied with the grisly murder of a child—something that seldom happened in the town of Pine River. The child's body had been hidden in a trunk, not unlike her gran's old steamer. The parents were the main suspects.

Kendra clasped the tablecloth to her cheek and willed the horrific memories away. With all of that going on, by the time she'd got around to worrying about Bill, he was long gone. Even though he'd taken the suitcases and moved out, in the back of her mind, Kendra had been convinced it was only temporary. A trial separation. A warning sign meant to get her attention. After all, this was *Bill*, her high school sweetheart, the father of her children; the man who'd answered *I Do* when asked if he did. But apparently he didn't. Not anymore. For better or worse? *Obviously not*.

When she realized he wasn't coming back, Kendra had sought solace in the only person she felt might understand, the one guy she could talk to about anything.

Woody was the one who'd been there when the child's remains were found in the trunk, he was one of the few that understood how difficult that image was to process and let go—especially in the dead of night. Especially when they suspected the parents had been producing child pornography with their own children.

But all that's in the past.

Her mind automatically went back to the day she was asked to hand in her badge and gun until the investigation into the store robber's suicide was completed. Only temporary, the captain had assured her. Only temporary. *Yeah, like Bill moving out had been only temporary. Sure.*

She carefully packed the kids' old clothing back into the big box. She patted it gently before returning it to the hall closet with a mental note to mention the items after Thanksgiving dinner. *If they show up.* Then she sat back with her spine against the wall. *Maybe Carrie will want to use the blanket to bring her baby home from the hospital. Maybe she'll want the tiny blue overalls, too.*

She stood carefully, head a little woozy from the wine, and steered her mind back to the present. Carrying the old tablecloth to the laundry room, she rinsed it by hand in the big sink with a bit of Woolite and cold water. Then she spread it out on a bed of thick towels to dry.

Tomorrow I'll press it with a warm iron. It'll be as good as ever. Too bad I can't rinse and iron my own wrinkled life that easily.

The walls began to close in. She put the TV on the classic movie channel, for background noise, and after a while the claustrophobia began to abate. In better days she would have put on music, now it all seemed to remind her of Bill and their youth.

One good thing about the old rented lake house, it had a huge dining room, and the table could seat twelve. She was looking forward to Thanksgiving, even if it would be awkward at first. Her only worry was that no one would come.

CHAPTER FIVE

Mr. McGraw

After his second camping trip, when he'd gone back to visit his best girl—and to make certain animals hadn't carried her away—Edgar drove home the long way, around Copper Lake and through the lake campsites. He wanted to stop at the little store for a hot coffee, but he thought that might be pushing his luck. The owner knew him. This had been one of his favorite places when he was a boy. The yearly campout with his grandpa had always been one of the highlights of his year—until the old man developed Alzheimer's and got sent away. *Put away is more like it.* Though he hadn't known that until much later, after the funeral. By that time his dad had been a part-timer, coming and going, running around with one woman after another, and his mom had been deep in denial. And deeper in the bottle.

A grim scowl took over his countenance. He'd been in junior high school then. It had been a turning point in his life. Not only had his grandfather left him, but it was also when he discovered girls. Unfortunately, he'd also discovered that girls—sort of like his absentee parents—wanted nothing to do with him.

The first girl he'd ventured to ask for a date—if one could call sitting together at the Friday football game a date—had laughed in his face. Then she had turned to her girlfriend and pointed and laughed some more.

He had often thought how glad he was that there were no cell phone cameras or social media back then—it was way too easy to imagine his humiliation scattered all over school in the space of a heartbeat.

Though one might think he would've taken out his frustrations on the same type of haughty stuck-up girls who'd laughed in his face, such was not the case, at least, not at first. In fact, when he initially encountered the freeze-out, as he had come to think of his brief period of female-species-interaction, he hadn't sought any sort of revenge. He'd simply turned all that hurt and anger inward. The insides of his thighs became crisscrossed with scars where he'd cut himself with his dad's double-edged Gillette razor blades.

The first cut had been accidental. He'd been standing at the mirror in his skivvies, practicing shaving—something he wouldn't have to do for a couple of years—when he accidentally dropped the heavy razor. On the way down, the thing had clattered off the edge of the porcelain sink, and the sharp blade had sliced into the tender meat of his inner thigh.

He'd been shocked that the razor had fallen so perfectly, slicing down the thin, pale skin with such fantastic accuracy. Then curiosity had set in, and he'd watched, fascinated, as the long shallow line had filled with bright red blood. When the filled line welled over and began to trickle down toward his knee, he'd sat on the edge of the tub and simply observed. The stinging hadn't set in until the blood had already begun to dry.

Then he had used the tips of his fingers to pull the edges of the cut apart so he could watch the blood well up again.

That had been the beginning.

There had been more humiliations, oh, not right away but over the next few months—and with each one a new cut would appear.

A score of humiliating incidents ran through his head. One of the most memorable had hit him like it did so many clumsy boys, in P.E. during Presidential Fitness week and the fifty pushups challenge. After that it seemed a domino effect: there was the time in Assembly when the kid in front of him had cut the cheese and blamed it on him, and later when he'd been called on to work an algebra problem in front of the whole class. He'd screwed it up of course. Who could think with all those eyes boring into his back and the spitballs flying, landing next to his head on the whiteboard every time he wrote another number or variable?

It occurred to him, years later, to wonder just what the hell the teacher had been doing the whole time he had been suffering at the board, but back then, he'd just wanted the floor to open up and swallow him like a trapdoor below the magician's stage. The worst part was, he knew he was way smarter than any of them. He could normally work any problem in his head, but not with everyone staring and throwing spitballs, especially the wicked bitch who had laughed when he'd tried to ask out her friend.

That night the cut he'd made had been the deepest one yet. He'd kept it bleeding for almost an hour. It had been easy to reopen it the next day when his mom and dad had yelled at each other about some woman who had called. That fight had gone on for a while, and then his dad had turned on *him*, calling him lazy for not taking out the trash. His mother had responded by drinking herself into oblivion and passing out on the couch. His dad simply left without looking back.

It had been the last time they'd ever spoken.

And it was all because of some woman.

Early that morning—a Saturday it had been—Edgar cut his wrists. The amount of blood had been quite alarming. But there had been no one there to dial nine one one; no one to gasp and say what the hell have you *done*; no one to rush to his side with a fluffy white towel to stop the bleeding. His father was long gone, and his mother would not have awoken if they'd carried *her* to the hospital with the siren wailing.

So after a few minutes in the tub, when the bleeding had slowed to a non-threatening trickle, Edgar had stood unsteadily, climbed out and bandaged the cuts with Band-Aids. Must not have got the artery, he thought. *Guess I wasn't serious about wanting to die after all.* But he wasn't *too* disappointed. He'd rather enjoyed those first moments of not knowing if the bleeding was letting up, or if he was going to go to sleep and never wake up.

He'd let the shallow wounds heal, and then he'd reopened them the next night when his mother went out with a "friend" leaving him to order pizza for supper, again.

That semester had been the beginning of a serious cycle of cutting and reopening that would carry him through the rest of that awful year.

His flesh had become his confidant, his own warm blood his savior.

***

Now, Edgar rolled his head around and around to work out the sleeping-on-the-ground kinks. He drove the exact speed limit coming in from the campground. No way did he want to be pulled over by the cops, certainly didn't want to get a ticket for speeding. Even the forest ranger at the entrance to the park gave him the creeps.

He thought back to the reason for his cop-phobia.

It had been his first kill, so many years ago, and it wound up being the one thing that could break his cycle of cutting. After Mr. McGraw, he had never cut himself again.

He'd been fifteen, his dad had been gone for good by then—but it wasn't anger that led him to kill Mr. McGraw. Nope, it had simply been an accident, a terrible, wonderful accident in which he had unintentionally whammed old Mr. McGraw's head with the trunk lid of his own car.

He'd been helping the old man carry in groceries. It was the middle of the day and he'd been skipping school again. He'd told his mom he was coming down with a stomach virus. His mother didn't care. She simply called him in sick and then went back to bed, skipping work the same way he skipped school.

Hunger had finally driven Edgar to leave the house. He wanted a bowl of cereal, but there was no milk. Disgusted, he'd headed to the neighborhood market on foot.

Old Mr. McGraw had caught him before he got there.

"Give me a hand with these, sonny?" He'd grabbed his back with both hands. "Ain't as young as I used to be."

"Sure, Mr. McGraw." He'd stepped into the old man's garage without a second thought. If the world hadn't intervened in Edgar's young life in the shape of crappy, self-absorbed parents and a face only a mother could love, Edgar might have grown into a super-nice guy. He didn't mind helping others. Unfortunately, that was the only time anyone ever wanted to interact with him—when they wanted something.

In the garage, everything was going fine until the last bag. He'd grabbed it out of the trunk and reached up for the lid just as Mr. McGraw had unexpectedly leaned in. "Oops, a stray can of tomatoes," the old man said. "Must've fallen out when I turned the cor—"

But he'd never finished that sentence because that was the exact moment Edgar slammed down the lid.

The sharp edge must have hit a nerve in the elderly man's neck. He went down as if he'd been shot.

Edgar was appalled when he saw the guy's dentures fly out of his mouth and strike the concrete floor of the garage.

Oh my God!

He'd leaned down and felt Mr. McGraw's wrist and throat hoping to find a pulse—although he wasn't sure he'd know it if he did—but he couldn't find anything.

Later, he would wonder whether he should have called the police right then, and an ambulance, of course, but at the moment it happened, he couldn't imagine answering all their questions about what he was doing in the old man's garage and then having to admit he'd killed the poor guy. He couldn't even imagine admitting why he wasn't home in bed like he was supposed to be. And then there was the fact that his mom was passed out cold. How would he explain that?

Somehow his hand had found the switch to close the garage door. As the dimness overtook him, he'd been blessed with a sudden bright idea. If Mr. McGraw never woke up, no one would know what happened. He could make it look like the old guy had been robbed or something.

With the lightning-speed of panic, Edgar raced into the house and grabbed a hand full of paper towels. He wiped every surface he could have possibly touched and when the old man groaned he'd picked up the nearest weapon, a two by four, and bashed his head in. Edgar was fully committed to the plan now.

If this was what the adrenaline of fear felt like, he liked it. He didn't want it to end. Edgar didn't think he had felt this good, this alive, *ever*.

After making certain the old man wasn't going to moan anymore, Edgar had turned on the overhead light. The amount of blood in the garage both alarmed and delighted him. Fortunately, Mr. McGraw had plenty more paper towels. He'd just stocked up at the grocery store.

Edgar made certain he cleaned up his bloody footprints, but he didn't bother to clean up the rest of the blood. He wanted it to look as if someone had surprised the old man and robbed and murdered him as he unloaded the groceries.

He dug around in the man's bloody pockets until he found his wallet. Then he removed all the cash—fifty-three dollars—and his bank card, which he planned to cut up and flush as soon as he got home.

As a precaution, he took the time to wipe down everything he'd touched a second time, and then he gathered all the paper towels he'd used and wadded them into his shirt. In the back of his mind, he could see himself burning them in the fireplace while his clothes and tennis shoes were sudsing in the Maytag.

He felt light. As if he'd just made a new cut that let all the poison out, for good. He had a sudden, unbidden image of his drunkard mother with *her* head all bashed in, but he pushed that away and fingered the fifty-three bucks in his pocket.

A smile crossed his face. He was still hungry, but he wasn't about to show his face at the corner market now.

He tiptoed back into the widower's kitchen and emerged with a half-gallon of milk. Mr. McGraw wouldn't need it after all he thought as he made his way down the alley toward his own home.

His mother hadn't moved so much as a muscle when he snuck back into the house. The disgust he felt for her only multiplied as he went about the business of cleaning his clothes and burning the evidence in the fireplace.

Now, a smile on his lips brought on by the memory of that first adrenaline high, adult Edgar turned onto his street. He'd navigated the maze of campsite lanes without even thinking about it. Reliving that first kill always gave him great pleasure.

No longer simply smiling when he drove into the empty garage, at this point he was grinning from ear to ear. Candy was out of town. It was the day of her sister's baby shower, and she had agreed to be one of the hostesses. She wouldn't be home until tonight, plenty of time for him to print out the pictures he'd taken of his best girl. *I know the perfect place to display them, too. Got a big corkboard wall just waiting.*

Thinking of his photo wall made Edgar pause. His best girl with her head resting in clover—that made him happy. And she'd still been mostly intact, but that probably wouldn't last much longer. Did he want her to be found? He had mixed feelings. All he knew for certain was that he missed that feeling of living in the shadow of danger the way he had those weeks after Mr. McGraw, and the hours, days, and weeks immediately after all the other girls he'd been lucky enough to become acquainted with over the years. The ones he still had to revisit, the way he'd recently begun to revisit his *best* girl.

Yes, maybe he did need them to be found—to satisfy some craving even he didn't understand—but on the other hand, he didn't *want* them to be found at all.

He wanted to keep them all to himself.

He was having way too much fun sneaking out to the mountains to play. If someone did find his best girl—or any of his girls—he wouldn't be able to visit them anymore. He dreamed of having them all together in one place, like his old bunker in the woods, the one with the big corkboard wall. But that was not feasible. If someone stumbled upon that, then all his girls would be gone at once. And that would not be good. Then he would be forced to start over from scratch.

This way, with the girls, spread out in a wheel shape, with the bunker at the center, if one happened to be found, the others would still be available to him. That way, he could add to his photo collage at will.

Between Candy going on and on about babies and becoming an aunt, and his work becoming busier and busier as ski season neared, Edgar *needed* his girls. He needed them as surely as a toddler needed a binky. But it would end soon, and he'd go back to his "normal" life without his girls.

CHAPTER SIX

Thanksgiving

The heirloom tablecloth fit the ambience of the old house perfectly.

Kendra stepped back and congratulated herself. The turkey was in the oven, sans foil, crisping. The stuffing had turned out pretty well. She'd followed her mother's recipe to the letter, something she'd never taken the time to do before. But she'd had Bill back then, and he'd always claimed he loved to cook.

She swiped a hand across her brow. Her hair had grown even wavier as she let it grow. From time to time she simply trimmed the bangs around her face and called it good. She'd kept it short for so long she had completely forgotten how unruly it could be.

Her new chocolate colored ironstone dinnerware— courtesy of Pottery Barn's online store—graced the table, along with several filler pieces from various Mother's Days and birthdays over the years. The candles were also new. They came from a local candle café in Stutter Creek. Kendra made it a point to force herself to get up and go out into the world every day. Even if it was just to buy candles.

Overall, she was very pleased with the way the day was shaping up. Carrie and her husband had arrived the night before. The mother-to-be seemed eager to share her growing belly with the soon-to-be-grandma. They'd stayed up late into the night, catching up. And Kendra's worries that the kids were angry with her for breaking up the family were finally laid to rest. No one blamed her; in fact, they blamed Bill for not sticking by her, for not even trying to work things out.

Just knowing that fact allowed Kendra to breathe a little easier. Everything had happened so fast, and she'd been so deep into the two cases—the murdered child and the suspect who committed suicide—that her personal life had taken a backseat. Now, it was all she could think about. Going from working twelve to fourteen hours a day to not working at all was extremely difficult. Like shoving the gearshift into park going downhill at ninety miles per hour.

But now, things were looking up.

When she brought out her new eyeglasses and put them on, both Carrie and Rory complimented her so thoroughly that she began to feel better about wearing them. Getting older is definitely not for sissies, she told herself. *And this is only the beginning.* She'd always been inordinately proud of her 20/20 vision. *I guess it's true; pride does go before the fall.*

Willa arrived around noon. She brought all the makings for broccoli-rice casserole, but she hadn't actually made it. Willa was in her first year of college at Texas Tech. She would be transferring to veterinary school in Galveston after she got her Bachelor of Science degree.

Tech was a four-hour drive from Copper Lake. "I left early this morning," she said, kissing her mom on the cheek. "But then I went the wrong way on the lake road and took the scenic route."

Kendra rolled her eyes and enveloped her younger daughter in a bear hug. Willa was marvelous in science, but she never had possessed a stable sense of direction. She still got turned around in malls and parking lots. "So, who is he, this boy that's making you drive the wrong direction? I assume you were either on the phone with him or thinking about your last conversation—"

"Oh, Mom," Willa giggled. "His name is Sam, and he's also pre-vet." Her eyes sparkled. "And he's very, very nice."

Kendra felt something loosen inside her chest. Seeing her younger daughter so happy made everything better. "Well, he'd better be. I'm just surprised he isn't in the car." She glanced out the window as if she believed he might be hiding there.

Willa ignored the joke and moved on to Carrie's wide-open arms. "Sissy! I can't believe you're going to be a mom. I'm so excited." She patted Carrie's baby-bump. "I'm going to be *Aunt* Willa." She looked up at her brother-in-law. "Congratulations, you two."

Carrie hugged her little sister enthusiastically. "You'll be the best aunt in the world. We'll go shopping for baby clothes and dress her up just like we did our baby dolls."

Kendra's eyes watered as she watched her girls interact. *They're both so beautiful. I can't have done too badly.* She joined in the hug-fest and took the grocery bag full of food from Willa at the same time. "I'll just get this casserole started," she said. "Your brother should be here soon. I think he's bringing a friend." She emphasized the word, friend.

"Oooh," the girls chorused. "You mean big brother is finally bringing someone home for the holidays?"

Willa began to dance around. "Bubba's got a girlfriend, Bubba's got a girlfriend, Bubba's got a—"

Carrie cleared her throat and grabbed her younger sister to halt her twirling.

"Nice to see you, too, Sis." Their brother stood in the doorway, stooping slightly to keep from bumping his head on the low lintel. He moved aside and held out his hand. "I'd like you all to meet Charlie."

They stopped what they were doing and stared at the beautiful young man with the shiny black hair standing behind Keith like a small shadow. "Hello," he said. His voice was soft and crisp at the same time.

"Charlie's from Spain. He didn't have any real place to go for Thanksgiving." Keith grinned. "Betcha feel kinda foolish now, don't cha, Wills?" He tapped Willa on the arm with a gentle fist to punctuate her old childhood nickname.

Kendra stepped forward and drew the young man into the room. "Welcome, Charlie," she said. "Make yourself at home." In the back of her mind, she was thinking about the four bedrooms. She'd sort of thought to herself that Keith's girlfriend could double up with Willa since Carrie and Rory would have one room, and she would have her own, of course. That left Keith to have the fourth one to himself. *But now what? It only had one bed.*

Carrie jumped in with an evil glint in her eye. "You guys can take the room across from Rory and me. It has a double bed."

But Keith wouldn't let himself be baited. His eye held the same evil glint. "Thanks, Sis. That's so generous of you. Just let us get our bags." He nudged Charlie further into the room. "Make yourself at home, bro. Told you my sisters were just like a barrel of monkeys."

Kendra had grabbed him before he got out. "Hey, you. Aren't you forgetting something?" She held out her arms.

"Sorry, Mom. *So* good to see you." He held her out at arm's length. "Diggin' the new hair. And the Ben Franklins. They suit you."

Kendra ran her hand through her hair, embarrassed that neither of her daughters had mentioned her longer hair, but her only son had noticed right away. "Thanks, kiddo. You really think the bifocals look all right? They don't make me look elderly?"

He shook his head, hugged her, and then paused to examine her stitched up hand. "Pinch it in your weapon?"

She laughed. She'd done that once as a rookie, pinched a chunk of flesh out of the webbing between her thumb and forefinger by attempting to speed-trip the hammer out on the shooting range. "No, I haven't done that in a while." She held the wound up like a badge. "This is my first official Halloween injury—got it carving a pumpkin." She lowered her voice. "Also one of the reasons for these." She indicated the bifocals. "Pretty bad when you can't see your own damn thumb, isn't it?"

Keith grinned. "Only you, Mom, only you." He started toward the Ford Bronco parked in the drive. "Seriously, where'd you get it stitched up?"

"At the clinic in town. You know that little urgent care place we visited the first and only time we tried skiing when you were a kid? They have a new doc." She flexed her hand. "He had me fixed up in no time." She glanced down at her hand, a frown on her face. "Would've been healed already, but I reopened it working in the garden. The doc was not happy about that. Had to completely redo them." She shrugged and tucked her hand behind her back. "Now, tell me how your last year of college is going."

Keith laughed. "It's going great. I'm looking at internships for the summer after graduation, and then grad school in the fall." His blue eyes were those of a boy excited over his first home run. "Can you believe I might get to design buildings for a living, just like I used to do with my Tinker Toys and Mega Blox when I was a kid?"

Kendra felt her heart fill with pride. All three of her kids were on the right path. Her prayers were being answered one by one. Regardless of what happened with her career, or with the investigation, or even with her marriage, this was what she would focus on. This was the main course. The rest was just broccoli-rice-casserole waiting to be made.

Willa elbowed her sister when Charlie and Keith took their bags into the bedroom, but Carrie took the high road and pretended not to understand the literal ribbing. She felt bad for teasing Keith about the room arrangements. "I love your new place, Mom." She gazed around the living area. "What can I do to help with dinner?"

Kendra got out pots and pans to steam the broccoli and boil water for rice. "Both of you come in here and keep me company while I finish this casserole." She smiled. "You know how I am in the kitchen." Her lack of culinary skills was legendary.

Together they made the casserole and talked about baby names.

Willa said, "For a girl I think Willa would make a fine middle name—not that I would want her to be called that— too confusing. But as a middle moniker it would be—hey! Who's that coming up the drive? Do I need to set another place at the table?"

Kendra glanced out the window. "I'm not expecting anyone." And then she recognized her old Mercury rolling up the drive.

"That's Detective James, isn't it?" Carrie asked. They were all familiar with each other. He'd been her mom's partner for several years. On more than one occasion, the kids had been delighted to deliver food and drink to the office when the two detectives found themselves pulling all-nighters.

"So it is," Kendra replied. She swept off her apron and headed out to greet him as he stepped from the car.

"Happy Thanksgiving." His deep voice was jolly as he shut the car door. "I see the kids all made it."

Kendra nodded. Hearing him call her offspring "the kids," made her smile. He was only fifteen years older than Keith. "Did I forget that I invited you?" She didn't believe in mincing words.

Woody grinned and shook his head. "Nah, your mental faculties are intact." He hitched at his belt, looked at the ground. "I just came to tell you that the preliminary findings of the investigation are in." He looked at her, and then tapped the corner of her new bifocals. "Nice," he said. "About time you started acting your age."

Kendra felt her knees softening. She plopped down on the porch step. The cool fall breeze played in her hair, tickling her neck and the tops of her ears. She wanted to acknowledge his acknowledgment of her new specs, but right at this moment, she couldn't think. "It's bad news, huh?"

He hesitated. "Don't get ahead of me. I just didn't want you to hear it from someone else."

Kendra felt her world shrink to a pinpoint. "Are they saying it was my fault? That it was a bad collar?"

Woody nodded then sat down beside her and looped an arm around her shoulders.

"Dammit. I don't want to cry." She pulled off her metal-rimmed glasses and took the handkerchief he offered. "You know how I hate crying."

He squeezed her gently. "It's only preliminary. I think his seemingly spotless record is what's causing them consternation. Well, that and his wife giving him an alibi."

She sniffled and blew her nose loudly.

"I feel as though we're being watched," he said. "I'm resisting the urge to turn around."

Kendra nodded. "It's the girls. No doubt they're plastered to the window. They think we're having an affair, probably."

Woody whispered, "Might as well, then. We could start tonight after the kids are all tucked in."

She snorted and wiped her eyes. "You're incorrigible. But since you came all this way, are you hungry? We're just about to put dinner on the table."

He stood and held out his hand. "I thought you'd never ask. And Ken?"

She looked up at him as he pulled her to her feet.

"We'll find something on him." He tapped his middle. "My gut says there's a reason he stepped in front of that truck. And not just to get away from that shrew he was married to."

Kendra shook her head and replaced her spectacles. "I'm beginning to doubt everything about this case. But do they really think I would push him—"

"That's enough talk about it today." He turned her toward the door. "I'll call you tomorrow, and we'll start strategizing. We've wasted enough time, but today's Thanksgiving. Let's just be thankful."

The door opened, and all three kids stepped out. Behind them, she could see Rory and Charlie flipping channels on the TV, searching for the ballgame.

"Show's over, kids." Kendra physically ushered them back inside the house. "Detective James will be joining us for dinner." She pretended not to notice the girls shooting looks at each other behind her back. She wasn't certain what they thought about the reason for her tears, or for the divorce—this was their first all-together gathering since the split—but she planned to speak frankly with each of them before the holiday was over.

"I'll set another place," Willa chirped. "This gorgeous table was made for family holiday dinners."

Kendra smiled at her younger daughter. She'd thought exactly the same thing when she was digging through the boxes looking for place mats and candleholders.

In the end, she'd dragged out the laminated mats the kids had colored in school over the years. Then she'd added her handcrafted pine cone candle holders and the candles she'd picked up in town. The centerpiece was a small pumpkin surrounded by pine boughs and autumn leaves.

"It looks very nice," Charlie said. "I love the centerpiece and the candles."

Kendra blushed uncharacteristically. "I think I channeled a little Martha Stewart there for a couple of days."

Everyone laughed and milled around the table reading the childishly scrawled thanks illustrated on the various placemats. *I'm thankful for my fambly* was written on one; *I'm real thanksul for everthang* was printed on another in bright blue crayon.

"That's what happens when you retire too early," Woody interjected. "You get crafty."

Keith moved a plate to better read one of the placemats. "Hey, Wills," he held up a crudely drawn turkey, "remember this one?" The caption below the drawing said *I'm thankful I'm not a turkey.*

Willa grinned. "I really was thankful not to be a turkey. I think that was the year I realized the connection between the bird and the meal."

Kendra's smile was a bit melancholy. "I loved it." She patted her youngest daughter. "Still do." *Just glad I got that box of keepsakes before Bill got to it.*

Carrie wiped a glittery tear from her own cheek. "I hope Dad is having a good holiday." She glanced at her mom with a guilty look. "I mean—all these little reminders of the past just sort of make it seem—"

Rory pulled her to his side. "Pregnancy hormones." He shrugged as if that would explain away the hurt they had all suffered. "She gets emotional."

Carrie shook her head to negate the "just pregnancy" excuse, but she didn't argue. "Sorry, Mom. I shouldn't have said anything."

Kendra blinked away her own leftover tears. "No apologies. We feel what we feel. It's hard. And I'm sorry I can't change it. I thought it was forever, too." Her voice trailed off to a near whisper at the end, but that was okay. She'd got it out there; she'd said to the whole room what she'd been planning to say to each child individually. *I didn't ask for this. I was as blindsided as anyone.* And on the heels of that she thought, *maybe I've been too considerate of Bill's feelings. He did this to all of us. Not just to me.*

She looked up when she felt Woody's stare boring into her. *Sorry, you had to witness all this,* she thought at him. *But you're the one who came on Thanksgiving. What'd you expect?* She left them to find their own places while she went back to the kitchen to take out the casserole, which Carrie had finished and put into the oven.

Willa appeared at her elbow like a little ghost. "Love you, Mom." She hugged her mother fiercely. "Don't worry. We all know who asked for the divorce. We don't blame you. It's still sad, though, isn't it?"

Kendra turned and enveloped Willa in a full on hug. It wasn't something they often did—not since her little-girl-with-the-skinned-knees days. "Thanks, sweetie. I know it's partly my fault. I took your dad for granted. I stupidly thought he was as focused on my career as I was."

"We *love* having a detective for a mom." On the verge of crying now, her voice sounded brittle. "We thought Dad did, too. A wife, I mean."

Kendra disentangled herself. "We'll get through this. It will just take some time."

Willa nodded. "I hope I'm half as strong as you when I grow up."

They both laughed, and Willa blew her nose on a paper towel and then grimaced at the rough texture.

Kendra picked up the casserole dish and indicated the tea pitcher. "Will you bring the iced tea?"

Willa washed her hands and then grabbed her mother's elbow. "Are you and Detective James, you know...?"

That stopped Kendra in her tracks. "Are we what?"

Willa had the grace to look at the floor.

Kendra didn't know what to say. Denial seemed the easiest route. "We're partners; you know that. We've been partners for years."

Willa didn't look up. "I know. I'm sorry, it's none of my business."

Carrie appeared as if summoned. She took one look at their faces and stopped. "Everything okay?"

Kendra nodded. "Of course." And then she hurried to the table clutching the casserole dish in both oven-mitted hands.

CHAPTER SEVEN
Appearances

Edgar appeared to be meditating. He sat on the floor with his legs folded and his hands, palms up, resting lightly on his knees. Candy knew not to disturb him when he was in this position. Even at Thanksgiving.

As sometimes happened—especially since the talk of babies had grown ever more pervasive—his mind would not become calm. It twisted and twirled and tricked him into going into the past where all his troubles had begun.

Fifth grade.

He sat in the award ceremony with his head down, staring at the floor. His no-show mother was absent again; too busy sleeping it off at home after being out all night with her new boyfriend. Ever since his dad left, she had gone from bottle to bottle and man to man.

Edgar picked at the cuticle around his thumb barely noticing when it started to bleed.

Slut. She always put him last. It happened every time a new man came into her life.

Edgar watched as Guy Fulton ran up and hugged his mother and handed her his certificate. I'll get him later, he thought. And he did. Guy never saw who tripped him and caused him to fall down the stairs after the ceremony.

Joey Pedrales sat by him at the award ceremony, which he thought strange. The teachers always made them sit in boy-girl order, but one would logically assume that said boy and said girl would be opposites. A noisy boy beside a quiet girl or vice versa. Instead, his teacher almost always paired him with Joey, someone even quieter than he.

Edgar didn't mind, though. Joey was one of the few people in the class who took nearly as much teasing as he did. She had a boy's name, and he had an old horror writer's name. That should have been enough to start a friendship. Unfortunately, both of them were simply too shy and self-conscious to let it happen. Besides, Edgar was seldom actually teased about his name—he was more often teased about his big nose and his even bigger Adam's apple. Brett Sayles, bully extraordinaire, delighted in plonking it with his hard forefinger as they passed each other in the hall.

As for Joey, they never even talked except the one time he had to say, "Excuse me," because he had accidentally elbowed her in the chest as when they both rose to leave at the same time.

They continued orbiting each other throughout junior high and into high school where Edgar finally found his niche in biology class where he learned to dissect things.

At first he worried because he enjoyed it so much. But then the teacher took a shine to him—or perhaps it was a touch of pity—and began to allow him some leeway. Before long he was like a lab assistant in charge of the specimens.

Edgar looked forward to the day he could dissect an actual human.

That memory brought him back to the real world.

He felt his open palms close into tight fists. *It's useless. No meditation today.* Besides the constant worries about kids, he was convinced the stupid holiday had something to do with his lack of focus. Edgar hated holidays of any kind. Contrived, useless excuses to overeat and sit in front of the television.

He opened his eyes and looked at his lovely blank room.

The walls were matte white. The single classic meditation cushion—a thick teal square of brushed cotton, with a perfect tassel at each corner—faced the floor to ceiling window that looked out on his serenity garden. He had done his research; he knew he needed to keep his center from collapsing, from imploding. The only way to survive day-to-day life without resorting to fresh girls—which he'd promised himself he would *not* do after he married Candy—had always been to meditate for at least twenty minutes every day.

But it was too late now. She'd pushed him too far.

He tried to get his distracted mind back on track.

Think about something else, think about med school, where he finally excelled.

It was in med school that he'd grown to love the feel of a femur in his hands. There was something serene about the shape of it, the smooth length of the shaft, the roundness of the head, the unexpected bumps of the greater and lesser trochanters. Then there was the way the pad of his forefinger perfectly fit the velvet valley of the patellar surface.

Edgar had quickly discovered that holding an intact femur in his hands was as close to happiness as he had been since his first cuts. Or his first kill. It was even better than the first time he'd stripped flesh from bone with his fingers.

But that had been after his best girl.

He hadn't been able to clean the bones completely. Even with the help of chemicals there had been a fair amount of meat left, but that was okay. He'd loved imagining how they would look after being in the ground for a while. It was only that *one* femur that he needed clean. So he could hold it. And carve it.

That thought, that imagining, had kept him in check for years, right up until Candy had forced him out of "retirement" with all her baby talk.

And now that he had brought his best girl back into the light—into the land of the living, so to speak—he was delighted he hadn't been successful in stripping her of her birthday suit completely. For the last few days, he'd found himself nearly salivating at the thought of uncovering the mysteries that lay beneath the soil where each of the others was buried.

He pushed up the sleeve of his shirt and looked at the numerical tattoo on the inside of his wrist. *Joey.* He didn't look at the tats on his upper thighs. They were much more difficult to see; they blended in with the old cut-scars perfectly. *Thankfully I made a precise record of each burial. I suppose my subconscious knew I would need to find them again, someday.* He rolled his sleeve back down.

Ommm.

He straightened the tassels on the cushion. They had to hang perfectly straight or his OCD wouldn't let him concentrate. The he got up and straightened the cords hanging down from the open blinds, and at last, the memories left him, and true meditation began.

Ommm.

CHAPTER EIGHT

Giving Thanks

The turkey skin was brown and crisp, the inside white and moist. "I can't believe it," Kendra admitted. "This is the best turkey I've ever made." She set the holiday platter at the head of the table.

"Martha Stewart strikes again." Woody chuckled.

Kendra pointed the carving knife at him. "Watch it, you." She waved the knife around menacingly. "I may not have my Glock, but that doesn't mean I'm unarmed."

Woody held his hands up in a defensive gesture. "Sorry, boss. I mean Martha."

She pierced the skin of the breast and began to slice. "Pass your plates, unless you want the leg, then you'll have to wait."

They all filled their plates, everyone talking and commenting at once.

"Looks great!"

"Are those crescent rolls? Haven't had those in for*ever*."

"Corn, pass the corn."

"Don't hog the sweet potatoes, *Carrie*."

"The baby wants yams. Give me back those yams!"

"Wait!" That was Keith. "We can't dig in until everyone says what they are thankful for this year."

The table chatter fell silent. No one expected Keith, Mr. Nonchalant-college-guy, to wax nostalgic. But there it was.

All eyes turned toward him.

He looked down at the placemat under his plate. His voice was serious. "I'm just thankful we're all together."

Sitting across from Keith, Charlie added, "I'm thankful for the holiday invitation. I wasn't looking forward to eating a turkey sub in the Student Union Building." He didn't smile when he spoke, but Keith did.

"A turkey sub in the SUB," he muttered playfully.

"I'm thankful I will soon be an aunt," Willa interrupted. She seemed to want to steer clear of any more serious talk about families.

Kendra looked around the table. "And I'm just thankful for *all* of you being here with me today." Her gaze lit briefly on each one of them—a butterfly—before landing, finally, oh-so-softly, on Woody James.

"Me, too," Carrie spoke up. "That's what I'm thankful for. I was so worried about how this would go, but it's turning into a wonderful holiday."

"Amen to that," Rory agreed. "I'm thankful to be part of such a wonderful family celebration."

That left only Woody James.

Everyone looked at him. He smiled self-deprecatingly. "Well, as the only member of the party not actually invited to this shindig..." He let that sink in. "I suppose I'm most thankful for the polite manners that prevented me from being turned away at the door."

They all chuckled, some a tad nervously, as if someone had been a just a tiny bit worried about what Detective James might say, and then the spell was broken and Kendra began to carve in earnest.

After the turkey was demolished, and the salads and other sides devoured with and without cranberry sauce, it was time for dessert.

Kendra had made a Scotch Cake—a fancy word for a chocolate sheet cake with a jigger of scotch in the batter—and everyone took a good taste of that. But Carrie had also brought her favorite caramel pie topped with whipped cream, and Willa had surprised everyone by bringing out homemade pralines. "That's the real reason I didn't get the casserole made." She wrinkled her nose. "These so-called easy pralines took all freakin' day—"

"Pinterest?" Carrie asked.

"Or Martha Stewart?" Woody teased.

Willa grinned. "I think it was a Martha Stewart recipe pinned to someone's board on Pinterest."

Kendra shook her head and shoved another praline into her mouth. "Whatever," she mumbled. "They're delicious—you've both outdone yourselves." She closed her eyes and enjoyed the candied sweetness surrounding the pecans.

She felt her daughters' eyes upon her, watching to see if they could find a connection between her and Woody, no doubt. But their concentration was broken by the obvious camaraderie between their brother and his soft-spoken friend. She opened her eyes.

Is he or isn't he? Are they, or aren't they?

Kendra could almost feel the question permeating the air. More than once, she caught Woody observing them, too.

What if they are more than just friends? Am I okay with that? I always said I would be, always championed the cause—who you love is no one's business but your own—but that's easy to say when the cause belongs to someone else. What if the cause is now sitting here in my rented dining room, am I still okay with it?

Keith glanced up, caught her eye, and winked.

She smiled. *That boy; always the charmer.* She rolled her eyes at him, and he chuckled. He was her only son and she knew she would always love and support him regardless of the issue.

It was easy to remember when he hit junior high school, and the girls had started calling nonstop every night and every weekend. Summers were even worse. It was day *and* night, then.

Bill—the one who was home most often—had activated a strict nine o'clock phone curfew. The fan club adoration was completely ridiculous, he said. And she had just grinned. *Keith* was ridiculous—ridiculously handsome, ridiculously kind, ridiculously irresistible, just like his father had been.

She had a sudden, unbidden, gut-clenching image of Bill on their wedding day wearing his tux with the royal blue cummerbund. Ridiculously sexy, wide white smile, dark almost-black hair, and those eyes. She'd chosen the royal blue to match the color of his deep blue eyes. She had nearly fainted—actually felt weak in the knees—when her father had escorted her down the aisle toward him.

Someone dropped a fork and brought her back to the present.

Kendra glanced around the table to see if anyone had noticed her momentary lack of focus.

Both Woody and Keith were looking her way.

Smiling, she popped another bite of praline into her mouth and closed her eyes again to shut them out.

CHAPTER NINE
Best Girl Joey

Edgar still sat on his teal-colored cushion attempting to meditate. But he, too, was fully back in the past.

He knew how fortunate he'd been to get his residency paid for through the Rural Healthcare Initiative. He'd signed a five-year contract to settle in Stutter Creek, where the clinic was located. The RHCI agreed to pay off one-fifth of his student loan each year until he'd completed his contract. The fact that he had grown up in Pine River only a half hour away was an added bonus. They thought it would help assure that he would stay permanently. It was difficult to find young doctors for small, rural towns. Most wanted to go to the larger cities where the money was so much better.

But they didn't know about his best girl, Joey. Didn't know she was right here, near his old hometown.

Their first summer home from their respective residencies, just after Edgar had discovered his fascination with femurs, their paths had crossed at the local Starbucks in Pine River. They'd made eye contact, and she had smiled.

Edgar's heart had almost stopped. But he'd quickly recovered. In college, in addition to the basic freshman courses, he'd also learned about true loneliness. Surrounded by thousands of other kids, he still didn't have a single friend. Much less a girlfriend.

But he did have a roommate, and though they weren't friends, he did clue Edgar into phone sex, and Internet porn, and Craigslist.

Edgar was a quick study.

When he went home that first summer; he was no longer the naïve little boy who had sat beside Joey all through elementary and into junior high. At the coffee house, when he blurted out an invitation to go to a movie, she had nodded yes. And when the night was over, and he invited her back to his home for a nightcap, she had surprised him by saying yes again.

But Joey didn't know his apartment was still in the basement of the big house he had shared with his mother. She didn't know he'd never even *wanted* to move upstairs after his mother overdosed. Nor did she know he had a separate entrance hidden behind the trumpet vines. Joey didn't know she would be his first girl, his very *best* girl.

However, since he *did* consider her to be the closest thing he had to an old friend, Edgar made sure she didn't suffer. Well, not counting that moment when she woke up in the middle, but that was completely unintentional. He just didn't have the knack for anesthesiology. Fortunately, he had a pillow that put her back under, permanently.

It had been much easier to get at the femur after that.

Edgar had hated having to sell the place after he married Candy, but moving her in there wasn't an option. He finally set fire to it one evening by making a pinhole in the gas line near the old furnace. The resulting explosion had been mainly confined to the basement, and insurance had paid off handsomely. Sort of the icing on the cake.

Fortunately, he and Candy had already taken possession of the rental on Robin Road, the one covered with trumpet vines. Of course, Joey had been moved to her new home in the woods way before the fire.

She was, after all, his best girl.

CHAPTER TEN

After the Meal

After the turkey carcass was stripped, and the remaining white meat put away for sandwiches, with all the leftovers going into Tupperware dishes for snacking later in front of the TV, Woody said he had to be going.

"Sure you won't stay and watch the game?" She was only being polite. Kendra knew his presence was a bit uncomfortable for everyone.

Woody shook his head slightly. "I've got files to go over before tomorrow. You know how it is."

Kendra nodded and started toward the door to escort him out. Behind her, she could hear the unnatural silence that had engulfed the room.

"See ya, kids," he called out. "Thanks for sharing your holiday—and your mom."

"Nice to see you again, Detective James," several voices replied in unison.

Kendra put her hand in the middle of his broad back and gave him a little shove. "You just love stirring the pot, don't you?"

He didn't reply, but she could see his shoulders shaking as he laughed under his breath.

At the door, he grasped her fingers lightly, forcing her to follow him onto the porch. "Keep in touch," he said. "I can't help thinking we'd get this mess solved a lot sooner with you there." He touched the black-sticker-stitches gently. "And I can't believe you cut yourself shaving."

Kendra smiled. "Pumpkin injury, and a little more, but we don't have to go into that." She cut that topic off and replied to his other statement. "As for the case, you know you can call me anytime. You've got my number." She let the door close softly behind them.

He held onto her fingers as he stepped off the porch.

Kendra stepped off with him. She had no choice. "C'mon, Woods. I haven't changed. I'm still me. Not helpless. Not some damsel in need of saving."

He chuckled softly and dropped her fingers. "I never thought that at all." He looked up at the sky, out at the lake, at the colorful fall leaves mounded in drifts beneath the trees. "Beautiful place. Suits you."

She didn't know what to say to that. Something between them had shifted, and she didn't know how to get it back on track. "I—" she began.

"I'd like to visit again," he interrupted. "Take you up on that offer to go fishing."

Kendra rolled her eyes, recalling how he'd invited himself to go fishing. "Call me," she said. She thought she'd been very clear on the subject of him visiting just to go fishing or hiking. But she'd been so glad to see him today that it probably negated everything she'd said earlier, about not wanting to spend time together because of Internal Affairs.

Nevertheless, she wasn't going to argue now. Not on Thanksgiving.

She turned to go back inside, but he stopped her and hauled her to him in a brotherly side-armed hug.

"Take care of yourself." His lips grazed her cheek, and she threw caution to the wind and brushed her lips across his cheek, too.

Then she pulled away, filled with regret.

"Why?" she asked. "Why are you pushing the limits? Making me push them, too?" She tapped the toe of her hiking boot on the bottom step.

"I don't know." He sounded sincere. "I suppose I just want a response. I just want to know that I haven't misread our relationship all these years." He didn't look at her. "I miss you, Ken."

The crisp air brought the bright gold fragrance of autumn to their nostrils. "I think I smell a little moisture in the air," she muttered. "Snow, perhaps."

"I miss you," he repeated. Then he squeezed her tightly a second time before stepping off the porch to where the old Mercury sat waiting like a portal into the past.

Determined not to watch him drive away this time, Kendra turned and caught a glimpse of the curtains rustling at the picture window.

She imagined the kids rushing back to their seats, giggling.

She strolled into the living room where Carrie, Rory, and Keith sat staring at the tube in earnest. Ignoring them, she continued to the kitchen where she surprised Willa and Charlie, who were deep in conversation as they finished off the crumbs of pralines in the bottom of their cellophane bags. Willa had gone all out and presented each person with his or her own orange or yellow see-through bag of pralines.

"Don't mind me." Kendra pulled out a bottle of wine.

Willa seemed oblivious to her mom's little front porch drama. "Charlie likes my pralines."

Kendra heard the note of disbelief in her younger daughter's voice and stopped near the sink. But outside the kitchen window, her eye noted the curtain of fine red dust hanging in the air above the road toward town. "We all loved the pralines, kiddo. You did great."

Willa shot her a thankful glance. "I hope Detective James remembered to take some with him." Then before Kendra could respond, Willa continued, "Charlie's going to be an electrical engineer. He hopes to work on those big wind turbines that are springing up all over the country."

Charlie ducked his head, embarrassed by the attention.

Hmmm, maybe not gay after all? Kendra held up her bottle. "Wine?"

Both kids looked at each other and nodded.

Kendra took two more glasses from the china cabinet and poured. She thought back over the years. Holidays had always meant celebratory wine.

Feeling like a third wheel, she took her glass back to the living room and plopped down between Keith and Carrie.

"You okay, Mom?" Carrie patted her mother's leg and then returned her hand to her own expanding midsection.

Kendra touched her daughter's belly lovingly. "I'm good," she said. "How about you? Pregnancy going well?"

Carrie nodded. "Just a little heartburn now and then." She shifted on the sofa and smiled. "I'm doing my yoga every morning." She took her mom's hand and laid it across her belly.

Kendra smiled, a faraway look in her eye. "I remember when I carried you. It was so much different than with Keith." She patted her son's knee with the other hand. "You were easy."

Keith smiled but barely looked away from the TV screen.

"You, on the other hand," she said to Carrie, "were a nightmare. I was sick from sunup to sundown, puking my guts out all over the station, even on crime scenes. It was awful."

Carrie laughed out loud. "I can't imagine having to go to crime scenes with a big ol' baby belly, and morning sickness, too. It's all I can do to get myself to my school studio each day." Carrie was the artist in the family. After a couple of years of art school at the local junior college, she had accepted a position as an art teacher at a local Montessori school. The tiny art studio was her pride and joy, and she had turned out to be a natural teacher.

Kendra nodded. "It was my first year as a detective. You were quite unexpected, you know." She shook her head. "I thought they were going to fire me for sure. Or knock me back to patrol." She stood suddenly. "That reminds me, here, hold my glass." She handed Carrie her wine glass. "I found a box of baby clothes when I was looking for Gran's tablecloth."

She went to her bedroom to retrieve the box she had placed on the bureau, but when she glimpsed her reflection in the old-fashioned mirror, it stopped her in her tracks.

Her hair was a messy silver corona about her head (*oh, why did I let it grow?*), and her cheeks were flushed from a combination of cooking all day and drinking wine. She was certain Woody James had nothing to do with her state of disarray.

Sitting on the edge of her bed, she placed the box on her knees and thought about the case that had brought Woody to the house. *What if they fire me now, because of this creep's suicide? How would that affect my retirement? Or should I save them the trouble and go ahead and retire early? Do I want to retire? What the hell would I do all day if I retired?* She imagined the future unrolling before her on a wave of nothingness. No work routine, no new cases, and no alarm clock.

It frightened her.

She and Bill had always planned to travel when they retired. Sea to shining sea, they'd joked. Big RV, maybe a little pull-along Jeep behind it, a couple of bikes, see the entire magnificent country they'd never had time to explore because of their work schedules—and because how much can you see in two or three weeks each summer?

Oh, they'd tried. Mount Rushmore one year, DC and Philly the next, then down to Texas to visit the Alamo, over to Cape Canaveral for Keith. She'd thought they were having a blast—at least that's how she'd felt at the time. So what if she checked her phone now and then? Sent and received emails with Woody and the sheriff from time to time? Didn't everyone do that?

She slipped her thumb under the edge of the box lid, and it caught on her stitches. The doc had done a great job—even though he had been pretty upset that she'd accidentally ripped them out the first time.

Just a few more days and she would return to get them taken out. Flexing her thumb and forefinger, she let her mind return to the contents of the box.

She reclosed the carton, carried it to the living room, and set it on the end table. No way was she going to interrupt the ballgame again. Rory glanced up, but his eyes didn't see her, they were unfocused, the way a nursing baby's are at feeding time. Men and their football, she thought. Of course, many women were sports crazed, too. *Just not in our family.* "We can look at these later," she said to Carrie. "I'm going to start the dishwasher."

Carrie heaved herself off the couch and followed her mother. "I'll help." She smoothed her knit shirt down over the baby. "If the Cowboys aren't winning, I don't want to watch." She laughed self-consciously as her father's words tumbled from her mouth.

Kendra flinched but tried to cover it. "That's exactly what Bill always said, If the 'Boys ain't winning, ain't no use watching.'" Then she went on. "Do you remember all those trips we took during the summers when you kids were small?"

Carrie picked up the box and took it with them to the dining room. "You mean our edu-vations? Sure. We had a ball—at least when Keith wasn't hogging the back seat or stinking up the entire car with his obnoxious bodily emissions."

Kendra laughed. "Edu-vations? Is that what you kids called them?"

Carrie nodded and began to gather up the handmade placemats. "We enjoyed them, though. We did. I especially loved Mount Rushmore when Dad went round and round the base of it ten times looking for the exit back to the highway."

"That was a fun trip—remember how angry Bill got when I offered to drive?"

"I sure do." Carrie laid the mats on the sideboard and inspected the antique tablecloth for stains. Luckily, they'd all been very careful. "Hey, Mom?"

Kendra looked up, her arms full of condiments and leftover serving pieces. The kids had all minded their manners and carried their own dishes to the kitchen as soon as they'd finished eating. Bill, the chief cook and bottle washer through the years, had taught them well. She waited for Carrie's question. "What is it, sweetie?"

Carrie hesitated. "Never mind." She folded the tablecloth gently and placed it on the sideboard with the placemats.

"What were you going to say?" Kendra waited another second. "It's okay, whatever you want to ask. I'm an open book." She must have seen the cheek kisses outside, Kendra thought.

"Did you and Dad ever think about taking a vacation without us kids? A weekend or anything at least?" She kept her eyes averted as she toyed with the edge of the lace tablecloth.

Not what I expected at all, Kendra thought. "Well, yes, we did." She pulled in a breath and sat down in her usual dining chair. "What are you, a mind reader?" She patted the chair beside hers, inviting Carrie to sit.

"Why do you say that?"

She waited until Carrie was seated. "Because I was just thinking, a few moments ago, about how your dad and I always talked about buying an RV and traveling the entire country—maybe even up into Canada—after we retired. And we did take a few little trips alone over the years. Remember that weekend jaunt to Vegas when you and Keith stayed with Gran and you came down with the chickenpox?"

Carrie fingered the lone chickenpox scar at the edge of her hairline. "I do remember that. It was before Willa was born. I guess I was about three or four—hey! I'll bet that's when she was conceived, right?" She gazed at her mom in earnest.

Kendra closed her eyes. Her daughter was right. It probably was when Willa was conceived. They hadn't planned on having any more kids after Carrie had surprised them, but after they arrived in Vegas, took in a couple of shows, had a few drinks, and played a few slots, they were both drunk and in high spirits, reveling in the luxury of a kid-free weekend. She'd recently stopped taking the pill because of a lump in her breast, and Bill, who'd said he packed the condoms, hadn't been able to find them when needed. He convinced her that at his age, he knew what to do to prevent pregnancy, but, of course, they were both too tipsy to make sure that happened.

"Who knows," she sighed. Open book or not, she wasn't about to discuss her ex-sex life with her pregnant daughter. "All I know is, that curtailed any more side trips for a while. Which was too bad because Bill always talked about going back again." She swished her hair off her forehead. "He did love to gamble."

"Curtailed our edu-vations for a while, too," Carrie said. "Remember how car sick Willa got when she was little?"

"Odd, isn't it?" her mom said. "I had terrible morning sickness with you, yet you never got motion sickness, not even on that dolphin watch tour we took around the Florida Keys, and then poor Willa came along—easiest pregnancy I ever had—and she's puking just looking at a backseat or a boat. Funny how she's able to drive without getting ill isn't it?"

"I read something about that one time," Carrie replied. "It has something to do with being forced to watch the horizon instead of not being able to see it from the backseat."

"Hmmm," Kendra thought aloud. "I sort of get it, but not really. I mean, what does that have to do with getting sick on a boat? Oh, well, I guess she's never had the opportunity to drive the bo—" She cut off that thought when she heard sniffling and realized Carrie was crying.

"Honey!" She left the table and hurried to her daughter, wrapping her arms around her. "What on earth is the matter?" She pressed an unused napkin into Carrie's hand.

"It's nothing, Mom," she dabbed at her wet cheeks.

"Sure seems like something."

Carrie wiped her eyes and cleared her throat. "It's just, well, I worry—I mean, look at me. I'm so big and," she held out the damp napkin, "my emotions are all over the place. How can Rory stand to look at me, to be around me? I mean, if you and Dad couldn't make it work, after all these years. What chance do I have? I'm such a mess!" Her voice cracked, and she choked back a sob. "And I didn't even finish college. My little sister will finish before me."

"Oh, sweetie." Kendra squeezed her again. That last statement almost made her laugh. "Don't worry about a thing. You are not a mess. You're the most beautiful mom-to-be I've ever seen. Your dad and I, well, we just took each other for granted. Me more than him, I suspect. You and Rory won't ever do that. You'll learn from my—our—mistakes. And why would you even care about a four-year degree when you're already doing the job you love?"

Willa came through just then. "Hey," she said, concern lacing her words. "What's happened?" She knelt in front of her sister and looked up into her face. Being the baby of the family, she'd always idolized her older siblings.

Carrie dabbed at her face again. "Everything's okay," she said. "Mom just brought out some old memories and my hormones couldn't handle it." She nodded at the box. "Let's see what we've got here."

As they were unpacking the precious little clothes, Kendra remembered their houseguest. "Where's Charlie? Wasn't he in the kitchen with you?"

Carrie began to hum 'Someone's in the Kitchen with Dinah'.

Willa laughed. "He went out the back door to explore a little bit. He said this is one of the prettiest places he's ever seen. I think we're going to walk down to the lake later."

"That sounds good," Carrie agreed. "I could use some fresh air, too. And a little exercise wouldn't hurt after all those pralines."

Willa's eyes gleamed. "Yep, we'll walk those off, and then we can come back and start on the caramel pie!"

Carrie ignored that and held up the little overalls with the tiny blue bear on the pocket. "Oh, look at these. I hope it's a boy."

Willa took the tiny clothes and held them to her cheek. "It is," she said. "It's a boy. Aunt Willa has spoken."

The sisters laughed, and Willa ran for a length of thread from the sewing basket. Carrie removed her wedding ring, and they tied it to the thread and held it over her pregnant belly. "If it goes in circles, it's a boy." Willa's voice was serious. "Side to side means it's a girl."

Kendra laughed. "You know, there are twenty-first-century ways to tell for certain."

Carrie grinned. "Where's the fun in that? Oh, look! It's going in a circle—"

"I don't think so," Willa argued. "That's a side to side motion if I ever saw one."

"Oh, my," Kendra covered her mouth dramatically. "Side to side and in a circle. That must mean twins—one of each!"

Carrie's eyes nearly popped out of their sockets. She took her wedding ring and slipped it back on her finger. "Seriously, I want to be surprised when the time comes, but it's NOT twins. That much I know." She glanced toward the living room where Rory dozed in front of the ball game. "I don't know what I'd do if it were."

After oohing and ahhing over the rest of the mementos, they repacked the box, and Carrie went back to the living room. "I'm taking it all," she said. "And I'll take good care of it so Wills can have it when it's her time."

Willa shook her head. "Gonna be a long, long time before I need any of that!"

Carrie laughed. "Famous last words…"

Kendra and Willa strolled down to the lake where they found Charlie skipping stones across the flat surface of the water. "I like this place," he said simply.

Kendra nodded. "It is relaxing, isn't it?"

Charlie skipped a few more stones.

Willa hung back. She seemed shy all of a sudden.

"I'm going a little farther," Kendra called. "There's a great little trail around this side of the lake."

"Coming with you, Mom." Willa caught up to her easily. "I don't know about Charlie," she whispered. "He's so nice, but…"

"Gay or straight, you mean?"

Willa nodded. "How could I *not* know?"

"You're asking the wrong person here, kiddo. I think my gaydar batteries expired years ago."

"I guess he could be both," Willa mused. "I mean. Do you think he's *bi?*"

Kendra had to clamp her lips shut to keep from spewing an offhand remark. "Well, I guess you could always ask your brother."

Willa frowned. "Yeah, like he'd tell me the truth."

Kendra crooked her elbow and linked her arm with Willa's. "If you want my honest opinion, I think if you can't *tell*, it's probably because he doesn't want anyone to know." Then she thought, *thank God I never had to deal with today's dating problems. Sheesh!*

CHAPTER ELEVEN
Lonely

They hiked the nearest trail and then headed back to the house where they were almost certain the ball game would be winding down. Halfway back, Charlie fell into step beside them.

"Hey," Willa said. "I hope we didn't run out on you."

He shook his head. "I didn't want to intrude on your mother-daughter time." He lifted his eyes bashfully toward Kendra. "I miss my own mother, my whole family. I think that's why Keith took pity on me and invited me along."

Kendra smiled. "I'm so glad he brought you," she said. "You are welcome at our home anytime." What a polite young man, she thought. I hope *one* of my kids is smart enough to see his worth. At that thought, she did chuckle. But she covered it well, with a throat-clearing cough. "Getting a bit chilly," she declared, zipping her hooded sweatshirt against the chill. "Can't wait to see what this place looks like come snowfall."

Both young people followed her gaze toward the upper reaches of the tall pines, perhaps envisioning them dusted with snow.

I'll remember this day, Kendra thought. It will be one of those bittersweet memories I drag out when I'm feeling nostalgic thirty or forty years from now. The day I'm moving into my assisted living apartment near one of the kids. It'll bring tears to my eyes as surely as the moment I pulled Carrie's old Easter dress out of that cardboard box.

She sucked in her gut, puffed up her nerve, and linked her other arm through Charlie's before belting out the opening words to "The Happy Wanderer" at the top of her lungs. Before they arrived back at the house, they'd also made it through a whole verse of "Frère Jacques," Willa's all-time favorite kids' song.

As they stepped up onto the porch, their arms unlinked and Willa grabbed her in another impromptu hug. "You've made it a great day, Mom. Thank you." Her eyes were shiny as she pulled away.

Two out of three ain't bad, Kendra thought. *Now, to find out what my only son is up to.*

Kendra let the two of them go through the front door ahead of her. She wasn't surprised to find Carrie asleep on the sofa with her head on Rory's shoulder and her persistently cold feet tucked beneath the blue-on-blue afghan that resided on the back of the couch. Kendra remembered the fatigue that had accompanied her own first pregnancy. The second and third weren't so bad, but the first one had been almost debilitating. She looked at Keith on the opposite end of the sofa and was rewarded with a sheepish grin. Rory didn't even notice. Upon closer inspection, he appeared to be napping, too.

Kendra patted Keith's shoulder when she walked by. Charlie and Willa had both headed straight toward the kitchen, probably on a quest for caramel pie, so she took a moment to visit the bathroom to freshen up. She didn't want Willa to think she was playing chaperone or anything, but before she closed the bathroom door, Kendra took one last look at the trio on the sofa. Something about the scene made her feel strangely wistful for their childhoods and the way they would glom together in front of the TV for one last show before bedtime. Of course, Rory wasn't there back then, but he'd fit into the family so seamlessly when he and Carrie married that it seemed as if he'd always been around.

Little did she know that soon the sentimental feelings and images from this very day—and days like it—would be the only things giving her the will to survive.

The rest of the visit went so smoothly Kendra was certain the kids had made some sort of pact to make the holiday stress-free, or taken a blood oath, perhaps, the way they'd done as little ones when they felt they needed to present a united front to their parents. Usually in the case of a stray dog or cat that needed saving.

The day after Thanksgiving, when everyone was loading up to leave, Keith gave Carrie a hug and gently patted her tummy. "Take care of the lump," he said. Then he ducked before she could whack him with her tote bag.

He turned to Willa. "Take care of yourself, little sis, and if you are going to be engaging in a long-distance romance with my roomie, always keep in mind that I can see everything on his Facetime—we have a *very* small dorm." This time, he didn't duck quickly enough, and Willa clouted him with the side of her tiny fist.

But she didn't deny the possibility of a long-distance relationship.

Kendra glanced at the quiet young man waiting patiently beside the car for his roommate.

"Can't believe you thought he was gay," Keith whispered in Kendra's ear as he hugged her. When he pulled away, after much too short a time, she could see the laughter in his merry blue eyes. "Or me either, for that matter."

"Oh, I never really," she began.

But he didn't give her a chance to finish. Instead, he simply shook Rory's hand, flung himself into the driver's seat and keyed the engine.

As he roared away, he and Charlie powered down the windows and treated them all to a smattering of Lady Gaga's anthem, "Born this Way."

Kendra put her hand on her hip. "I believe they enjoyed making sport of us."

The girls nodded.

Carrie shrugged. "Do you think he'll ever grow up?"

"God, I hope not," Kendra replied. "At least not until I do."

Her daughters looked at her with confusion in their eyes. But Kendra didn't elaborate. It was just an offhand remark meant to make everyone smile; instead it had hit almost too close to home, as if she were about to embark on a new phase of her life just as Keith was. And so I am, she thought. *Maybe retirement is my next phase, or I could go into security or private investigations or—*

"—gotta be going," Willa was saying. "I love you, Mom. Take care of yourself."

"You, too, kiddo. Don't drive too fast and no—"

"Texting, I know." She slung her shoulder bag into the front seat and followed it. "I'll call you when I get home."

Kendra leaned in and hugged her through the window. "You better not forget."

Willa hugged her neck and assured her she wouldn't forget, and then she whispered, "Love the specs, by the way. Very scholarly." Then she drove sedately away, and it was time for Kendra to say goodbye to Carrie and Rory. Somehow it was harder to let her elder daughter go. "I know you'll take care of each other," she said, including Rory in the sentiment, "but I just hate to let you go. The next time I see you might be when you're going into the hospital—"

"Oh, Mom," Carrie's eyes grew huge. "Don't say that. I know we'll see each other before then. We have to. I don't want to go through my whole pregnancy without you there." Her lower lids glistened.

Kendra patted her arm. "Of course I'll see you, what was I thinking? I could drive down after Christmas if the weather stays pretty. Don't you worry about a thing."

Carrie nodded. "I feel like a little kid again, wanting my mommy around all the time."

Rory pulled her to his side. "You're going to be a mommy, too. A GREAT mommy!"

Kendra swooped in and planted a big kiss on her cheek. "Yes, you will. You're both going to be amazing parents. I just know it."

Rory tucked Carrie into the front seat and gave Kendra another brief wave as he climbed into the driver's seat. Carrie flapped her hand out the window a few times and then they were gone.

Kendra felt like an idiot, standing in the drive, waving as they disappeared, but she couldn't make herself go inside. She stood a few seconds longer, watching the dancing spiral of leaves stirred into action by the motion of the vehicles. Then she turned and shaded her eyes. It wasn't late yet, but already the lake was beginning to shimmer metallically.

She stepped onto the porch and pushed her way inside the empty house. The silence enveloped her as surely as if cotton wool had been stuffed into her ears.

She put on the radio but once again, music just seemed to exacerbate the fact that she was alone. Picking up the TV remote, she turned to one of the national news channels. More horrific beheadings by a new terrorist group. A racially motivated riot over a police-involved shooting in a small Missouri town, and another airline disaster in Malaysia.

No good news, she muttered. Time to retire and retreat. Become a hermit.

She grabbed a bottle of water from the fridge and headed for the shimmery lake. It seemed to be her only place of solace anymore.

CHAPTER TWELVE

Tag

Ella placed an ice-choked glass of water in front of Chet Boone. "Morning! You all ready to go?"

He smiled up at her, storm-cloud eyes twinkling. "Yep. You sure you can spare the Nickster for a couple of days?"

Ella laughed. "At this point, I would throttle you if you tried to back out." She held a menu up and whispered to him behind it. "He's been driving me crazy packing and unpacking his gear." She hastily put down the menu and glanced around as her son came through the kitchen door with an omelet and a glass of milk.

"Hi, Mr. Boone." He plopped down in a booth nearby. "I'm ready; I just have to eat breakfast. Mom said I couldn't go if I didn't."

"Smart Mom," Chet replied. "I think I'd better have the same. We've got a long hike in front of us, you know."

Nick nodded.

"You guys off on a job?" The voice came from a table near the window.

Chet turned his attention to the dark haired man. "Hey, Doc. Yep, we've got a report of a cougar getting too close to the campground up at Copper Lake."

The doctor wiped his mouth with his napkin and stood, thumbing through his wallet for money. After looking at the bills he pulled out, he dropped a twenty on the table. "You two be careful out there. I don't want to have to stitch up any big cat scratches."

Chet smiled, but Nick took him seriously. "Oh, Mr. Boone won't let anything happen to us. He knows all about big cats and bears and all the predators that live in the forest.

That's why he's a wildlife biologist." He attacked his omelet with vigor.

The doctor tipped his head back and chuckled. "Of course he does." He headed for the door. "Nevertheless, it sounds like a lengthy job. Guess you'll be gone a while. Hope you've got plenty of bug spray and a good first aid kit." He hesitated at the door as Chet replied.

"We sure do, Doc. But we'll be back tomorrow night—maybe even earlier. Nick has school on Monday. Anyhow, cougars are pretty nervous. It's probably already back up the mountain by now."

The doctor nodded and waved one hand in acknowledgment. Then he ducked out the door and headed to his car.

"He gets an early start, doesn't he?" Ella poured Chet a cup of coffee in a thick white mug.

"Sure does—and even though I know he's an avid hiker, I never run across his camp in the forest. I'm going to have to ask him which trails he prefers. At least he seems to know what he's doing."

Ella nodded and went behind the counter to finish Chet's omelet. "The only time I see him is when he stops by to get a bite before hiking. Well, that and driving down the road, of course."

"That's right, he lives just around the corner from you."

"Yep, I see him and his wife every now and then. We don't socialize, though." She set a plate in front of Chet and glanced at Nick. "Slow down, son. Chet hasn't even started yet."

Nick glanced up with a sheepish grin. "I can't wait to go fishing and catch our supper and cook it over a campfire again." He took a deep drink of milk and wiped his upper lip with the back of his hand.

Ella smiled indulgently. "Are you sure you want to go, Nick? I sense a bit of uncertainty in your voice."

Chet laughed.

"Mo-o-m." Nick rolled his eyes and stabbed another bite of omelet with his fork.

Ella patted him on the shoulder and started back to the kitchen. She couldn't believe Chet was so patient with her boy. He actually seemed to enjoy Nick's company. There was no doubt that Nick enjoyed his—it was as if Chet was the father he'd never had. She thought back to the last conversation she and Chet had shared on that subject.

"I can wait," he'd said. "After what you and Nicky have been through, I wouldn't blame you if you never trusted another man." His eyes had darkened. "Especially since I wasn't even there to help."

Ella had assured him he was there when needed—afterward—at the hospital. Besides, it felt good to know that she and Nicky could handle whatever life threw at them. She shuddered remembering how awful the break in and attack had been.

Now Chet was telling her he'd wait for her. Ella hadn't known what to say. He'd told her he wanted an exclusive relationship and that even though they'd only know each other a few months, he was positive they were meant to be together—all three of them. I *want* to be Nicky's dad, he'd said.

That statement had thrown Ella a curve. She'd known the two seemed to share a remarkable bond, but for Chet to come right out and tell her he wanted to be Nick's father… that had been quite a surprise. They'd talked all around the subject of living together, and even of getting married *someday*, but that was all in the future. Right now, she was very satisfied with the way things were. And that was another surprise, from deep inside *her* this time.

She picked up the plates and cutlery but had no more time for reflection. After hugs and kisses from Nick, and a quick but chaste peck on the cheek from Chet—her customers were watching—the two of them picked up Nick's equipment and left.

Ella waved and blew them more kisses as they climbed into Chet's state issued pickup.

She had just finished wiping the booth where Nicky had sat when the tiny bell over the door jingled again. Picking up the coffee pot, she turned to see Nicky's biological father, Tag, standing in the doorway.

Her first instinct was to flee. She hadn't seen the guy in over ten years. And if she never saw him again in the next ten, it would still be too soon.

But it's my restaurant. I can't run. Maybe he's just passing through like so many folks in Stutter Creek. Maybe he won't even know it's me.

Ella sucked in a breath, straightened her spine, and decided to take the bull by the horns. "Hello, Tag." Her voice was icy. She tried not to notice how his hair was the exact same shade of toffee as Nick's.

Still looking every bit the cocky football star he'd been in high school, the man smiled. "Ella. Good to see you." He held out his hand.

She stuck a menu in it and led him to a booth in the back. "I'm sure you're just passing through. I'll bring you a cup of coffee while you wait." She turned on her heel and stalked back to the coffee station for a mug.

Tag sat there in silence. He seemed genuinely surprised that she hadn't welcomed him with open arms the way she'd done back in high school.

When she took his coffee back to the table, he cut right to the point. "I'm here to talk about our son," he said. "I saw a news report about what happened to the two of you."

Heart pounding, head spinning with disbelief, Ella bit the tip of her tongue to cut off her intended retort. *Our son? You mean the baby you wanted me to abort?* Then she pulled herself together and replied, "You'll have to call me later after I get off work. I can't sit down and discuss anything right now."

She couldn't imagine why he had suddenly appeared out of nowhere, but it couldn't be good. It was too easy to recall how he had reacted when she'd told him she was pregnant all those years ago in high school. "I'll pay for the abortion," he'd said. "You know I've already got a college football scholarship. Nothing's going to interfere with that."

That wasn't the last time she'd seen him. She recalled how nervous she'd been at graduation when she'd looked down and caught him staring up at her as she walked the stage. Probably trying to see the baby bump, she remembered thinking. But they'd never spoken again. Now, here he was. *What could he possibly want?* She didn't believe for a moment that he wanted to be a father after all these years.

Ella wrote her cell number on a slip of paper. "If you want to talk to me, call me after seven tonight."

Tag took the paper, read it, tucked it into his jacket pocket, and ordered breakfast.

Ella fried the eggs, toast, and hash browns in record time. She couldn't stop thinking how he must have passed Nick and Chet on the street as they were leaving.

She had his order out to him in minutes. She wanted him gone. She was certain she could feel his gaze eating into her flesh the entire time she moved around the dining area, waiting on the other customers. But she didn't have time to worry about it because just then Kendra Dean came through the door with her coffee thermos held high.

"Going for a hike?" Ella greeted her.

"Fishing," Kendra said, patting her canvas fishing vest to illustrate her words. "I went for a little hike yesterday and found a sweet spot with a drowned tree—it has to be a catfish hole." She smiled. No one here knew her reputation as a stone-cold workaholic. Most folks in Stutter Creek thought she had genuinely embraced retirement out at her Copper Lake home. She wasn't sure why, but she wanted to propagate that idea. "Thought I'd get one of your breakfast burritos to take along."

"Good idea," Ella replied. "John Stockton came in first thing this morning. He and Danny were headed out to the creek to fish. Said the trout should be jumping." She hesitated with her head cocked to one side like a spaniel. "There's something different about you today. New hair-do?"

Kendra laughed and pulled her glasses off her nose. She held them out for Ella's inspection. "Just got these a few days ago. Bifocals. Can you believe it?"

"Could be worse," Ella laughed. "Could be trifocals."

Kendra rolled her eyes and replaced her glasses. "I'm sure those will be next, but after slicing open my hand just carving a jack o' lantern, I suppose I should be thankful I've got these."

Ella glanced at her injured hand. "When do those come out?"

Kendra followed the café owner's gaze. "Heading over there this afternoon. Sure glad they take appointments on Saturday."

"You just missed the doctor," Ella mentioned. "He was in earlier, too."

"Seems like trout aren't the only things jumping around here today." Kendra looked around the dining area. "Is there anyone I know who *hasn't* been in yet?"

As if on cue the back door opened and a woman's voice called out, "Morning, ladies."

"Just in time," Ella replied. "Can you whip up one Super-Cop Special, please?"

"You bet," the older woman called back. "And good morning to you, Detective Dean."

Kendra glanced toward the kitchen where Martha, the previous owner of the café, was tying a snowy apron around her rotund middle. "Morning," Ken replied. "Good to see you back. How was your Thanksgiving down in Florida?"

"Wonderful," Martha sighed. "Kids and grandkids galore—Allie says hello and sends you a big hug."

"Fantastic," Kendra replied. "She doing okay?"

"Doing great. Got her nursing degree, got married, now she's expecting her first baby. She can't wait to be a mom." She clucked her tongue against her teeth. "Thanks to you and Detective James—"

"Don't forget John and Beth Stockton." Kendra smiled. "And Turk the Wonder Dog. And Chief Brown, of course."

"Of course," Martha nodded, washing her hands. "It took a lot of teamwork—but you all saved my Allie. Saved her life." She cracked two eggs onto the hot surface of the grill.

Ella rolled her shoulders and took a deep breath. It had been a busy morning already. As usual, she had been chief cook, bottle washer, waitress, and cashier since she'd opened at six-thirty. She was always glad when Martha arrived; she came in later now than she did when Ella had first bought the place. In fact, she had told Ella she was seriously thinking of retiring and moving to Florida for good, but she just couldn't seem to tear herself away. Ella was glad. She knew she could run the place now, with just her part-time help, but she had grown to care about the sweet woman. She truly enjoyed spending the days with her.

From the corner of her eye, Ella saw Tag stand and drop a bill onto the table. She waited for a moment to see if he'd left the entire amount or just the tip. Some folks—like the doc—simply left cash on the table, but most preferred to pay with plastic at the cash register.

Tag must have left the whole amount. He nodded at her and walked toward the door, back as straight as tempered steel. What had he thought would happen, she wondered? *Did he really think I would be delighted to see him? That I would fall all over myself the way I'd done when he asked me to the senior prom? Did he even have a clue about the little boy who would have worshiped the ground he walked on if he'd been given half a chance?*

Ella felt angry tears threatening to crack her resolve, so she busied herself ringing up his check and making change. Ten dollar tip. Not too little, not too much. Just right as Goldilocks said, right before she broke baby bear's chair.

"Order up!" Martha called.

Ella straightened her own spine and hurried toward the pass-through window, glad of the distraction. The less time she had to think about Tag, the better off she'd be. But of course, that was wishful thinking. All day long his image kept creeping into her head. He still had that golden-boy look as if nothing bad or unpleasant ever befell him, as if the silver spoon he'd been born with still fed him three squares a day. Soon her thoughts were running as wild as rabbits in a vegetable garden. *What if he said he wanted to be a father now, what if he said he was sorry, what if he said he'd made a mistake, and now he wanted a relationship?*
What if, what if, what if …

CHAPTER THIRTEEN

The Dogwalker

Edgar placed himself in position in his white room and let out all his air.

Candy was going on about her sister again. He thought they'd put this all to rest. No children. Ever.

But apparently women have the right to change their minds.

She just wouldn't shut up about it. His sweet little Candy was gone. Now she seemed brittle, like old spun sugar that would shatter at the slightest touch.

He stood it as long as he could. The more she nagged about the patter of little feet, the more he felt drawn to the woods.

Just like that day last September when he'd found himself driving aimlessly through the neighboring communities looking at the scenery. In truth, he'd simply been putting off going home. The baby brouhaha had only just begun.

He'd been driving, subconsciously drawing nearer and nearer to the hub of his "good girl" wheel when he'd spied a young woman trudging beside the shoulder of the rural road.

She had seemed disgruntled and breathless as she slogged along holding onto a tall dog on a short leash. The dog resembled a young Scooby-Doo. Its long pink tongue lolled from one side of its mouth giving it the appearance of a permanent goofy grin. To Edgar, the big pup appeared to be walking the girl instead of the other way around. If he hadn't taken the scenic route to avoid going home, he might never have seen the pair at all.

When he first pulled up beside her, she tried to ignore him.

"Miss? Oh, *miss*." He leaned over so she could see his concerned expression through the open window. "I know this might sound strange, but I'm a doctor, and I couldn't help but notice that you seem to have had a little too much sun. Why don't you let me give you and the pooch a ride home? I'm on my way to my clinic, but I couldn't drive past and leave you looking as if you're about to pass out."

The young woman swiped her purple-hued hair off the back of her splotchy red neck. She really did look as if she had gotten too much sun.

"No," she replied, nervously twirling a sapphire ring on her third finger. "I'll be all right. Thanks anyhow." She sped up and tried to move even farther off the roadway. She obviously didn't trust him.

Edgar chuckled. "That's all right, but here," he held up an unopened bottle of water. "At least take this so you won't get too faint. I hope you don't have far to go."

She looked at the bottle of water and licked her lips. "I – well, it is quite a ways back—my fiancé will be getting home soon. He'll wonder—"

Edgar knew he had her then. He could hear the *want to* in her voice.

He nosed the car over just slightly in front of her and held the bottle out the passenger window. A quick glance in his rearview assured him no other cars were coming.

She took the bottle being very careful not to get close enough for him to grab her wrist. "Thanks," she said. "You really a doctor?"

Up close, Edgar could see that she was not used to exerting herself in the middle of the day this way. Especially not in the dog days of summer. She was just a little too heavily made up for that. He couldn't wait to hear her story.

"Of course I am." He held up his lab coat. His ID badge was clipped to the lapel. "What are you doing out here so far from home?"

She unscrewed the cap from the water bottle and gulped greedily.

Edgar couldn't take his eyes off her throat muscles as she drank. She was wearing short-shorts and a tiny tank top.

He opened a second bottle of water for himself.

At last she lowered the bottle and nodded toward the dog in response to Edgar's question. "Clyde got out—again. Only this time he wouldn't stop when I called. Chased the silly thing for half an hour before I caught him. S'posed to be at home making supper for my boyfriend. We were going to go to a party, but he was late."

Edgar nodded sympathetically. He made it a point not to look at her. "Good looking beast," he joked. "Had a dog very much like him when I was a kid. Named him Scooby." He took another swig of water. "Crazy mutt liked to get out and run the neighborhood, too. I was forever having to bail him out of the pound." The lies rolled off his tongue so easily he almost convinced himself.

The girl looked at him a little closer. "You telling me the truth? You really had a Great Dane like my Clydie?"

Edgar nodded again, still making certain not to look directly at her. "Best darn dog I ever had. Courage was his middle name—when I could keep him at home that is." He chuckled as if they shared an inside joke. "Well, I hope the water helped. You two should really find a tree, grab a little shade for a while before you pass out or spike a migraine."

Drool dripped from the tip of Clyde's long, long tongue.

"And be sure to share some of that with him, too." He indicated the puddle of drool on the dusty shoulder of the road. "Looks like he could use it."

The girl glanced down at her furry companion. It was obvious she hadn't given his thirst a second thought. "Oh, poor baby." She looked at the remaining water. There was about a quarter of the bottle left. She held out her palm and poured water into it. Clyde's pink tongue lapped it eagerly, but most of the liquid wound up on the ground.

Edgar saw his opportunity "Well, good luck to you. Hope that little drink helped. Enjoy your party." He put on his blinker and made a show of checking his rearview mirror as though to pull out onto the highway.

"Wait!" she called. "Umm, Mister. I mean, Doctor... do you, would you happen to have one more bottle of water? I'll be glad to pay you. I just don't think Clydie got enough. He's a big dog, you know." She dropped the empty bottle and stabbed one hand into her back pocket as though in search of cash.

Smiling, Edgar flapped his hand at her. "Keep your money! I've got a whole case of water in the trunk. I'm a weekend, hiker. I always keep water on hand. Wouldn't be without it." While he spoke, instead of pulling back onto the highway, he snugged the car in a little closer to the shoulder. He put the gearshift into park and opened the driver's door still being ultra-careful not to give her so much as a casual glance. "I'll let you have a bottle for Clyde and another for yourself. Then I've got to be on my way. Patients are probably getting im*patient*." He laughed self-deprecatingly at his feeble attempt at wit.

She stepped a little closer to the car. "I really appreciate this—"

"There's a collapsible bowl left over from my last hike," he interrupted. "It'd be perfect for Clyde." He stretched his arm into the trunk as far as he could and then pulled back with a groan of pain.

"You okay?"

Edgar grimaced. "Fine," he said through clenched teeth. "Injured my back last weekend. Too much weight in my pack." He dug his fingers into the muscles of his lower spine. "I should have known better. Me, of all people."

"Let me get it," she said. "I'm just grateful you stopped at all."

Edgar stepped aside so that she would have unobstructed access to the open trunk. "Help yourself," he said. "The bowl slid toward the back—"

She leaned in as far as Clyde's short leash would allow and Edgar smashed the trunk lid down on her head exactly the same way he'd accidentally done old Mr. McGraw all those years earlier.

The edge of the lid coming down on her skull caused Clyde to jerk free and run all the way to the safety of the woods before he stopped and looked back.

Edgar didn't have time to worry about him. The girl had collapsed half in and half out of the trunk. Without missing a beat, he picked up her bottom half and flopped it over into the trunk before slamming the lid down again.

He remembered wondering if she was dead, or just unconscious. And then he realized he didn't know and didn't care. The hub of the wheel was only a few minutes away.

As he sauntered around to the front of the Toyota, he began to sing, "Ding dong the wench is dead, I rapped her head, and now she's dead. Ding dong the little wench is dead." He felt lighter and happier than he had in days. His wife wanted a baby. She just wouldn't shut up about it. But he had *his* baby. She was in the trunk. And *she* wouldn't be a stone around his neck for the rest of his life.

He glanced around once more as he pulled out onto the roadway. Then he cranked the stereo up and listened to his classic jazz station as loudly as he could stand. If there were any noises from the trunk, he didn't want to hear them. *Don't want to hear them, nope. Don't want to know. Not yet. Be a surprise. A nice, big surprise just like a new dad watching his wife give birth. You don't always know what you're going to get.*

If he'd looked in his rearview mirror one more time, he would have seen the puzzled look on Clyde's face as the big pup watched him drive away.

Edgar inhaled and opened his eyes. His white room and green serenity garden outside the window came back into focus, and he smiled. Carving her femur had been exceptionally sweet, much better than dealing with brittle spun sugar.

CHAPTER FOURTEEN

Into the Woods

Kendra paid for her order and left them with a little wave. She craved a few moments of serenity in the woods surrounded by birdsong and the gentle lapping of waves against the rough shore of the lake.

She climbed into her pickup and started the engine. It was still warm from the drive in. Stupid to come into town for a burrito and then turn around and drive back to the lake. Just shows how screwed up my thinking is lately. What a waste of gas. Oh, well. Too late now.

She thought of trying to make the hike all the way to the creek that gave the town its name, but knowing that she might run into John and Danny Stockton squelched that desire. Not that she didn't like them, quite the contrary, she sincerely admired the whole family. She just didn't have a head for company today, didn't think she could enjoy small talk. All she wanted right now was a bit of peace before she got up her nerve to call Woody and tell him she wanted to see the case files. She knew it was against the rules of her suspension, but she also thought she could help him figure it out.

As she ruminated, she let the pickup truck meander back toward the lake. The burrito was delicious, and the hot coffee both soothed and invigorated her. Nevertheless, she eventually came to the conclusion that no matter how much she enjoyed the lake's peace and quiet, she couldn't deny a deep longing to get back to the real world. The one she'd lived in for the past twenty years. *Hard to go from ninety miles an hour down to zero without suffering some sort of whiplash. And if I don't start doing something soon, that whiplash is liable to paralyze me.*

Burrito finished, she began to watch for the turnoff to the lake store. With the holiday behind her, and nothing much ahead of her, Kendra felt the need to simply stand in one spot, drop a line in the still morning water, and think things over. The more she thought about looking at her case files, the more she'd begun to crave it.

Maybe this is a bad idea. Maybe I should just take my lumps, go ahead and retire, whiplash or not. Maybe that's what my subconscious is telling me by making me yearn for these other things. Like fishing. Maybe it's telling me to slow down. Live for myself for a change. She glanced up toward the sun. Dammit. I'm really not thinking straight. Why did I agree to go back in and get the stitches removed on a Saturday? Now I'll have to drive all the way back to town after I'm through. Nope, definitely not thinking straight.

At the entrance to the camp store, she wheeled the pickup into the empty parking lot behind it and strode down the inclined drive with a purpose. In her head, she was already casting that first hook into the water, counting the number of slowly expanding circles widening around the dancing bobber.

"Can of night crawlers, please."

The store clerk, a slack-jawed teenage boy who kept one eye on his wide-screen Galaxy phone the entire time, sauntered over to a white, coffin-sized cooler and filled a small tin can with worms. The tin can still had a Pork-n-Beans label wound around its middle.

"Buck fifty," the boy said, holding his hand out without looking up.

Kendra debated shorting him on purpose, just to teach him a lesson, but she knew it wouldn't do any good. He probably wouldn't even have to make up the difference. The store owner would undoubtedly suffer the small loss.

She snapped the rubber band around the makeshift foil lid, which the boy also provided without comment, and then stuffed the can into one of her voluminous fishing-vest pockets.

Leaving her truck in the lot behind the store, Kendra drained the last swallow of coffee from her thermos and tucked it into the cab. She then retrieved her gear and began the short hike to the spot where she had decided to begin. It was one of the places she'd scouted out yesterday.

By the time she found the spot, her head felt clearer.

The water was still. The early morning breeze barely rippled its skin. In the evening the sunset made the lake gleam like a polished copper pot, but in the early morning hours it was ghosted by a fine white mist that rose up from the surface of the water like a cadre of thinly veiled spirits dissipating in the cool autumn air.

Kendra set her tackle box and old-fashioned creel on the ground and removed the worms from her pocket. She immediately baited her first hook and then pulled on soft leather gloves. Her stitches protested a bit, but the gloves would protect them. She relished the thought of getting the darn things removed, for good.

Standing at the edge of the water in her hiking boots, Kendra cast her worm as far toward the center as possible. Copper Lake was a big, wide lake. It was impossible to see the other shore with the veil of mist obscuring her vision, but she knew how much line to play out to hit the deeper water. "Hit 'em deep where the big fish sleep," she murmured.

Slowly, patiently, she reeled the worm back toward the shore giving it a little jerk every few feet to make it dance along beneath the surface of the water. In her minds eye, Kendra imagined a large catfish with its mouth open ready to latch on to her dancing worm.

But it didn't happen.

For some reason, she caught not a single fish. Nor had even a nibble.

After an hour of trying, Kendra gave up and picked up her gear. The cool autumn morning was beginning to give way to a cool autumn mid-morning. The temperatures were in the upper forties—not bad for nearing winter she thought. Not bad unless you own a ski resort. She'd heard lots of grumbling in the grocery store and café about how poorly the season was apt to be this year. Should have a foot of new snow by now most folks said, but so far, nada.

Kendra walked on down the edge of the shoreline watching for old logs and tall weeds. That's where the big cats will slumber her dad always said. *And by God I want fish for supper tonight.* She could almost smell the crunchy fried odor of cornmeal battered fish sizzling in the pan.

About a third of a mile away from her original spot, Kendra spied the ancient drowned tree at the edge of the water. Moss grew abundantly on one of the thick, barely-visible branches, and weeds appeared to have a stranglehold on it below the water line.

That's where you are, old granddad, she thought. *That's where you live.*

Quietly, she set her tackle box down and speared another wiggly onto her hook. Wading out just a bit farther than before—very quietly since she knew catfish were easy to startle—she carefully flipped her hook toward the hoary mess. Probably just get hung up and lose my hook, she thought. *But maybe I'll get lucky. Then again, maybe I'll catch a snake.*

She glanced at the prickly vegetation. *Perfect home for water moccasins. I've got my boots on, though, and I* want *a fish. I don't want to go home empty-handed.* She glanced back the way she had come. Bill had often jokingly referred to her as bull-headed even to the point of danger. Never tell her not to do something, he'd say. That's like waving the proverbial red flag.

Is it true? Am I stubborn to the point of excess, to the point of danger?

She reeled her ineffectual hook back to the shore and then cast her line gently toward the far edge of the weeds. Idiot, she thought. *Just asking for a tangle—*

She felt a bump on the hook and automatically gave it a little jiggle.

Another bump and she was certain a catfish was stalking her worm.

"Come on, you," she muttered. "Take the bait."

She reeled slowly and then *wham* the fish took the worm, and she jerked upward to set the hook.

Gotcha!

The stillness of the lake was suddenly shattered by the fish's life or death struggle. It tried to slip the hook and disappear back into the depths of the weedy hole, but Kendra was having none of that. She kept a continuous tension on the line, not too steep, just steep enough to keep him coming in.

"Don't tangle, don't tangle, don't tangle." She repeated the words like a mantra as she brought the big fish closer to shore.

Every now and then she could see its steel gray back breach the misty surface of the water. "Fishy, fishy in the brook, Mommy caught him with a hook, Daddy fried him in the pan..." she wound the reel up harder. "And baby ate him like a man."

She remembered reciting the nursery rhyme to her kids when they were on their own fishing/camping trips way back in the day. Reciting it now felt hollow. That part of her life was no more. Every time she looked back in memory, something leaped up to bite her as if *she* were bait on a hook.

Kendra eased the catfish closer to shore. She could see the barb lodged firmly in its lip. "You're mine now, sucka," she muttered. But she said it without vigor. Somehow the fight had gone out of her instead of the fish.

Without debating the issue, Kendra yanked the thing out of the water and landed it on the bank. The big fish crashed into the dry grass at the edge of the water. The flip-flopping death struggles made her stomach churn, and she had a brief moment to wonder if her fishing days were over forever or if this were simply a momentary pause.

She placed a booted foot on the creature's whiskered, alien head and reached down to remove the hook. Kendra was glad for her leather gloves, she had the hook out in record time, and then she rolled the big cat back into the water with both hands. It wriggled once and disappeared into the deep.

God, what's wrong with me? I love fishing. I wanted fried fish for supper.

She stood on the bank and felt something slip away as surely as the old fish had slipped back into its weed-choked home.

Shrugging off the mood like a pesky insect, Kendra picked up her fishing gear and started back toward her rented lake house. As she turned, she caught a hint of movement from the corner of her eye.

Chill bumps rashed the backs of her arms.

She stiffened but tried not to make any sudden movements. If someone was watching her—and her sixth sense told her they were—she didn't want the person to know she was aware of them.

Slowly and deliberately, she reached into one of the numerous pockets on her fishing vest and flicked off the safety on her Glock. She didn't remove it, but she did fit the grip into her palm inside the voluminous pocket.

Now, she turned toward the area where the movement had occurred. The gooseflesh was gone, but her senses were on high alert. She raised the pistol nonchalantly inside the pocket. It won't be the first time I've fired through fabric, she thought, and it probably won't be the last. *Unless I retire, that is.* She shoved that idea back into its little mind-box to deal with later. The tackle box and empty creel both grasped in one hand, she began a slow walk back along the edge of the lake toward the camp store where she'd left her truck. She kept the Glock raised and ready inside her vest pocket, glad she'd finally given in and invested in the model 19, it was quite a bit smaller and lighter than the model 22 she'd trained with. But, thankfully, she didn't have to use it. She didn't see or hear anything out of the ordinary.

Could've been a deer, she thought, but her sixth-sense said otherwise. She had learned never to ignore that sixth sense. Most called it a cop's intuition.

Kendra let her eyes take in her surroundings, looking surreptitiously for a landmark. *There.* Her gaze fell on the splintered remains of a standing, lightning-struck tree, then she meandered on her way, hand still on her weapon as if she hadn't seen or heard a thing.

When she was certain she was no longer visible from the spot at which she'd first experienced the gooseflesh, she tucked her fishing gear beneath a low spreading juniper bush and slowly began to make her way back. At times, when there was little vegetation or a gap in the trees, Kendra found herself almost crawling.

Pulse racing, she had to mentally remind herself to get a grip. As a detective, she hadn't done a lot of searches the way she had as a young—skinny—patrol officer. She'd done her share, just like helping out on the case in which a killer had kidnapped Martha's niece, Allie.

This was a bit more difficult. Okay, a lot more difficult she thought. Not a spring chicken anymore. Not exactly skinny, either. She grimaced as a sharp stone gouged her knee.

Rising to her feet again, Kendra consciously slowed her breathing and pulled the Glock out of her pocket, automatically checking the magazine as she did so.

She stopped behind a thickly branched Douglas fir and pushed her too-long bangs off her forehead before starting across the last few feet of open ground toward the blackened tree. Her new glasses kept slipping down on her nose, and she vowed to get the frame adjusted as soon as possible.

There were no sounds except for the occasional chirp and call of birds high in the trees. She no longer felt watched. Due to the heavy carpet of fall leaves, she thought she would be able to hurry across the ground without making too much noise. Now and then, however, her foot would find a small dry twig or a pinecone but other than that, the woods were Sunday silent.

Kendra discerned no movement. *Maybe it was a deer after all. Or some other four-legged creature.* In the few weeks she'd been here, she'd explored almost every inch of the lowland area between her rented house and the lake, and she'd seen plenty of deer. But she'd never once felt her cop's intuition kick into overdrive the way it had a few moments earlier.

After breaking an exceedingly large dry twig, she placed her feet more carefully (a *bull in a damn china shop*), watching the cushy earth for signs of disturbance. There was so much ground cover it took her eyes a while to make out a place where a sapling branch had been broken almost but not quite all the way through the pale inside of the fresh wood practically shouting *look at me.*

Kendra nodded, assuring herself she was indeed on some kind of trail, just as her eyes located a pinecone that had been smashed flat by the heel of someone's large shoe, the triangular seeds fanned out in a spiky brown corona on the ground.

For the first time in weeks, she felt alive. Her lips were drawn together into a thin, concentrated line, and if the kids had seen her, they would have been shocked at the transformation from Martha Stewart back to Detective First Grade Kendra Dean. But if Woody could have seen her at that moment, it would have done his heart good. He would have known there was no way she was ready to retire.

Letting her gaze take in the whole of the forest—as far as she could see at least—Kendra waited. If anything moved, she wanted to see it before it saw her.

When she felt certain there was nothing nearby, she continued up the slight incline toward the base of the mountain. She hadn't explored anywhere other than the area between her house and the lake so she didn't know how far up she should go. She knew the campground was somewhere nearby, so she followed the scant trail until it met another, this time going back down.

Probably the trail back to the camp store and my truck, she thought. But she wasn't ready to go back. Not just yet.

She reached into her pocket and took out her cell phone. No signal. In a clearing, she might get lucky, but with these trees, no way.

She continued upward.

Halfway up the incline—she could see where the base of the mountain began because the soft rise became steeper and scragglier—Kendra began to relax her guard. Her breathing returned to normal. So far, so good, she thought. If anyone had been there, they were obviously long gone. *Most likely a hiker or camper not in the mood for company. Just like me when I started out, hoping not to run into anyone.*

She reached the base of the mountain and was surprised to see an old blacktop forest road. Kendra didn't know the area well at all, but she'd had no idea a road ran this close.

Glancing behind, she was doubly surprised to see how far up she had hiked. *Go on and find the campground? Or go back to the camp store where I left the truck?* The first thought appealed to her, mostly because she was convinced someone had been nearby and also because she was the type of person—okay, detective—who had an almost inordinate need to be familiar with her *entire* surroundings.

She hesitated but a moment. The road beckoned, and she stepped out of the dim forest onto the blacktop, coming out of the shade and into the sunlight.

The shape of her shadow on the pavement told her the morning was gone. Her belly reminded her how long it had been since breakfast.

Nevertheless, she began to walk, her breath puffing out into the cold air like tiny ghost bubbles as she exerted herself more and more. Soon, she rounded a bend and came upon one of those carved Smokey the Bear signs that said, Please Don't Burn Down My Home. A little farther on, a wooden post held up a triangular marker telling her she was entering Stutter Creek campground.

As if on cue, her ears picked up the sound of water stuttering over a rocky creek bed. *That would be the famous creek that feeds into Copper Lake and also gave the small town its name.* Of course, she'd seen portions of the creek many times. It wound its way down the mountain and ran almost directly alongside the small town before ending in the lake.

She hadn't seen this section, though, nor this campground and she wondered if this was anywhere near the legendary Crybaby Bridge she'd heard about. I'll want to check that out later, she thought. She knew Woody would be thrilled—he was practically addicted to those ghost hunter shows on cable.

While keeping an ear on the creek and an eye out for campers, Kendra rounded yet another bend in the road and found herself directly opposite the RV campground. A large Road Master RV occupied one unit, and there were three more spaces that were empty.

A little further along, the park road terminated in a small open area that led to another trailhead. Another sturdy wooden sign said Cougar Ridge 6 miles. It also sported a carved wooden map depicting a hiking trail weaving in switchbacks up the steeper face of the mountain.

Have to be pretty experienced to go up there, she thought.

There was one car in this parking lot, an old Chevy with what appeared to be camping gear strapped to the luggage rack.

There were no people around either the RV camp nor the trailhead.

Guess they're off hiking or perhaps fishing in the creek. Too cold for swimming. What else does one do this time of year?

She decided to continue up the trail just a little further since there was really nothing pulling her back to the house except her empty belly.

Another hour of steep hiking and her belly was roaring. Her head was beginning to ache, too. It was easily past noon now, and she hadn't expected to be out past mid-morning. In fact, she'd thought she'd be on the way to the doc's clinic by now.

She noticed an ancient sign nailed to a tree that said she was about to trespass on private property, but she really doubted that. It's just a leftover. Didn't the state own the whole mountain these days? The sign seemed to mock her. *Am I lost?* She thought it quite possible, but all she had to do was turn around and follow the trail back the way she'd come, right?

Her feet stopped seemingly of their own accord. It is a sign, she thought, both literally and figuratively. Take it for what it is—whoever or whatever was watching me is gone—he got away. *Time to call it quits and go home. It was fun while it lasted, but seriously, boredom is probably what caused the goose bumps. Boredom. Just not used to sitting around doing nothing all day. No wonder my mind is conjuring up bad guys. I need action—or at least some sort of commotion.*

She turned abruptly, ready to give up—something very foreign to her charge-ahead nature—and found the ground spinning crazily beneath her feet. *Uh oh, headache and dizziness, early signs of dehydration or altitude sickness. Maybe a bit of both. Went a lot higher up than I intended. With nothing to drink but a few sips of coffee. Thank God the weather is cool. Can't believe I didn't bring water—not a hiker—just a washed up old detective who can't seem to think straight about anything.*

Kendra looked for a spot to sit and rest. Several yards off the trail, she spied a deadfall of brambles and branches and figured there would be a log or tree stump nearby. The fall was deep in shadow, and that appealed to her throbbing head. On closer inspection, the little area on the other side of the deadfall appeared to be carpeted with soft sweet clover.

Kendra didn't see the bones until she was sitting practically face to face with the skull.

CHAPTER FIFTEEN
Edgar's Girl

Edgar thought he had the forest all to himself. He'd followed the wildlife biologist and the kid until he was sure they were headed away from his area, and then he'd doubled back and tramped up the mountain to where he'd reached his best girl.

She was still just where he'd left her.

He caressed her femur and snapped a few more pictures in the early morning light. Only he had access to the rough private road leading to this site. It was one of the main reasons he'd purchased it so many years ago.

Feeling refreshed, he retraced his steps back down the trail to his car. It was parked in an overgrown turnaround a couple hundred yards inside the entrance to his land. He climbed in and carefully turned the vehicle around so that it was pointed back down the mountain.

The chain was still across the road just like he'd left it, the ancient metal sign dangling from the middle.

Privat Prop ty—Tre passers Will be Pros cuted

Several letters were missing, shot away, no doubt, by kids with pellet guns. Rust had taken over most of the rest of the sign, but Edgar didn't care. It had done its job all these years. He wasn't going to start worrying about it now. Besides, there were other signs, wooden ones, which marked his boundaries in other places.

He unlocked the chain, laid it on the ground, drove the Toyota through, stretched the sign and chain back across the road and relocked it behind him. He didn't always use this entrance; there was another road, even higher up, with a footpath. But he was in a hurry this morning. He hadn't intended to follow Chet and Nick before checking on his girl, they'd actually led him quite a distance away from her, but after hearing their conversation in the Drugstore, he'd had to make certain they weren't going near his spot.

He drove slowly around the lake with his window down, the cool morning air fresh against his face, his mind full of images of bones. *Now I can get through the rest of the day,* he thought. *No matter what comes along.*

And then he'd seen *her* tramping around.

Carrying her fishing gear toward the lake, she never even noticed him. But he saw her, and all his self-preservation hackles stood on end.

He'd been suspicious of her sudden appearance in Stutter Creek to begin with, but his rational mind convinced him he was just being paranoid, so he'd gone on about his business. But when Candy started raving about babies, he'd been forced to revisit his girls, and now here *she* was—the detective—practically in his back pocket. Paranoia? Or something more?

He parked the Toyota in the nearest turnaround and backtracked to the area where he'd last seen her.

Sure enough, there she was, casting a line toward an old tree stump. *Idiot,* he thought. *Everyone knows you don't cast your bait into a tangle of branches beneath the water.*

He watched her for a while. *Obviously not a fisherman.* So what's she doing out here all alone? If she isn't fishing for fish, she must be fishing for *him.*

It wasn't difficult to make himself invisible.

But then she began to hurry away, and he was certain she'd seen him after all.

When she stowed her fishing gear under a bush, he knew it was time to go. He melted back into the forest—his home away from home—and made his way back to his car. His heart seemed to fill his entire chest. He felt alive, on edge. Better than cutting, he thought, much better than sitting home waiting on Candy to drop another baby bombshell. Unfortunately, he couldn't hang around to see what the detective did next. If he were too late arriving at the clinic, tongues would wag.

He was sorry he'd agreed to the weekend half-days. It was one of those things that seemed like a good idea at the time, especially with ski season coming up. A good way to get back into the swing of things, so to speak. But now, it just seemed inconvenient. At the moment, he'd like nothing more than to track this woman—this detective—through the forest like a hunter tracking his prey.

Looking down at himself, he was glad he'd thought to grab the extra set of scrubs from the bunker. He always kept extra clothing there, in his oversize antique doctor's bag. His work in the forest was messy.

He used the wet wipes to wash away the dust and grime from traipsing around in the woods, and then he changed his clothes right there in the car. Stowing the dirty ones in a net laundry bag in the floorboard would remind him to take them in and wash them when he got home. It would also remind him to replace the set the next time he went to the bunker.

The drive back to town was not nearly as enjoyable as it should have been. He couldn't help but feel that the sudden appearance of the detective was because of him and his girls. And it worried him, greatly.

But there was nothing to be done at this very moment. Best to think it over, and then decide what action was necessary.

He drove into the parking space behind the clinic and prepared himself to meet his staff.

"Good afternoon," Nurse Green greeted as he walked in through the back entrance. "Not too many walk-ins, yet." Her eyes twinkled merrily. "But I'm sure that will change once they realize we're actually open." She laughed heartily and continued on her way to the waiting room.

Edgar nodded, relieved to be in his routine. "Do we have any actual appointments, or will it be all walk-in?"

The nurse stuck her head back through the door she'd just opened and said, "Detective Dean is supposed to come in to have her sutures removed. Remember you had to redo the sutures back before Thanksgiving? Oh, and Willie Garza has an appointment. Thinks he may have broken his big toe." She tapped a folder. "Bet he got mad at Lucinda and kicked the wall, again."

Edgar chuckled, but it was forced. He couldn't believe the detective was coming in this afternoon. Another coincidence? He'd wondered about how she'd reopened the wound the first time, but he had put it out of his mind. Now, though, could it be possible she was coming in again just to keep tabs on him? He would have to check with the receptionist to see when the appointment had actually been scheduled—and whether the detective had changed it.

If it turned out that she was keeping tabs on him, something would have to be done.

CHAPTER SIXTEEN

Girl in Clover

Kendra's mouth fell open, and her heart dropped into the pit of her stomach when she realized she was looking into the empty black eye sockets of a skull. Oddly, though, this skull was not half-buried in the earth the way one would think it should be. Nor was it scattered in pieces as if it had been dug up and deposited there by wild animals. No, indeed, this skull appeared to be right where it belonged, sitting at the top of a fully formed skeleton reclining on a bed of clover, hands clasped on what would have been its chest.

The detective's headache was forgotten. Her dizziness was also forgotten, washed away by a wave of adrenaline. She didn't scramble backward in an attempt to put distance between herself and the remains the way most people would have done. Instead, she pulled out her iPhone and began to snap picture after picture from every angle. Then she realized she had a signal, so she immediately dialed nine one one and told them who she was and what she had found.

In less than a minute, Sheriff Gray Puckett called her back. He was already on his way. Kendra could hear the ding-ding-ding of the seatbelt alarm as he climbed into his cruiser. When he asked her why she was in that particular area— on a workday—she told him everything about being on paid leave. Kendra had nothing to hide. She also told him about going fishing and getting the feeling that someone was watching her. When they hung up, she immediately called Woody and told him what was going on.

"I was going to call you about those case files," she said. "But I may not have too much time after all." And then she told him what she'd found. She thought about sending him the pictures she had taken but was afraid Sheriff Puckett might not appreciate her sharing evidence before he'd had a chance to see it.

"Wow," Woody exclaimed. "What'd you do, get so bored you just searched until you found a case right there in your own backyard? I mean if you wanted to work I would've driven the files over myself—"

"That's quite enough," she said, stemming the flow of sarcasm. "I was just out fishing when I felt this sudden certainty I was being watched."

"Are you there alone, now?" Woody interrupted.

Kendra immediately grasped his fear. "Yes," she said, "but I've got my weapon, and I've scanned the area, no one is around. No one alive that is." She glanced down at what she was fairly sure would turn out to be a woman. No one ever arranges men's remains this carefully, she thought. *Men's remains almost always show evidence of sudden violence, gunshot wounds, bashed in skulls, shattered bones. These remains appeared to be posed, right down to the odd placement of the thigh bone on top of the victim's ribs. Other than that, there were surprisingly few signs of violence about the remains at all.*

"I'll be right there," Woody said.

Kendra hesitated. "I think we should wait until your presence is requested by the sheriff. I don't want to step on any professional toes. Especially since I'm already on suspension."

"Couldn't I just pretend I was in the area like you were?"

"Yeah," Kendra snorted. "I want everyone to think we were together up here when we stumbled across the remains."

Woody started to argue, but eventually he relented. "All right, but call me the minute you can. I want to know everything."

Kendra agreed, and they clicked off.

The sheriff arrived about thirty minutes after she hung up. Apparently he knew a few drivable trails that got him closer to the action before he had to start hiking. Nevertheless, he sounded like the big bad wolf coming up the mountain. He was not a small man, and it was obvious he had pushed himself to his limits hurrying up the narrow trail.

Kendra could hear him from half a mile away. After she had given him another cursory overview of why she was there and what she'd been doing, the sheriff began to photograph the scene with a slim digital camera. He also examined her feet and photographed the soles of her shoes to compare with the footprints that were visible here and there around the remains.

"Forensics will be here within the hour," he said. "But I always take as many pictures as I can since things can change so quickly in outdoor settings."

Kendra liked his way of doing things. She'd met him years before, at a law enforcement conference, but she hadn't worked with him. He had only been sheriff—an elected office—for a couple of years.

Before long, the forensics team arrived and spent another couple of hours videotaping and photographing the scene and the remains. One techie even made a pencil sketch of the entire area. "Old school," the young woman said. "Our instructor told us it was a surefire way to force our eyes to see all the details of a crime scene." She grinned at Kendra. "I hate to admit it, but he was right. If I wasn't sketching it out, I never would have noticed this odd little brush I found over there." She pointed at the edge of the deadfall with the eraser end of her Ticonderoga.

She held the sketch up for Kendra to see. The girl had some talent, Kendra thought. She had captured the lay of the land very well, right down to the position of the bones and the glossy brown bristles peeking from beneath a dead branch. I wouldn't have noticed it even then, Kendra thought. *To me, it just looks like a clump of dry pine needles.*

She walked to the deadfall and touched the bristles without moving the brush itself. She could feel their springy suppleness, and she made certain not to touch the handle. That's where fingerprints would be if there were any.

"Came out of some kind of kit, I'll bet," the girl said. "I've seen collections of brushes similar to this in the college bookstore."

Kendra glanced at the tech's ID badge. *Brandi Dagwan.* "Tell me more, Brandi."

The girl smiled sheepishly. "Well, I minored in art and design. Brushes and art supplies intrigue me." She looked down at the small brush again. "I don't know these bristles, though. Maybe it *isn't* for artwork." She pointed at the stiff-but-soft bristles again. "But if we find out what kind of bristles those are, that might be a lead, right?" Her eyes met Kendra's.

"Good thinking," Kendra said. "It sure could be a lead. Especially since the brush doesn't appear to have been exposed to the elements for very long."

The techie nodded, a look of satisfaction on her face.

Kendra was impressed with the county's forensic team and made a mental note to tell the sheriff so. Before long, Dr. Lois Campanelli, a recently retired physician, and the county's Medical Examiner arrived—also out of breath—and pronounced the skeleton officially dead. Then she took a small brush of her own from a container that looked suspiciously like a tackle box and leaned down to get a better look at the thigh bone resting on the skeletal ribs.

Ahh, Kendra thought, no wonder the technician assumed the brush she'd found came from a kit. The M.E. appeared to have a whole tackle box full of them.

Dr. Campanelli brushed the bone gently. "Well, it was certainly nice of the perp to leave our friend here near the trail. I don't believe I could have gone much further without a mule to carry me. Hmmm, what have we here?"

Everyone within earshot stopped what they were doing and looked over. The note of disbelief was evident in the doctor's voice.

"Something stranger than what we've seen so far?" Sheriff Puckett asked.

The blonde woman merely extracted a large magnifying glass from her tackle box and leaned down again.

The sheriff shifted from one foot to the other. He wasn't used to having his questions ignored.

"Look here," she handed him the magnifier. "What's that look like to you?" She had a gleam in her eye to match the one in her voice.

Sheriff Puckett peered at the dirty bone. "Well, I'll be damned. Are those numbers?"

The woman nodded. "They appear to be etched right into the bone. That had to be done with a very sharp instrument—"

"Like one of those carving tools sculptors use?" the sheriff interrupted.

Dr. Campanelli shrugged. "Possibly, hard to tell. All I know for certain is that the femur is the hardest bone in the human body. It would take an exceptionally fine, sharp tool to carve into it that precisely." She ran her gloved finger across the marks almost lovingly. "That's detailed work." She took the magnifying glass from the sheriff's thick fingers and peered through it again. "Do you see this?" With the point of a mechanical pencil produced from her coat pocket, she indicated a tiny circle carved into the bone after what appeared to be the last number.

"What is that? A zero? It's a lot smaller than the other numbers. I can read those pretty well, except for the ones still crusted with mo—"

The doctor gritted her teeth. "It looks like a degree symbol to me." Her tone implied she was talking to an imbecile. "Haven't you ever read a map? That clearly says 35° 05' 98" N. That is a latitudinal coordinate." She wrote the numbers in her pocket spiral. "I'm thinking these other numbers must be longitudinal, 106° something, something, something W. I just can't make out the digits before the W." She tapped the tiny carving gently, to make certain he saw what she was talking about. "Some hikers use UTM now, Universal Transverse Mercator, but if I'm not mistaken lots of folks still use these coordinates to locate places." She tapped the bone with her pencil once more. "That's how you write latitude and longitude all right. Look it up on that fancy phone you've got there."

Kendra saw the sheriff's face go from red to bright red to eggplant purple. She was certain he was about to explode. *How rude, showing him up in front of his staff. It's almost as if they have some sort of history.*

She hoped they could keep it cordial, whatever the problem was, because up until that point, everything had been progressing smoothly.

Sheriff Puckett turned to one of his deputies and gave him some rapid-fire instructions.

The Medical Examiner bent even closer to her work, but Kendra noted the slump of her shoulders and the flush that had crept up out of her collar. *I'll bet she already regrets those things she said and that tone of voice she used. What was she thinking?*

She didn't have time to wonder because the M.E.'s assistants began to gather the bones and place them in a body bag on a stretcher.

Kendra watched as Brandi Dagwan replaced her sketchpad with a digital camera and click, click, clicked away as the bones were carefully placed into their snug new home.

She overheard Dr. Campanelli telling one of the techs to wrap the femur separately to make sure nothing damaged the coordinates carved into it. "Hope I wrote them right," she was saying. "Hard to tell for certain. Need to get it into the lab for a more thorough inspection."

"Lois!" Sheriff Puckett said. His voice was somewhere between harsh and hopeful.

She turned; her reading glasses perched precariously on the end of her nose and arched her brows. "Yes?"

"You'll let me know as soon as you make out those last few numbers or symbols ..."

The M.E. turned back to her work waving one hand in the air dismissively. "Of course I will," she muttered. "Why wouldn't I?"

Kendra noted the dark look that passed over the sheriff's face. It was obvious he wasn't used to being treated like an underling.

"Is she always that pleasant?" Kendra asked Sheriff Puckett after they'd walked a distance away.

He laughed, watching the sun disappear behind the mountain. "Sometimes she's even worse." His voice was almost jolly as if he'd thought it over and decided to forgive the cranky M.E.

Kendra pulled her fishing vest tighter. The lowering sun dropped the temperature quickly. She was used to the rapid drops in temperature at the higher altitudes—she'd live in the northern New Mexico area most of her life—but she wasn't used to simply standing around, waiting. Before she realized it, she was bouncing up and down on the balls of her feet to get warm.

"Lois lost her husband a while back to cancer, short, sudden, and savage. Took a lot out of her. She retired to take care of him; then it was all over almost before it began. Her kids were after her to move to Texas to be closer to them." He glanced over his shoulder as if to make certain no one else was listening, then he continued, "She cried on my shoulder a time or two, strictly off the record, been mad at me ever since." He chuckled again.

Kendra smiled self-deprecatingly. "Some of us girls just don't like to show weakness—of any kind. Especially in this business. Took us too long to get here to let anyone see our vulnerable sides—much less our soft underbellies."

The sheriff looked at her closely, as if he hadn't bothered before. "That what it is?"

She nodded. "Most likely. You've seen her at her worst; now she holds it against you."

He shook his grizzled head, pulled off his hat, and wiped the brim thoughtfully before replacing it on his head.

Kendra wondered if the hatband indentation around his head was painful. It appeared to be permanent.

"You sure that's it?" He shifted from one booted foot to the other as he spoke.

"Not positive," Ken replied. "I don't even know her." She stopped bouncing for a moment. "But I know grief changes people—and I know I don't like being thought of as weak or ineffectual." She bit her bottom lip, unsure how much personal info she should confide. "That's one reason I came all the way out here—I mean to Copper Lake—I couldn't take all the looks of pity back home." She ducked her head and resumed bouncing. Woody probably knew that about her, but she'd certainly never straight up told anyone else. She might've told Bill, if he was still around, but of course he wasn't so that was beside the point.

"Hope you're right," the sheriff replied gruffly. "I thought I'd offended her in some way."

Kendra's phone buzzed, and she sent it to voice mail thankful she'd had the presence of mind to turn off her ringtone. She glanced at the missed call alert. It was Woody, so she sent him a quick text. "Still at the scene w/sheriff. Call u soon." She knew he'd understand. He was probably just making sure she wasn't alone with the possibility of someone still watching.

It took another hour for the technicians to finish cataloging the scene, another hour after that for them to gather and repack all their equipment except for the lights. They would be the last things to go.

"'Preciate you staying," the sheriff told her as he took one last look around the well-lit scene. "I'll walk down with you—my car's in a little turnaround on a private state park road not far down the trail. I'll deliver you back to your vehicle—"

"Thank you, Sheriff." Kendra was honestly grateful. She'd been wondering if she could find her way back in the dark. She'd have to make a note to retrieve her fishing gear tomorrow, in the daylight.

They made their way down to his car with the aid of a deputy and a large flashlight. She sat in the sheriff's car while he stood outside the vehicle scheduling who would stay on scene and who would go back to their regular duties. There were only half a dozen deputies to cover the entire county. Overtime was in the making. The sheriff intended to keep the scene protected until daylight when they would go back over it again to make sure they hadn't missed anything.

While she waited, she returned Woody's call.

"Hola," he answered. "How's it going? Didn't mean to interrupt."

Kendra felt her body relax at the sound of his voice. His drawl and the fact that he seldom got excited always had a calming effect on her. They'd been partners for a few years. Still, it always surprised her when she realized how integrated they had become. Like a single unit. "It's okay," she replied. "About to leave the scene. Headed to the camp store to pick up my truck, then over to the sheriff's office to make my official report."

Woody exhaled. "Okay. Good. I wish I could be there. I've thought of taking a couple weeks' vacation and hanging out at Copper Lake—"

She tried to interrupt, but he continued. "I know what you're going to say, but I don't care what anyone thinks anymore. I'm finding out that not seeing you every day is way harder than I thought it would be."

Kendra tried to speak again. "Woods, I—"

But he continued once more. "Don't worry. It isn't going to happen. I'm covered up in this case—we finally got into his computer, Ken, your suicide perp. The techs are going through it now. I know we will find something on there that will tell us why he stepped in front of that truck."

Kendra breathed a sigh of relief. He hadn't given up on her even though she'd practically given up on herself. Still, things were complicated enough already. "You just know it, huh?"

He chuckled. "Yep. My detective's gut says so. I can't rely on yours right now, so mine has been working overtime—you know, the way a blind man's hearing will grow sharper or a—"

"Uh huh. I think I get the picture." She didn't know what else to say.

Woody was also silent for a moment. "I'm going to figure this out," he said.

"I know you will." Her voice was solemn. After fifteen years, she suddenly wanted a cigarette. This seemed to be one of those moments where she should light up. "Thanks, Woods. I hope you know how much I appreciate it."

He broke the tension. "Don't worry. You'll owe me. When it's all said and done, you are going to owe me. Big time."

A flash of his crooked grin entered her mind—his crooked grin and a slow dance in a small bar. But she pushed that last part away. "I'll call you tomorrow," she said.

They broke the connection and Kendra smiled for the first time in days. *At last, a glimmer of light at the end of the tunnel.*

The sheriff drove her back to her vehicle in near silence. He seemed deep in thought, and she didn't intrude upon his contemplations.

She followed him to the station in her truck and made out her short witness statement as a civilian. It was much easier and faster than the one she would have had to prepare if she'd been on the job.

By midnight, she was back at home in her pajamas treating herself to an Irish coffee topped with a dollop of heavy cream.

After the day she'd had, Kendra felt she deserved it.

CHAPTER SEVENTEEN

From the Stutter Creek Sentinel
HOLIDAY HORRORS!
Skeletal Remains Found Near Copper Lake
Carving on femur appears to be map coordinate
Is this the work of a killer cartographer?

The sheriff's face was eggplant again. "Who the hell leaked this information to the press?"

It was the day after Kendra had found the remains. Of course, they couldn't keep *that* a secret, but they had fully intended to keep the part about the map coordinates a secret.

Still fuming, the sheriff bellowed, "Killer cartographer? Who writes this shit? If Bob Linney came up with this crap, I'm going to have his balls in a sling. Killer cartographer, of all the stupid shit I've heard, this has got to be the worst. No wonder the damn paper is on its last legs."

The sheriff's secretary had called Kendra early that morning and invited her to the office for a meeting. Kendra had no idea *this* was the topic of the meeting. Not being a subscriber to the weekly newspaper, she had not seen the headline.

Everyone in the room shook their heads. Of course, no one was going to admit being a blabbermouth. It could have been anyone. A deputy could have mentioned it to a spouse, or one of the technicians could have been overheard discussing it with the M.E. as they rearranged the bones on the examining table. For that matter, it could have been any one of the dispatchers or secretaries who were privy to reports that had to be filed and shared.

All Kendra knew for certain was it was *not* her.

She joined the others in shaking their heads negatively. "Not I," she muttered, returning the sheriff's look when his thunderous gaze met hers. She hadn't even told Woody about the carving. That wasn't the kind of information one shared on a cell phone. All she'd told him was how she'd found the remains practically right in her new back yard.

While she sat ruminating, the rest of the staff left the conference room. That left only her, one remaining detective, and the sheriff to brainstorm on the white board. "Could it be an old graveyard?" Detective Simpson asked. "Maybe some teenagers dug up the bones as a dare or something?"

Kendra nodded. "That sounds like something kids would do if they knew the remains were there. Then they took it a step further and carved on the femur just for fun. To give folks something to talk about."

"Does sound like a teenage prank, doesn't it?" The sheriff observed. "But damn, that carving is precise. And the doc said it would take a special tool, not just a pocketknife. That suggests planning." He stopped for a moment, seemingly to mull something over. "As soon as it's completely cleaned, we'll be able to read it better. Right now, we can only make out the first set of numbers—what Lois insists is the latitude."

Detective Simpson looked at Kendra. "She also said it appears the carving is old. That it wasn't done after the bones were dug up, but before they were buried."

Kendra nodded. "That kind of rules out high school prank, doesn't it?" She glanced up. "I mean that makes it seem certain that the killer did it, right?" She didn't want to sound too cocky, to step on anyone's toes, but what else could it mean?

"That's what we thought, too," Detective Simpson agreed. "But it's nuts. And no, I didn't really think there was an old graveyard that far up the mountain, but I like to be thorough. Rule out every possibility." He shifted his weight in the chair, which emitted a loud, metallic, squeak. "Right now we don't even know if the person *was* murdered. Not for certain."

Kendra looked at the sheriff. He nodded, too.

For the next hour, the three of them sat and discussed every possible scenario they could imagine.

She drove home after the meeting feeling drained and confused. The sheriff hadn't actually asked for her assistance, which is what she'd been hoping for when the secretary called. On the other hand, he *was* keeping her in the loop, in a roundabout way. Should I volunteer to help out, she wondered. *Or should I simply hang back and see if they ask?*

Without giving herself a chance to overthink it, Kendra made a U-turn and headed back to the sheriff's office.

She marched in, smiled at the secretary's affable expression, and strode right into the big man's inner office without knocking. "I'm available," she told him when he glanced up from the file he was reading. "I'm here on leave, and I'm going bat-shit crazy from boredom. What else can I do to help?"

Sheriff Puckett leaned back in his chair and laced his fingers over his generous belly. "Sit down, detective. Let's chat."

By the time the chat was over, Kendra was on unofficial loan to the Brewer County Sheriff's Office. Her boss in Pine River said it was all right as long as she didn't sign any reports or make any arrests on her own. In other words, she was incognito, an unpaid consultant.

Kendra liked the sound of that.

On the way home, she stopped by the drugstore.

"When are you ever going to get those stitches out?" Ella asked as she handed her a menu.

Kendra fingered the stiff black stitches. "Soon," she said.

"You must be awfully busy. Weren't you headed over to the clinic the other day when you were here?"

Kendra nodded. "Something came up that day." She didn't mention that it was the day she had found the human remains. Very few folks knew she was the one who had found them—and she wanted to keep it that way. In the paper, it had simply said "a hiker" found them.

Ella didn't question her further; she simply brought her ice water instead of the coffee she had ordered.

"You all right?" Kendra asked.

Ella nodded. "Sorry, just a bit distracted." She tugged at her apron. It was clear from the look on her face that she was debating saying more.

No secrets, Kendra thought. Can't have secrets with a nutcase running around digging up old bodies. She patted the table across from her. "Want to talk?"

Ella glanced around the café. It was a slow period between breakfast and lunch. She slid into the booth opposite Kendra. "Nick's real father is in town."

Kendra's thoughts whirled, but she kept her face impassive. With everything that was on her mind, it was hard to switch back to the idea that other folks had problems, too. At last she spoke. "Not from around here, I take it?"

Rubbing an imaginary spot on the shiny table with the corner of her apron, Ella replied, "No. He's from Albuquerque. In fact, this is the first time I've seen him since before Nick was even born." Her gaze met Kendra's. "The two of them have never met, and I think I'd like to keep it that way."

Kendra sipped her ice water and Ella rolled her eyes and thumped her forehead with the heel of her hand when she realized she still hadn't brought the coffee Kendra had ordered. She jumped up to retrieve the pot from the Braun coffee maker.

Placing a cup before the detective, she filled it with the steaming brew. Then she took a second cup and filled it for herself.

While Kendra stirred Coffee-Mate into her cup until it resembled beige milk, Ella told her the entire sordid story of her high school fling with the captain of the football team. When she finished, Kendra sat quietly, thinking.

An older gentleman entered and chose a seat at the long wooden counter.

Wordlessly, Ella hurried behind the counter where she drew another glass of ice water and picked up a menu from the rack. As Ella exchanged pleasantries with the regular customer, Kendra thought about how the kind café owner had been used and abused by two different men in her short lifetime. At least my husband was never cruel or abusive, she thought. And he certainly never regretted our children or wanted me to abort them. *What a horrible ordeal that must've been.*

She felt her backbone stiffening. It always felt that way when she sensed injustice, especially when directed at someone as decent and kind as Ella Webb, not to mention her adorable son, Nick.

When Ella returned to her table, Kendra asked for a description of Tag and the vehicle he drove, but Ella had no idea what he was driving. She was able to give Kendra a description of him, but she assured her that she was certain he was no danger to herself or anyone else.

Kendra wasn't convinced. In the back of her mind, she wondered if he could somehow be connected to the appearance of the bones. But her gut said no, there was no logical reason to think that. He was from the city. According to Ella, it was the first time they'd had any contact in over ten years. Coincidence, she thought. *For once, just a simple coincidence.*

CHAPTER EIGHTEEN
Edgar At Home

Edgar read the paper with his morning muffin. He wasn't having breakfast with Candy today. He was finding it very difficult to be in the same room with her these days. He had tried to accept her intimations the night before. Even though she'd dressed in his favorite silk kimono with nothing underneath, he simply couldn't get past the idea that every time they made love she was hoping for a tiny miracle. A tiny miracle, her words, not his.

It *would* be a miracle, he thought. Especially since she was on the pill and had been since they'd met. He knew the only way he could ever feel comfortable with her again now was if one—or both—of them went under the knife. And he really did not want to go there. He didn't want to have to explain all the scars and self-tats on his body. But unfortunately, his wife refused to entertain even the thought of having her tubes tied.

"It's a small, painless procedure," he'd told her. "Since the invention of laparoscopic surgery, it's now known as a simple Band-Aid operation." But she wouldn't even discuss it. He reminded her of their agreement about children, but he hadn't had the foresight to get a prenuptial contract to that effect. He'd been naïve. And now she was balking. Wouldn't talk about it at all, just tried to sway him with silk and wine.

If it did happen, she wouldn't be the first mommy-to-be who had gotten pregnant against her partner's wishes. She also wouldn't be the first one who met with an unfortunate accident. *Surely it won't come to that.* Candy might not be thinking straight at the moment, but he was certain she'd never deliberately get pregnant. Not against his wishes. *So why can't you get it up for her then, if you're so certain she's trustworthy?*

Fool me once, shame on you, fool me twice—nope that won't happen.

Ever.

He folded the newspaper and laid it on the sideboard. Candy was still sleeping. She seemed to be doing a lot of that lately.

Leaving the remains of his breakfast on the dining table, Edgar stole out to the garage and opened the door as quietly as possible. He always went for a run or a hike on Sunday morning and this morning was no different. Except this morning what he wanted was to get out to the woods and check on his other girl. The Holiday Horrors headline thrilled him, but at the same time, he couldn't believe he would never see his *best* girl again.

You knew it would happen. If you didn't want her found, why did you bring her back?

He began to smile. *Of course, this is what I wanted.* He started the engine. *Certainly takes my mind off Candy and all that nonsense about children.* He rounded the corner at the end of Robin Road and glanced at the house where Ella and Nick lived. *Wonder if she's still alone?*

He recalled how Chet had stopped by the café to pick up Nick and take him camping. He'd made it a point to ask when they were expected to return, and that day was today. Unfortunately, he'd been much too busy with other things to take advantage of the situation. But they aren't expected until this evening, he thought. And that's several hours away. *But Candy is at home, sleeping. She isn't out of town—she could wake and look out the window or come looking for me. She has been acting so odd lately; her behavior has become completely unpredictable.*

Such temptation.

So close to home.

It almost makes up for the idiot detective not showing up for her appointment yesterday.

***

The fragrance of homemade spaghetti permeated the large country kitchen. Ella luxuriated in having the house all to herself on this glorious Sunday afternoon. Monday through Saturday she devoted to the Drugstore Café. But the café was always closed on Sunday, so she had the whole day to herself. Nick and Chet were due back tonight. Nicky had school tomorrow, so they had to return pretty early. *They will both appreciate the smell of spaghetti when they walk in the front door.*

She had just taken the pot of boiling pasta off the stove when she heard a sound behind her. Ella whirled around and stared at the huge black rubber doggie door. She stood perfectly still waiting for the sound to come again.

It had sounded like a laugh or a harsh sneeze covered with a sudden hand.

She stared at the door. This can't be happening again.

The first night she and Nick had spent in this house had been full of spooky noises, but today it was just her and Andy. Nick had informed her the pup's real name was Andy, not Slimebucket. He'd named his new pal for the Greatest *Dane* he could think of, Hans Christian *Andersen*. The big mutt was crashed out on his extra-large doggy pillow fast asleep.

Ella forced herself to focus.

All the doors were locked. After last year's episode, she never failed to lock them, but anything could fit through that giant rubber flap. *What the hell was I thinking getting a dog door that big? Oh, yeah, thinking I didn't want to clean up Great Dane poop in the kitchen.*

Indecision paralyzed her, and she stood like a statue waiting for something—an arm or perhaps a head, at the very least, a hand—to come through that flap.

She held the hot pan directly over the opening.

Nothing happened.

The silence was broken only by an occasional doggie snore from beneath the table.

The pot of pasta began to tremble.

She grasped the thick black handle with both hands and waited another few seconds. Time spun slowly through the room on sunbeams flickering with dust motes. There were no more sounds.

Did I imagine it? Wouldn't Andy have heard someone sneaking around outside?

She let out a shaky breath.

Will I ever get used to being alone again?

Quiet as a ghost she stepped back, pulled the metal insert from beside the refrigerator, and slid it into the guides on the doggie door. Now, nothing could come through. Her other hand, the one *still* holding the pan of pasta, began to shake, but there was no way she would set it down. Hot water could be a tremendous equalizer if necessary.

She backed across the kitchen, never taking her eyes off the door even though she'd secured the flap. Her neighbor, Norma, who lived down the lane, had assumed she and Nick would be moving into town after the fiasco with the stalker. In fact, no one thought the two of them would want to stay in the house, not even after the doors and windows had all been repaired or replaced.

But Ella adored their old rental, and the landlord said there was a good possibility the owner would sell her the place if she were interested. Besides, Nick loved the rural setting, especially now that they had Andy.

"I refuse to give in that easily," she'd said after living in a motel while repairs were made. "That would be like letting him get the best of us." She didn't tell Norma, but that was also the reason she kept Chet at arm's length. *I'm a mom and a new business owner, it's time I took control of my life instead of being dependent on—or afraid of—some man.*

At last, satisfied no one would be coming in the doggie door, Ella set the hot pasta in the sink. Pulling out the small key she wore on a thin chain around her neck, she reached into the back of the cabinet and unlocked the lock box holding her Smith & Wesson revolver. She had another in her bedroom just like it.

Without hesitation, she flipped open the cylinder and checked to make sure it was loaded. Checking the load was one of the first things the firearms instructor had taught her. She exhaled and crossed the old kitchen slowly, holding the gun down at her side the way she'd been taught.

Andy snored loudly.

Ella hesitated.

No, that was definitely not the sound I heard. Maybe I should hire Turk the Wonder Dog to teach Andy how to be a watchdog.

Making her way through the house, she mentally pictured all the doors and windows again. The front door is locked. *I always lock the front door.* She checked the hallway door that led upstairs to the attic. This was the door her stalker had burst through after cutting the power and plunging them into darkness. But it was no longer just a flimsy wooden door. With Chet's help, she had replaced it with a hollow core metal one set into a reinforced frame. They'd even installed a dead bolt on it. Then they had fitted the attic windows with iron bars.

She'd thought about putting bars on all the windows, but once again, that had seemed like giving into fear completely.

Besides, what if we need to get out quickly the way Nicky had during that awful confrontation?

At the time, all the renovations had seemed to border on ridiculous—as if she were making them prisoners in their own home. But now, alone, Ella wondered if she'd gone overboard on the macho thinking. *Maybe I should've moved us into town, near other people in a neighborhood rather than out here in the boonies. No matter how much we love it. That weird organic sound. What could it have been?*

She gripped the revolver tighter and continued through the house, checking each and every room with the gun held at the ready. She looked under beds and in closets. She also made it a point to glance out each and every window—making certain they were locked of course—to see if she could spot a peeping tom.

There was nothing.

At last, she steeled her nerve and unlocked the attic door.

It was difficult to go up those narrow stairs even in full daylight.

She hesitated, and then placed her foot carefully on the first step. *Do any of them creak, or squeak?* She forced her foot onto the next stair and the next and the next until the last step, which opened directly into the large, now-tidy space.

In her mind, she pictured someone crouching, waiting to knock her senseless when her head appeared above the landing. But only the sound of her own breathing reached her ears. She felt as if she were in a vacuum. *No wonder I can't hear anything. There's no air to carry sound waves.* Her chest began to tighten. *No panic attack. No. I will not have a—*

She stepped into the large space and did a quick survey of the slope-ceilinged room. There was no place to hide. She, Nick, and Chet had cleaned it out completely.

Ella felt her chest muscles loosen.

Her gun hand felt watery as if she were on the verge of melting.

She turned and galloped back down the stairs. At the bottom, she relocked the attic dead bolt and headed toward the front door to continue her search outside. *I know I heard something. And I'm not going to stop until I find out what it was.*

For a moment she thought of calling the police department—maybe her old buddy, Officer Rodriguez, would be on duty—but what would she say? She'd heard someone laugh? They knew her history, they would probably come out right away, but she was pretty certain there would be nothing to find. And what would she do the next time she heard an errant noise, call them again?

Why do I always doubt myself? I'm a big girl. I can check outside in broad daylight. As long as I have my .38 that is. I could even call Norma to come down, she'd be here in a heartbeat, except it's Sunday. Norma is at church.

She took another deep breath and unlocked the front door.

When the warm sun struck her face, Ella felt like an idiot holding a gun. She stuck the revolver in her oversized apron pocket. It's not like anyone will see me, she thought. Lilac Lane was fairly deserted, except for Dr. and Mrs. Stevens, who had moved into the old house across the way. The previous owner, poor Mrs. Benefield, fell and broke her hip shortly after Ella and Nick moved in.

She now lived in an assisted living home. While she was in the hospital, the doctors had determined she was suffering the early stages of senile dementia, too. The house had gone up for sale shortly after that.

Ella glanced toward the doctor's house, but all she could see above the trees was a tiny portion of the roof.

She walked around the corner of the house. The fall leaves crunched underfoot, but she thought the temperature was quite pleasant for this time of year. It was only her second year in Stutter Creek, but Ella was fairly certain winter had come earlier last year.

On the side of the house, she looked up at the now-barred attic window. The trellis holding up the lilac vines was still in place. She loved the lilacs. The fragrant purple flowers grew profusely on several of the houses on the lane. Apparently, the plant spread very easily. Over on Robin Road, tubular orange trumpet vines still held sway.

She continued to check the exterior of the house.

So far, so good.

Everything appeared secure. She rounded the far corner just in time to see the rear of the doctor's car headed down the road toward town. She automatically raised her hand to wave but apparently he didn't see her.

Ella was relieved to see the doc's car. If anyone were creeping around, he would have seen him. She went ahead and checked the back of the house just for good measure. There were no signs of footprints or anything amiss. Of course with all the leaves covering the yard, there was no place for footprints to be seen, *but what was this?*

Ella bent down and looked more closely at something on the ground. *Just an ink pen.* She picked it up and stepped onto the shadowed deck to try her back door. The lock was secure, but she shivered nonetheless. Back here, where the sun was partially blocked by the house, the air felt much colder.

She tried to push open the doggy door, but the metal plate was solid.

It was nothing. My overactive imagination. It's the first time I've had the house to myself since I can't remember when.

Just as she turned away from the door, she heard another sound—from inside the house.

It was Andy, whining.

She'd left him asleep under the table, but he must have heard her jiggling the doorknob. "Hang on, Andy," she comforted through the door. "Mommy's coming."

She dropped the ink pen into her pocket and hurried back around to the front of the house. Could it have been Tag? Could he have been standing there and then lost his nerve? But wouldn't he have tried the front door first?

As she entered the house, Andy dashed past her to get outside. She laughed and shook her head at the clumsy pup. Then she heard her phone ringing in the kitchen. She hurried inside and grabbed it before it could go to voicemail. It might be Chet saying they were on their way home.

"Hello?"

"I'm sorry I didn't call last night." Tag's voice was shaky. "I – I sort of lost my nerve."

Ella sucked in air. *It's as if I conjured him simply by thinking about him.* She had wondered why he didn't call after his visit to the café, but she was also glad that he hadn't. She had hoped her abrupt manner had scared him off.

"What do you want, Tag?" Ella didn't try to hide the annoyance in her voice.

There was a moment of silence.

She thought of just hanging up, but then he spoke.

"After I heard about the ordeal you and Nick went through, I guess I just wanted to make sure you are both all right."

Ella harrumphed. "Why? Why would you even care?" She replaced the .38 in the lock box as they talked.

"I've thought of you many times over the years, El." He waited for a response, but she didn't grant one.

There was another awkward pause.

Ella's finger hovered over the END icon.

"I know I screwed up all those years ago," Tag said at last. "I want to meet Nick. He sounds like a great kid—"

"Stop right there," Ella interrupted. "Nick is a *fantastic* kid. He's *my* fantastic kid. I raised him. Me. Alone. You wanted me to get an abortion. You didn't want any part of him or me—"

"You're right," he interrupted. "I was a kid myself—"

"Like I wasn't?" She wasn't about to cut him any slack. In fact, she was still on the verge of hanging up.

"I'm sorry," he whispered. "I really am. Just hear me out, please."

She waited.

She debated telling him to crawl back under his rock and stay there, but in the back of her mind she thought she would let him have his say and be done with it. Be done with him, once and for all.

He began to talk.

"My life has been nothing, Ella. It's like God is punishing me for turning my back on you. I tore my ACL in practice that first year in college, lost my scholarship, flunked out of school, took a job in my dad's car dealership, started drinking—"

Something suddenly dawned on Ella. "Are you in AA or some other twelve step program, is that what this is? You're at that step where you're required to make amends with people you've wronged?"

"It isn't that," he said. "Yes, I'm an alcoholic and I've worked the steps, but that isn't what this is about." He inhaled deeply.

Ella wondered if he'd just lit a cigarette or something more potent.

"When I saw the news report it started me thinking about what could have been, and then I just couldn't stop."

"Surely you have your own family by now."

"Never had any other children," he said flatly. "My wife left me when I was at the bottom, before AA."

Ella felt a momentary flash of pity for him. But that didn't change the fact that he had never been Nick's father and never *would* be. Not now. Not ever. Over the years, she had come to the conclusion that it takes more than just a sperm cell to make a man a father. "I'm sorry you missed out on such a wonderful kid." She was torn between wanting to spare him and wanting to stick the knife in and give it a hard twist. "But there's nothing for you here now. You aren't on Nick's birth certificate. That's how you wanted it. I've never even told him about you, so you need to just move on with your life like you did so many years ago."

What's that clicking sound?

She looked down at the ink pen in her other hand. She had pulled it from her pocket and begun to click the button nervously as they talked.

Ella made herself stop.

She laid it on the table. *Stutter Creek Urgent Care Clinic* was inscribed on the barrel. Ella thought it odd for a moment, but then she realized Tag was speaking again and the ink pen was completely forgotten.

"—could try again. How about if I take you and Nicky out to dinner in Pine River, and we all get to know each other?"

Ella's mind went momentarily blank with rage.

When she was able to formulate a sentence, she spoke slowly and clearly. "Have you heard nothing I've said? We. Don't. Want. You. You are not going to *ever* be a part of our lives. Never. You wanted me to kill my son. I will never forgive you for that."

There was absolute silence on Tag's end of the phone.

Ella pressed END and stood there, shaking with fury.

CHAPTER NINETEEN
Kendra at the Clinic

The waiting room was filled with kids, and each one was sneezing, coughing, or sniffling. "Flu season already?" Kendra asked the receptionist. "Or *hopefully* just fall allergies?"

The receptionist rolled her eyes. "Every year when school begins they start piling in with their runny noses and fevers. All those stuffy classrooms."

Kendra smiled. "Any chance I can just wait outside since I'm only getting stitches removed?" She felt like Howard Hughes.

The girl handed Kendra a blank yellow sticky note. "Give me your cell number and I'll text you when it's your turn."

"Thanks." Kendra wrote her number on the square of paper.

She sat in her pickup and surfed the internet until her iPhone buzzed in her hand. It had only been a few minutes.

Kendra expected it to be the receptionist telling her it was her turn. Instead, it was a text from Woody.

"Hey, boss," the message began. "How about coffee and a sandwich this afternoon? I've got some news."

"Sounds good," she replied. "You must have ESP. I was just going to call you."

Woody sent back a goofy smiley icon and wrote, "Your place or mine? I really do have a file for you. It's only a couple of months old."

Kendra typed a single question mark.

"Missing girl from the Gypsum neighborhood in Yellow Bend," he replied. "Family just getting around to reporting her."

"Must be estranged."

"Very. When mom's new squeeze became her stepdad, the girl split. Last known address was a trailer park w/a boyfriend. He claims he thought she had moved on because the dog was missing, too. The real reason he didn't report her was because he's been in jail all this time."

"Tell me more," she typed.

"She was last seen walking her dog—a half grown Great Dane."

Kendra sat up straighter. "A Great Dane? From the *Gypsum* area of Yellow Bend? That's just the other side of the forest. Isn't there a road bordering the forest that leads right into that little hellhole?"

Woody sent back a thumbs-up icon. "I knew you'd make the connection." He continued typing. "There's an old Farm to Market road. Runs right around the edge of the forest until it dead-ends into the Gypsum Mobile Home Park. Guess what else borders Gypsum?"

"Tell me," she demanded.

"A deep ravine—"

Kendra's thumbs flew over the keypad. "It can't be," she wrote. "Nicky Webb's dog was found at the bottom of that ravine. It was so steep he couldn't scramble out. Or maybe it's because he was injured or something. Anyhow, that would be *too* coincidental, wouldn't it?"

"Not at all," Woody replied. "It isn't coincidental if the dog was found near the spot where his master was abducted. If indeed that's what happened."

"But that would mean she was abducted between Copper Lake and Yellow Bend."

"Most likely. 'Course it's possible Nick's big pup isn't even the same dog—"

"Bullshit," Kendra typed. "I've had one coincidence recently; that's my limit. We both know coincidences only happen to folks who aren't paying attention to details."

Just then, a new message popped up. It was the receptionist telling Kendra to come right in.

She sent Woody a hasty text as she exited the truck, "Sounds very interesting in light of what I found in the woods. I've got to run now, but I'll come to you this time. Lisa's Café, six p.m.?"

"I'll be there," he replied.

Kendra clicked off and strolled into the clinic, her mind no longer on the task at hand. Instead, it was on the set of remains and their proximity to the ravine where Nicky's dog was found.

Dr. Stevens came in almost as soon as Kendra had been seated and had her blood pressure taken. "How've you been?" He extended his hand, palm up.

At first Kendra thought it was a weird way to shake hands, and then she realized he was waiting for her to show him her stitches. She laid her hand in his large bony palm, and it practically disappeared.

"Looks fairly good." He admired his handiwork. "But they are a little embedded. I expected you on Saturday."

Kendra heard the admonishment in his tone and was surprised. How many physicians kept track of when their patients' appointments were? She thought only the office clerks kept track. Maybe it was an ego thing. Big fish in a small pond, expects his patients to follow his advice to the letter, without question. Or maybe the Saturday appointment had been out of the ordinary, although at the time it had seemed run-of-the-mill.

Whatever the reason, it irked her to be scolded like a schoolgirl, but she shrugged it off. "Well, doc, I was a little busy."

His eyebrows went up, and she decided perhaps that had just been his clumsy way of starting a conversation. *Maybe*

I'm just prickly. She'd had instructors like that back at the academy—and in most of the refresher courses she'd taken over the years. The "don't question me I'm a detective" sort. *Hope I haven't turned into one of those old fogies.*

She gave him the benefit of the doubt. "Tell ya the truth, Doc, I uh—well, I'm the one who found the human remains in the woods." She couldn't resist adding, "And guess what? One of the bones had been etched so precisely it appeared to have been carved by a scalpel or something."

Dr. Stevens stopped what he was doing and searched her face. "Is that some sort of detective joke?"

Kendra felt a chill settle over her. The temperature in the room seemed to have dropped. Even his voice had gone cold. "Yeah," she said, relying on instinct. "Sorry about that. Poor excuse for a joke wasn't it? Truthfully, I just forgot my appointment." She averted her eyes knowing, even as she did so, that she was exhibiting one of the classic "tells" of a liar.

"Not funny. In bigger cities, you'd be charged a fee for missing an appointment without calling to cancel." If his voice got any colder, his words would freeze in midair.

It took Kendra a serious act of will power to keep from simply walking out. Instead, she clenched her teeth. "Won't happen again," she replied.

The doctor smiled widely. "Ha-ha! That was *my* little attempt at humor. Didn't mean to offend."

"Well that's one thing we obviously have in common," Kendra said as the door opened. "Neither of us should quit our day jobs to go into comedy."

A gray-haired nurse rolled a tray of instruments into the room. "Okay, what'd I miss?"

Dr. Stevens shook his head. "Detective Dean and I were just joking around." He ignored the shocked expression on the nurse's face and spoke directly to Kendra. "After I remove the sutures, the nurse will give you some salve to apply nightly to soften the scar." His smile mocked her. "Wouldn't want it to interfere with your gun hand now, would we?"

Kendra forced a laugh. "No worries on that account, Doc. I'm practically retired. Appreciate the thought, though." She wanted to make light of the situation, but she didn't know how without coming off as a complete smart-ass.

The nurse produced a pink plastic basin and instructed Kendra to hold her hand over it while she swabbed the area with scarlet liquid from a squirt bottle. The soapy liquid turned yellow when she rubbed it around Kendra's hand with a 4x4 square of cotton clenched in a tong-like hemostat.

After rinsing the whole mess with another squirt bottle of purified water. The nurse dabbed the area with a second square of cotton to dry it. She told Kendra to continue holding her hand open while she unwrapped the instrument portion of the tray.

Beneath the clear plastic were several instruments that Kendra assumed had been sterilized. She wanted to ask if the instruments—an oddly shaped pair of tweezers and a small scissors with the tips bent at a forty-five degree angle—were sterilized for reuse or if they were new every single time, but she didn't want to seem interrogatory. It was just her inquisitive, detective's mind. It never shut off. But the doctor seemed so prickly she didn't think he'd appreciate her questions.

It was the same way in her everyday life. She had an overriding curiosity about her surroundings that was never ending. Nosy Nate that's me. Just like the folks who would be tramping around the woods in search of bodies after reading today's paper. If I weren't in law enforcement, I would probably be right out there with them.

While Kendra sat woolgathering, Dr. Stevens donned a pair of thin latex gloves pulled from an open purple box on the wall.

Without another word, he took her hand and opened it even further to expose the row of neat black stitches. Skin had grown over one or two of them. "Try not to move," he said as he grasped the end of a stitch with the oddly shaped tweezers. He drew it up away from her flesh and with his other hand he snipped the miniscule knot—*what are stitches made of these days, Kendra wondered, surely not catgut the way they once were (which was not actually cat gut at all, but an abbreviation for cattle gut)*—and pulled it loose. He did exactly the same on the other four. In two minutes, he was done. A tiny drop of blood appeared where the skin had been broken to get at the ones that were embedded, but that was all.

I could've done that at home, Kendra thought, saved the insurance company a couple hundred bucks. But judging by his reaction about the missed appointment, he definitely would've taken umbrage to her performing her own suture-removal. *Best to stay on good terms with the local doctor. Never know when he might be needed again.*

She flexed her hand a few times. "Thanks, Doc. Feels as good as new."

The nurse washed away the tiny drop of blood and gave her a tube of ointment accompanied by a big smile. "Rub a small amount on the scar each night to keep it from tightening up." She packed up the rolling cart with the basin and the instruments. Pushing open the door with her backside, she left the room.

Dr. Stevens rolled off his gloves, stepped on the foot pedal to open the trash receptacle, and dropped them inside. "Nice seeing you again, Detective." His smile was almost believable this time. "Take care of yourself."

Kendra noticed for the first time how many teeth the doctor had. *All the better to eat you with my dear.* Kendra didn't know where that thought came from, but she chalked it up to intuition. *Something about him just screamed Big Bad Wolf.* "Sure thing." She tilted her chin up in a parting gesture that felt almost masculine.

He nodded and pushed open the door with his shoulder.

Kendra noticed how all the personnel seemed to avoid touching the doors with their hands, so she made it a point to open the door with her shoulder, too.

At the checkout window, she paid her twenty-dollar co-pay and immediately, in the back of her mind, a warning sign flashed. What about insurance if I take early retirement? Haven't even thought of that. I'm way too young for Medicare, and private policies are so expensive. Just have to take another job. Security maybe, or private investigations for some big company, like an insurance company. Might not be around here though. Might have to move to another county. Or another state. Would that be like running away—and what if the civil suit finds me liable somehow? Legal fees would bury me. I wouldn't be able to retire—I'd have to work forever just to pay them off.

She tried to cut off the sudden onslaught of worries. It was all so ridiculous. Even now she had trouble believing it had happened.

After the arrest, when she had been preparing to transport the suspect to the county jail, that's when the guy had bounced out in front of the UPS truck like a little kid's ball. It had happened so fast, and he'd been so cocky, she'd simply never dreamed he could be suicidal.

Kendra shook the bangs off her forehead and tried to shake away the memories as well. Then she slid into the driver's seat of her Ford and headed back toward the lake.

On the way home she stopped by the Corner Store, filled the truck with gas, and picked up the gallon of milk she'd forgotten to buy the day before. She chatted with Juanita, the owner, for a moment and then she took the long way home since there was nothing more pressing to do until her meeting with Woody at six.

She pulled into the garage of her lake house, killed the engine and closed the overhead door. She was suddenly looking forward to a cup of coffee and maybe one of those cinnamon rolls she'd made from scratch last night after returning home from the sheriff's office. She'd needed something to do to occupy her mind and her hands. *Another Martha Stewart moment Keith might've said. Whatever. I might even crack open one of those books I picked up from the library last week.* She stepped out of the pickup, surprised at how cool the garage felt. *Winter is definitely on the way.* She pictured herself lighting a small fire in the well-used fireplace.

In the kitchen, she poured out the old coffee and made a fresh pot. Glancing at the clock, she willed the hands to fly. *I'll need to leave by five fifteen to meet Woody.* She dropped her phone and handbag on the end table near the stack of books.

As she pulled her favorite coffee cup—the one with the Pine River Sheriff's Office logo on it—from the cupboard, the phone began to hammer out the opening riff to the song "Bad to the Bone." Woody had programmed the silly song on her phone late one night while they were on a stakeout. It always made her think of Arnold Schwarzenegger in the movie *Terminator.*

She picked up the phone and plopped down on the arm of the couch. Carrie's name appeared on the Incoming Call screen.

Kendra clicked the Accept Call icon. "Hey, kiddo, how's everything going?"

"Fine here, Mom. How's everything with you?"

Kendra's motherly instincts rose to attention. "A-Okay here. What's wrong?" She didn't like to pussyfoot around, especially with an unexpected call from a very pregnant daughter.

Carrie laughed. "I'm all right, really! I'm actually calling with some good news."

"You've found out you're having twins after all? The string test was right?"

Carrie chuckled. "Umm, no, thank the Lord. But I think you'll like it anyway."

"Good," Kendra replied. "So what is it?"

"Well, it looks like we'll get to have Christmas together after all." She hesitated for a split second. "Isn't that wonderful?"

"Fantastic. What's the deal with your dad?" She knew there had to be some reason for the odd little hitch in Carrie's voice.

"Always the detective, aren't you, Mom?"

Kendra waited.

Carrie let out a sigh. "He's going to Vegas for Christmas."

Kendra waited some more. Her mind was racing with possibilities, but she didn't want to blurt out anything inappropriate.

"Mom? You there?"

She exhaled. "Yeah. I'm here. Are you kids all right with this?" Her fingernail found the new scar tissue in the web between her thumb and forefinger and tested it gently.

"We're delighted," Carrie said. "I couldn't stand the thought of you out there alone at Christmas."

Kendra grinned. She'd been feeling that way since Thanksgiving. "I'll get the tree up right away," she said. "We'll have another big meal, maybe Keith will bring his friend Charlie again—"

Carrie laughed softly. "Maybe he will. I think Willa would like that—don't know about Sam, though."

Kendra cut off the small talk. "Why Vegas? Who's going with him? Do you know?"

"I'm not positive, Mom. He just said he wanted to get away, and he wondered if we would mind."

"He always did want to go back to Vegas. We just never made the time. I guess he has all the time he needs now." She didn't say it to Carrie, but in her mind she was certain he wasn't going to Vegas alone. Their neighbors had divorced last year. Las Vegas hadn't made them happy. They'd married there, and went back every year on their anniversary. Kendra remembered how devastated the wife had seemed after her husband had moved out.

She couldn't help but wonder if Leda, the new divorcée, the one she'd once partnered with in a raucous game of charades, had cried on Bill's shoulder while she had been busy scraping bad guys off the pavement. *Wouldn't that be about right, the detective who couldn't see what was going on right under her own nose?*

"Okay, Mom, well. That's all I called to tell you."

"Thanks, sweetie." She didn't want Carrie to hang up. She wanted to quiz her about her day and about everything that was going on, but she didn't want to sound clingy, or needy.

"You staying busy?" Carrie asked softly.

Kendra hated the tiptoey sound of worry she heard in her elder daughter's voice. "Of course I am. You know me. In fact, I wish you were here to eat a homemade cinnamon roll with me. I'm becoming quite the baker if I do say so myself."

Carrie chuckled. "Martha Stewart rides again, huh?"

"Yeah … something like that."

They broke the connection with promises to talk again in a day or two, and Kendra headed for the kitchen where the smell of coffee beckoned her like an aromatic beacon. But before she could pour her first cup, her text message alert chimed merrily.

It was from Woody. "Can we make it nine o' clock? Paperwork is kicking my butt."

"Of course," she typed. "Now I know why you miss me so much." She'd always been a stickler for staying on top of paperwork.

He sent her a row of smiley icons with eyes crossed in agony.

She poured her coffee, grabbed a roll, and headed for the living room to build the fire. On the way, she snatched her old gray hoodie off the peg beside the garage door. The night had definitely developed a chill.

CHAPTER TWENTY

Meditations on the Previous Summer

Dr. Stevens couldn't concentrate after Kendra left the clinic.

He quickly prescribed antibiotics and allergy medications for the remaining patients and then told the staff he would be available by cell phone for emergencies. They knew that meant any other walk-ins would be instructed to make an appointment for the following day unless it was an emergency. Their stock answer would be, "Doctor's been called away, come in first thing tomorrow."

It had been a double whammy.

First Candy had called to tell him what a huge success the baby shower had been, and then Kendra had walked in telling him she was the one who had found his girl in the woods.

He recalled the jolt of adrenaline that had coursed through his body when the tiny Stutter Creek Sentinel had broken the story. HOLIDAY HORRORS indeed, he thought. *I'll give them some holiday horrors.* A plan began to take shape in his mind.

Seeing those words in print had generated one of the most intense feelings he had ever experienced. Better than sex. Almost as good as holding a fresh femur in his bare hands, nearly on par with Mr. McGraw, his first "accidental" victim. It was this feeling that made him decide it was time to unearth another girl. He had to find out if the feeling could be duplicated.

And maybe I'll dress her up a bit, just for the holidays.

As for the detective, he had been immediately suspicious. He hadn't been surprised when she'd missed her original appointment on Saturday. In the back of his mind was the idea that she must have snipped the stitches herself—she seemed that type.

But once she was in the exam room, and they began to chat, the more certain he became that she'd been baiting him to get his reaction. Nowhere in the news article had it said she was the one who had found his girl. When she'd blurted it out, he came to the conclusion that she suspected him and was trying to trip him up somehow.

After that idea occurred to him, Dr. Stevens decided his wife had been doing the same thing, baiting him to get his reaction. "I'm sending some pictures to your phone," she had told him on the way home from the baby shower. "Just wait until you see all the tiny clothes and other things." Her voice had been as chipper as he'd ever heard it. "Oh, Eddie," she'd cooed. "Having a tiny baby to care for must be one of the most wonderful things in the world."

Edgar had felt that his silence spoke volumes, but whether Candy heard what those volumes were saying was another question in need of answering. So he had been blunt. "I hope you haven't forgotten our agreement." Then he deleted all the pictures without opening them.

Candy's phone voice lost its luster. "Of course not. I just thought, after all these years, maybe you had changed your mind. Or had a change of heart."

"Why would I?" His tone had not been angry, just very, very even. "If I wanted children," he reiterated. "I would adopt a child without a home. One in need of a decent mother and father. There are so many children in unhealthy situations. No need to bring more into the world."

Candy had gently interrupted him. "I know you had an awful childhood—"

"You don't know anything about it!" he'd exploded. "Don't ever pretend to understand anything about my childhood."

Candy had stopped talking completely.

Edgar had always been careful to keep that side of his past hidden from Candy. He'd mentioned it only briefly as a way of explaining why he had no contact with his family. After that, he'd been the perfect husband, as long as she abided by his rules.

Obviously, he could no longer trust her. Actually, he could no longer stand to even look at her.

And now the detective was becoming a problem, too.

After he turned off his cell phone, he drove directly to his special place in the woods. He used one of the old private entrances only he knew about.

Once there, he walked through the forest without bothering to watch his footprints or check to make sure he was alone.

He knew where he was going; he'd tattooed it on his thigh in permanent India ink. But as he walked, a text came in from Candy.

"CALL ME!" her words shouted.

Edgar ignored her.

"PLEASE CALL," she'd shout-texted again. "I THINK I'M PREGNANT! IN FACT, I'M POSITIVE!"

Edgar stared at the words in horror. *No!* His mind whirled with rage. *It isn't possible!* His fingers tapped the keypad furiously. "I'm not stupid," he wrote. "You've been on the pill since we married." He pressed send without thinking. In his head he thought, *I check her little compact pill holder daily. She hasn't missed a single one. Unless she's throwing them away instead of taking them.*

That thought struck him between the eyes like a ball peen hammer. *Would she betray him that blatantly?* She's a woman, his subconscious screamed; they get what they want any way they can. He thought of his mother and her men friends.

She'd done anything and everything to get what she wanted from them after his dad left.

"They aren't foolproof, Eddie." Candy had turned off the all-caps now that she had his attention.

"We'll talk about this when I get home," he shot back. "Don't mention it to anyone until I've had a chance to examine you myself. There has to be some mistake."

Candy sent him a sad face icon, but he ignored it and shoved the phone deep into his pocket.

His best girl was gone, and he really *needed* the feel of a femur now.

He licked his lips and swigged from one of the bottles of water he kept in the Toyota's trunk.

Part of me must have wanted her found, he thought. But in his analytical mind he knew he'd most likely left her uncovered and exposed because it was just so exciting to visit her when he knew the consequences if they *were* found out. He figured it was the same sort of thrill a cheating spouse feels every time he or she meets their lover at the Motel 6 on the edge of town.

But now his best girl was gone.

Detective Kendra Dean had deprived him of her.

Fortunately, there were plenty more to soothe his soul. He checked the coordinates he'd plugged into his Garmin handheld GPS.

It was very accurate.

Only a few more steps.

He adjusted his backpack so that it sat a bit more comfortably on his shoulders. He always kept it in the trunk. The extra items had been added only after he'd read the Holiday Horror headline.

His spade bit into the loamy soil and Edgar lifted away the blanket of earth as gently as a new mom unwrapping her own babe.

Why would she trick me? His anger resurfaced with the bones. *Why would she get pregnant knowing I detest children? Doesn't she love me at all?* For a moment, he marveled at the very thought. There was no such thing as love—he knew it was really just a social idea like cleanliness or good manners or religion. And Candy certainly tried to make everyone believe she was a religious person—but if his understanding was correct, and he knew that it was, the Bible taught that the wife must obey the husband, not go against him and deceive him as if he were too stupid to know the best path for their family. *He* was the head of this family. Not her. Not the woman. Him. He must be obeyed.

Edgar placed his hands upon the femur he'd just uncovered. It was always the last thing he covered, therefore, the first thing he uncovered. The rest of the bones were in their correct places, but the femur he always positioned squarely in the center of the body, near the spot where the heart once lived.

Now *that* was love.

And this one hadn't even been in the ground that long. But he had taken an extra amount of time stripping away the flesh before he buried her. The act of pulling the long strips of meat from the bone was akin to the *ommm* he chanted during meditation. It was a self-soothing balm for his tortured psyche.

Caressing the carving on the long bone, Edgar lifted it from the soil. She has to go, he thought. Candy has to be taught. She doesn't control me. I'm the one in control—and if we were to have children, that control would be out the window.

He'd seen plenty of frazzled parents with their screaming brats in the clinic. Granted, those kids were usually sick, but not always, sometimes the brattiest ones were not even the patients. And then there were the kids they saw in restaurants.

Kids just complicated life. The way he had complicated his own parents' lives. The way he'd driven his father to leave and his mother to hide in her booze and her pills and her endless parade of men.

No. There would be no children.

He gently excavated each bone and dusted it with one of his coco-bristle hand brushes, from the set he'd bought online at ArchTools, the archaeology store. He'd also bought a bone-carving tool, but it hadn't had the finesse of his trusty scalpel.

Of course he took extra care with the femurs—both of them since there was so little flesh to get in the way—and he was delighted to find that his index finger still fit perfectly into the valley of the patella.

Edgar laid each bone reverently beside the shallow grave. No clover this time. Instead, this bed would have a pillow of pine boughs. Above his head, a woodpecker tapped out a hungry rhythm. The evergreen forest felt close, yet huge. It was a pagan church.

Edgar had to stop several times and simply sit with his fingers pressed to the ends of the femurs. This was his idea of indie-foreplay. Before long, his right hand crept down to his fly and unzipped, while his left hand continued to caress the valley of the patella.

After he had pleasured himself, his blood pressure fell back to normal, and endorphins flooded his system. His twisted version of happiness engulfed him so completely he had to stop and take stock before he could go on.

A few moments later, he resumed his work.

In keeping with the holiday theme, Edgar wrapped strands of tinsel around the darkly staring skull. When he was finished, his girl appeared to be dressed in a macabre silver turban. In each eye socket, Edgar placed a shiny red Christmas ornament.

He stood and looked at his second-best girl. She was quite striking with her bulging red eyes and silver turban nestled in the pine boughs. Something's missing, he thought. She looks almost naked.

Then he remembered the last item in his backpack. It was a long knitted Christmas stocking depicting Santa perched high atop a mountainous toy-stuffed sleigh. Pulling the sleigh were the requisite eight tiny reindeer. He placed the femur inside the stocking and then tucked it between the bony fingers lying cross the rib cage. There, he thought. *Let those idiots at the newspaper chew on this. Holiday Horrors? How about this for some Holiday Horrors?*

His soothing work took only a few hours.

Afterward, his adrenaline was lessened, but something still burned inside his head. Should I have moved her closer to the known trail? What if no one finds her here? She's much farther off the beaten path than my best girl was. But maybe that will be better in the long run. If she isn't found, that will be good. She'll be that much easier to revisit. She'll be my own Christmas present. Just mine.

Anxiety creased his brow as he hiked back to his car and headed for town.

Do I want her found or not? That is the question...

He decided not to worry about it.

There's plenty of daylight left. Maybe I've got time for a brand new girl.

CHAPTER TWENTY-ONE

The Kidnapping

Kendra had taken the Christmas tree out of storage in the garage—it was a fake one but a good one—and had also dragged the boxes of decorations out. But then the spirit had left her, and she'd decided to put off the actual trimming of the tree until the next day when she wasn't quite so tired.

She'd just settled herself into the corner of the sofa with her book, coffee, and cinnamon roll when she heard a knock at the front door. *Who could that be? I'm not expecting anyone. Woody! I'll bet he got loose early and came on over even though his last text said to meet in Pine River at nine.*

The doorbell followed up the knock.

"I'm coming," she called. "Keep your shirt on."

Out of habit, she peered through the peephole, but it was not Detective Woody James she saw standing on the front porch, knuckles raised to rap the door again.

No wonder he couldn't wait long enough for me to put my coffee down. Doctors are always so impatient. She ran a hand through her messy hair. *What could he possibly want? I just saw him at the office a few hours ago.* She flexed her stitch-free hand reflexively before opening the door.

"Well, hello—" she began.

The doctor slammed her to the floor with a forearm across her throat, and all Kendra had time to think was *he's the killer.* Then she saw his other arm coming down. In it he was holding a police-type leather SAP—a flexible Billy club weighted with lead on one end. She had a split second to realize it was just like the one in her own storage locker, and then she went out as surely as if someone had flipped her ON switch to OFF. The last thing she remembered was the smell of fresh coffee and cinnamon.

***

Woody tried Kendra's cell phone over and over. They'd agreed to meet at Lisa's Café at nine o'clock, and now it was almost ten.

Ken was seldom late, and she would never break an appointment without calling.

He looked at the file he'd placed on the table for her to examine. The file about the woman—and her dog—who were missing from just outside Yellow Bend, the next town over from Stutter Creek.

"Why did you wait so long to report your sister missing?" the desk officer had asked, but he told Woody when he looked into the woman's eyes it was obvious she was a drug addict. "Tweaker," he'd said. "She probably couldn't tell yesterday from six months ago."

What she did tell was chilling. "I didn't come earlier 'cause I thought she was with Brad, her fiancé. But then he come by my house looking for her. Said she ain't been home in months. Nor that big ol' pup she rescued neither."

The officer said she'd wiped her leaky nose and added, "I'm afraid he's done somethin' to her. To the both of 'em. She ain't never been gone this long."

That's when the desk officer had turned the case over to Woody because it appeared to be a county matter.

And then Woody had called Kendra and arranged this little rendezvous.

But now she was an hour late and *still* not answering.

All at once, he'd had enough.

He gathered up the file, left the waiter a twenty, and hurried to the car.

He thought about activating the grill lights and busting every red light in two towns to get out to the lake, but there weren't that many stoplights to begin with so he simply played it cool, did the hesitate and look, and then went on through without lights flashing.

The closer he got to Copper Lake, the more difficult it became to tame the electric eel of fear that lit up his gut. He hit redial for the third time. "Answer, damn it. If you're in the shower when I get there, you are in big trouble, lady." He thumbed the OFF icon when her voice mail came on again. He'd already left a message; he didn't need to leave another.

When his tires hit the dirt shoulder of the blacktop road, Woody realized his mind was wandering, and his foot had grown heavy on the gas. He slowed considerably and steered back onto the pavement. She has to be there, he thought. Where else would she be at this time of night? Woody realized he had no idea what sort of nightlife she led now that she was basically single. *Still, she wouldn't leave me hanging. And if she is stuck somewhere between Stutter Creek and Pine River, wouldn't she have her phone?*

His foot pressed down again.

In record time, he drove straight through Stutter Creek and was soon turning into the lake house drive.

The house was dark, but he couldn't tell if her vehicle was there or not, the garage doors were solid, no windows to peek through.

He leaped onto the wide porch—the same one where he'd sat and comforted her only a couple of weeks earlier—and knocked heartily while ringing the bell at the same time. When that didn't elicit a response, he dashed back to the car, retrieved his Mag light and shined it through the filmy rose-colored sheers covering the window.

The living room was empty. Thin moonlight hinted at an undecorated Christmas tree standing forlornly in the corner awaiting its star and tinsel. From the outside looking in, Woody had the feeling he was peering into the negative of one of those snow globes. *Maybe if I shake it, the light will come on, and she will magically appear.*

His flashlight picked up the shape of the bare tree again, and he realized the room must not be completely dark. He leaned to the side and sure enough there was a slight glow coming from the fireplace. As if a fire had died down to embers.

Woody rapped on the glass with his flashlight. "Kendra Dean. Ken! You in there?" Cold sweat broke out beneath his shirt. He had a sinking feeling in his belly. Kendra was never without her phone. And no way would she ever go off and leave a fire burning in the fireplace.

He pulled out his phone and hit redial again.

From inside the nightmare snow globe, he heard the first chords of George Thorogood's iconic anthem, "Bad to the Bone." Woody could see the iPhone lighting up as the music played. It lay on the end table near Kendra's small handbag. He wouldn't have noticed it if the phone hadn't lit up.

Panic clutching his gut, Woody strode back to the front door and lifted his foot to kick it in, then he remembered something Kendra had taught him—look for the easy way first—so he reached out and turned the old-fashioned door knob.

It was unlocked.

Stepping aside to keep from being a perfect target, Woody pulled his weapon and pushed the door open with the tips of his fingers.

The interior of the living room was shrouded in gloom. He could smell the pine logs in the fire mingled with the sweet smell of cinnamon and coffee.

He held his Maglite on top of his gun so it would blind anyone looking at him.

Time stopped.

The faint moonlight illuminated the sheer-curtained windows but did little to dispel the lurking shadows.

He located the light switch beside the front door and flipped it on. Woody wasn't familiar enough with her new home to know if things were *exactly* as they should be, but to his detective's eye everything appeared to be neat and tidy except for the nude Christmas tree in the corner, the glowing embers in the fireplace, and the half-eaten cinnamon roll beside the cup of coffee on the end table.

He stuck a finger in the coffee.

Cold.

And then there was her cell phone lying beside her handbag.

He also noted the open book face down on the sofa. She'd only read the first couple of chapters.

Maybe she decided to stop and decorate the tree. There were three cardboard boxes beneath it. One was marked *handmade decorations*, another was marked *Christmas balls*, and the third was marked *lights*.

Still doesn't explain why she isn't here now, unless she's in the garage or the attic retrieving more boxes. *In the dark?*

He strode to the kitchen and immediately noticed the coffee maker still on. He turned it off and opened the door leading to the garage. Try as he might, Woody couldn't dispel the feeling of ghosts looking over his shoulder—the living ghosts of her children as they'd been at Thanksgiving. It was as if they were all there with him, urging him to hurry and find their mom.

Her pickup was in the garage, the engine as cold as the coffee.

He dashed back into the living room, grabbed up her handbag, and dumped out the contents. When he spied her key ring, he plucked it up and hurried back to the garage to make certain she wasn't slumped over behind the wheel of her truck. The tinted windows made the cab seem like a cave. Woody unlocked the driver's door and climbed inside.

The clean, crisp smell of her perfume lingered in the fabric of the seats.

Woody inhaled deeply, remembering how he'd once breathed in her whispered words in the hallway of a Holiday Inn.

His heart thrummed inside the cage of his ribs.

She's off on a hike, his mind insisted. She went for a hike and went farther than she intended. She'll come bursting through the front door any minute and proceed to chew my ass from here to Kingdom Come for jumping to conclusions.

But that idea didn't ring true.

Ken would never go hiking and leave her phone at home, and the front door unlocked. Especially not at night. *Not when she was supposed to meet me over an hour ago. No way.*

He closed and relocked the pickup and made his way through the rest of the old house checking every room, every closet, and under every bed.

He even checked the attic.

Still nothing.

Nothing out of place, nothing overturned. No sign of a struggle. No sign of life.

Back in the living room, he stopped to think it through. *Maybe she got a call, and someone came and picked her up.* He grabbed her cell phone and thumbed through the recent calls. He saw where she had talked to the county sheriff's office several times since last week, and then he saw a few calls he didn't recognize.

He finally got to the place where she had called the clinic this morning. *That must be where she was when we were texting.*

The voicemail showed only his message from a half hour earlier.

He switched over to text messages; scrolled past the ones they had exchanged, and found one even more recent. It was from Carrie. *"I told the others about dad going to Vegas and guess what? They both agreed to meet back at your place for Christmas just like we talked about earlier. It will be great! Love you…"*

Woody scrolled back through the earlier calls, and sure enough, there was one that matched Carrie's number from a few hours earlier. He felt an immediate wave of revulsion for Bill. Who the hell went to Vegas at Christmas? He would never go off and leave his kids on a holiday, no matter how grown up they were.

He thought of Willa's round little face and Shirley Temple curls, and he couldn't keep from smiling. He'd known her since she was just a junior high school kid, and she'd stolen his heart from the beginning. In fact, he had a deep affection for all of Kendra's children, even Keith, who looked so much like his handsome father.

Woody shook his head and slipped the phone into his pocket. He knew it was time to call in Chief Brown or Sheriff Puckett. This was all too coincidental. She'd found a body, and now she was in need of finding. He took her phone back out, looked up the sheriff's number, and dialed it from his phone.

His insides ached as he stood in the empty living room with the naked Christmas tree. He listened impatiently as the sheriff's phone began to ring.

Where could she be?

CHAPTER TWENTY-TWO
Hope These Aren't My Cuffs

Kendra awoke in darkness. The floor was rough cement, and her handcuffed wrists were shackled to a metal ring on the floor. *I hope these aren't my cuffs,* she thought groggily.

She tried to turn her head to take in her surroundings and was greeted with a sadistic pain that began over her right ear and shot straight down the side of her jaw into her neck and even down into her shoulder. *Damn bastard. He could've killed me. Maybe he will yet.*

She turned her head slowly. Her eyes were beginning to adjust to the dimness. It wasn't completely dark; there was a faint source of light coming from somewhere. Kendra tested her wrists as quietly as possible. She had no idea if she was alone or whether he was sitting nearby watching.

I must've scared him today in his office when I blurted out what I had found. Why else would he have taken me? It is time for me to retire. I knew better than to tell a stranger what I'd discovered—even if he is the town doctor.

Now, I have to figure out how to get out of here. No way I can live after I've seen his face—he hasn't killed me yet because he wants to know if I've told anyone. Wants to know if I'm certain it's him, or whether I just suspect. And stupid me, I didn't suspect. Not at all. Not until he crashed through my front door with murder in his eyes and that damn SAP in his fist. Shit. I knew those bone-cuts looked surgical.

She listened intently. If he *was* nearby, he was being very quiet. She looked at the ring to which she was shackled. It was set into the floor. *Who did that? Who had a big metal ring bolted to the floor? Maybe I'm in some kind of warehouse or something. Concrete floors, cold and damp—maybe it's a basement. That would make sense. What connection would a doctor have with a warehouse? But a basement would make sense, especially since I'm pretty sure he surgically removed that girl's femur and then carved those numbers and letters into it.*

Kendra inhaled deeply through her nose. If there had been a murder committed here, she was sure she'd be able to smell it. People don't die cleanly. There are always body fluids; blood is one part of it, and the coppery scent of copious amounts of blood is one smell impossible to forget, especially when there is enough that the odor colors the air and coats the tongue.

She inhaled again. In addition to the odors of damp mold and spiky mildew, she was fairly certain there was the faintest tang of blood.

It was difficult to be certain, though. The mold was so prevalent it tickled her nose until she was certain she would have a sneezing fit. As a last resort, she leaned her head down and pinched her nostrils closed. She didn't want him to know she was awake yet, but folding herself in half that way made her head pound so badly she almost passed out. *I'll never hit another creep with my SAP unless it's completely unavoidable.* Her stomach roiled as the waves of pain washed through her head.

At last she sat up slowly, sneeze averted but stomach and head paying the price. *I hope nothing is bleeding inside my skull. Might have a concussion—but how bad? How can I get away if I can't even move?* The thought of standing up, if she were even able, seemed completely beyond her physical capabilities.

Eyes closed, she concentrated on breathing in and out, slowly, carefully, until the nausea began to subside. In moments she was dozing again, head lolling against the damp, cinder block wall at her back.

When she woke again, light oozed into her eyeballs through the thin skin of her lids. For seconds upon seconds,

Kendra put off opening her eyes. *My vision will be blurry. He will be crouched right in front of me, and there will be two of him—maybe even three.*

The longer she tried to make her eyes stay closed, the more they wanted to pop open regardless of the consequences.

"Hello, Detective. Welcome to my world." The voice came out of nowhere.

She recognized the doctor's terse speech. Kendra suspected his dialect was studied as if he'd picked it up in college along with his medical degree.

"Here you are, in my little abode."

He spoke so faintly she had to focus to hear him.

"You're wondering why you're here." It was a statement rather than a question. "But when your head clears—and by the way, I know you're awake—you'll think of the reason. You'll know why I couldn't leave you rambling around Stutter Creek spouting all that nonsense about surgical cuts on bones. Those are my map coordinates if you must know. They remind me where I buried the others."

Kendra didn't open her eyes. "How can you put coordinates on one victim that leads to the next?" Her raspy voice sounded as if it had been dragged over an old-fashioned cheese grater.

"Planning," he chuckled. "Good planning. You see, my girls keep me sane. They keep me on an even keel so to speak. If not for my girls, I'd be, well, I'd probably be on death row by now. Or dead by my own hand. Oh yes, I once thought of that. But that would be giving up, wouldn't it? And I don't give up. Ever." He hesitated, then continued. "Did you know what you were doing when you told me about my girl? Did you know it was me? Or were you just flinging information into the air like a dandelion shedding its seeds?"

Kendra didn't let him goad her. Play it safe, she thought. *Play it safe.* Tips from her hostage-negotiation training began to surface in her feeble mind. *Make the captor know you as a person. Make him see you as a human being. Use his name; make him use yours. Find a connection, or create one.* "I thought you were simply my doctor. My friend." She drew in a shallow breath. "Dr. Stevens. Edgar. I'm retired. I stumbled upon your girl when I was out fishing." Her head hurt, it was hard to think. "I – I felt someone watching me. I followed my intuition. Was it you, watching?" She hugged her knees to her chest. Her bottom was so cold her hip bones were beginning to ache. *At least give me a blanket or something. That will be my first goal: a blanket. Baby steps.* "If it wasn't you watching me, then I'm not the only one stumbling around out there..."

"Hah!" His laugh was short, harsh. "You don't fool me, Detective. My own mother would turn me in if she were still alive. But then she also would've hired some hack to write a movie of the week about me and the girls while she collected all the money—"

Kendra continued her controlled breathing. She'd already caught the plural reference to his *girls*. He'd already told her the carvings on the bones were map coordinates leading to other victims. She couldn't believe he was telling her all this. *But then, I am a captive audience, and who better to tell your secrets to than someone you know will soon be dead?*

He wasn't finished talking. Apparently, he was only getting started. "Come to think of it, I have dear old mom to thank for *all* of this."

Kendra featured him waving his hand around as he spoke the words "all this." But she still didn't open her eyes, not yet.

"She overdosed, you know? Such a sorry, clichéd excuse for a life. Somehow, I managed to crawl up out of it. Even though her death meant I got put into the system."

His speech trailed away, and Kendra had to resist opening her eyes to see if he was still there. Then he began to speak again.

"I modeled this place on my old room. That's rather queer, I know. But it's comforting, bringing my girls here. I guess you're one of my girls, now. Although I didn't intend it that way." He hesitated again. "You know, *Detective*, she always made me sleep in the basement, even when I was just a little tyke."

Kendra didn't respond. The way he used her title bothered her. It was as if he knew the hostage negotiation rules, too, and was flaunting them at her.

"Yes. She made me stay downstairs in the dampness, with the spiders, while she partied upstairs. I snuck up a time or two. Got my eyes blackened for my troubles. But she did me a favor in the long run—when she died, that is—because my foster father kicked my ass. Kept me in school. Made me excel, go to college. Too bad he didn't live to see me graduate."

He laughed another harsh, short laugh that made Kendra feel certain he'd had something to do with his foster's dad's early death.

"Dear old mom," he continued. "Dying young was the best thing she ever did for me."

"What about your biological father?" Kendra didn't care; she just wanted to keep him talking. Every sentence out of his mouth was another moment she was still alive.

He totally ignored her question. "My foster family. If not for them Edgar would've been a high school dropout rather than a respected doctor. He didn't let them down, but then, they never knew about the darkness he hid inside himself, nor the damage it did every time it leaked out. Not until it was too late, that is."

Kendra wasn't surprised at what he was saying, but she became even more alarmed when she heard him begin referring to himself in the third person. *He's just one candle away from a total meltdown. And when that happens, I'm toast.*

"You didn't know all that, did you?" he asked. "You couldn't know all that. No one does. Not even my lovely wife. Especially not my lovely wife. I trusted her with everything else—and still she betrayed me." He stopped talking, and Kendra waited.

And she waited.

Then she waited some more.

She counted to sixty, three times—at least she thought it was three. Twice she got confused and lost her place. The pounding in her head had leveled off to a dull roaring ache, but she still didn't want to open her eyes.

The light went away.

One moment it was there, the next it was gone.

She was in darkness again.

It's a trick, she thought. *He wants me to open my eyes because—*

Because—

She couldn't think of a reason why.

It made no sense that he would want her to look at him.

I'm not thinking clearly. That's the problem. Was he even here, or did I imagine all that? She opened her eyes to cold darkness. He was here. That was real. This is all real. *I'm trapped in a basement of some sort, chained to a metal ring in the floor, but there was light when he was here, I know there was.*

She closed her eyes and dozed again.

As she dozed, she felt herself transported back to Thanksgiving, the day she and Willa had walked around the lake with Charlie. Even dozing she could recall the vision of those tall spiky pines dusted with the premonition of snow.

She remembered thinking that they were making memories that day.

CHAPTER TWENTY-THREE

Alvin and Scrubby

Alvin Ackerly and Scrubby Bukowski became friends in first grade at Stutter Creek Elementary because they were almost always seated near each other.

The two boys were now in high school. They'd grown up together. Scrubby's mom even let Al come home with Scrubby every day after school until his mom could get by to get him after work.

Al's dad had taken a soft turn on a hard curve and driven right off Jumper's Point late one night when Al was just a kid. The old man might've had "a little nip of gin" (as the old Jeanne C. Riley song said), but since he didn't take out anyone but himself, the investigating DPS trooper simply wrote it off as an "accident due to icy conditions on a mountain road." He knew from experience that some insurance companies would refuse to pay out if alcohol was mentioned.

For a while, after Al lost his dad, Scrubby was afraid he was going to lose his best friend. Al's mom kept talking about moving to California to live with her sister while they "got their feet on the ground." But that deal fell through when his mom took a seasonal job at the Alpine Ski Lodge. Fortunately, the lodge's owner took a shine to Mrs. Ackerly and kept her on after the ski season. Al told Scrubby he was pretty sure the owner and his mom were "screwing around."

Those were Al's words. He wasn't sure how he felt about his mom seeing another man even if his dad had been dead for six months. "Isn't there some rule about waiting at least a year?" he'd asked Scrubby.

Scrubby had simply shrugged and readjusted his fishing pole. "I don't think there are rules," he'd said. "But I'm only a kid, what do I know?"

Al hadn't pursued the matter. He was glad they were staying in Stutter Creek, but he was upset that his mother wasn't more torn up over his father's death. He was a little surprised that *he* wasn't more torn up. But his dad had been a real yeller. He'd have a snort—as he called it—and then he'd get happy. Then he'd have a few more, and the fighting would begin.

Al didn't miss the fighting. But he never admitted that, to anyone. Not even Scrubby. It was too much like saying he was glad his dad was gone.

Anyhow, that was all in the past.

Today, he'd stuck his thumb out like a hitchhiker when Scrubby drove up in his new Challenger.

"Day-*um*," he'd said, putting his thumb away and leaning in the open window. "You weren't kidding when you said you'd just bought the hottest car in the Creek." His eyes were bright, and if he felt a momentary pang of jealousy, he was able to tamp it down very quickly.

"You shoulda been there," Scrubby said, the spikes of his hair poking out every which way. "But Dad just picked me up early and surprised me with it." He ran a hand around the leather-covered steering wheel lovingly. "I'll be making the payments, of course." He let that sink in for a moment.

"Of course," Al muttered.

A look of concern scuttled across Scrubby's freckled face. "It might be tough, going to school and working, but it'll be totally worth it. Besides, it's only a couple of years till we graduate."

Al opened the door and climbed inside, closing the door behind himself. "Lucky bastard." He smoothed his hands across the leather seats reverently. "It's just like new, ain't it?"

Scrubby nodded. "Only thirty-eight thousand miles. Dad says that's nothing. Guy that had it just couldn't make the payments on time, it was about to be repossessed." He put the car in gear and executed a perfect U-turn in front of Al's house. "Got the fishin' gear in the trunk." He checked his rearview. "Not the 'crawlers, though—"

"You sure you want to go fishing? I know we had plans but hell, we can take my old truck later." His mom had managed to get him an old truck to get back and forth to school. It ran most of the time. "Wouldn't want to mess up that new car smell." He punched his buddy lightly on the shoulder.

Scrubby grinned. "It does smell new, doesn't it?" He ran his hands around the steering wheel again. "Bet they sprayed something in it. No way it could still smell new being almost a year old already."

"I dunno. Guy obviously took good care of it—" He had a momentary flash of how awful it must've been for the guy to give it up. But it wasn't his problem. He just hoped his buddy could make the payments. He was almost afraid to ask how much they were, but he knew Scrubby would tell him eventually. He couldn't keep a secret if his life depended on it.

"He sure *did* take care of it." Scrubby revved it up a little.

Al grinned. "Let's go out on 141. See what she can do."

Scrubby nodded and put his foot down.

The smile never left his face as he headed toward the highway.

He didn't speed, much, but he did let the Dodge walk when the road was straight. "I just can't believe she's mine," he admitted, using the female vernacular the way Al had done.

After they pulled into the parking area behind the camp store, Al whistled admiringly as they got the fishing poles out of the trunk. "Dude, seriously. We have to take my heap from now on. What if we catch a big ol' stinkin' catfish? I'm not going to feel right putting it in this trunk. Man, this thing is *pristine*." He looked down at the spotless carpet. "Midnight blue through and through. Day-*um*. I think I'm in *love*."

Scrubby pulled out his tackle box. "Yep, got a nice trunk." He hesitated. "Maybe you're right. Maybe we won't actually catch anything today."

Al laughed and clapped him on the back.

They were halfway up the park trail—headed for a little-known fishing hole at the deeper end of Stutter Creek—when Scrubby stopped. "You know, I haven't been to this spot in a long time." He wiped his forehead with his palm. "I forgot how far it was. I'd just as soon be cruising town as stomping around out here with Blue sittin' all lonesome down there in the parking lot."

"Now you're talking." Al switched his tackle box to his other hand. "I was thinking how good a milkshake would taste about now. I mean, here it is Saturday afternoon, and neither one of us has to work. Shouldn't we be showing off your new wheels and checkin' out Darla Faye's uniform shirt down at the Tastee-Freez?"

Scrubby turned and headed away from the trail. "You don't have to tell me twice," he said. "C'mon, let's take the shortcut back to the camp store. Tastee-Freez, here we come. By the way, I hear Annabel Mendoza just went to work there." To himself he muttered, "Bet she rocks that shirt, too." He continued chuckling under his breath as he meandered off into the woods.

After a couple of miles, he hesitated just long enough to knock his knuckles on the old Private Property sign for good luck. It had been years since he'd taken out some of those letters with his BB gun. "Remember when my dad would bring us up here to fish and sometimes he'd let us bring our guns and plink that old sign?" His question hung in the air without a response.

That's when he realized his buddy was no longer tramping along behind him.

"Al? Hey, *Alvin*!" He made himself sound like the guy in the old Chipmunk's movie when he yelled "*Alvin*!" That was something he hadn't done since junior high. *Prob'ly stepped behind a bush to pee.* He peered all around in the forest gloom.

What he saw when he looked back was quite a surprise to Scrubby. He raised one hand to his face to shield his eyes as if the sun could be causing this odd vision. But there wasn't much sunlight this deep in the forest. What he saw was very simple, it was his good buddy, Alvin Ackerly, staring slack-jawed at something on the ground.

Scrubby started back toward him at a jog. He hadn't seen Al's face look like that since they were kids, and he'd had to deal with the news of his father's untimely death.

"How long til Christmas?" Al's voice was dreamlike.

"Christmas? Why?"

"'Cause I just found someone's present."

Scrubby dropped his tackle box and sprinted to where Al was standing.

"Son of a *bitch!*" he breathed. "Is that what I think it is?"

Al nodded.

"Is it for real?" Scrubby's voice cracked.

Al nodded again, but his words weren't so certain. "I guess it could be a prank. But I don't think so." He turned wide eyes toward his buddy at last. "That's a chick, huh?"

Scrubby pulled out his cell phone and took a picture. His hands were shaking so bad he snapped several more, just in case. "I'll send it to my dad—no, wait, better call the cops first, right?"

Al, still slack-jawed, simply went back to staring at the grinning skull with the big red Christmas balls for eyes.

Scrubby spoke even while pressing nine one one on his smartphone. "I think it is a chick. I mean a girl. Or a woman." He looked at his friend helplessly. "Looks like she had long hair."

Alvin swallowed noisily. "That's a Christmas stocking she's holding. Why would anyone do that? Who would be crazy enough—?"

At that, his sentence broke apart, and he glanced around as if he'd heard someone sneaking up on him from behind. "Shit." He wiped his suddenly damp forehead with the sleeve of his flannel shirt. "Let's get out of here."

He started down the trail, fishing gear completely forgotten.

***

The dispatcher on duty alerted both Chief Brown and Sheriff Puckett as soon as the call came in. "Another set of remains," she told them on three-way. "I've dispatched a unit. She'll be standing by with the two boys."

"Good job, Marissa," the sheriff said. "I'm on my way."

"I'm almost there," Chief Brown chimed in.

Since he arrived first, Chief Brown followed the sheriff's deputy up the side of the mountain to the scene. "Thank God it's daylight," he said as they left the trail and made their way through the underbrush.

The two boys stood off to one side, well away from the remains, fishing gear now piled at their feet. The chief recognized Alvin Ackerly. He remembered when the boy's father had gone over the cliff. He was pretty sure the other kid was the one known as Scrubby because of his bushy brown hair.

"Boys." He nodded at them in acknowledgment, and then edged closer to the strange scene.

The bones glimmered whitely in the depth of the forest. They weren't hidden; in fact, they were obviously laid out for all the world to see. The eye sockets contained two shiny red Christmas balls, and a Christmas stocking was fitted into the grip of the finger bones. A halo of tinsel had been wound around and around the gory skull. Someone went to a lot of trouble on this one, the chief thought. And then something else occurred to him. The Holiday Horrors headline from the most recent edition of the Stutter Creek Sentinel.

The article had insinuated that there might be a reason the remains were found right before Christmas. The reporter even went so far as to postulate a theory that it could be an anti-Christian hate crime. Or at least something designed to send a message to Christians during the holiday season.

The chief wasn't sure about that. He didn't like jumping to conclusions. Besides, how did this tie in with their previous idea that it was something to do with cartography? He secretly wondered if they had a second nutcase on their hands. A copycat. Someone who simply wanted his or her fifteen minutes of lunatic fame.

Sheriff Puckett appeared beside him like a large, solid, phantom. "Good God," he said. "That's some weird shit going on there."

"Is that your professional observation?" the chief asked. He and the sheriff went back a few years. They weren't exactly the best of friends, but they were courteous coworkers. And that was more than a lot of law enforcement agencies could say.

Sheriff Puckett made a noise of derision and started snapping pictures with his digital camera. "Crime unit on the way?"

Chief Brown nodded. That was one reason they worked together so often. The county and city had been forced to combine their resources in order to afford the forensics, team. "Looks like a woman's hair," he said. "Odd how the perp left the scalp intact isn't it?"

"Seems to be the only place with any real flesh still attached." He put a hand to his midsection. "Kinda wish I'd skipped the blackened catfish for lunch."

The boys apparently could take it no longer. Together, they sidled up to the two lawmen. "Can we go now?" Scrubby asked.

Chief Brown stuck out his hand. "Scrubby, you boys did a good thing calling this in like you did."

The teenager shook the chief's hand tentatively. "It was a shock. We were on the way to go fishing when we found it." He glanced toward the remains and then abruptly looked away.

The sheriff examined him carefully. "Y'all see anyone on your way up here?"

Both boys shook their heads. "We didn't touch it either," Alvin said. "I don't even like being this close." He shuddered as the words left his mouth.

The sheriff recognized him just as the chief had. It was a small community. "I don't blame you boys; I wish none of us had to be here." He looked down at the sad Christmas tableau. "But somebody did this. And it's up to us to find out who, and why."

Chief Brown grunted his agreement, and then he turned on the large flashlight he had carried up from his car and began to examine the ground around the staged scene. "You guys can head back down." He turned to the deputy. "Escort them back to the trail. Make sure they make it all the way down to the sheriff's office, please. Call their folks, and then get them started on their written statements."

"Yes, sir," the deputy replied, motioning for the boys to accompany her.

"And stay on the edge of the path going back." He indicated the leafy part of the trail. "Don't want any more footprints than necessary—be sure and tell the crime unit, too." Under his breath he muttered, "What sick son-of-a-bitch wants to do something like this?"

Sawyer Puckett stood like John Wayne, gun belt low on his hip, one arm cocked out at the elbow. "What d'you make of it, Rog?"

The chief wagged his head. "Man, I don't know what to think about this mess. We've had some kooks through here over the years, but they were usually just passing through." He continued to examine the area with his light. "This one's been here a while, to do all this. And he seems to be mocking us doesn't he?"

"You mean the newspaper article?"

Roger Brown nodded. "He definitely reads *The Sentinel*." He shook his head and wondered aloud why so many lunatics seemed to be attracted to his little part of paradise. "You think it's getting crazier everywhere? Or is it something about our little corner of the world that attracts them?"

The sheriff grunted. "I have no idea. I just want to find the asshole."

Together they made certain the area was secured, and then they discussed who had command of the investigation. They both knew it was the sheriff's jurisdiction, just like the first one—since it was located outside the city limits—but Roger Brown had been on his way back into town when he heard the call go out. That's why he had arrived first. That's also why he hadn't been able to check out the first one when she was found—he was out of town.

The sheriff turned back toward the trail, but the chief hated to turn his back on the skeleton. From the corner of his eye, he could see the pale bones shining whitely, their red eyes reflecting his light right back at him.

CHAPTER TWENTY-FOUR

Reminiscing About Dancing

When Kendra awoke again, she opened her eyes without thinking. She was shocked to find herself not in a damp, dark basement, but in what appeared to be a shadowy cinder block bathroom with all the fixtures removed. She tried to lift her hands, but they were still shackled to the floor.

She peered down at the ring. It looked like one of those metal towel racks that bolt directly onto the wall; only someone had bolted this one to the floor instead.

The room was dim again rather than completely dark.

Where is the light coming from?

She sat up a little straighter to try and work the kinks out of her spine. She was tall, and the way she was attached to the floor made her bend slightly to one side. Already a deep ache had settled into her hips and spine both from the cold floor and from the way she was forced to sit.

If it is a towel rack, she thought, they sometimes hook into the base at a split in the middle rather than being one solid metal ring. She tested the metal. It seemed solid but it wasn't yet light enough for her to see it clearly. *Worry about that later.*

She twisted her aching neck carefully to look at her surroundings. Sure enough, the walls were raw, gray cinder block, the floor rough concrete with a hole that could be a drain or a place where a toilet might have once stood. There was also a painted cabinet in the corner that appeared to contain a single sink. It was impossible to know if the sink and faucet were hooked into a water supply, the pipes—if there were any—would be hidden inside the cabinet.

At the thought of water, her throat closed up as though she'd swallowed a fistful of sand.

She closed her eyes for a few moments.

When she opened them, the light had grown strong enough for her to locate its source.

Toward one end of the room, way up high was a small, filthy, skylight. So far as she could tell, it was the only window in the room.

"Doc?" Her voice came out weak. "You here?" Her thirst was so great she felt feverish, but that might have been due to the ache in her head. She'd decided to play his game by ingratiating herself to him. She hoped to convince him she was in awe of his physician/friend status. But there was no reply.

High above her, the light suddenly went out.

Clouds over the sun? She shivered and hoped there were no spiders in here with her. Everyone knows spiders come out when it's dark. And roaches. She hated roaches even worse than spiders. Could there be rats? *Oh, God, why did I have to think about rats?*

Eventually, her eyes readjusted to the dimness, and she was able to discern that her environment—while stark—was at least bug and rodent free.

Kendra began to look for ways to get free. She ran her fingers all around the bolted ring in the floor but found not a single loose seal. He'll be back, she told herself. *He has to come back to check on me. No way his ego would allow him to leave me here alive. That's not how this type of game usually works.* She thought back over the half-dozen serial killer cases she had worked over the course of her career. Actually, she'd only really worked two of them; on the others she'd simply been a consultant.

As her mind worked, she began to work her body as well. She started with her sore neck and head. Ever so slowly she rolled her neck and practiced rotations of her head to try and work the pain out of the muscles. Then she simply worked her way down her body from her shoulders to the tips of each finger and then to her spine, waist, hips, legs, and feet. When she got down to her hips, she did her best to recline on her side and execute a series of leg lifts. At one point, she even managed to roll onto her belly and relieve the pressure on her spine that way.

One of her greatest fears—aside from a brain bleed or concussion from that damn SAP—was the onset of leg cramps in her thighs and calves. She sometimes suffered from those even on her good days. She certainly didn't want that excruciating pain while she was shackled to the floor unable to stand up and stretch them out.

Her exercises took the better part of an hour, and then Kendra began to worry about dehydration. Fortunately, if a bathroom became necessary, there was that hole in the floor nearby. Surely that's what it was intended for. But without water, she doubted she'd be forced to use it. She wondered if it was attached to any sort of drain, and then the ramifications of having a drain in a bunker—for surely that's what this was—came to mind as she recalled the metallic odor of blood.

Have I gotten used to the smell already? Or is he doing something to kill the odor? Just how much time am I losing each time I nod off?

To keep from obsessing about her current situation, Kendra let her mind rove freely. It immediately went back to the scene where she'd found the remains.

She recalled the way the M.E. and the sheriff had seemed to be at odds with one another. He'd said it was due to her grief over losing her husband, but could it be more than that?

She sifted through her memories to see if the M.E. had been present at the other cases she had worked with Sheriff Puckett. There hadn't been that many since this wasn't, until recently, her county. And she couldn't think of another case the three of them had worked together.

Kendra cut off her remembering there. She thought a lot of both Lois Campanelli and Sheriff Puckett. She didn't want to go back over the harsh way the two of them had interacted, even if she had made light of it for his sake. It detracted from the job, and it was unprofessional. Kendra hated unprofessional. *On the other hand, we all have lives away from the office. Or at least we should have.*

She stretched to the extent her handcuffs would allow, and then her mind found its way back to a night she and Woody had spent on the road—outside the job—as they had transported an AWOL private to Fort Leavenworth. It seemed the private had gotten drunk and sliced up his buddy at a bar in Lawton, Oklahoma, but since Fort Sill no longer had a correctional facility, they had to take him all the way to Kansas. He'd gone on the run not even knowing if his "friend" was dead or alive. He'd gotten as far as Pine River when he was caught. It was nothing sexy, not even very exciting, just drugs and drink and too much testosterone.

She remembered Woody saying, "And now he'll probably spend a few months in jail and lose his good conduct medal." Woody had been driving for a change.

In the passenger seat, Kendra had been catching up on reports on her laptop. "Guess he'll get a dishonorable discharge, too," she replied. "Even though his friend will recover and didn't press charges. Sure screwed up his future, huh?"

"Yeah." Woody had moved his perpetual toothpick to the other corner of his mouth. Giving up smoking had been difficult.

"Hope he doesn't become another statistic—you know, another homeless veteran—when he gets out." She pulled down the vanity mirror and had a peek at their prisoner. They were driving a patrol car instead of their usual unmarked Mercury. The heavy mesh screen between the back and front compartments laid an eerie pattern across the young man's sleeping face. "God," Kendra murmured, "look how young he is. He could be one of my kids."

Woody shook his head. "Yours would never do something like that. He made his choice when he took a knife into that bar and proceeded to get shit-faced." She knew Woody had little compassion for drunks and druggies. "You make your choices; you live with your consequences," he said.

Kendra nodded. "I know you're right. It just seems like such a waste." She opened her laptop and tried to get back into the report she'd been writing.

Now, sitting on the cold concrete in her own strange prison, Kendra recalled being out of sorts on that trip, but she couldn't remember exactly why. Whether she'd had words with Bill, or whether she'd missed another one of the kids' school functions, she didn't remember exactly—it had happened so often—but she did recollect feeling as if she'd devoted her life to a job that had few rewards. Taking the young private to prison was downright depressing. It had probably played a large part in her solemn mindset.

The three of them had left Pine River at four o'clock in the morning. It was a fourteen-hour drive. She and Woody switched drivers every few hours and only stopped for B&B—burgers and bathrooms—when absolutely necessary.

It was well after midnight by the time they deposited their prisoner with the correctional officers and filled out the necessary paperwork.

"How about a nightcap?" Woody had suggested, rubbing his neck and lower back while waiting for the clerk to verify their credit card at the Holiday Inn.

Kendra nodded. Her own back had begun to feel like ground meat after the long drive.

She dropped her bag in her single room, freshened up a bit, and met him in the lobby.

"The hotel doesn't have a bar," he said by way of greeting. "But I asked the clerk where we could get a nice, quiet drink, and he directed me to a place called Woody's Watering Hole on Cherokee Street."

Kendra gazed at his smirky grin. "For real?"

Her cohort raised both hands in an I-surrender gesture. "Not lying." He indicated the young clerk with a nod of his head. "You don't think he's pranking us because of the name, do you?"

Kendra shrugged. "One way to find out." She started out the door. "He does know we're cops, right?"

Woody laughed. "He should. He's the one who ran the department's credit card."

Kendra's spine cried out for relief as she attempted to find a better position on the cold cement. The dull ache reminded her of how Woody had rubbed her shoulders when they were sitting in the dark little bar.

After ordering their drinks—beer for him, White Russian for her—Woody had excused himself to the men's room.

When he returned, his path led directly behind her chair. He must have noticed her rubbing at her neck and shoulders because he stopped and gave her a thirty-second massage.

"Ahh," she said. "Everything's in knots."

"I hear ya." He rolled his own head around slowly. "Not used to riding fourteen hours with a perp sitting behind me. Even if he was behind wire and asleep most of the time." He took his seat across from her again.

Kendra shrugged and met his grin with a tired one of her own. "The things we do for the job." She took another sip of her drink and inspected the nearly deserted bar. "Thank God there's not much going on."

Woody nodded. "I'll be ready to hit the sack after this." He glanced around, too. "It'd be our luck for a fight to break out. Guess we're taking quite a chance having a drink when we're technically still on-the-job."

Kendra raised her short glass. "Here's to taking chances."

"Amen." Woody clinked his beer bottle against her glass.

When a slow song came on the jukebox, he stood and held out his hand. "Take another chance?"

She took a long, slow sip of her drink and then set it down before placing her hand in his. It's only one song she told herself. But a flame ignited in her belly as she allowed him to pull her in close. He didn't press her body to his; he simply curled his large hand around hers and held it against his chest while the music led them around the tiny dance floor. When she chanced a glance at his face, she was surprised to find his eyes were closed.

She relaxed and rested her temple against the shelf of his chin. Even now she could still recall the way she felt in his arms as if she'd just arrived home from a long, arduous, journey. Kendra also remembered wondering how long it had been since she and Bill had gone dancing. How long it had been since they had held each other so tenderly and carefully.

As they danced, her mind had wandered. She recalled wondering if this new wrinkle in her and Woody's relationship could simply be a response to Bill's 'needing some space,' or whether it would have happened anyway. *Was I wrong to always keep the horror stories from work in their own little compartment, never sharing what was going on? Was Bill right when he claimed he'd always been in our marriage alone?*

When the music stopped, she and Woody had both opened their eyes.

What the hell am I doing she wondered as she dropped his hand and looked away.

Woody touched her elbow and steered her back to the table. His blue eyes revealed nothing. If he was doubtful or confused by her sudden withdrawal, his face didn't show it. By unspoken agreement, they turned down a second drink when the waitress appeared.

Woody pulled out cash and paid for their drinks. "Don't think this needs to go on the company card, do you?"

She smiled. "Probably not." She thought of offering to pay for hers, but it seemed too much trouble. "I'll get it next time," she said.

Woody simply nodded.

On the way back to the hotel, he switched on the Mercury's wipers to sweep away the moisture that had accumulated while they were in the small bar. He punched the button to scan the radio stations.

When Amy Lee's operatic voice soared from the speaker singing "Bring Me to Life," he hesitated.

"That sounds good." Kendra leaned her head back against the headrest. "I've always loved Evanescence."

Woody turned it up, and they drove through the darkness toward the Holiday Inn.

Now, dozing fitfully on the concrete, Kendra let the epic song play through her head. It was appropriate, she thought as the lyrics came to mind. He *had* brought her to life after the shock of Bill's announcement had worn off.

"I like that station," she remembered saying. "And I didn't mind the dance either." Then she'd reached across the console to lay her palm on top of Woody's hand. "But we both know it wasn't a wise thing to do."

In the moonlight filtering through the smeary windshield, she'd seen Woody's jaw tighten. "You're right," he'd said. "It wouldn't be wise to fall in love with someone whose company is the one thing you look forward to each and every morning when you roll out of bed."

Kendra's stomach had tightened. Regretfully, she'd pulled her hand back into her half of the car. "Woody, I—"

He waved her words away. "No need to say anything. I understand. You have a husband and a family." He'd turned toward her. "But I'll tell you this and then I'll never mention it again."

She waited, half hoping he'd change his mind and not say it.

At last he'd said, "The way you felt in my arms tonight is exactly the way I knew you would feel." He opened his car door and jerked his lanky frame out of the small space.

Kendra had remained sitting with her mouth open and her mind spinning.

He'd waited until she exited her side of the vehicle, and then they'd walked into the hotel together, a blanket of silence enveloping them as surely and softly as the misty night.

The moist air had reminded her of home. She'd breathed it in and then they were there, sharing the elevator with a couple of women who had just arrived for a weekend wedding. The women had talked nonstop about the bride and whether she would be able to fit into her wedding gown when the time came. "Only if she lays off the donuts," one snickered.

Kendra remembered feeling sorry for the bride if these two were supposed to be her friends. She also remembered feeling a boatload of guilt about her own situation, thinking, *who am I to judge? I'm supposedly* married *to my best friend and look at the way I'm treating him.*

She and Woody had stepped off the elevator and stopped outside her room, which was across the hall from his. "I'll set my alarm for six." She jabbed her key card into the narrow slot above the door handle. "I don't think we have to leave as early as we did coming down here."

Without a sound, Woody trailed the tips of his fingers down the middle of her back from the base of her skull to her waist. It was the sort of careful caress she might have expected. "Thanks for the dance," he whispered.

She looked down at the navy and maroon swirls of the hallway carpet. Then she turned, and he'd been so close she couldn't draw a breath.

He opened his arms, and she leaned into his embrace, but this time she didn't rest her temple against his chin.

She looked into his guileless blue eyes, and then she stood on tiptoe and buried her hands in his thick, wavy, hair. She pressed her lips to his and whispered against his mouth, "This will have to be the end of it."

Woody inhaled her words and crushed her to him as if he would never let her go.

CHAPTER TWENTY-FIVE
Calling Sheriff Puckett & Keith

The sheriff sat in his county-issued cruiser and listened intently to Woody's voice. "Missing?" His gruff voice cut across the night miles. "What do you mean, missing? I just saw her in my office this morning."

Woody's voice was just as gruff. "I tell you, sheriff, in all the years I've worked with her, she's never skipped a meeting without calling. Besides, I'm here at her house now. I've got her purse, her keys, and her cell phone." He paused. "The only thing missing is *her*."

"Pickup's in the garage, huh?"

Woody could tell the sheriff was picturing the scene in his head. "Yes," he said. "Nothing awry except for the interrupted snack, and the fire left burning in the fireplace. Plus the front door was unlocked."

"No sign of a struggle?"

"None that I can see."

"Have you called friends to see if anyone picked her up—?"

Woody shook his head even though he knew the other man couldn't see him. "She just moved here. Didn't have any special friends that I'm aware of. C'mon, Sheriff. I know she found those remains the other day; this is way too coincidental. Besides, Kendra Dean doesn't do this. She was supposed to meet me hours ago to go over some files. She would never have left me hanging without a phone call."

Sheriff Puckett was silent.

Woody hated to admit Kendra had told him about finding the bones, but that was minor now. He waited. Standing in the middle of Kendra's deserted living room, he waited.

At last the sheriff spoke. "A second set of remains was discovered not an hour ago. I'm still at the—" He would've said more, but Woody interrupted.

"My God, is it her, is it Ken?"

"What? No, no, no." The sheriff must have realized the leap Woody's mind had made. His voice gentled. "These are older remains, another set of bones. They're in the same rough area of the forest as the first set, though. I'm sure you know what that means."

"Multiple victims," Woody muttered. He didn't like to use the term serial killer. Two victims wasn't a series, he hoped. But what did that mean in terms of Kendra's disappearance. "I'll work her case," he told the sheriff. "Sounds like you've got your hands full there."

Sheriff Puckett agreed. "Start by calling everyone she knows. Does she have family, kids?"

"Yes, I've got their numbers here in her phone." Woody pulled it out of his pocket. "I'll begin with them. And I'd like to put out an Attempt to Locate."

"Of course," the sheriff said. "Anything you need, just talk to Marissa, the dispatcher, or call me back. I'll be out here for the next few hours, waiting on the Medical Examiner and forensics team."

"I'd like to come out if I may." Woody hadn't intended to say that, but it seemed only natural that the two cases were related.

Once again the sheriff was silent.

After a moment, he said, "I don't have a problem with that. Either Chief Brown or I will come out to the lake house just as soon as one of us can get loose here. Then we will escort you up here to the scene."

"Thank you, Sheriff, I appreciate that—"

"I'm sure she'll turn up," he said. "In fact, I'd just enlisted her aid with the first case. Seems a pretty savvy detective to me."

Woody squeezed the phone. "Yes, she is. The best."

Sheriff Puckett grunted affirmatively; then they clicked off.

Going strictly on instinct, Woody took Kendra's phone and scrolled through her contacts until he found Keith's name and number. Ordinarily he would've called the last person Kendra had spoken to, which had been Carrie, but he couldn't be certain the young mother-to-be would be coherent over the phone with news like this. Best to get Keith's input first.

When Keith picked up, Woody didn't mince any words.

"Keith, this is Detective James. Have you heard from your mom today?"

Keith sucked in a huge breath of air then let it out slowly. He'd been a cop's kid long enough to know when the conversation started off with a question like this; it could only mean one thing. "Why? Is she missing?"

Woody hesitated. "I don't know if missing is the correct terminology at this point, but I do need to know if you've had any contact with her in the last several hours."

"No," Keith said. "I haven't talked to her in a day or two. The last time we spoke she told me she was planning on going fishing the next day and that the only thing on her agenda after that was getting her stitches removed. You know, that hand injury she had."

Woody stood in Kendra's empty living room nodding and wondering if that was the reason she'd had to run when he'd been texting with her. Everything had been fine at that point.

He looked around the homey living room. He could feel the essence of the strong-willed woman all around him. Not one for frills or frou-frou, she'd surrounded herself with photos of her children and mementos of their lives together.

On the back of the sofa was a crocheted afghan in shades of vibrant blue. That looks like Ken, he thought. That looks like something she would make or at least something that was made specifically for her.

"Detective James? Are you there?"

Woody gave himself a little shake. "Yes. Sorry. Just thinking. So I guess you don't know about the discovery she made during the fishing trip."

"Discovery?" Keith's voice was both surprised and fearful. "What sort of discovery? She was supposed to be on leave. Or vacation. Or something."

"Oh, this was an accidental discovery. Unbelievable, but accidental."

Keith exhaled. "It was something bad, wasn't it? Sure it was. What other kind of discovery would lead to you calling me like this? Was it a dead body or something?"

"Not a body, exactly," Woody admitted. "More like remains. Remains of a woman placed just-so in the woods as if awaiting discovery."

"And Mom found her. And now she's missing?"

An involuntary groan escaped Woody's lips. He didn't want to be having this conversation with anyone, much less with Kendra's only son. "She was supposed to meet me in Pine River at nine. When she didn't show, I came here."

"You're at the house now?"

"Yes, I came right over, but she isn't here. The front door was unlocked, so I came on in."

"Mom never leaves a door unlocked. What else did you find?"

Woody exhaled. Keith had begun to sound just like his mother, the detective. "Everything. Her purse, her wallet, and her cell phone. There appears to be nothing missing from the house—"

"Except her," Keith replied.

Woody hesitated. "Yes, except her."

For a moment, silence coated both phones.

Keith cracked it first. "What about her truck, is it there?"

"Yes." Woody's voice was a rough whisper. "I keep thinking she could just be out hiking. That's how she found the remains, hiking home after fishing, and I don't see her hiking boots so I was hoping she'd mentioned something to you—"

"No," Keith interrupted. "No, like I say it was all about fishing and stitches the day I talked to her."

"Stitches," Woody said. "That's where I need to start. Do you know where she was getting the stitches taken care of?"

"Yeah, she went to that clinic on Main Street. It's been there for years. Got a new doc. At least I think she said he was new."

"Okay. That gives me a starting point."

"Can you tell me about the discovery she made. The remains?"

Woody almost said no, he wanted to be done, to be on his way to the other crime scene, then to town to look up the doctor that ran that clinic, but this was Keith, her son. "It was the bones of a young woman, arranged on a bed of clover as if she were sleeping." He started to tell him more, but he knew that would be a mistake. All he needed to know right now was that his mom was missing.

"God," Keith said, "that means there's a lunatic in the area, doesn't it?"

"It doesn't look good," Woody admitted. "And I had hoped to give her some good news for a change.

Keith seemed to have trouble processing the change of topic. "I'm sorry. Good news?"

"Yes," Woody said. "I just got word that the burglar Ken arrested—"

"The one who offed himself and got Mom suspended?"

"Yeah, that one." He waited a beat, wondering if he should share this with Keith, too. After another second, he plunged ahead. "I think we found out why he killed himself."

Keith waited.

"His computer was full of child porn. They even found an image of the child-in-the-trunk, the one that gave your mom—and me—so many sleepless nights. The creep appeared to be part of a huge ring. Of course, his wife claims she didn't know. But you can bet she'll drop the case against Ken now."

"That *is* good news for Mom, so awful about the children, though." He hesitated as if wanting to say more. At last he said, "I can't wait to hear you tell her. I'll drive to Carrie's and pick her up, then go down and get Willa. I don't want to tell either of them on the phone. We'll be there in a few hours. Maybe you will find her before I have to tell them."

"I will certainly try, Keith, I—" Woody began. But Keith severed the connection.

Woody looked at his phone. Be careful kid. Drive carefully.

He clicked the off button and slid the phone into his pocket, and then he pulled it back out and scrolled down until he found Bill's number.

The phone went straight to voicemail so Woody simply left his number with a message to call if he'd talked to Kendra recently. In the back of his mind was the old cop's adage, when a wife goes missing, look at the husband first.

He didn't really think it was a possibility in this case, though. Their split wasn't that acrimonious; mostly it was just sad. Besides, there were those remains to consider...

CHAPTER TWENTY-SIX

Kendra's New Home

Miles and miles away, as Kendra laid dozing and reminiscing on the painfully cold concrete floor, the good doctor was about to start on patient number three at the clinic. He was jolly today. Even the snotty noses of Mrs. Brown's three kids couldn't ruin his good mood.

He had a new girl. And she would be right where he put her, waiting on him when he got off work this evening. When the chunky mother in the tight jeans ushered her three leaky dumplings into the exam room, he wanted to remind her this was an urgent care clinic, not a pediatrician's office, but due to his current good fortune, he didn't even bother.

The rest of the day flew by. He could hardly wait to get all the patients out the door so he could concentrate on his good fortune.

That evening, he suffered through dinner with Candy-the-betrayer, and then he informed her he was going for a drive to think things over. He was disappointed, nay, *disgusted* with her. He made no bones about that. The question he'd posed to her was what did she plan to do about her little situation? He wanted no children. Never had. He'd made that *abundantly* clear. Now the ball was in her court. She could either agree to get rid of the fetus—he told her he'd be glad to take care of it in the clinic after hours—or he would be forced to take other measures. Her timeline was one week. After that, he would assume she'd made her decision.

"You mean you'd divorce me simply because I want a family?" Candy's voice was incredulous.

Her husband didn't answer. She knew his wishes, and she deliberately went against them. As far as he was concerned, the matter was closed to discussion. Now it was time for action.

Once in the car, he was in such a hurry to get back to Kendra; he didn't even bother to turn on the radio. He hummed and muttered all the way to his little hidey-hole. His cop-phobia was gone. The fact that he now *owned* a detective added a whole other level of excitement to the game-of-girls.

Or maybe he'd just been married and sedate for so long that he'd forgotten what excitement felt like. After all, those other girls had been *ages* ago.

All except the dog walker of course.

She had been strictly spur of the moment opportunity.

His thoughts dissolved into memories of that warm and sunny afternoon.

In no time at all, he was approaching the "driveway" of his home away from home.

The sun was going down, and the spiky shapes of the fir trees loomed over everything. Everyone at the clinic knew he loved camping and hiking, but no one knew about his little hidey-hole bunker. He'd dug the pit the summer he moved back to take up his position as physician of the new clinic. His property was part of a planned camping development that had never panned out. He'd picked up the acreage for a song. It was too steep and rugged for a cabin (probably why the planned development hadn't worked out), and hunting was not allowed, so once he'd scouted everything out, and discovered no neighbors nearby, he'd parked a decrepit old camper in the middle of the acreage and tore out the floor.

Then he'd begun to dig.

At first, he'd convinced himself it was merely a dooms-day-prepper kind of thing, a passing fancy that went along with his other OCD tendencies. But deep down, he knew why he was digging the hole beneath the camper. He was doing it because he figured at some point in the very stressful future he would need it for a girl.

Digging that hole had kept him sane all the years of his marriage to Candy—all those barren years when he'd sworn off the other women. But now, the stress-bubble was about to burst. She'd betrayed him. He could no longer trust her.

He was extremely thankful he'd followed his intuition and completed the bunker. Or as he liked to think of it now, *Kendra's new home*. It even included his memory wall of photos.

Edgar hiked up the rough deer trail to the tiny clearing. His "driveway" was simply a dark leafy place off the road where he was able to stash his car for a few hours at a time. Driven into the place, under the shelter of the low branches, the car was indiscernible to any passersby. Besides, it was on his property, his private property.

He stood for a moment, just outside the clearing, listening to the near silence of the dusk. The old camper was long gone. He'd sold it for a few bucks once he'd completed the hole. Now, there was nothing to show that there was a room beneath his feet except for the black iron post—known as a deadman—to which the camper had been anchored.

Even using his handheld GPS, it sometimes took him a few tries to find the hole, especially in the near dark. But that was okay, if a wayward hiker ignored the No Trespassing/Private Property signs, they wouldn't notice anything amiss.

The trapdoor to his lair was fitted with a thick Plexiglas square set into a heavy wooden frame. The small door was flush with the surface of the ground, and he'd painted it the exact color of the forest floor before making certain it was covered with a thick layer of leaves and debris. He'd even brought bags of potting soil and planted moss on top of the door to further disguise it. The Plexiglas he had smeared with mud to make it invisible. Some of that mud had been wiped away with his comings and goings, and that was all right.

He didn't like using his flashlight, though he had one if needed; instead, he liked to sneak down in the near-darkness. Catch her unaware. He also relished the idea that when the sun rose she would be treated to just enough light to see the hopelessness of her situation.

He also wanted her to get an idea of how much work he had put into his little project. She was a detective, not some frail dog-walker. He wanted her to be in awe of him.

The vent pipe that allowed fresh air into the little hidden room stuck up a few inches above the ground about ten feet away. It was painted green and brown camouflage colors to match the surrounding forest. He knew it was possible— perhaps even likely—that the small pipe would someday become clogged with leaves or dirt, thus cutting off the fresh air going down into the hole, but that only added to the excitement of wondering what he would find each time he arrived. *Would she be dead, or alive, or somewhere on that fine line in-between?*

Edgar didn't care—they would all wind up planted in the forest eventually. The not knowing was actually part of the pleasure of anticipation.

In the case of the dog-walker, except for a few moans, she'd never awoken after he slammed the lid down on her head. That had been a total surprise. Old Mr. McGraw had awakened, and he'd required a few whacks with a two by four, but little miss dog-walker must have been more fragile.

His one regret was that he hadn't known about the beauty of the femur when he'd accidentally-on-purpose killed Mr. McGraw. His first kill and he hadn't even got to hold the leg bone.

Sometimes, when he was stressed at work, he would take five minutes, go into his office and assume the meditation pose. The staff knew not to disturb him then. They'd all received the cutting edge of his tongue when they'd forgotten. But a couple of the nurses secretly admired him and thought he was so wise to meditate that way—weird but wise—that one of them even tried it at home. It hadn't worked for her. She'd told a coworker she'd felt like an idiot chanting *ommm* out loud, but it sure seemed to keep the cranky doctor from blowing a gasket.

What the staff didn't know was that Edgar could never really meditate there, not in such a public-type place. He needed his white room at home for that. Instead, what he was doing in his office was simply going away for a while, decompressing through memory, actually causing himself to recall and relive each of his victims and their femurs. He even fantasized about going to the cemetery and retrieving old Mr. McGraw's femur so he could hold it and carve it and add it to his memory-collection. But for now, that was way too risky so it remained just that, a fantasy he could pull out when he really needed it.

CHAPTER TWENTY-SEVEN
A Belly Full of Dread

Since Sheriff Puckett was technically in charge of the second crime scene in the woods, Woody agreed to wait for Police Chief Brown at Kendra's house. They were going to go over the entire house looking for blood, fingerprints, or clues of any kind.

Woody crept through the house as he waited, but he felt like a trespasser, snooping through Kendra's things when she wasn't there which was, of course, stupid. But the feeling was there nevertheless.

At last he simply took a brief inventory of every room, noting the distinct lack of signs of a disturbance, and then he sat on the front step and waited for the chief.

Once he arrived, the two of them went over everything again, and while an officer dusted the door for fingerprints, Woody and the chief came up with a plan for interrogating the employees at the Stutter Creek Urgent Care Clinic, the last known place Kendra had been besides her own house.

Within a few hours, Woody was leaned back in the Mercury as cars pulled into the parking lot at the clinic. After leaving Kendra's house, he'd driven straight there and napped in his car. He and the Chief had come to the conclusion that it might be better to surprise the doctor and all his employees rather than waking them out of their slumber last night.

It was beginning to rain; just a light mist, and the temperature had dropped during the night. *Kendra's out there somewhere. I hope she isn't exposed to the elements.*

Congratulating himself on his patience, Woody waited until the doctor and staff had arrived and started their day.

He made certain they'd had time to settle in and get things ready. He wanted every one of them to be taken off-guard.

There were already several patients waiting in the lobby when he pulled open the door, flashed his identification at the receptionist, and dragged the sign-in clipboard forward so he could read it.

Fortunately, the receptionist had not removed the previous day's sheet.

Kendra's name was listed as one of the earlier appointments from the day before. "I need to see the doctor on duty." He shoved the clipboard aside.

The girl didn't move fast enough to suit him, so Woody pushed through the connecting door and started down the hall toward the examination rooms.

"Sir, please, you can't go back there." The receptionist's voice was strident.

Woody knocked on the first door he came to. When no one answered, he turned the knob and looked inside. The room was empty but for the white-papered exam table.

"Here, here!" A voice bellowed. "What's going on?"

Woody turned to see a nurse with iron-colored hair bulling her way down the hall toward him. She removed her reading glasses as she came, as if he'd torn her away from important paperwork.

"I need to see the doctor, immediately. It may be a matter of life and death." He didn't wait for her to reach him, he went right to the next door, Exam Room 2, and knocked on it.

Behind him, the nurse said, "Where are you injured?"

Woody ignored her and would have opened Exam Room 2, but a white coated man yanked open the door. A scowl took up most of his long narrow face. "What's the meaning of all this?"

Woody glanced down at the doctor's long fingers curled around the silver doorknob. The man's bony wrists stuck out the ends of his coat sleeves a good three inches.

When he saw where Woody's gaze went, the doctor pulled his hand back quickly. But not before Woody saw the thick, twisted scars.

Suicide attempt. If he were female, I might even guess self-mutilation. But not many men are cutters. Most were just too squeamish about the sight of blood, especially their own. He is a physician, though.

He looked up at the doctor's face. The scowl had been replaced by something even more alarming, *secrecy.* The question was, were the secrets because of the scars, or because of something else?

Woody let his gaze travel down the man's arms to his hands and then back to his face. *I haven't even identified myself, and I already get the idea that he's hiding something.* He pulled his identification out and held it up. "We need to talk."

The man's face paled. He stepped into the hallway and glanced back as he pulled the door shut.

Woody had a momentary glimpse of a young woman standing next to a feverish-looking child.

"Please get Miss Devon a sample bottle of children's Claritin and instruct her how to give it to young Richard when his allergies act up. Be certain to tell her she can simply buy it over the counter from now on." He didn't look at the gray-haired nurse as he spoke. Instead, he glanced at Woody and then nodded toward a door at the end of the hall marked OFFICE. "We can talk there."

Woody led the way. He didn't wait to for the doctor to open the office door; he twisted the knob and went right inside. Manners were not part of his repertoire in this situation. He wanted the doc off his game. This man—these people—may have been the last ones to see Kendra before she vanished.

Dr. Stevens entered the room and closed the door softly.

He walked around behind his desk and indicated a chair for Woody.

Woody remained standing.

Before the doctor could speak, Woody said, "Detective Kendra Dean was here yesterday for suture removal." He let the formality of his words sink in. "Tell me about her visit."

Dr. Edgar Stevens sat in his plush leather office chair, causing it to squeak ever so slightly. He cleared his throat and straightened a manila folder so that its corner fit the right angle of his desk.

OCD, Woody thought, maybe that's why he seems so nervous. He wondered whose patient file was in that folder. *Could it be Kendra's?* His hand itched to snatch it up and thumb through it, scatter it across the desk and watch the doc deconstruct.

The doctor cleared his throat again. "Let me get Nurse Green in here, she assisted me in the procedure." He leaned over the desk and made as if to press the intercom button on the desk phone.

Woody beat him to it. His large hand shielded the button. "I want to hear from you first; then I'll get to her."

That seemed to bring out a bit of ire in the doc. "See here, now. I don't know why you've burst in here like this, demanding this and demanding that. I will not answer any further questions until I know why you are here." His previously pale face now sported rosy twin splotches of anger—one on each cheek.

Funny, Woody thought; he hasn't yet asked why I'm inquiring about Kendra or if something is wrong with her. *Let me see if I can goad him a bit. Find out what he's hiding besides scar tissue.* He totally ignored the doctor's threat not to say anything without explanation. "What time did Detective Dean leave your office?"

Dr. Stevens drew his mouth into a thin, hard line. "You will have to check the patient records—that's Ms. Green's job, documentation."

"Why are you angry?"

The doctor exhaled and stood. "You burst into my clinic, demanding I leave my patients in the middle of an exam—"

"Claritin?" Woody's words were dipped in sarcasm. "Not exactly brain surgery."

The doc tried to give it back to him. He looked Woody up and down. "And I don't see any life-or-death injury on you." He looked away, apparently having held his own for as long as he could. "In fact, I'm not sure you even have the authority to be here—I don't recognize you as being from Stutter Creek."

Woody rounded the corner of the desk and stopped an inch short of crashing into Dr. Edgar Stevens' face. "Kendra Dean hasn't been seen since she left your office." He wasn't entirely certain that was true, he was simply going on instinct, and his instinct said something was not right with the good Dr. Stevens.

The doctor took a step back. His Adam's apple bobbed as he swallowed nervously. "We took her stitches out and she left. No big deal. The wound had healed beautifully. Gave her some anti-scarring cream." He surreptitiously tugged at his coat sleeve as he talked.

So, Woody thought. No big deal, huh? No big deal except for the fear-sweat that had popped out on the doctor's forehead like tiny stick-on diamonds. "Where was she headed when she left here?"

The doctor furrowed his brow. "How would I know? We weren't having tea."

"What *did* the two of you talk about? Did she mention her plans for the afternoon?"

Dr. Stevens drew himself up to his full height. He had managed to put a couple of feet of space between himself and Woody. "We talked about the weather. We talked about the woods. We talked about life in a small town." He glared at the detective.

"The woods, huh? Now, why would you discuss the woods?" Woody had honed in on that phrase for reasons unknown. Pure gut reaction.

Dr. Stevens shook his head. "I don't know. Hiking. Camping. I can't recall. It was just small talk, that's all."

Woody turned abruptly and left the office. He wanted to get to the nurse before the doctor could. From the corner of his eye, he saw Dr. Stevens' shoulders slump. As if he'd held himself up as long as possible under the onslaught of Woody's fury.

Nurse Green wasn't hard to find. She had apparently been doing her best to listen through the wall of the room next door. Oddly enough, she only recalled how Kendra and the doctor had seemed to be sharing a joke about something when she walked in. "It seemed strained though," she said.

Woody wasn't surprised the woman didn't remember them talking about hiking and camping and all that. But he was surprised at the easy way she admitted that the conversation had seemed strained. In his experience, most nurses would rather die than paint their employer in a bad light.

"What made you think the conversation was strained?"

The nurse chuckled without mirth. "You'd have to know Dr. Stevens. He isn't the joking sort."

Woody thought that over. He could certainly believe it, but that made him even more suspicious. "Did Detective

Dean say where she was going when she left here?" He had no beef with the nurse; she seemed genuinely confused.

She cocked her head to the side as if thinking back. "No, not that I recall. Has something happened? I hope not. She seems to be one of the good ones."

Woody clenched his jaw. "That's what I'm trying to determine, and you're right. She is one of the good ones. The best." He left the nurse staring after him and went directly to the front to talk to the stunned receptionist.

She was no help at all. The only thing she could remember was how Kendra waited in the truck rather than in the waiting room with all the sniffly kids. He took down the receptionist's phone number so that he could mark it off the list of recent texts on Ken's phone.

From the end of the hallway, Woody spied the doctor peering out of his office, but neither of them acknowledged the other. I don't know what it is about him, Woody thought. *But he's definitely hiding something.*

He finally made his way back to the car with nothing to show for his efforts but a belly full of dread.

CHAPTER TWENTY-EIGHT

A Little Line of Red

When the detective left, Edgar tried to resume his normal routine, but the day was shot. He snapped at nurses, pissed off Mr. Longoria, who just came in to get his blood pressure medicine refilled, and even made the little Powell twins cry—simultaneously.

His eyes were hard chips of flint on either side of his nose. They stared out from under his furrowed brow as if contemplating murder with every glance. One new patient actually asked the nurse why the doctor was mad at her.

Edgar was on the edge.

He fingered the twisty scar on his wrist. The detective had probably seen it, but that wasn't what he'd been worried about. The tattoo just north of the scar, that's what he'd been attempting to cover. Why he'd put it there, where it was so easily visible, he couldn't say. It had been a moment of hubris, a way of celebrating and prolonging the thrill of the kill.

Raising the sleeve of his lab coat, Edgar caressed the tiny numbers and letters: 35.0598° W. 106.6197° N. Those were the coordinates for the location of his first girl, Joey. His *best* girl. The one he'd recently uncovered in a moment of desperation. The one who was now in the hands of the Medical Examiner thanks to the nosy ramblings of Detective Kendra Dean.

He somehow made it through the rest of the patients without hurting anyone, but for the first time in years, he found himself in his private bathroom with a plastic-sheathed safety scalpel in his hand. He didn't know if it was the thought of cutting the letters and numbers into his arms that made him yearn for the pain, or whether it was simply all the stress brought on by the detective's visit.

Just a little cut, he assured his reflection as he undid his trousers and let them fall to the floor. *A little line of red to make me feel better. It will let the poison out and allow me to think more clearly.* He chose a spot that was in an easy-to-bandage area inside his thigh.

The rude detective had been right about one thing; he had attempted suicide when he was a teen. It was after Mr. McGraw but before Joey. After Joey, he never again felt the need to die.

He closed his eyes as endorphins leaked into his system. Just the act of getting ready to cut was enough to soothe him.

When I had my girls, I didn't have to cut.

His head jerked up, and the surprise on his mirror-face was so comical it almost made him smile. I have a girl. I have a girl. I have a woman-girl-detective just waiting for me to return. How did I forget that, too much stress? Doesn't matter. Doesn't matter anyhow.

He exhaled and pulled up his trousers. The bathroom was cool, but his skin was slathered with sweat. Even though he hadn't made a single mark, his hands were shaking so badly he could barely retract the scalpel back into its blue plastic sleeve.

Wait, he thought. What if that detective follows me when I leave?

He stood indecisively for half a minute.

If he does, I'll wait. I'll wait until nightfall.

When the last patient had gone, the cleaning crew came through with their buckets on wheels and chemicals in spray bottles, and Edgar knew he'd waited long enough.

"Going hiking," he texted his wife. "Stressful day. Need some air."

It wasn't unusual for him to avoid going home. Since the baby business had become such a hot button topic between them, he'd spent more and more time in the woods with his girls. So far he'd unearthed two and had been thinking about the third when Kendra intruded and made him change his plans.

He unlocked the Toyota and climbed inside. It would be too noticeable if he stayed while the cleaning crew worked. He'd never done that before. If the big detective was watching—Edgar stopped and glanced all around the area as he backed out of the parking lot—he would surely be suspicious about that.

There was very little traffic at this, the dinner hour. The sun had started its downward slide and was almost completely cosseted away behind the mountains. Most working people were already off work and home for supper. A few would be at the Drugstore Cafe or at one of the lodge restaurants in town. A couple more weeks and all the seasonal lodges would be open. The little town would be hopping with skiers and snowboarders and families looking for adventure.

That meant the clinic would be open until midnight every night, and the clinic's other doctor, Kirstin Gundersen, would be back from Norway. Dr. Gundersen split her time between her home in Oslo and the ski resort in Stutter Creek. She had also signed a contract with the Rural Healthcare Initiative, and she often said becoming a physician was her way of being able to ski three-hundred-sixty-five days a year. She also let everyone know that once her contract was up she would be headed back home without a second thought.

Edgar didn't mind sharing the clinic with Dr. G. Trading shifts every other week gave her daylight hours to ski, and it gave him daylight hours to tramp around the forest. He'd gotten to the point where he relished working the night shift because it gave him so much time to play.

That brought a smile to his face as he was leaving the parking lot. Things would be all right, he decided. The big detective didn't know anything, or he wouldn't have left without taking him to the station.

Edgar's nerves began to settle. The man had been grasping at straws. Maybe she told him she'd been to the clinic before she disappeared, but there was no way anyone could know I went to her house. Perhaps I should have taken the drugstore owner instead. But the sight of that huge dog lying beneath the kitchen table had seemed too risky. Especially since it appeared to be the same kind of dog the girl had been walking. That was just too close to karma for him.

While he calmed himself down, his phone beeped, and he jumped so hard he banged his skull on the interior roof.

It was only a text from Candy. "When will you be home?"

Edgar smashed the phone against the steering wheel. *None of your business, slut.* He gripped the Otter Box-protected phone and inhaled deeply. The device didn't appear damaged. He couldn't *afford* to damage it. Getting a new phone would require a trip to Pine River and he didn't have time for that right now.

He set it on the passenger seat and then grabbed it back up. "You have no right to question me," he texted back. "I'll be there when I get there." He sent the message and then turned off his phone. He was a doctor. He knew how unsafe it was to text and drive.

For a while, he meandered aimlessly through the countryside, watching carefully for signs of someone following him. *What if the big detective put a GPS tracker on my car?*

Nah, they don't have the manpower to just follow people at random, much less use tracking technology. This is not New York or D.C. it's just tiny Stutter Creek, New Mexico.

But no matter how he tried to convince himself otherwise, the doctor's fears would not be alleviated until he pulled his vehicle into a secluded turn-around and searched the Toyota from top to bottom. He even took the flashlight from his camping gear in the trunk and lay on his back in order to search the undercarriage.

When he was satisfied there was nothing attached, he replaced the flashlight and carefully closed the trunk lid. For a moment, he simply stood behind the car, reminiscing about the sound the lid had made when it connected with the dog-walker's thin skull.

Some people were so fragile.

She'd never awakened. And there was nary a drop of blood to clean out of the trunk. But if there had been, the clinic cleaning crew had super chemicals for that very purpose—he'd borrowed a bottle just in case. They also had sodium hydroxide-based drain cleaning fluids that were very good for hurrying decomposition of flesh. But that hadn't been necessary, either.

He looked up at the moon, momentarily amazed that it was up already, and then he realized he'd been standing behind his car for several moments for no reason.

Edgar shook himself like a wet hound and climbed back into his car. He realized that he'd been going in circles around his sanity-wheel, getting closer and closer to the center as he circumnavigated the county and the road leading to the hub—his bunker—Kendra's new home.

CHAPTER TWENTY-NINE

Thirst

Kendra watched the light grow dimmer and dimmer through the little skylight. Her head was better, but her thirst was a demon intent on torturing her every waking moment. Her throat felt swollen inside. She wondered if it was simply due to excessive thirst, or if she'd suffered some injury when he knocked her unconscious. She tried to cough, but something tickled the back of her throat. It felt as if she'd swallowed a spider.

That thought made her choke, and she leaned forward gagging and spitting.

Something soft and stringy materialized in her mouth.

In a panic, she scraped a fingernail across her tongue and was appalled to see something black appear on the tip. *A spider leg! I did swallow a spider!* She began to hack and spit in earnest. *It must have crawled into my mouth as I slept.*

Unable to cough up anything else, Kendra held the suspicious article up to the meager light. Not a spider leg, too soft, didn't break apart. Her stomach lurched. It's a hair, soft and black, curly. Oh My God. No, wait. It's only a thread, has to be. But how did it get in my throat while I was unconscious?

She spat and spat and coughed and hacked and spat some more wishing all the while for a single sip of water to ease her aching throat.

Eventually, she dozed in and out, and each time she woke, she struggled to find a new position on the concrete that didn't make her feel as if she were sitting on nails.

Kendra tried not to think about the piece of thread *(it wasn't a hair, no, it couldn't be)* in her throat. Instead, she began to search for a way to escape, but the handcuffs were tight, and the metal ring was solid. There was no way she was going to physically escape.

Wits then, she thought. Have to outwit him somehow. Assuming he comes back. But she thought he would. No way he could stay away knowing he had a new plaything. She was sure that's what he was doing. Playing. The remains she'd found had been arranged so perfectly; it was obvious he'd taken his sweet time with them. Obvious that he enjoyed it, too.

She listened intently.

Every now and then she was certain she heard something. She thought she was in a crude bathroom inside some old basement. Kendra tried to picture such a setting in her mind. She came up with plan after plan of how to trick him into setting her free.

Shifting her position again, her leg met something that felt suspiciously like a water bottle. Her heart began to beat faster as her tongue darted out of her mouth of its own volition. *Could it be?* She edged her butt around until she was able to get the thing under, and then between, her knees. *Yes! It was a plastic bottle and the way it rolled made her certain there was liquid inside.*

Suddenly, there was a slight creak.

Kendra sat up as straight as her shackles would allow, closing her knees together, hiding her precious find.

Her eyes strained to see in the near darkness. "Doc? That you?" Her voice was a croak. "I wouldn't mind a drink of water, and a moment to stretch my legs. Is there a bathroom I could use?" She listened for some reply, some movement that would tell her he was there.

But all was quiet.

She did *sense* something, though.

She thought it might be a wave of fresh air as if the door that had been opened led not to the upstairs, or to another room, but actually to the outside. It was just a quick whiff of soil, damp and earthy. *Am I in the woods?* She thought it possible—especially knowing he'd already placed the remains of one victim there—*but if I'm in the woods, what am I in, an underground bunker?* Her years of detective work caused her to make leaps of thought easily. She trusted her senses. Especially her sense of smell—it seldom let her down.

"I know you're there, Doc. I can smell you." The darkness seemed to eat her words. They simply disappeared into the nothing. *Was he sitting just outside her realm of vision? Watching her, thinking of things he'd done, or would do?* The idea made her shiver with disgust.

There was no reply.

"You've been hiking through the woods." Her voice cracked, her sore throat protesting by closing up. "You smell nice, like good rich soil." She didn't know for sure about the hiking, but based on where she'd found the bones, she figured he was a hiker. And there truly was that earthy smell. Mostly, she just wanted to catch him off guard, make him think she knew more than she did.

Kendra wasn't positive this was the right track to take—to make him think she was smart, like him—she was going strictly on feelings and training she never thought she'd have to use for herself. She had a feeling his ego might be her only hope.

"I like that smell," she continued. "That's why I chose to live near the lake. Nature is much more dependable than people, don't you think? I mean people let you down. They betray you—"

Looming out of the dimness like an evil phantom, he shoved his sharp-nosed face toward hers. "What do you know about betrayal?"

Kendra thought fast. "Why do you think I live at the lake, alone?" She let that question hang in the air for a moment.

Apparently, judging from the way he'd leapt on the word "betray" she had hit a nerve. "I didn't want to leave my job in Pine River. I was betrayed. Forced to step aside because some lowlife took the coward's way out after I arrested him."

There was silence except for his slightly elevated respiration.

Kendra took that into account also. He's in good shape, she thought. So he could've hiked for a while, could have even rested before coming inside, but her gut said that wasn't the case. Her gut said her little dungeon wasn't too far from a road. *If I can just get loose . . .*

"I know about your case," Edgar said at last. "You mentioned something about being on leave the first time you came into the clinic."

Good! Now he's thinking of me as someone he knows, as his patient, rather than just his next victim. "That's right, I'd forgotten how we enjoyed chatting the first time we met. I may have told you too much." She hesitated as if thinking it over. "Some things are *supposed* to be kept secret, aren't they?"

Edgar brayed laughter. "I know what you're doing, *Detective* Dean. But it won't work. I'm sorry to tell you that you have stumbled into my world, and there's only one way out. Your negotiator tactics won't work on me. I've read the books."

Kendra decided to try another approach—shock. "Well, could I at least be made comfortable while I wait for you to kill me? Is that too much to ask?"

"And what would make you comfortable enough to welcome death?" His soft voice came from directly in front of her. "I could bring you a sedative. Is that what you're hoping for?"

Kendra felt his moist breath on her face. It wasn't fetid, but it *reminded* her of something fetid, something dank and rotting. "Just a drink of water, that's all I ask." Her mind flashed to the plastic bottle between her knees, and it was all she could do to keep her voice steady. "And a chance to go to the bathroom."

He laughed again. "You think I'm stupid, don't you? Or maybe you just think you're very, very smart."

She resisted the urge to utter a sarcastic reply. His demeanor was so calm and dispassionate it was terrifying. *He really is going to kill me and carve my bones. I have to try something else ...but what?*

Pressing her back into the cinder block, Kendra moaned slightly. Her gut told her to try seduction. Anything to keep her alive long enough to figure a way out. But the sudden image of the hairy looking thread on the tip of her finger almost caused her to start gagging again.

"What are you doing?" he asked.

It occurred to Kendra that if she couldn't see him, he couldn't see her either. "Nothing," she whispered. She tried to make her voice husky rather than just rough. "I just, well, I sort of like the handcuffs. But I suspect you knew that already or you wouldn't have put them on me so perfectly."

There was a small silence, and then his face loomed at her again. "What are you talking about?"

She hoped she had read his demeanor correctly. Although he was married to a beautiful junior pillar of the community, Kendra suspected he was quite a pervert when it came to sex. In her previous dealings with pervs like him, Kendra was able to put them into two distinct categories. They either married their mothers and beat them and treated them like shit, or they married the polar opposite of their mothers and then put them up on untouchable pedestals like some sort of goddess.

In his case, she assumed the latter. She'd seen his wife a time or two around town, and the young woman had a kind face and a nice, open, smile. She certainly didn't appear to be the sort of woman who would go in for any Fifty-Shades crap—which is exactly what Kendra believed would turn Edgar on. He'd be all about control and pain. So what sort of intimate life might he have with the beautiful, wholesome, Candy?

Kendra could only imagine him as a wham-bam-thank-you-ma'am lover, one who would finish quickly and then run back to his internet porn; or in his case, his playthings in the woods. *Did he play with the corpse while it was fresh? Or only after the flesh was gone? Doesn't matter. I have to try something. He's going to kill me anyway. I know too much to live.*

"Oh, come on, Doc. You don't have to pretend with me. I'm a detective for God's sake. I know what depraved acts guys like you do with women before you kill them. I've seen it all." She jangled the handcuffs gently. "This is just the least of it. Come on, what are we waiting for? If I'm going to die, I might as well enjoy my las—"

His fist came out of the darkness. It rocked her head back against the cinder block, split her lip, and closed off her speech. "I thought you were different, but you're just like my mother and all the other whores except my Candy. And now she's even worse." He didn't hit her again; he simply disappeared into the gloom.

Barely able to make out his form, afraid to make any sudden movements, Kendra watched from beneath lowered lids for the man who was her captor to come back into view.

A few moments later, Kendra felt the soft gush of fresh air followed by the lingering scent of the forest. *Guess sex was the wrong tactic.* She licked the blood off her lip and pretended it was water.

The back of her head throbbed in unison with her mouth and jaw. The water bottle taunted her beneath her knees, but she was afraid to try for it yet. What if he came back—or wasn't even really gone? What if it was a trick?

When her mind cleared a bit, she began to go back over their "conversation" in her mind. *Betrayer. Candy?* He said she was worse than a whore now. What could that possibly mean? The comment about his mother was not much of a revelation.

She ran her tongue over her lips again and was not surprised to feel them swelling considerably. At least her nose had been spared. Eyes closed, she let her mind wander, hoping it would come up with something she could use. But the pain in her head and jaw made clear thought difficult. *If only I had some water. And an aspirin or three . . .*

Rolling the plastic bottle from side to side with her knees, she managed to work it far enough toward her lap so that she could reach it with her shackled hands. She shook it gently. If her estimation was correct, there was maybe an inch of liquid in the bottom of the bottle.

Shivering, Kendra loosened the lid and leaned over sideways so she could dribble the fluid into her open mouth.

It was gritty as if scooped from the bottom of a stream, but Kendra didn't care, it was wet. After a split-second's hesitation, she upended the near-empty bottle and swallowed it all. Something in the water scratched at her tender throat, and she wondered again what could have caused the internal soreness, but it wasn't worth worrying about. All she wanted now, it seemed, was to sleep. Her head pounded, and she was beginning to feel a distinct queasiness in her gut as well.

It was still dark when Kendra woke again, stomach roiling. She ran her sandpaper tongue out to wet her lip, but it was no use. The liquid in the bottle had not helped at all, if anything, it had made her feel worse.

She leaned to one side and dry heaved, bringing up little more than yellow strings of bile. Her lips felt twice their normal size, but she didn't feel much pain.

Leaning back against the wall, her fingers once again played over the surface of her surrounding area. They encountered the rough, cold, concrete floor, the empty plastic bottle from which she'd drunk the scant, grainy, liquid, and the slick metal plate to which she was shackled. There was also a bumpy thing on the flat plate. What was it? Her fingers played over it, trying to figure it out. But her head was so swimmy, she couldn't think straight.

She dozed.

When she came around again, she had no idea how much time had passed. For once, she wished she hadn't stopped wearing her watch. It had been far too easy to check and recheck it after she had moved to the lake where time seemed covered in molasses.

On a whim, she picked up the plastic bottle, unscrewed the top, and sniffed. There was no odor. She wondered— belatedly—if the bottle could have contained urine or something from one of his other victims. Was it possible he had purposely put the bottle there, knowing how thirsty she would be? Without an odor, she had no way of knowing what might have been inside. When she turned it up over her opposite palm, nothing came out. Not even a drop.

Surely it was only water. *Doesn't matter anyhow. I've already drunk it.*

She screwed the top back on and tucked the bottle behind herself. *If worse comes to worst, I might have to urinate in it myself.* She was actually quite surprised that she didn't have to go yet. Then again, she'd barely sipped at her coffee last night when he'd burst in and slapped her with the SAP. And then the two swallows she'd had from the gritty bottle hardly qualified as a drink at all. She sat up straighter and was startled by a knife-sharp pain between her legs. It felt as if she'd done the splits—at her age—and lived to tell about it.

She ran her hands over her groin and thigh muscles, probing gently, relieved to find that everything seemed normal, just extremely sore. What she didn't like was the fact that her jeans were unzipped. They were twisted, too. She did her best to right them, but with her hands shackled, it wasn't an easy task.

Damn concrete. Cold. Damp. Have I been here longer than one night? Is that why I'm in such pain?

She shook her head and grimaced at the wave of nausea eroding her senses. It reminded her of the one and only time she'd drank herself into oblivion—high school graduation night with Bill, her high school sweetheart and soon-to-be-husband. *How could I be hung over? I haven't had more than one or two glasses of wine in weeks...*

But she didn't have time to think about it. Her eyes would not stay open. In moments she was breathing deeply, head lolled over on one shoulder.

When she awoke yet again, Kendra was relieved to find herself still alone. She knew that when he returned it might be her last night on earth. He wouldn't keep her captive forever—although some men had tried that very thing with other women, like the three in Philadelphia who had been locked away for decades.

Her head felt a little better. While on the brittle edge between sleep and waking, a thought had occurred to her, sort of a WWMD—What Would Martha Do—moment.

She bent her chest as low to the floor as possible—unzipped her sweatshirt—and managed to get a finger inside the breast pocket of her shirt. She'd taken off her bifocals and stuck them in her pocket after reading a couple of chapters in front of the fireplace.

Ahh, there they are.

Shocked that the glasses had survived her rough treatment, she almost sighed with relief. She wasn't about to put them on, but she had an idea that gave her a tiny bit of hope. For a moment, she wondered why she hadn't thought to look at the spider leg/hair/thread with her bifocals, then she would have known for sure, but it was too late now. She had thrown it away in disgust.

Now, she ran her hands over the floor.

The bumpy thing her fingers had encountered earlier was a screw. Her fingers went back to it now. Nearly flush with the floor, the thing felt very tight, but it was worth a try. If she could get the metal plate loose—the one holding her towel-rack-ring to the floor—she might be able to surprise him as he came down the stairs next time. If she could get the jump on him, she might have a chance. But to do that, she needed some kind of screwdriver.

Without another thought, she pulled the glasses out of her shirt pocket and popped one of the earpieces off. The joint end of the earpiece grew thicker where it met the hinge. She fitted that section into the slot of the flat-head screw and gave it a test turn.

The thin metal began to bend.

Kendra stopped twisting and tried to think of a way to reinforce the slim shaft. She took it out of the slot and pressed the end of it down against the concrete floor until it began to fold back onto itself. *Thank God I opted for the metal frames even though the guy assured me they were out of fashion.*

She heard a scraping noise and immediately stopped her labor. As a precaution, she slipped the mutilated earpiece under her bottom. Then she leaned over and placed the glasses back into her pocket.

Fresh air swooshed down from above.

There must be a ladder in the corner. That's why I can't see him descend.

She waited.

One heartbeat.

Two.

Three heartbeats.

Fear oozed out of her pores like pilfered whiskey the morning after graduation. She held her breath and stiffened her spine.

And then he materialized out of the darkness like before.

"You pissed me off." His voice vibrated with barely controlled rage.

"Don't you know who I am?"

Kendra waited. This wasn't her first dance with a madman. She didn't want to push him too far—yet.

"Is that a rhetorical question?" Her tone was light, nonthreatening, but coming through her swollen lips, it sounded like "Iss zat a ra'torical queshun?"

Either the sound of her slur or the sight of her bruised lips and jaw caused him to retreat back into the gloom. "I'm your *doctor*," he said. Then he repeated it as if to convince himself. "I'm *your* doctor."

The Hippocratic Oath popped into Kendra's mind. *First, do no harm...*

Could the good doctor be remembering it, too?

She sat perfectly still, not sure if he was talking to her, or to himself. As he backed away he repeated the phrase *I'm your doctor* and his voice took on such a singsong quality that *I'm your doctor* began to remind her of that old song; *I'm your captain...yeah yeah yeah yeah.* Who sang that? The Doobie Brothers? Grand Funk Railroad? *Oh my, God, why is my mind going all loosey-goosey on me now? These may be my last moments on earth—is he over there sharpening his carving tool while I sit here humming old rock songs? No, wait. He won't kill me down here. Then he would have to carry me up the stairs. That wouldn't be very smart. But is he as smart as he thinks he is? Or could he be angry enough to act first and think later? Come to think of it, since he is a doctor he could just carve me up and carry out the pieces. Not too much difficulty there—besides, we already know he likes to carve on bone.*

She shifted her weight and felt the makeshift screwdriver beneath her.

It felt a little bit like hope.

CHAPTER THIRTY

Stingy With Its Secrets

After a few moments, Kendra realized she was holding her breath.

Her pounding heart throbbed in her swollen lips. Her scalp itched with anxiety and she couldn't even raise her hands to scratch.

Where is he? If only I had my Glock... But of course, she didn't, all she had was a cramp in one thigh and the broken earpiece off her glasses.

She waited so long she dozed off again. When she awoke, her neck felt as if someone had folded it the way she'd folded the metal earpiece.

The earpiece! What if she'd scooted it away while she slept? What if it he had seen it? Picked it up, or kicked it aside just to torment her?

With trembling hand, she reached under her thigh and felt around. The tips of her fingers encountered rough concrete, a circular object, and nothing more. She pushed the circular object down into her jeans pocket. It felt like a ring, but she couldn't examine it now, she had to find that piece of folded metal.

Frustration and anger spewed to the top of her head like a geyser. *Stupid, stupid, stupid! Where could it be?*

Then it dawned on her; there was a *second* earpiece on her glasses.

Feeling as if time had slipped past and was somehow now of-the-essence, Kendra leaned forward toward her shackled hands. The pain in her head and lips swelled to a new crescendo, and she began to claw at the crooked spectacles folded into her breast pocket. They seemed to be hung up on something.

That's when she felt another swoosh of fresh air.

No time!

Frantically, she shoved her fingers under her thigh as far as they would go—*if my legs weren't half-numb, I could feel the damn thing*—and there it was, the tiny metal earpiece that now felt somewhat like a squared-off fishhook.

How can he be so silent? Is he a ghost? A demon?

She found the screw and frantically jabbed the half-folded metal down into the slot. It began to turn. It was working! She was going to get loo—

His face materialized in front of her again.

The moonlight had crossed over the tiny window-up-above and it no longer poured down on top of him but lay softly behind him, a light blanket of the finest see-through gossamer. Like the bad guy in a fairytale, one of the really dark ones like *Hansel and Gretel* or *Little Red Riding Hood*.

"What are you doing?" he asked. "What have you got there?"

He reached for her hands.

Could he see that she was holding something? Her theory about how he couldn't see her if she couldn't see him must not be true.

He pushed his face down even farther—

No! You can't have it. It's all I've got!

Her fingers continued to scrabble at the screw.

Only one more second and I'll have it out. One more—

"Give me that!" His voice filled the room, careened off the cold walls.

She gave it to him.

She turned the folded metal earpiece into her palm. It was strong. It protruded from her clasped fist like the point of a sharpened key. She jabbed upward directly at his looming face as hard as the handcuffs would allow.

He screamed and fell back, both hands covering one eye. From his throat, he gargled something that sounded like *I'll kill you*, and then he gathered himself and rushed toward her again. But his one-eyed depth perception was off.

Her well-placed kick caught him directly in the groin.

He went down as if he'd been shot.

Kendra slotted the earpiece and began to turn the screw again, but the makeshift tool was now wet and slippery. She wiped it frantically along her pants and tried again. *If he gets up now, I don't have a chance.*

But he wasn't getting up just yet. Huddled into a fetal-shape on the floor, he had one hand covering his injured eye, the other cupping his wounded testicles.

Keeping one eye on the downed doctor, Kendra worked at the screw with both bound hands. Suddenly, the tension on the screw relaxed. At first she thought the earpiece had simply twisted back on itself, but no—the screw had actually turned once, then twice, then three times. Excited, Kendra grasped it with her fingertips and unscrewed it the rest of the way.

The doctor began to puke on the concrete.

Kendra pushed the screw aside and yanked upward on the metal ring.

The entire bottom part of the plate came away from the floor and then stopped.

There was a second screw at the top of the plate. Of course there is, she thought. *I should have known that from the placement of the first one! Idiot!* She began to berate herself again even as her fingers slipped the end of the "screwdriver" into the new screw.

The acrid odor of vomit permeated the damp air.

She tested the screw. This one was tighter. The folded metal "tool" began to bend under the pressure.

The doctor wiped his mouth with one hand and pushed himself onto his knees. Now he was head down, forehead touching the floor. "I'm blind," he mumbled. "You *blinded* me." He threw up again and rolled back over onto his side.

Good! Hope I did. After what you've done it's nothing.

The second screw began to give.

And the earpiece broke.

Tears of frustration sprang to her eyes, but she didn't give in to them. She simply thrust her chest down toward her hands, yanked the rest of the mangled spectacles out of her pocket and ripped the other earpiece away.

Like a madwoman, she jammed the thicker end of the earpiece down onto the concrete and folded it, hard. From the corner of her eye she could see the silhouette of the doctor struggling to his knees again. Kendra stuck the new screwdriver into the slot of the screw and twisted with all her might.

Moonlight outlined the abstract patterns of nastiness on the concrete. The earthy smell of fresh air was gone. It was replaced by the putrid odor of bile and something else, something even darker.

The screw let loose. It must have been stripped at some point. It popped out of the metal plate and fell to the floor. Kendra kept her grip on the small earpiece-tool and pulled herself to her feet.

Her legs were weak, but adrenaline coursed through her veins and helped her remain upright.

The doctor seemed to realize what was happening. He lurched to his feet, too.

Kendra didn't hesitate. Handcuffs still attached to the ring, metal plate now swinging freely from her wrists; she took two huge strides forward and executed a perfect kick to the side of the doctor's knee.

He crumpled again, one hand back to cupping his injured groin, the other slipping free of his damaged eye.

She delivered another kick to his face, but her boot glanced off his wet cheekbone.

The doctor howled in agony.

The black rage of revenge had a firm grip on Detective Kendra Dean. She was intent on killing him on the spot.

But he had a murderer's luck and an overabundance of survival instinct. He rolled just far enough to avoid being stomped.

Kendra gripped the metal plate between her palms and smashed down with all her might. The corner dug a trench into his skull.

He stopped moving.

Kendra dealt him one more kick to the throat and then she stumbled backward across the sticky, moonlit floor. *He's dead. I crushed his larynx. Maybe fractured his skull. He's done.*

When her backside banged into the black iron step of the set-in ladder, she had an immediate intuition: *what a labor of love this must have been.* She imagined how he must've whistled happily as he bolted the iron ladder to the cinder block wall.

Twisting around, she grabbed the rail and hoisted herself toward the sky. The metal plate banged against the metal rail and did its best to hang her up on every step. She gripped it in one palm and gripped the railing with the other—still handcuffed together.

As she mastered the climb, she spied what appeared to be a corkboard covered with pictures. The images were murky in the darkness, but she was certain she knew a killboard when she saw one. He took pictures of his victims and displayed them here, where he could peruse them at will. They were aligned in perfect, obsessive, columns and rows.

Kendra's stomach did a slow roll. She could only imagine what he did while standing there, gazing at his board. She gritted her teeth and continued climbing.

He still hadn't moved, but she thought she heard a groan.

I should go back and check for a pulse. We may need him alive to find the other victims.

No. Woody will do that. I've done my part. Besides, if he had a pulse I might have to hit him again, and that would not be self-defense. It would be murder. She felt like Gollum arguing with himself in The Hobbit. Her cop side won out. I'm not a victim. I'll just lock him down here. Send in better-equipped officers. I'm a cop. I can't kill an incapacitated man, no matter how vile.

The fresh earthy smell drifting in from the square opening above her head drew her like a magnet. It seemed to second her decision to leave him. Freedom smelled like earth. Damp earth and moonlight.

She hoisted herself up out of the cinderblock hole and glanced back down.

Lock him in and send Woody back to get him.

She perched on the edge of the hole to allow her blurry vision to clear. In the moonlight, she imagined how her face must look. She could feel a bloody smear drying across one cheek.

After breaching the hole, Kendra continued to sit on the edge to get her bearings. She wasn't surprised to find herself in the middle of the midnight forest. The moonlight seemed strong, but not strong enough to show her the path back to the road.

It did show her the small trapdoor, though. The square of wood had been folded open on a strong hinge, the hasp obviously meant to fit down over the upright loop built into the opposite side.

The padlock must be in his pocket.

She pulled her legs out of the hole and looked back down.

From here, it just looked like a tube of darkness. She could no longer see the splash of moonlight that had illuminated the gory floor only seconds earlier.

She glanced up at the sky. A bloated gray cloud obscured the moon. Great, looks like a rain cloud. That's just what I need. As if the autumn temps weren't cold enough.

A noise from the darkness brought her back to the present.

Sounds like he's dragging himself toward the steps. Not dead after all.

Kendra automatically slung one leg back into the hole, determined to go back and finish him off once and for all, but the sound of his voice made her hesitate.

"Come back here," he coughed. "I've got something for you."

She heard the distinct sound of a hammer being pulled back.

Gun!

She quickly jerked her leg back out of the hole and tried to stand.

Edgar began to croak in that singsong voice she'd heard earlier: "I'm coming for you, Kendra Dean. Coming for you *Detective*. You can't get away from me, only I know where we are. You'll never make it out alive." He coughed, and she imagined him puking again. "I was going to give you a fighting chance. I admired you, Detective Dean. But now, you're dead. Now, you're fucking *dog meat*."

For a moment, Kendra allowed herself to be tricked into listening, but then she realized he was only singing to make enough noise to cover the sounds of his movements. She slammed the thick door shut—*there must be something to wedge in the latch*—and glanced down at the little earpiece tool in her hand. It almost made her laugh. *Something bigger than that.*

How did I not know he had a gun? Because he never threatened to use it. Still, not a very smart thing to do, leave a perp armed and alive. Thought he only had the knife, or whatever he used to carve up the bones. Bad assumption. Rookie mistake, head injury or no head injury.

She mentally kicked herself into gear.

"Fuck you," she muttered. "And the horse you rode in on." She grabbed a stout branch lying nearby and forced it in between the metal loop and the hasp of the lock. "That should hold you." She scoured the area around the trapdoor for any sign of a trail. But there was nothing whatsoever. The night was too dark, the forest floor too stingy with its secrets.

CHAPTER THIRTY-ONE

Hunt Her Down, Put Her Down

Down in the hole, the good doctor nursed his wounds.

His eye had bled copiously, but after a couple minutes of palm pressure the bleeding had stopped. Now he felt like Humpty Dumpty waiting to be put back together.

At least he wasn't blind. Whatever piece of metal she'd stuck him with had been too short to actually pierce his eyeball. It had simply gouged a jagged furrow in the delicate skin beneath his socket.

She won't get away.

He stumbled back across the floor toward the iron ladder. The heft of the gun felt very comforting in his hand. He'd kept it stored in the cabinet in his antique doctor's bag along with several bottles of pills and some emergency cash. He also kept a change of clothes inside. The trapdoor padlock bulged in his pocket.

I will hunt her down, and I will put her down. I will carve more than just her femur. She will be the first. This time, I'll carve the coordinates all over her face.

The detective had proved to be more of an adversary than he'd imagined.

How had she managed to get those screws loose? He felt of his head where she'd hit him with the metal plate. The one he'd been certain was securely attached to the floor.

She'd made it to the top before he'd managed to get the gun, then when she heard him cock it, she'd slammed the trap door closed and plunged him back into the murky darkness. Fortunately, he still had his flashlight.

He shined it up toward the Plexiglas and was overcome with rage. In a heartbeat, he pulled himself up the ladder. "Coming for you detective," he called again.

But she wasn't there.

He pounded his fist against the muddy Plexiglas. It gave but did not break. He'd never expected anyone to try and break out from the inside, nevertheless, his OCD had made him check and recheck that it was strong enough to bear weight in case someone accidentally walked over it. What was keeping it closed?

Smashing his face up against the glass, he roared at the dim night sky. The Plexiglas felt cold to his cheek. He hung onto the ladder like a bleeding monkey and examined the previous few hours in his mind. She had nothing she could have locked it with. Not even a belt. She'd been wearing jeans, a chambray shirt, and a gray hoodie for a jacket. That was all.

He looked at the 9mm in his hand. It was his only hope. He released the magazine full of ammunition and began to hammer at the Plexiglas with the butt of the empty weapon.

After a few whacks, he gave up. The wound beneath his eye had started to bleed again. Coming for you, Kendra Dean. I'm coming for you just as soon as I break out this damn window.

He sang to himself as a way of staying calm when what he really wanted to do was jam the bullets back into the cylinder and blast his way out. He knew that would work, but it felt like an act of desperation. And it would be extremely loud in the forest. This, on the other hand—felt like beating his head against the wall. The thick plastic window became a roadmap of scars, but it held. It was much tougher than he'd realized. Just like her.

Finally, he gave up, limped back down the ladder, and jammed the magazine into the gun. He fired upward and blew the Plexiglas out into the night.

Anger drove him back up the ladder, and he pulled himself out of the shredded trapdoor and tumbled over, suddenly dizzy, cupping his wounded genitals as pseudo-stars peppered the edges of his vision. The night air cooled his injured face. If not for that, he most certainly would've passed out again.

He huffed and coughed and attempted to work up enough spittle to clean off his slimy tongue, but he'd vomited everything in his gut onto the concrete floor below his feet. There was no moisture left.

In an attempt to alleviate the sour taste, he stuck his tongue out and wiped it with his sleeve. That only served to dry it more. *How did I let this happen? She's not better than me. She's not even one of my best girls. She's nothing but a thorn in my side that has to be stopped before she ruins everything.*

Slowly, controlling his breathing the same way he did in his meditation room, the doctor straightened and glanced around. Even with all that had gone wrong, in the back of his mind was a certain dark glee he hadn't felt in a long time. He supposed it was the thrill of the hunt. Like when he'd taken the dog-walker in the middle of the day. The possibility of being seen by any passing car had simply added to the fun. He'd been lucky that day.

And I'll be lucky, today, too. Then she'll pay. Big time. And I will enjoy every second of it.

Back under control, he began to smile. He gulped in the damp night air and set his sights on getting back to his car. She can't have gone far, he thought as he lurched along. It reminded him of the night he'd met Lola, another victim who had tried to fight back.

He'd found Lola on the back page of Craigslist. Lola probably wasn't her real name, but that was fine by him. He wasn't interested in her name, only her femur.

They'd met at the Dollar Motel on the highway, and he recalled how Lola had begun to undress slowly and provocatively in the seedy motel room.

He had stopped her with a plea to allow him a little leeway. "I like baths," he'd said. Then he'd filled the bathtub with warm water and invited her to get in first.

She'd been more than willing when she saw the pile of cash on the nightstand, and in moments she was his. He'd been captivated by the way her hair had fanned out around her face as she lay back in the warm water just before he pushed her head under. She'd struggled briefly, but the move had taken her by surprise and she'd inhaled deeply as soon as she'd gone under.

It was over in minutes.

Edgar dried her, redressed her in her see-through blouse and short skirt, and "helped" her to the front seat of his car. He didn't dare put her in the trunk in the motel parking lot. He simply drove to his special place and started his work.

On the drive there, he'd wondered if he could get her down the ladder, but after dragging her from the car to the trapdoor, he'd been too spent to do anything other than open it up and push her in. He didn't care that she tumbled to the bottom hitting every iron rung on the way down. Why should he? She was way past caring or screaming.

After he followed her down, he had closed the overhead panel, set up his gear, and operated happily by the bluish light of the moon through the Plexiglas. Combined with the LED light emanating from his battery-operated Coleman lantern, it gave the entire work area a cozy late-night-den sort of feel.

His shadow on the gray cinder block wall reminded him of the mad scientist movies he'd loved as a kid, right down to the wild hair falling over his brow. The only thing different was the steady lantern light rather than flickering firelight. Mad doctors always had flickering firelight, didn't they?

He remembered how he'd chuckled to himself as he worked. Operating in the moonlight was his greatest pleasure. Some men played golf, others tennis or poker. Still others had mistresses to keep them sane.

Edgar had his girls.

It hadn't taken long to remove the femur. All it took was a sharp scalpel, a firm hand, and the know how to separate the bone from the surrounding muscles and tendons. In no time at all, he was holding the treasured thigh bone in his gloved hands.

The rest of Lola's body he had dismembered and carried back up the ladder in trash bags. She had gone into the ground without benefit of any chemical decomposers. He had liked wondering what stage she was in as the months and years progressed. Besides, he never *really* expected to unbury her one day—but, of course, it had always been a distant possibility. Why else would he have carved such detailed directions on each girl's femur?

Staggering through the damp forest, his mouth watered as he recalled how he had cleaned and lovingly placed the woman's femur in the corner of the bunker to dry.

From his antique over-sized doctor's bag, bought on E-bay for a ridiculous but completely understandable sum, Edgar had removed his newest, sharpest, scalpel. It took a fresh one each time. The thighbone was so dense and so incredibly *hard* that even the minute amount of carving to which he subjected it quickly wore away the point.

And now she was tarted up once more. This time like a little holiday whore. A fantastic Christmas gift for someone. He wondered who the lucky one would be. Who would find his little treasure this time? And what would the press make of his new holiday decor? He couldn't wait to find out.

But first he had to deal with Detective Kendra Dean. She couldn't have gone far still shackled and drugged. I should have given her more of the Rohypnol. But she'd seemed to be very sensitive to it. And I never wanted to kill her that way. Where was the fun in that? I wanted her at least partially aware of what was happening. Now I just have to keep my head. Out-think her. She cannot be allowed to get home.

Pep talk over, he began to smile.

CHAPTER THIRTY-TWO

The Interview

Chief Brown held the newspaper clipping in front of her. "Mrs. Stevens, do you think your husband is The Cartographer?"

More Holiday Horrors
Second Skeleton Found
Carving on femur just like the others
Is this the handiwork of The Christmas Cartographer?

Candy held a crumpled tissue in her fist. She glanced at the paper, and then looked away. "Of course not. My Eddie is a good and decent man. He's a doctor for goodness sakes. Why would anyone think he's this – this serial killer? Just because he went on a little trip—"

"When was the last time you saw or spoke to your husband, Mrs. Stevens?"

"I – I spoke to him on the phone night before last. Actually, we texted. He said he was going for a hike. Said he had to get some air."

Detective James sat perfectly still, his face impassive, hands immobile. The chief had allowed him to interview the doctor at the clinic, so it was only fitting that the chief was taking the lead on this. He was afraid his judgment might be compromised. Nevertheless, his silence spoke volumes. He knew absolute passivity was one of the best weapons in a detective's arsenal of interrogation.

Candy twisted her hands together nervously. The silence did seem to unnerve her. The crumpled tissue shed bits of itself onto the industrial colored tile. She began to babble. "Eddie can be very close-mouthed sometimes, quite Zen, you know? He often goes on camping trips alone, says it's necessary to recharge his batteries. He also meditates, every day. I was told not to ever disturb him when he is meditating, but sometimes all of that just isn't enough. That's when he goes for a drive or on one of his hiking trips. Says he has to reconnect, that's it. Not *recharge*, reconnect."

Woody watched her face to see if she was lying or covering something up. He could detect nothing. The woman seemed nervous all right. But he felt it was simply a facet of her personality and not a deliberate attempt at deception.

"Your husband sounds quite high maintenance," the chief said. "But I suppose that isn't too surprising. Being a physician is a high-stress career."

Candy nodded. "That's it. That's it exactly." She dragged the tortured Kleenex between her fingers. "He told me when we were engaged that all he ever wanted was a quiet, beautiful home and a good wife to take care of him. He hated a lot of noise and confusion. I think his childhood must have been very chaotic." She stopped talking, but her hands didn't stop maiming the tissue. Her eyes cut down and to the left.

"Go ahead, Mrs. Stevens." Woody's voice was soft, conciliatory. "Is there something else on your mind?"

Candy pressed her lips closed as if to trap the words inside her mouth.

"It's all right," Woody said. "Really. You can help him by helping us."

She shook her head setting her soft blond waves bouncing gently. "But why does he need help? Why is he under suspicion? Don't you think I'd know if my husband was a – a killer? A *murderer?*"

Woody shrugged and tilted his chair back just slightly. He propped his right ankle on his left knee and fingered the slightly wrinkled crease on his slacks. "There are a couple of things we know about the remains that we haven't told the press." He pulled a slim silver toothpick holder from the inside pocket of his jacket. He took his time unscrewing the tiny cap before he shook out a single slender pick and positioned it just so in the corner of his mouth. He'd started carrying toothpicks when he was trying to quit smoking years earlier, and then he'd discovered it was a good way to delay an interview or interrogation, a good way to watch the other person squirm.

Candy clasped her hands together and took a deep, steadying breath. She seemed surprised when the wounded tissue came apart in her hands. Looking down at the two separate pieces, she smashed them into her palm and wadded them into a ball as if to hide the evidence. "What," she asked. "What sort of things?"

Woody plopped his chair down suddenly. The sound of metal chair legs on tile was almost as loud as a gunshot in the small room.

Candy jumped as if she had, indeed, been shot.

Woody smiled.

Chief Roger Brown grunted and scooted his chair back away from the table. "We appreciate you coming in on your own time like this, Mrs. Stevens." He shot a warning glance at Woody James. "There's no need to get upset. No one is accusing your husband of anything. He's just a person of interest. We think he might have some information about the case, and we'd like to talk to him again if we can."

Woody stood abruptly and stalked around the room. He couldn't believe the doctor had fled. They'd never expected that. He was such a high profile character in the small town that they had simply assumed he would stay right there where they could find him. *Stupid assumptions. Kendra would kill me for that rookie mistake.*

"I expect Eddie home at any time." Candy's voice quivered. "He has never stayed away more than a day or two before."

The chief rubbed a finger across the dip at the center of his top lip where a bead of sweat seemed to have made a permanent home. "Have you spoken to your husband since he's been gone, Mrs. Stevens? Other than the text telling you he was going hiking, I mean?"

Candy cut her eyes down again. "No. Not once." She looked at the furry white mess in her palms.

"Is that unusual?"

Down went Candy's gaze toward the floor again.

That's the *tell*, Woody thought. The telltale sign that she's either lying or holding something back. *Don't say anything, Chief. Give her some wait time; just wait for it.* He strolled behind her chair and let the sleeve of his jacket brush the back of her head ever so slightly. She shivered as if in a sudden draft. The chief closed his mouth and clasped his calloused hands on top of his strained-shirt belly.

After a few more seconds of silence, Candy rubbed her palms down the thighs of her nubby tweed pants and started to talk. "He never stays gone more than a night or two. Even the clinic doesn't know how to get in touch with him. I just don't understand it. Ever since I got home from my sister's house—she just had a baby, you know—he's been different. Cold. Uncommunicative." She dabbed at her eyes with the remains of the tissue, and then grimaced as she realized the puffy mess was sticking to her mascaraed lashes.

"I take it that's unusual. The what did you say, non-communication, part?"

Candy nodded. "He didn't even want to...didn't even try to..." She glanced up helplessly. "He didn't even *kiss* me when I got home."

Woody spoke up from the shadowy corner of the room. "No nookie at all, huh?" He wanted to shock her. To see if she was as naïve and innocent as she appeared, or whether the ingénue façade was just an act.

Candy coughed but couldn't seem to answer.

The air in the small room grew stale. The two men waited patiently. At last the shaky woman whispered, "Edgar doesn't want children. I knew he didn't, but I let myself get pregnant anyway. I just caught the mommy bug I think. My sister was so thrilled with her news, and her husband was over the moon. I wanted that. I wanted Edgar to look at me the way Joseph looked at my sister. But he didn't." She drew in a ragged breath and whispered. "He looked at me with *horror* instead."

The chief and detective exchanged glances over her head. Woody thought of a previous case in which an FBI profiler instructed them to always look for a trigger when someone goes on a killing spree. *Could the baby be the trigger that made him start digging the bodies up after all these years? Or is it something entirely different?*

Woody finally sat down opposite Candy again. "How far along are you, Mrs. Stevens? If you don't mind me asking."

Her gaze dropped to the left and down. "Just four weeks," she said. "I told him as soon as I found out, but I think I made a big mistake letting this happen."

"I'm sure he'll come around." Woody tried to make his voice soothing. "Husband's react differently, but if he loves you..."

Candy jumped on that immediately. "Oh, he does. He does love me. But we had an agreement, and I broke it."

The chief nodded, and Woody knew they'd made some headway. There was only one more thing. "Can you tell us where Dr. Stevens liked to go hiking?" They had the coordinates for the next body, but so far the doc had not surfaced anywhere near it. They were thinking **A)** it wasn't him after all or **B)** he knew they were there, and he had moved on to a new girl altogether.

Woody really hoped it wasn't the latter.

CHAPTER THIRTY-THREE

The Pull of the Bones

When he found himself going in the direction of Lola's gravesite, Edgar threw caution to the wind and powered on. The pull of the bones was strong. He wanted to hold her femur for a few moments. He knew that would calm him and allow him to think his way through this mess.

In the back of his tortured mind, he'd come to the conclusion that Kendra Dean somehow knew where his girls were buried—all of them—and that she was probably headed there now. It was almost impossible for him to wrap his head around the fact that she had bested him down in the hole. His thinking had become skewed.

She had even begun to take on a slightly supernatural quality.

He took a different route this time; an old unused road that was barely navigable.

If the rain comes, the way it's threatening, the road will be impassable.

He dragged a sleeve across his forehead and hoped for the best. The cold didn't bother him in the least. His flannel lined hiking clothes were the best money could buy.

It had secretly thrilled him when the newspaper article had referred to him as *The Killer Cartographer*. But now it made him nervous. Kendra Dean had figured out his latitude/longitude carvings much too quickly. She was pretty sharp. Perhaps she'd seen his tattoos. That's why he hadn't killed her right away. He had wanted to know everything she knew. *My mistake,* he thought.

I won't make that mistake again.

I'll soon remedy that situation. Even if Detective Dean isn't there, I'll take a moment to add a few new carvings to

Miss Lola. Throw a monkey wrench into their investigation, and then it won't matter what she told them if indeed she did. Especially since she will soon no longer be available for consultation.

There's no way she can find her way home.

I know she can't find Lola either.

I have got to get a grip...

The bloated moon floated high in the sky.

The thought of re-carving Lola's femur was like a drug. He wanted it badly. Wanted to hold the bone between his knees and the scalpel between his thumb and forefinger. He could picture himself there beside her, beside the lovely Christmas scene he'd created for her, and the pleasure he'd given himself while he worked.

He was practically running by the time he made it to the spot. But Lola was no longer there. Instead, he encountered a scene from a nightmare. Bright yellow police tape surrounded an empty bed of pine boughs. The tape had been wound from tree to tree to tree in a rough rectangular shape.

He could see no deputies; nevertheless, he didn't dare approach the area any closer. Somehow they'd found her. Someone had found her. How had they located her so quickly? Had he given himself away? He hadn't expected his second best girl to be found for a week or two, maybe even a month.

Was it Kendra Dean? Had he inadvertently told her where Lola was located that day in the clinic? Had she told someone else before he'd grabbed her? No, he was certain he hadn't mentioned the location. He'd merely mentioned hiking as a favorite pastime, right? He'd begun to seriously question himself and his actions. *Am I cracking up? Is the stress having that much effect?*

He hunkered down behind a fallen log and stared at the spot surrounded by the vibrant yellow tape. New snow glimmered beneath the strong moonlight.

Where is my Lola? Is she in some cold drawer at the morgue, or lying on an autopsy table being touched and handled by strange hands? Is someone fondling her, caressing her femurs at this very moment?

His mind galloped ahead at breakneck speed.

Or is this a trap? Did Kendra Dean find a way to contact them? Is it possible she told them and now they're trying to trick me into doing something stupid? Do they think they can outsmart me?

He glanced around to make certain he was alone. His lifelong paranoia reared its ugly head in a way it hadn't done in twenty years. He felt about to burst as if the very next breath he took would cause the top of his head to explode like an overfilled balloon.

Ommm.

He tried to calm himself down.

Ommm.

He closed his eyes and concentrated on his breathing.

In, out, slow, slowly, slower, there.

Almost normal.

He opened his eyes and looked around once more. Nothing seemed out of place except for his missing girl and the hateful yellow tape. Like a zombie, he made his way back down the path toward the Toyota. Everything was going wrong. First the detective, now this. It's only been a couple of hours. How could she have notified them? He had to find out if Kendra Dean had somehow made it home or to a phone. Time to go to town. Time to put an end to speculation, put an end to everything.

CHAPTER THIRTY-FOUR

Stutter Creek

Looking around again, Kendra had a sudden thought. *I need to leave clues so we can find this place again.* She fumbled in her ripped pocket and pulled out several loose threads. These she wound around a branch hanging at eye level. Only someone looking for clues will see it, she thought. *Most people will be looking at the ground, but I'll know where to search when I come back with a team.*

Then, running on instinct, she set off down the mountain at a decent pace. She was grateful for the adrenaline still coursing through her veins. Now if only the moonlight could get through the clouds and trees as easily. So far the rain had held off, but the swollen clouds still played cat and mouse with her only source of light.

She was just beginning to think she was completely free when she heard the muffled crack of a gunshot echo through the trees.

It's him. He's out; he made it out.

She took off again. All she knew was to go downhill.

Half an hour later, she had slowed considerably. Nothing looked familiar. She seemed to be going deeper and deeper into the woods. *That would be about right, escape the killer and die falling off a cliff.*

For a brief instant she let herself imagine the doctor crawling out of his dark hole and coming after her—she tried to be quiet, but in the darkness, hands still shackled, metal plate clutched between her palms to keep it from swinging against her thighs, it was hard to avoid stepping on dry branches and crashing into the underbrush. How much of this is poison ivy, she wondered. But it didn't matter. She had no alternative but to keep moving. She was determined to put as much distance between herself and Dr. Stevens as possible. She wanted to get Woody and the sheriff out here and arrest him before he got desperate and committed suicide like the burglary suspect who was the cause of all her problems.

As the night wore into the early morning hours, Kendra left more and more string clues until her hoodie pocket was hanging loose.

What will I leave next? She thought of the ring she'd shoved into her pants pocket. In the paltry moonlight, she worked the tips of her fingers into her jeans and fished it out. It was definitely a woman's ring. A simple gold-plated band set with a large sapphire.

Kendra tried it on and found that it only fit her pinky finger. A young woman belongs to this ring, she thought. *Where is she? Could she be the one I found resting in clover?*

She sat on a nearby slab of rock to catch her breath and rethink her options. The come-and-go moonlight had disappeared completely. *It really is darkest before the dawn. I can't go on stumbling around.* She ran her shackled hands over her scratched face and arms.

There had been a terrible moment when she'd come to a particularly dense growth of underbrush, which she'd had to bull her way through.

It had turned out to be the rocky edge of a steep drop. It was just like the one she'd imagined in her mind. She had barely saved herself by grabbing onto the well-rooted bushes.

Kendra could still feel the whistle of the wind that whooshed upward as she'd stood with trembling hands thrust into the scratchy bushes that saved her. For once, the handcuffs and metal plate had actually helped her as they tangled in the brush.

After that, she'd found the level slab of rock upon which to rest. *It'll be light in another hour or so. A little shuteye will be a good thing.* After long moments of dozing, she became aware of the sound of water stuttering over a rocky bed.

Stutter Creek?

The realization that she was hearing the same sound she'd heard a couple of days ago on her fishing trip, when she'd been certain someone was watching her, made her sit up and take notice. The sound gave her déjà vu chills. Like an episode of *Twilight Zone*, it felt as if she'd returned to the beginning of a strange and terrible dream. It brought Kendra wide-awake.

Once she'd wrapped her head around the idea that she was, in fact, hearing the loud burbling of the creek, she was surprised she hadn't noticed it earlier. She supposed her near fall had frightened her so much she had developed a sort of tunnel vision, or perhaps tunnel hearing would be a better description. All her senses had been devoted to simply putting one foot in front of the other to get safely down the mountain. When she realized the sun was trying to peek through the trees, she was doubly surprised.

Waking completely from her uncomfortable doze, Kendra pulled the hoodie tighter and wondered if she'd really heard the crack of a gun a while earlier, or whether it had simply been the soundtrack of a dream.

She wanted to get up and go on, but she was so exhausted she lay her head back down. Just a few more minutes. I'll get up after a few more minutes. Did he really tell me he was going to carve me like he'd carved the others? As in more than one?

He'd laughed maniacally when he'd told her that part, but she had been so busy trying to unscrew the metal plate from the floor that she hadn't thought about it. Now, she rubbed her arms with her hands. *I have to tell Woody there are other victims out there somewhere.*

She pulled her knees up tighter against her body and drifted away, but as she drifted, her last conversation with her partner came floating back to her, and she wondered: *Could the sapphire ring belong to the young woman from Yellow Bend? The one who'd gone missing while walking her dog?*

Violent shivering woke her a second time.

Kendra covered her mouth with her hands and blew into them in an attempt to warm up. *Must've dozed longer than I thought.* The air was so cold her muscles were almost locked in place on the frigid surface of the rock slab. *Better than that damn hidey-hole, though.* When she thought of what the murdering doctor had intended for her there, her empty stomach roiled and her fingers curled around the sapphire ring protectively. She said a brief, silent prayer, which she was certain was too late to help the owner of the ring. Then she focused on the here-and-now.

Food would be good. Water, too. No, not water. Hot coffee with one of Martha's Super Cop Specials just like I had yesterday—or was it the day before?

She forced that line of thinking to a halt. It wasn't productive. *Getting home, that's what I should be thinking of. That, and nothing more.*

Joints popping, muscles creaking, she heaved her middle-aged body off the unforgiving rock and headed toward the sound of the creek. Dozing with her hands shackled together had forced her shoulders into an unnatural position that deepened the ache that had already taken over her entire spine. *Can't worry about that. Just lucky I didn't take a bullet as I was climbing that iron ladder.*

In a few moments, the sound of the stuttering water had grown so loud it made her feel renewed. Just knowing she was near the creek that gave the town its name made her feel as if she were almost home.

When the brushy bank came into view, Kendra broke into a run.

She stumbled down to the water's edge and stuck her hands into the ice-cold early-morning water. The handcuffs clinked together as she splashed the water onto her face. The silver metal burned when it touched her skin and the ribbed knit of her hoodie sleeves absorbed the water like sponges. The metal plate seemed to weigh a ton.

She hesitated to actually drink, knowing the possibility of ingesting giardia or some other water-borne parasite, but all at once thirst overcame her, and she swept the water into her mouth from her cupped palms. After a few tooth-chattering mouthfuls, she sat back, satisfied but chilled.

Now I can go on. But first...

She dug into her ragged pocket until she found more loose thread that she wound around a bush. Now that it was daylight, she began to worry about the doctor trailing her. Every shadow and every tiny sound made her look over her shoulder. She also began to wonder how she'd managed to avoid some sort of road or trail. *I must've gone the exact opposite direction in the darkness—if he even had a trail to the hellhole that is. Of course it would be out in the middle of nothing, but still, how far could one drag a body? Unless they were alive when he took them there. Like me.*

Not wishing to follow that line of thinking just yet, Kendra began to jog along the bank of the creek to warm herself. Her breath huffed out in front of her mouth in misty exhalations. *Following the creek is better than any trail. Especially since it's going down the mountain. It's only a matter of time before it parallels the town, or at least a park road.*

She stumbled off balance for the hundredth time. *If only I could get rid of these damn cuffs, or at least the plate dangling from them. Then I could make some real time.*

That's when the moisture that had been threatening finally began to fall, and with it, the temperatures fell, too.

Great.

She stuck her shackled hands into first one hoodie pocket and then the other, in an attempt to warm them. It was nearly impossible with the plate still attached. *Lord, I swear I won't complain about anything else, just please make the rain stop.*

After a few moments it did.

Then the sleet began.

Soon, it changed to snow.

CHAPTER THIRTY-FIVE
Breaking the Pattern

Candy was so relieved when she got back home that she immediately went into the kitchen and put the kettle on for tea. Trying to cut back on caffeine now that she was pregnant, she had stocked up on herbal teas.

She took down her favorite china, poured the hot water, and stood dunking the tea bag over and over as her mind whirled.

Could he be the killer they were talking about? No! Not Edgar. Not the man she'd married, laughed with, lain with, and was now pregnant by. Just not possible. He was different, perhaps. Maybe even a little strange, but a killer? No wa—

"You shouldn't have gone against my wishes." Edgar's voice sounded sad but stern. As if he were scolding a puppy for soiling the floor.

Candy whirled around one hand swiping the teacup off the counter and sending it crashing to the kitchen floor. "Eddie—you startled me." Her other hand flew to her chest, patting at the place where her pounding heart threatened to break through.

Her husband's face was a mask of mud and blood and gore. One eye was gashed just below the socket. Blood had congealed in his lashes, clumping them together in stiff spikes. His hair was matted to his scalp, and the blood on his clothing appeared as stiff and fake as Halloween makeup.

He limped toward his wife, safety scalpel clutched tightly in his fist.

The overhead lighting added to his aura as a madman. He hadn't found Kendra, but here was someone who needed killing almost as much, maybe even more.

"Eddie," Candy began again.

He raised the scalpel, ignoring the crunch of china beneath his shoes.

Candy's hand reached for the kettle of hot water.

"Don't even think about it."

She grabbed the kettle and slung it toward him in a wide arc.

Scalding water sprayed across the room from the spout.

He dropped the scalpel and covered his eyes with his hands. His reflexes were good. Only a few drops reached his face.

Candy dashed from the room still holding the hot kettle. She didn't let go of it until she was in the bedroom behind the locked door.

Her husband pounded the door with his fists. "Come out, Candy! I wasn't through with you!"

Panicked, she glanced around the room in search of an escape. Her cell phone was on the kitchen counter. The bedroom windows were covered with heavy drapes. Candy yanked them open and shoved up the old-fashioned window sash. She threw one leg over the sill and was halfway out when the door disintegrated behind her.

With an unholy roar, Edgar rushed across the room and dragged her back inside.

Biting and scratching, Candy fought back to the best of her petite ability, but she'd never had the self-defense training of an experienced detective.

She never had a chance.

***

Edgar closed the window and placed his wife's body in the bathtub. After removing her femur, he poured cleaning fluid on the rest of the corpse.

Now he had a new girl to replace Lola, the one who had been found too soon.

He cleaned the thighbone and sat in his lovely meditation room for the last time. It didn't take long to carve the coordinates. He even added something extra just for fun.

Then he made his way to his private bathroom and stood under the lukewarm spray until all the filth of the last few hours had been washed away.

The things they make me do.

Such a mess.

He rolled Candy up in the floral bedspread and dressed himself in clean clothes. He moved slowly and methodically. There was no need to hurry. After he'd escaped the bunker and made it back to the Toyota, he had made it a point to loop around the lake in order to come through town from the opposite direction. He'd wanted to drive past the Drugstore Café, the makeshift headquarters where all the Kendra-searchers had gathered.

Even that late into the night, the parking lot had been full. Through the plate glass window, he'd seen clumps of people, some he knew, many he didn't, sipping coffees, picking at what appeared to be breakfast plates and burritos. It was obvious Kendra hadn't been found yet. If she had, they would've been going home to sleep.

He remembered thinking how much the drugstore owner owed him. *This has been good for her business, all those hungry searchers. Too bad I won't have time to collect on that debt.*

Now, he strolled through his home saying goodbye to his old life.

After he had finished with Candy in the bathtub and cleaned himself up, he'd had a Dagwood sandwich, a bottle of Sam Adams, and a couple of Lortabs from the bottle he kept on hand for emergencies. He also took stock of his many injuries. He owed Detective Kendra Dean for those.

Once he had Candy in the trunk, his new life began. *Out with the old, in with the new.* He knew exactly where he was going to bury her since he had already carved the coordinates on the femur of the previous girl. But this time, he hadn't had the luxury of stripping the flesh. The cleaning chemicals were all he'd had time for. That was okay. At least she wasn't looking at him when he rolled her up in the bedspread like a burrito. Not that it mattered. She'd brought it on herself by doing exactly what they'd agreed they would never do.

So much for love.

Now the question was, where to go afterward? He couldn't very well return to the clinic with his face all torn and bruised. And the house was off limits forever, way too much blood, and she would be missed eventually.

He thought about it the whole way up the mountain. Thought about it while he wrestled her petite body from the car to the site, dragging the ends of the bedspread through the new snow. He mulled it over while he dug the new grave. His mind tested theory after theory while he unwrapped her and rolled her remains into position. And he was still thinking about it while he shoveled the earthen blanket back into place.

Then it hit him.

The answer to everything.

It would take some effort, but it was definitely doable. He'd treated several of the less fortunate Stutter Creek citizens over the past year. Those who lived beneath bridges in the summer and in the homeless shelter when the snow came. The ones who appeared at the clinic if brought in by someone else.

He knew of two men close to his own age with no fixed address and no next of kin. If one of them went missing, who would notice?

And as luck would have it, the taller man could have been his stunt double. *All I have to do is place a fresh male corpse in the Toyota, drive it over a cliff and make certain it catches fire, so there will be no fingerprints left to identify it.*

He continued to ruminate as he smoothed the torn up ground and covered the spot with a few loose branches for camouflage. He stood over the grave breathing in the sweet scent of pine and freshly turned soil. *I may also have to lose the head so there will be no dental records, but that shouldn't be a problem.* He made a mental list of all the places he could dispose of a head, or at least the teeth. Then he laughed out loud, throwing his own head back in eerie imitation of a wolf howling at the moon.

All I have to do is spread some of my own DNA around the crash site and voila! I'm history. Gone forever. By the time these Barneys connect the dots, I will be in Mexico or Central America. Doctors in some areas of the world are so revered they don't even need credentials. And who knows, maybe I'll get new credentials under my new name once I get there.

He gathered his folding shovel and bloody bedspread and made his way back to his secret parking place near the bunker. He'd come to the conclusion that without Kendra Dean, they might never connect the dots. *I might not even need a new name. I'll be a ghost, a phantom, a whisper in the night, an urban legend.*

He approached the car, grinning. The Lortabs he had taken to dull the pain of his gouged face and bruised body had made him a bit loopy. But it was a *good* feeling. It gave him exactly the right amount of fearlessness needed to stow his gear and head back up the trail in search of that wily detective.

Wily. Like Wile E. Coyote, and just as inept. And I am The Roadrunner. Running down the road all day. Running down the detective. Running down my future.

Still ruminating about cartoon characters, the doc shoved the cumbersome bedspread into the trunk of the car. Burn it, too, he thought. It would have taken a much deeper hole to bury all that bloody, downy fabric. And with the snow coming down faster and harder all the while, a deeper hole just wasn't in the cards.

He sat in the front seat of his car for a few moments, luxuriating in the warmth and the cocoon-like silence created by the falling snow.

He had always known this day would come.

And he welcomed it with open arms.

The thrill of the hunt.

Everything else paled in comparison.

CHAPTER THIRTY-SIX
Falling

Kendra watched the flakes drift to earth like tiny feathers. She could feel the temperature dropping rapidly. She'd been following the sound of the creek for miles and miles but a few times she'd lost sight of it when the trees and brush became so thick that she had to traverse around them up onto the side of the mountain. Now, she sat beneath the wide sweeping branches of a Douglas fir and tried not to think about another coming night.

Her head spun, and her chest felt caved in. *Drinking from the stream might have been a bad idea.* She felt hot and cold all at the same time.

She had dozed off and on throughout the past day and night. If her thinking was straight—and she wasn't certain about that—then this was the second day since she had pulled herself up out of the hole.

Is the doctor still locked in there? Could he bleed to death from the eye wound or maybe the head wound? Wouldn't that be wonderfully ironic, to die in his own hellhole?

That thought gave her a momentary flash of hope.

But then her realistic side took over. The gunshot. There *was* a gunshot. That had to be him blasting his way out.

Besides all that, she didn't think he'd been on the verge of death, but then she wasn't a medical person. She actually hated going to the doctor. The stitches in her hand had been her first doctor visit in years. *And look where that got me.* Her family had always teased her about being so ridiculously healthy.

Look at me now, she thought. *Sick as a dog, barely able to function. Feel as if I've developed pneumonia, or what I assume pneumonia would feel like.* Stiff and sore from trying to sleep on the ground or on a slab of rock, and worst of all she had sipped from the burbling creek on more than one occasion. *Is it giardia, is that why I'm so lightheaded? Or is it just from hunger?*

The questions tangled in her mind like the strands of string she kept wrapping around branches and bushes.

Just keep the sound of the creek on my right. That's how it was when I started out. It will lead me back to town. It has to.

She stumbled a few more steps before she fell over a tree root covered by the thickening snow. At the last split-second, Kendra flung out her hands and managed to take most of the weight on her shackled hands rather than her chest.

The metal plate scraped a path in the snow.

She lay where she fell, chest heaving, eyes watering from the pain in her wrists. *Hope nothing is broken. That would be the icing wouldn't it?*

After a few moments, her breathing slowed back to normal, and she became aware of a sweet scent like newly mown grass. She opened her eyes.

Beneath her nose, a clump of clover peeked through the thin veil of snow.

Kendra licked her lips.

She was fairly certain clover was edible, and the snow looked clean and wet, very inviting. She stuck out her tongue and licked the clump of snow-dusted leaves.

Before she knew it, she was pulling up handfuls of the soft leaves, stuffing them in her mouth and digging around for more. The moisture of the snow on the leaves was like a tiny balm to her feverish mouth and throat.

Slow down, her better sense insisted. *Take it easy. This could be as bad as drinking creek water.* But slowing down was out of the question. She hadn't eaten anything since the bite of cinnamon roll in her own living room days earlier.

When she realized she was crawling around on all fours licking everything in sight to get the most snow to wash down her clover, Kendra had a sudden vision of white bones and pink flowers. *They had been resting in clover. Clover just like this.*

She sat back on her haunches and swiped her fingertips across her mouth. The pines and firs met overhead, and the constant lullaby of the wind in the canopy had practically melded itself into her DNA.

Her gut cramped, and she pressed her hands to her mouth. *I will not puke. I will not!* She willed the clover back down and searched for a dry spot to rest.

The feathery snow fell faster and thicker. *Need something to catch it in. Let it melt into good water.* But she had nothing. She spied a relatively dry spot under a close-needled fir and crawled beneath the low overhang. It was cave-like and cold, but it wasn't wet, yet. Best of all the thickly needled branches held on to the feathery flakes. *If nothing else I can simply scrape off the branches and let the snow melt in my mouth.*

Reaching up, she broke off the tip of a branch and tilted the snow into her open mouth. It was cold and momentarily soothing. *But I don't want to do that too often. It will freeze me from the inside out.* She thought of a book she'd read a few years earlier—*Into the Wild*—about a young man who had tried to survive on his own in Alaska. He had frozen to death inside the shell of an old bus.

She tamped the thought down the same way she'd tamped down the clover. That won't happen to me. This is northern New Mexico, not Alaska. And I've only been out here a couple of days, not weeks, or months.

She peeked out of her little cave and tried to see the night sky. *If only I could see the moon, or at least the stars.* But she couldn't. The trees were too dense, the falling snow too fine and thick.

Glancing down at the tip of the branch she'd broken off, Kendra noticed how it resembled the point of an arrow. She reached out of her makeshift home and placed it on the ground so that it pointed toward the direction she had been traveling. *Now, when I wake, I won't simply crawl out and take off in the wrong direction.*

She curled into a comma and fell immediately into an exhausted slumber, lulled by the soughing of the pines and the clean scent of the fresh snow. In her fevered dreams, she imagined herself coiled around the naked bones of a woman laid out on a bed of half-eaten clover. Her stomach churned, and she moaned in her sleep.

When she awoke, everything was white. The silently falling snow had covered the entire ground. She could no longer see plants or leaves or twigs—the snow appeared to be at least a few inches deep.

As she came more fully awake, Kendra became aware of the condition of her body and her surroundings. She had no idea how long she had slept, but it was still night, and the snow had crept into her makeshift cave and her sweatshirt and jeans were cold and damp. *So much for my thread clues. They're invisible now.* Attempting to sit up, she discovered the earth was a magnet and her body a twisted bar of iron.

Powerful tremors overtook her.

Get out and move or stay still and freeze to death.

She dozed off again.

An hour later she came to, like falling off a bed. One moment she dreamed about lying on the beach on a deserted island, white sand beneath her crusty cheek, gulls circling overhead, crying that harsh, throaty sound that always made her look up, shielding her eyes against the sun. The next moment she was sitting up, shivering, slapping her palms together—making her bracelets jangle—in an excruciating attempt to get the blood flowing again.

The square of metal still dangling from her cuffs seemed to have taken on weight, and her teeth chattered painfully. Is that the precursor to hypothermia? No, she thought, it's when the body stops shivering and chattering that hypothermia has set in.

Kendra forced herself out of her cave and used a nearby tree as leverage to struggle to her feet. She hobbled two steps and fell heavily. Her feet were completely numb. They would not support her. *Oh my God, how long was I asleep?*

Sitting back against the tree, she pulled one foot into her lap. The pain was incredible. A thousand pins and needles flooded her toes.

Pulling off her boot, Kendra gritted her teeth and rubbed and slapped her at her flesh. She couldn't tell which hurt worse, her hands or her feet. The left side of her face also had a numb-coming-back-to-life spot. *Frostbite? Worry about that later.* She continued rubbing and slapping her frozen foot until the pain was so intense she had to stop.

Then she started on the other one.

Idiot!

Holding on to the scaly trunk of a pine, she tested her feet again. Painful, but better. She gritted her teeth to slow the chattering.

Get moving again, that will help.

Slowly and carefully, Kendra made her way down the slope, hoping the lower elevation would get her out of the snow. At least it has stopped coming down, she thought. That's something to be thankful for—she had a flash of memory from Thanksgiving—Woody and the kids all saying what they were thankful for—and a cold tear slipped from the corner of her eye. She swiped it away and concentrated on putting one foot in front of the other. The scant moonlight reflecting off the snow lit the ground almost as well as a flashlight. *That's something else to be thankful for.*

She was more than a little surprised when she suddenly felt the urge to urinate. *How can that be? The only thing I've had to drink is snow.* Nevertheless, she felt the unmistakable urge, so she hobbled into the nearest stand of pines—not for privacy, there was no need for that in the middle of the night in the middle of nowhere—so that she would have something to brace herself against. She certainly didn't want to wet her clothing any more than it already was, plus, she hoped it might be a bit warmer in amongst the trees.

But she needn't have worried about any of that.

When she squatted—back, and thigh muscles screaming in protest—and felt the first tentative drops of urine begin to flow, she almost cried out.

A tongue of fire lit her insides as surely as if she'd douched with kerosene. *What the hell?* Instinctively, she cut off the trickle and glanced below the crotch of her panties at the frozen ground beneath. It was no longer white. Instead, Kendra saw that her steaming urine had stained the snow a delicate, pastel pink.

"Sonofa*bitch*." Her voice wasn't loud, but in the midnight forest it was strong. She thought back to the swimmy way she had regained consciousness back in the hole. *I was worried about a concussion causing the nausea and headache and blurry vision. I think that bastard put something in the water he gave me. He's a doctor; he had plenty of access to roofies or even worse.* She remembered how he'd jokingly offered her a sedative at one point. *How smart he thinks he is. He'd probably already given me one. I wonder if he filmed himself abusing me?* In her experience, perverts often filmed their acts of depravity in order to replay the deeds later. *And I let him live. I left him down there alive.* She pictured him with the gun she'd heard. *He was going to kill me.*

First he kidnapped me, and then he raped me. I guess the next logical thing was to kill me and strip my bones like the ones I found in clover.

And to think, I tried to use sex against him. No wonder he didn't consider me a threat. He'd probably already had me by then. That must have been some powerful drug.

Shaking like a ninety-year-old woman after a marathon, Kendra reached down and scooped up a palm full of snow and patted it into her fiery crotch. The snow felt great—for about a second—then she began to shiver all over again. She flung the snow away and finally managed to get her pants back up, the cold square of metal slapping her thighs as she struggled.

Fury caused a rush of adrenaline to flood her system and brought with it a certain amount of heat. The shivering subsided, and she felt more clearheaded than she had in days.

Stepping out of her pocket in the pines, Kendra embraced the frigid night. *He won't get away this time. Maybe I wasn't thinking clearly when I let him live, but I'm in my right mind now.*

Crotch burning, heart hardened, she began to retrace her steps.

I'll find that hole again. Be damned if I run away from that pervert. I'll kill him first. Then I'll retire. The burning pain made her realize that all the bumps and bruises and soreness in her thighs and back muscles had not been completely due to sleeping on the cold concrete floor after all. *Exactly what did he do?* She felt violated in more ways than one. The not knowing was the worst.

Snow began to feather down again, but Kendra had worked up quite a sweat. She wasn't sure if that was good or bad—she had a vague recollection of her grandmother telling her not to get overheated and then go out into the cold, but what choice did she have? Already, she felt warmer than she had all day.

She remembered placing a pine tip arrow outside her pine-cave before she fell asleep earlier, but she'd forgotten to look for it under the snow.

Maybe I'll just get lucky, she thought. *Or I could continue to follow the sound of the creek.* The sound was almost inaudible now, though, and she wondered if it ever froze over. *Is that why I can barely hear it?* The sighing breeze had stilled. It felt as if the night were on hold, waiting for her to do something. Anything.

She clenched her hands into fists in an attempt to warm them.

Was that the sound of the creek? Or was it the wind high up in the canopy? It was so dark she couldn't see the treetops. Couldn't tell if they were swaying or still. Down here there was no breeze, but what about up there? Wasn't there always a breeze at the top?

Which direction should I go?

Kendra started walking. She was fairly certain it *was* the muted sound of the creek to her right. Not just the breeze in the trees.

One good thing about the snow was that it made the ground visible.

One bad thing about the snow was that it disguised humpy tree roots and fallen branches.

She quickly learned to walk with a shuffle so that her toes met all obstacles first. It caused her leather boots to become even more soaked than if she had been walking normally, but Kendra saw no way around that. *If I lose a few toes to frostbite, it will be a small price to pay.*

All her powers of concentration focused on the subtle gradations of white and gray at her feet. Kendra didn't see the lip of the ravine until her numb toes were already over the edge and then she was sliding and tumbling, arms

outstretched in an attempt to snag something—anything—
to keep from hitting the unseen bottom.

The snow muted the crashing noise of her slide. It
happened so fast she never even cried out though every
frozen stone scraped and gouged at her skin as her hoodie
and shirt rucked up beneath her arms.

In the back of her mind, she could imagine the sadistic
doctor cackling madly at how terrible her escape was turning
out.

CHAPTER THIRTY-SEVEN

The Twilight Zone

Keith's Ford Explorer made the turn into The Antler's Motel parking lot. Charlie rode shotgun. Carrie and Rory were right behind them in their own vehicle.

The trip to Stutter Creek had been short and stressful.

After getting his sister and brother-in-law registered and settled, Keith called Willa. He told her that their mother was missing and that he and Charlie were on the way to Texas Tech to get her. He explained that Carrie and Rory were staying in Stutter Creek to be nearby in case of news.

Willa's voice carried within the confines of the small motel room even though Keith had not pushed the speakerphone icon. "Why didn't you call me sooner? I could be halfway there already!"

Keith tried to explain that they hadn't wanted her to drive up alone, but she was having none of it. They could hear her dragging open drawers and rattling hangers as she presumably threw articles of clothing into a suitcase.

"I should go to her," Charlie murmured as Keith ended the call. "You stay here with Carrie."

Keith looked at him suspiciously. Charlie and Willa's friendship was not a secret, but the depth of feeling in Charlie's voice took him by surprise.

"You sure?" he asked. "She's the youngest. I feel like I should be with her." Charlie shook his head. "I got this." He pulled out his phone and touched a name. "It's me," he spoke into the phone. "I'm with your brother, about to head your way." He listened before he spoke again. "Yes, I've decided to leave Keith here and come for you. Stay put until I get there." He touched the END icon. "I should have brought my car," he said.

"Take ours," Rory insisted. "Keith will have his. We can all get around with him."

"I'll leave immediately." He clasped Keith's shoulder. "I'm sorry—" he began.

But Keith cut him off. "No. Don't say it. Mom's all right. She's fine. We just have to find her. There's a logical explanation—"

Charlie nodded. "Of course. I didn't mean that. I just meant I'm sorry I can't go with you now. But I'll be back, with Willa, as soon as possible." His normally shy personality had taken a backseat to his friend's distress. "Should you notify your father?"

Keith walked him out to the parking lot. "I suppose I should. But I don't want him here. If not for him Mom might still be in Pine River where she's supposed to be. If he'd just stood by her."

Charlie had heard about their impending divorce but he didn't know the details. Even though all three kids were adults, their parents' split had affected them deeply. "Totally understandable. Your call, all the way."

"Thanks, man," Keith said. "I can't worry about him right now. I just have to get out there and start looking. Damn. She's been so upset lately with the divorce and then this thing with her job—which is a nothing but a load of crap, by the way—that I feel guilty letting her be up here all alone."

"She's an adult and a detective," Charlie replied. "Besides, judging by the way she and Detective James acted, I doubt she was all alone."

Keith turned to him with fire in his eyes.

Charlie held up both palms. "Just sayin', man. Just sayin'. I mean your Mom's a cool lady. I don't know the problem with your father, but she's independent. I doubt she would have wanted a babysitter."

Keith's shoulders relaxed. "Okay. Yeah, I get what you mean. Still, it's my *mom*. Where could she be?"

Charlie couldn't answer that. He climbed into Keith's Explorer and gave him a little wave.

Keith dialed Woody's phone but got no answer. He left a voice mail and then went back inside the motel to get Rory's keys. He figured Carrie would want to go with him to their mom's house or the sheriff's office—whichever place they could find Detective James, but it was already nearing one a.m., and she appeared to be wiped out. He hoped she would agree to stay in the motel and rest until morning.

As he walked back through the motel lobby, Keith caught the crackle of a police scanner and a voice directing deputies to the location of a crime scene.

"What's the crime?" He kept his voice casual.

The clerk turned to him with wide eyes. "Another body found in the woods. Third one in a week." The young man turned his gaze back to the scanner as if he could see what the officers were talking about. "They use codes, but everyone knows what they're saying. 11-44 is scanner talk for dead body, coroner needed."

Keith leaned casually against the counter. "Wow, pretty exciting for such a small town. You say three bodies were found in the woods?" He didn't know how much the clerk knew about his mom, so he played it safe.

The guy swept spiky green-tipped hair off his forehead. "Yeah, all of 'em north of Copper Lake." His eyes gleamed with excitement. "I also caught a couple of references to a 10-57 which is regular old ten code for a missing per—"

Keith didn't let the kid finish. "My mother is missing." He tried to sound grown-up as if he wasn't about to burst into tears. "That's why I'm here. The detective called me—how do I get to the scene?"

The clerk's face clouded. "Well, I don't know exactly."

Keith dashed behind the counter. "I need to get *there*." He didn't threaten the boy, simply took up all his personal space.

"I – I think if you drive out the highway toward the north you can—hold on." He picked up the business phone and dialed a number on speed dial.

Keith hoped he was simply calling the manager, but from the clerk's side of the conversation, he was pretty certain the guy had just called the cops.

He turned and started toward the room where he'd left Carrie and Rory.

"Mister," the clerk called. "Wait..."

Keith glanced back over his shoulder.

The green haired kid stood with one hand over the receiver. "They're sending a deputy to pick you up." He looked down at the registration card in his hand. "I told them your name and they said your mom *is* the one who is missing. Everyone has been searching for her. Apparently a Detective James told them to be expecting you."

His knees weakened and Keith sank onto the small sofa opposite the check-in counter. "Thank you," he said. "I'll go tell my sister." But he didn't go right away. For a few moments, he sat where he was, trying to gather his wits about him.

At last he felt able to stand.

He headed back to Rory and Carrie's room and was thankful to see his sister asleep on the bed, fully clothed. He told Rory what he'd learned, and Rory gave him the keys to the Taurus with instructions to stay in touch.

"I will," Keith said. "The clerk said the deputy would pick me up, but I'd rather follow him to the scene. I don't want to be without a car."

He waited outside the motel wishing he had something to calm his nerves. He'd smoked cigarettes a few times over the years but never—thank God—got hooked. Right now, however, he wished he'd taken them up. This was the time for a cigarette—this waiting time.

In the back of his mind, a prayer/chant had begun. *Please, God, don't let it be mom, don't let it be her, it can't be her.* But his prayer wasn't doing much to ease his conscious mind. It was just too coincidental. Missing mom, new remains. Two plus two...

When the deputy arrived, Keith introduced himself. "I'll follow you if that's all right. I may have to leave and come back to pick up one of my sisters or something. I don't want to be stranded."

The deputy nodded. "Sheriff Puckett is at the scene. He said to escort you there immediately."

Keith wanted to thank him for being so courteous, but his voice wouldn't cooperate. He couldn't believe they were going to the scene of a dead body—a body that might turn out to be his mother.

I've entered the Twilight Zone, that's all.

This can't be real.

CHAPTER THIRTY-EIGHT

In A Hurry

"This one is fresh," Sherriff Puckett said. He looked at Woody's drawn face and sunken eyes and stopped talking. "I agreed to let you up here because I know Kendra Dean was your partner."

At the word "was" Woody's face drained of all color.

"Now, I didn't mean it like that." The sheriff rubbed his mouth. "I simply meant she was your partner back in Pine River."

Woody nodded, but couldn't seem to speak. He motioned toward the freshly turned earth with one hand.

The sheriff continued. "John Stockton's dog found the grave. Amazing he could find it under the snow. But like I say, it's fresh. They were leading one of the search groups when Turk alerted. John said they were headed up from the lake." He rested his hand on his holster. "Thankfully the dog is well trained and didn't simply start digging—" He looked back over his shoulder. "I dug just enough to make certain it was what we thought. Now we'll just wait for the forensics team."

Woody's head bobbed again. "I know them. John and Turk helped us catch that maniac at Blue Cave a couple years back."

"Lots of psychos in our little corner of the world," Sheriff Puckett intoned.

"Epidemic," Woody agreed.

As they spoke, Sheriff Puckett quietly steered Woody away from the partially opened grave.

"I know what you're doing." Woody's voice was steady. "And it won't work. I *will* be here when they take out the corpse. But it isn't Ken. No matter how fresh it is." He stopped talking as if to catch his breath. "I'd know if she were no longer of this earth."

The sheriff didn't question that statement. He was a self-contained man. Other people's relationships didn't concern him. Nevertheless, he tried to keep Woody a little distance away, just in case. After all, no one had seen Kendra Dean for three days, and that was a long time to be missing in the forest. Especially with the drop in temperatures and the new snow.

The Medical Examiner made it to the scene in record time.

Woody stood a few feet away while she instructed the technicians how best to finish opening the grave.

The bones were cold. The frozen ground had cemented them into place as surely as if a layer of concrete had been poured around them.

Lois Campanelli finished sweeping away the last remnants of soil before laying aside her whiskbroom. The remains weren't clean this time.

A halo of crunchy hair created an icy no-color nimbus around the melted facial features. Most of the skin had sloughed away or puddled in the eye sockets and mouth. It appeared the dead woman had somehow attempted to swallow her own face.

The M.E. stood slowly, joints audibly protesting the cold and the fact that she'd been crouched there for several long minutes. A grimace of pain crossed her face.

"I can do that," one of the assistants said. "You don't have to—"

She looked at the helpful young tech. "Thanks, I'd rather do it myself." She turned to Woody and the sheriff. "I can't say for certain, but I think it's a much younger woman—"

Woody stared down at the dirt-encrusted corpse. "It's not her. I know it isn't. This one is much too short. Ken is almost six feet—"

A crashing noise arose from behind them.

The sheriff and the two deputies immediately crouched and drew their weapons.

Keith's voice was frantic as he lurched out of the trees toward them. "Is it her? Is it my mom? Detective James, is it her?"

Woody looked up just in time to grab Keith and keep him from tumbling headlong into the grave. "It isn't her, Keith. It's *not* your mom."

The handsome young man broke down into sobs.

Behind him, the out of breath deputy who led him there from the motel struggled to keep up. When he saw the sheriff with his weapon drawn, his face blanched. "Sorry boss, when he saw the lights, he just took off."

Sheriff Puckett placed his service revolver back into its holster and snapped the safety strap down before digging a large white handkerchief out of his back pocket.

Woody thought he would offer it to the sobbing Keith; instead, the sheriff raised the front edge of his Stetson and used it to mop his hairline. In the bright glare of the portable crime scene lights, Woody could see beads of sweat trickle onto the big man's forehead when he raised the hat. He thought Keith was very lucky he hadn't caught a bullet just then.

He continued to hold Keith upright. "Where are the girls, are they here?" He looked around as if expecting to see pregnant Carrie trudging along behind them.

Keith shook his head. "Carrie and Rory are at The Antler's Motel in town. Charlie's on the way to pick up Willa, but I couldn't wait—the motel desk clerk has a police scanner."

The sheriff scowled. "Small town."

Keith cleared his throat and wiped his face on his sleeve. "Are you certain it's not her?"

Woody kept one hand on the boy's upper arm. "We're positive, son. Your mom is still out there, somewhere. We'll find her, soon." He introduced Keith to the sheriff and the group at large, but after that, no one quite knew what to do with him. The M.E. and her technicians—along with the two deputies and their shovels— continued uncovering the fresh remains.

"Wait a minute." Woody leaned down into the light. "I recognize that piece of cloth." *Where have I seen that recently?* He wracked his brain for a flash of memory, but it wouldn't come.

Then suddenly it did.

He'd seen the same nubby tweed pattern only yesterday.

"*Mrs.* Dr. Stevens," he said. "She had on a pair of tweed pants when we interviewed her down at the station. I'd swear it was that same fabric."

"Yesterday?" Brandi Dagwan's voice held a note of disbelief. "You mean this woman was alive yesterday?" She glanced back down into the hole at the melted face and fleshless torso. "Look at the decomposition. There's a bit of fabric on the legs but if she had on a blouse, it's gone already."

"Chemical," Woody insisted. "Some kind of acid, I'd bet."

Lois Campanelli nodded. "I suspect you're right. I don't want to say for certain until we get her back to the lab, but yes, I'd say that was extremely likely and look," she indicated the femur lying atop the rib cage. "This time the coordinates are barely scratched into the surface. The dirt hasn't even settled into the marks."

"He was rushed," Woody observed.

"In a hurry to get her in the ground," the sheriff agreed.

CHAPTER THIRTY-NINE

Perchance to Dream

Kendra hit the bottom of the ravine like a tow sack full of bricks. She felt a lump rising on her head. She must've hit a million rocks on the way down.

She lay perfectly still in the moonlight, her breath jammed up inside her lungs so hard they felt solid. Finally, she was able to inhale but the breath was so shallow she was certain she'd punctured something.

After a time, her breathing eased. She sat up gingerly. Her hoodie and shirt were twisted and torn. Every time her fingers met her skin there was pain, raw, scraped, frozen, pain.

She tried to see the places on her torso where she had ridden most of the way down, but it was too dark. Her fingers came away sticky, though, so she knew there was blood.

After a few minutes, she swiped a hand across her lips. Seeing no blood-tinged foam, she assumed her lungs weren't punctured after all. She pushed herself up and then immediately staggered and sat back down with a thud. Her vision swirled like Van Gogh's stars. Maybe I have a head injury, she thought. *Maybe Van Gogh did, too.*

Reflected moonshine allowed her to see where she had slid down the side of the ravine. It reminded her of the penguin slide at the zoo. Except her slide through the snow ended in dirt and rocks and small scratchy bushes instead of icy cold zoo pond water.

The thought of water made her remember she'd been trying to follow the course of the creek. She pushed herself to her feet once more. Nausea invaded her belly, and she bent at the waist and dry heaved until she was certain she would either faint or die. *My poor head, all those rocks. Or is it dehydration? Woods, where are you?* That thought snuck up on her. She was certain he was looking for her, but she'd never depended on anyone to save her before. Why start now?

Breathing carefully, standing hunched over like an old woman, Kendra forced herself to focus on her surroundings. Is that noise the wind, or the creek? She couldn't tell. There seemed to be a roaring in her ears that came from inside her head rather than outside. *Damn.* She struggled to remain upright while the ground tilted and rolled beneath her feet. Closing her eyes didn't help. Her body swayed even worse. She opened them just in time to see the ground before it slapped her in the face.

This time, the pain was immediate. She'd landed on her chin and cheek, on her swollen lips. The trickle of blood tasted warm and salty. Kendra rolled over and stared up at the blurry swath of stars. She had broken her glasses in order to escape from the mad doctor. Her hand went to her shirt pocket but it was empty. She had no idea where she might have lost the remaining pieces of her specs.

She lay still again, willing the world to stop spinning.

After awhile, her body took her down to sleep.

Perchance to dream.

CHAPTER FORTY

Playing With Us

I should have killed the prick at the clinic, Woody thought. Now he's out there on the loose and I have to find him again. He massaged the muscles in his lower back. And this time he knows we're on to him. Has he got Ken?

A small voice spoke up. "If this is Mrs. Stevens, shouldn't we be blanketing the area with her husband's picture? Along with that of Detective Dean, of course—"

Woody looked at the girl's Forensic Assistant badge hanging around her neck on a special lanyard. "Thanks, Tana. We've got that covered."

Brandi elbowed her coworker in the ribs and the girl had the grace to look at the ground. "Sorry, Detective. I get excited sometimes. I just admire you and Detective Dean so much—I mean I was there after she found the first set of remains. She was so awesome."

Once again Woody noticed the word was. He let his gaze wander back to the remains they'd just uncovered. Blonde or gray? Was the corpse too petite, or was he simply being optimistic? No, Ken's bones would definitely have more heft. She was tough—not a lightweight. Plus, there was that tweed fabric. Ken would never wear tweed.

He glanced back at the young assistant.

Her cheeks were polished red apples.

"No problem," he said at last. "This isn't Detective Dean. And by the way, I like to see enthusiasm in my coworkers. And Ms. Dagwan," he looked directly at the senior assistant, "let me know if either of you come up with any more ideas we might not have thought of, all right?"

Brandi nodded. "Of course—"

Moment over, Woody knelt and laid a thin sheet of tracing paper on top of the victim's exposed femur and began to rub it gently with the nub of a pencil.

The two assistants watched in silence.

The Medical Examiner crouched over the shallow grave opposite the big detective. She motioned for her girls to add more light to the scene, and they quickly obliged by redirecting one of the portables they had hauled up from the equipment van.

Woody rubbed the femur patiently. The tracing paper and pencil were things Kendra had always insisted they keep in their clipboards. They sometimes used them on the job to raise messages on "blank-appearing" paper notepads as well as old, worn serial numbers on weapons and other crime scene items.

As he worked on the bones, Woody let his mind wander in order to keep it from reminding him he was handling a woman's thighbone.

He recalled doing gravestone rubbings even as a kid when his dad had taken the family to visit Tombstone, Arizona. They'd also visited Billy the Kid's grave in Fort Sumner, New Mexico. The whole trip his mother had chided his father for teaching the kids to "worship outlaws."

Thinking of their "outlaw" vacation reminded him of Stutter Creek's historic Drugstore Café, a place where Billy the Kid and other outlaws had sometimes hidden from the law in a crawl space beneath the kitchen floorboards. The Café even boasted an official plaque on its old wooden sidewalk immortalizing that very fact.

Woody roused himself from his reverie and held the tracing paper up to the light. His eyes met those of the M.E., and her eyebrows went up, but he didn't try to discuss the findings in front of the others. Another thing he had learned from Kendra was to keep things as quiet as possible for as long as possible. "Too many cooks spoil the broth," she had often preached during his rookie days.

When they were out of earshot of the others, he handed the rubbing to Lois Campanelli. "More latitude and longitude lines?"

The woman shook her head. "I don't think so. There *are* numbers, but they are different somehow." She held the paper up and pointed to a letter.

Woody could make out what appeared to be 88 W 15 N 17 D. His eyebrows went up again. "If these are latitude and longitude coordinates like before, then he wrote them backward. 88 degrees west is the longitude, and 15 degrees north is latitude. They should be reversed. But then we have what appears to be 17 D? What the hell is D? That's not a compass point no matter how it's written. Or carved."

The confusion in his voice made the woman laugh. "You're reading between lines that we aren't even sure are there yet."

He frowned. He was itching to get out into the woods with the other search groups looking for Kendra, but he also knew the best way to find her was to find their perp. So he held onto his patience like a treasure. "Enlighten me, please."

Keith trailed behind them.

The M.E. continued walking. "D isn't any sort of direction. Not one that I know of, at least." She shrugged. "I'll plug the numbers into my GPS and see what pops up."

The sheriff ambled along talking on his cell phone.

Woody stopped every few feet and looked back at the scene. It was lit up like a movie set with all the assistants hard at work to uncover the remains while preserving as much evidence as possible.

He took the paper back from the M.E. and studied it as they walked. The bright lights extended onto the trail from battery operated "snake lights" hanging from the lower branches of trees. "I don't get it," he said. "What could it be? Why is it different?"

"This one is very recent," Sheriff Puckett said from behind them. "That means he's had to change his M.O."

Woody and the M.E. turned toward the sound of his voice. Even though the trail was lighted, the dark shapes of trees were close, the leafy smell of mold even closer. As he was thinking about their surroundings, and wondering where the hell Kendra was (he wouldn't even let himself entertain the thought that she *wasn't* simply lost) the snow began to make itself known again. The fine flakes quickly changed back to feathers, falling faster and thicker.

"This can't be right," the M.E. said. She touched the screen on her Garmin as if to recheck the data.

"Can't find the location?" Woody was barely able to curtail his sarcasm.

"Oh, I found it all right. But it sure isn't around here."

"Let me guess," Woody said. "It's the middle of the ocean."

She shrugged. "Not exactly. It appears to be Central America. Honduras, I think. If I plugged the numbers in correctly, that is."

"What the hell?" Woody reached for her Garmin to see for himself.

"Playing with us," the sheriff said. "Screwing with us just like he did with the Christmas present and the woman in clover. Letting us know we're out of our element. That he is smarter than we are."

"That's right," the M.E. replied. "The first two sets of remains were above ground, uncovered, and perfectly arranged. This one is completely different. And I don't *even* know what to do with 17 D."

"I'm sure he'll let us know, somehow." Sheriff Puckett removed his hat and shook snowflakes off the brim.

Woody recalled how the man had been drenched in sweat only a few moments earlier. He felt his own pulse rising. He longed to be in the car, going somewhere, doing something, rather than standing around speculating, doing nothing—but again, he reined in his emotions. Focus, he thought. *Focus.*

"I just realized there are no degree symbols," the M.E. murmured. "All the other bones had degree symbols after the numerals. This time, there are no degree symbols, we simply assumed these were map coordinates like the others." She swiped stray hair off her forehead. "Maybe it isn't Honduras after all. But you know, when those two boys found the second set of remains, it was easy to go back and suss out the missing number on the femur of the remains Kendra had found—the one we call Clover Girl—and the coordinates matched up. Apparently the killer had carved the second girl's grave coordinates on the femur of the first girl."

"So is it possible the coordinates on the second set of remains somehow correspond with this set? Or could there be something else missing?"

Lois held her hands up in a you-got-me gesture. "We'll soon find out. I've got a tech attempting to clean the femur without damaging the carving. Let's see if he has come up with anything." She pressed a number on her cell phone and spoke to someone in the lab. She then pulled up her GPS system and typed in the coordinates as he gave them to her. "Here goes." She typed the numbers from the second set of remains—the Christmas gift—into the search bar and immediately got a hit on a topographical map. She held the phone up to the sheriff. "Does this location ring any bells with you?"

The sheriff took her phone and looked at the coordinates she had entered, and then he took out his phone and looked at the coordinates he had sent to the dispatcher. "Nope. It isn't this one. He's *more* than one step ahead of us."

The M.E. sighed. "That's what I was afraid of. So why change the numbers on this femur? Just to keep us on our toes?"

"Maybe," Woody said. "But we also saw how hurried this one appeared to be—maybe that's why the carving is so different—or maybe you're right and he's just playing with us." He stopped walking. "Or what if there is another body? One in between the last one and this one? Or even more than one? I don't think we were supposed to find this one right away. So far he's been *unburying* the ones he wants us to find, and this one was obviously just buried."

The others remained silent.

Finally, the sheriff spoke. "We need Chet Boone here. He knows these woods like the insides of his own eyelids. He might be able to figure out what 17 D represents." He began to poke at the keypad on his phone. "I'll ask him to come down to the station. John Stockton is supposed to meet us there to make his official statement."

They started down the trail toward the roadside turnaround where most of the vehicles were parked. The sheriff said, "We can always put the numbers into the big screen back at the station—pull up a satellite map. See if that gives us any clues."

Yeah, Woody thought grimly. *Maybe the gravesites will all line up like a giant arrow pointing to the exact spot where we can find Kendra.* He chided himself for being so negative, and then he realized Lois Campanelli was speaking again.

"Besides the strange un-coordinates carved into the femur this time, let's think about the other differences in this body versus the first two."

"There's the condition of the body," Woody said. "None of the others had been treated with chemicals—"

"That we know of," Lois interjected. "So far the other remains were mostly skeletal. This one is much more recent."

Woody tried to say something else, something about how strange it was that the perp seemed to plan out his burial sites, but his voice would no longer fit past the huge lump of fear sitting on the back of his tongue. Just knowing the guy was still out there, killing, was enough to make him doubt his convictions about the identity of the remains.

Lois must have heard the break in his voice. She patted his arm. "Actually we haven't got *all* the postmortem results yet. Three corpses in six days is about two too many for our tiny department—but we're doing the best we can. However, what I was going to say is that those other bodies may have been treated with chemicals at one time. Over the years, the stuff could have simply seeped into the ground."

Woody nodded. He was doing his best to hold himself together, but the longer they discussed the bodies and the remains, the more he wanted to jump in the car and start searching. It wasn't logical, it wasn't the way he was trained, and Kendra certainly wouldn't have approved—if she were here. *But she isn't. And that's the whole problem.*

Nevertheless, he couldn't shake the feeling that she was somehow nearby. He knew her far too well to ever believe she would have gone down without a fight, without leaving a trail of destruction in her wake, but this body they'd just uncovered. It was definitely recent. And it was definitely wearing tweed. That plus the fact that the doc—who was supposedly the last person to see Kendra face to face—hadn't been seen since the day he had interviewed him at the clinic added up to one very fat coincidence.

And we don't believe in coincidences now, do we?

That little niggling voice sounded suspiciously like Kendra's.

He rolled his shoulders and straightened his spine. Don't worry, Ken. I will find you. Even if it's the last thing I ever do.

Keith caught up to him and asked what the medical examiner had been talking about with the coordinates and femur carvings, so Woody gave him a thumbnail version of the case so far. "That's really all we know at this moment except for the fact that the last place your mom was known to have visited was the doctor's clinic—and then she was supposed to meet me in Pine River to review another case, and when she didn't show, that's when I discovered she was missing."

"And she was the one who found the first set of remains six days ago, is that correct?" Keith stared into Woody's face as if it were very important that he understand the timeline here.

Woody knew how he felt. Sometimes details were the only things one could cling to at times like this. "That's exactly right, Keith." He gripped the boy's shoulder. "So now we've got to concentrate on putting all these little nitpicking puzzle pieces together so we can get an idea of exactly what this creep has done and where."

Keith dropped his gaze to the ground, and Woody knew he was struggling to keep his emotions in check. "Thank you." His voice was rough. "But there are lots of others out there searching, right?"

Woody assured him there were. Practically every able-bodied person in Stutter Creek and half the law enforcement officers from Pine River were out and about—doing as much as the moonlight would allow. The sheriff and Roger Brown, the Chief of Police, had both made it very clear that no civilians were to be wandering about the woods alone or even in pairs after the sun went down. "We can't risk an accident on account of someone's being overzealous. Detective Dean wouldn't be on board with that. Not at all."

Fortunately, with John Stockton and Chet Boone heading up the daylight civilian search teams, Woody felt confident that everything that could be done would be done. The only thorn in his side was the fact that with the discovery of each new victim, that many more officers were pulled away from the search in order to work the crime scenes.

But there was nothing he could do about that. It simply meant he would have to work that much harder to put the clues together.

CHAPTER FORTY-ONE

Feel It in His Bones

The four of them arrived back at the sheriff's car, and Woody spied Rory's Taurus parked a little way further down the road. He asked the sheriff to wait a moment while he walked Keith to his vehicle.

"I'm going back to the motel," Keith said. "I left you a voicemail with my number."

Woody nodded and pulled out his phone. He was surprised he hadn't heard the call. "I'll let you know when we find her. We will, you know. We've had teams of searchers out for the past two days, combing the mountains and the area around the lake. But we can't do much at night, and now this…"

Keith looked away. "I know you'll do everything you can. By the way, I called my father. He's on his way, too." He looked at Woody. "I thought it was the best thing—"

"Of course it is," Woody agreed. "I tried to call him myself the day I realized she was missing." He left off without saying he had never received a response. He hadn't heard his phone earlier; perhaps Bill hadn't heard his either.

Keith started to get into the Taurus and then stopped. "Mind if I ask you something?"

Woody's gut clenched. He knew what was coming. It felt like Thanksgiving dinner and the unasked questions. "Go ahead. I'll tell you anything I can."

With one foot inside the vehicle, Keith gazed out over the hood toward the dark woods. "You and my mom...are you the reason my dad left?"

Woody resisted the urge to spout off a smart remark about how the man had deserted Kendra in her darkest hour—after the robbery suspect had committed suicide—

instead he replied, "I don't know what happened. Your mom never spoke badly of your father, not even once. I think she was as surprised by his departure as anyone."

Keith looked at him then. "Seriously? She never told you they were having problems?"

Woody shook his head. "That's the thing I admire most about your mother, although she expects me, and everyone else in law enforcement, to strive for perfection on the job, she is also the most forgiving person I know when someone screws up—unless you cross her on purpose." He grinned. "And then it's time to give your heart to God because—"

"—your ass belongs to Mama. Yes, I know that side of her very well myself." Keith swiped at his eyes with his sleeve again. "You love her, don't you?"

Woody hesitated a split second too long. "I think the world of her." His face belied his words, but he didn't feel like this was the time to stir the broth.

He assured Keith he'd be in touch as soon as they knew anything more, and then he watched as the young man drove away, a very different individual from the cocky college student he'd been on Thanksgiving Day. Woody hated that change. It made him feel helpless. When the Taurus was out of sight, Woody walked back to the sheriff's cruiser and climbed into the back seat.

The sheriff was speaking. "Sure glad those SCA kids worked on these trails all summer. They were clear right up to the point we had to get off the path and onto the private property. To be honest with you, I didn't even know anyone could own private property up here." He cleared his throat gruffly. "I thought the state of New Mexico owned this whole mountain."

"Student Conservation Association, huh?" Woody couldn't keep the concern from his voice. "Bunch of teenagers on summer vacation?"

The sheriff grunted in affirmation. "Yeah, they come every year when school is out—it's a government funded program, they clear debris, stuff like that—" he went suddenly silent.

Woody filled in the gap. "You would know if any of them had gone missing, right?" He had a sudden image of tanned teens with backpacks roaming the woods with a serial killer in their midst. "I mean you would have been the first to know."

"Of course I would," the sheriff agreed. "But that's three sets of remains we've got now, and only one report of a missing person—the dog walker from Yellow Bend. I'd say it's time we head back over to Dr. Stevens' home. Based on that swatch of tweed, I'd say we need to find both him *and* his wife." He adjusted his hat. "And I'll sure be glad to find out who owns that chunk of land these poor gals keep turning up on. Got Stu Armand down at the tax office now, going through the records."

Woody settled back in his seat. "My gut says the dog walker is not victim number two, the Christmas gift. She hasn't been missing that long. But if he used a chemical to decompose her, then maybe—"

The sheriff started the car. "I think it's possible. Anyway, we got a DNA sample from her sister for comparison just in case. Too bad it could take six weeks or more for the results to come in. And that first set of remains, the one Detective Dean found, are so old we'll be lucky if we ever identify them." He picked up his radio mic and told the deputy on scene to call him if necessary.

"There's a pattern," Woody said. "And a trigger that made him start displaying his wares so-to-speak." He took out a small spiral notebook and began to make notes using the scant light of the moon. "Let's look at the differences again. First, this body was fresh. Second, the carvings were different. No degree symbols—no little circles at all—and he was very careful to include those on the other bones."

The M.E. added, "And then there's the matter of that third number, 17 D. What that is, I have no earthly idea. But it certainly is not a compass point in this world. Maybe on Mars or some place."

Woody scratched the stubble on his chin. The lack of sleep was beginning to catch up to him.

"Hope we don't have a damn copy-cat," Sheriff Puckett said. "Someone who simply read about it and decided to try his hand at bone-carving."

"Yeah," Woody snorted. "Some idiot who doesn't know how latitude and longitude should be written."

Lois Campanelli shook her head. "That's pretty far-fetched." She adjusted the heater vent and held her hands in front of it, rubbing them together as she spoke. "I tend to agree with your first opinion, Sheriff."

Woody looked at the sheriff.

"That he is toying with us? I'm afraid that makes the most sense to me, too, especially if it is the doc. And if this is his wife—then he's probably done. There's no going back. He's always struck me as an egotistical prick anyhow. And then there's that Christmas theme on vic number two. That was downright twisted."

Woody spoke up, "All right, then. We all seem to be in agreement that the numbers may not be latitude and longitude coordinates, right?"

Both heads nodded. "Definitely," the M.E. said. "We already know that if they were map coordinates that location would be in Central America anyway."

Woody stretched his long legs out sideways and sat back to think things through.

The sheriff said, "Got the judge out of bed to issue a search warrant. We'll pick it up on the way. I understand your office has a couple more detectives on the clock."

"Yes. We're staying in touch by phone. In addition to off-duty officers volunteering to search, we also have the Missing Persons detectives going through Ken's files, checking to see if this is somehow connected to any of her previous cases." He pulled a toothpick from the silver holder in his shirt pocket. When he had it positioned just right in the corner of his mouth, he continued, "But we all know it isn't. That's just being thorough. Her finding that first set of remains—that was the catalyst. Even though it was just a case of bad luck, stumbling upon them out here near the lake."

He leaned back in the seat and the warmth of the heater lulled him into a doze. It had been a long couple of days. On top of the extra hours he'd been putting in on Kendra's other case, the suicide, Woody couldn't remember the last time he'd slept more than a few minutes.

As he drifted away, Kendra appeared beside him in the back seat.

She entered his head and began to talk as if she'd been in the conversation all along.

"I don't think these are latitude/longitude coordinates, either. But I'm not jumping to conclusions."

Woody knew he was asleep, but he didn't want Kendra to stop talking, so he played along. Even in his dream state, he played along. "Okay. I get that," his dream-self agreed. "Obviously this clue or whatever is completely different. But why? What changed?" He imagined himself shoving his toothpick from one corner of his mouth to the other. For a moment, that almost woke him, and then his tongue found the pick he'd stuck in his mouth before dozing, and that somehow solved the dream/reality overlap.

Finally, he said, "If we figure out why this one's different, we might figure *him* out."

"Right," Kendra replied. "That is one thing we agree on." She slipped into the driver's seat—which was somehow no longer filled by the large frame of the sheriff—and Woody felt the car engine begin to rev.

"I need coffee," driver-Kendra said. "Let's hit The Drugstore."

He felt the car begin to roll, but he couldn't keep his sleeping persona from glancing back at the scene. "Coffee, now? Are you sure? I've never known you to be the first to leave a scene."

"It's the new me," Ken said. "Less about control, more about delegating authority." She looked at him—he was now in the passenger seat instead of the back seat—and he felt as if her stare must surely wake him. "What?" she demanded. "I can do that. I can delegate. Or don't you remember?"

Woody stared back at her. Somehow *knowing* he was dreaming was almost too much to handle. "Who are you and what have you done with my old partner?"

The dream-Kendra snorted. "Smart ass. Just drive."

He looked ahead and found that *he* was now in the driver's seat.

So he drove.

Kendra rolled her window partway down.

The wintry air circulated through the car and once again, Woody felt sure he would awaken in the back seat of the sheriff's car, legs cramped and toothpick dangling.

"Look at us." Kendra pulled down the vanity mirror on her side of the car. "I'm old, and you're getting there. These late nights are taking their toll."

Woody rubbed the stubble on his chin.

She sighed. "Wonder when the old brain cells will start to die off—or have they already? What the hell is that third number, Woods, 17 D? It makes no sense."

To his surprise, she produced an overlarge, cartoonish looking smart phone and typed the numbers into Google, and then Bing, then every other search engine she could pull up.

"Listen." She read her findings. They varied from a mini-John Deere excavator known as the 17D (which Woody had once rented to help his dad dig a backyard pond for his mom), to a vaccine for yellow fever called 17D, to a B57-17D Flying Fortress plane from WWII.

She even found some metro lines known as 17D, but they were in Minnesota and neither of them thought that could possibly be a connection. "It has to be something right here under our noses," she said.

Woody was amazed that his sleeping brain could come up with all those things—even though he realized all that information had to be stored in his brain already, somehow. And then he was amazed all over again that his sleeping brain somehow *knew* he was sleeping. *I know about the John Deere because I used one of those in the past, but what about all those other things? Are they real, or is my exhausted mind simply making them up?*

Then another thought struck him. *Is any of this real?*

He began to doubt the dream—I'll wake soon, he thought—I have to.

Beside him, Kendra opened her ever-present mini spiral notebook. It looked suspiciously like the one he'd been jotting notes in a few minutes earlier.

Where are you, Ken? His mind asked. But the dream-Kendra ignored him and began to brainstorm words beginning with the letter D. The first word she wrote was Direction. "Maybe he's deliberately trying to deceive us," she said. Then she wrote *deceive* followed by more and more words. She said each one aloud as she wrote it.

Direction

Deceive

Deliberate

Deception

Depth

Death

Deep

Dig

Die

Die trying (Woody added that one, which made Kendra's eyebrows go up dramatically.)

Deal

Dream

When she said that last one, Kendra looked at him with an expression that was almost comical. Then she said, "That reminds me of how I found those first remains on that lovely bed of clover. You remember that, don't you, Woods?"

Woody did indeed remember it. They had planned to meet after that, but then things got squirrely, and they'd never had the chance. He looked at her dreamy form in the passenger's seat and was surprised to see tiny pink flowers in her hair.

"Dirt," she said, adding the word to her list. "Snow covers up the dirt, you know. It covers everything."

Woody felt something in his chest lurch as if he'd just seen a ghost. To the list, he told Kendra to add Down, as in down in the dirt.

And Done, as in "I'm done, this is my last one. I've killed sixteen others; this is number seventeen, the last one. 17 D. Seventeen and Done."

"Where did that thought come from?" Kendra asked.

Woody shrugged. "I heard it somewhere."

Kendra closed her eyes. "Trying to think like a killer isn't easy. Besides, it's all conjecture. Sometimes they fit a profile, sometimes they don't. This one seems to be very methodical and very smart. So smart that he keeps changing the game in the middle—changing horses in midstream as they say."

"So smart."

"He *thinks* he's so smart, doesn't he?" she asked out loud.

Woody waited to see if there was any more before he answered. "Well, I guess he is pretty smart. He's killing and getting away with it. Then leaving us all these cryptic carvings as clues—"

"Stop with the alliteration," she demanded.

"I don't even know what that means."

Kendra opened one eye. "Seriously? You never took high school English?"

"I surfed," Woody grumped. "I read a few books. Diagrammed a couple sentences or something."

Kendra guffawed, and Woody felt certain she was right there beside him. "But you write such eloquent reports," she joked. His reports were famous around the station for their brevity and their colorful, phonetically misspelled words.

"I just assumed—"

She stopped him in midsentence. "Never assume. We both know better than that. To assume just makes an ass of u and me. We first assumed that he's some kind of mapmaker or something, but we need to stop assuming anything."

Woody was perplexed. "But we already know it's the doctor." Or am I just assuming that? Is that what she's trying to tell me? Just because she saw him before she disappeared doesn't mean something else didn't happen after she left there. Maybe that isn't even his wife in that grave. Could the tweed be the red herring? Oh my God, what if the two of them are in it together?

He shook his sleeping self mildly, and then tried to make his body sit up straighter.

"Go on," he said.

Kendra kept talking as if he hadn't spoken. "What if he's a gamer? And those coordinates are for one of those geo cache games or something—you know, for others to find? Hidden away from view. I've heard you can be right on top of the coordinates and not find the treasure. Know what I mean?"

Woody nodded. "Or maybe he does the carving as art. He could be an artist, right? An artist *and* a doctor. I mean the remains are staged so perfectly, like pictures in a gallery."

Kendra nodded. "Right, right. We've been assuming too much. Letting the press lead us around by our noses. The Cartographer. Bah. The numbers may not have anything to do with maps at all other than those first coordinates—and they could have a totally different meaning than we realize. In fact, could the killer be a woman? Could there be more than one killer?"

Now that they'd broken the first chain, she was on a roll.

Woody kept his thoughts to himself. He knew when she was on a roll it was best not to interrupt, even if she were nothing more than a dream. He grinned around his toothpick, caught himself doing it, and literally wiped the smile away on the pretext of removing the toothpick from his mouth. He was so thrilled to have her back again; he wasn't about to jeopardize it by waking himself up.

They pulled up in front of The Drugstore, and he cut the engine.

Kendra's eyes were far away; it was obvious she was studying something inside her head.

"Ready, boss?" He opened his door and climbed out. This was the woman he'd fallen for all those years ago. Super smart, super focused, super sexy.

Since she hadn't moved, he walked around and opened her car door even though she hated that.

She unbuckled her seatbelt. "What am I? Friggin' helpless or something?"

He pushed another grin off his face with the palm of his hand. "Apparently you are. You've been sitting there like a zombie. What do I have to do to get you out of the car, wave a raw steak under your nose?" He stood back when he said that.

Kendra stepped out and flipped him the bird.

Woody closed the door behind her. "So tell me more about this alliteration stuff. I'm seriously suspicious that you're just trying to make an old surfer-dude feel foolish."

Kendra ignored him and opened the door to the café. The little overhead doorbell tinkled merrily.

Woody jerked awake.

The toothpick fell from his mouth, and the spiral notebook slid down to the floorboard. The ballpoint pen was still clutched tightly between his fingers.

The seatbelt alarm was dinging *bing bing bing bing bing* as Sheriff Puckett got out of the car.

Woody turned and stared at the black mountain. They had left the artificial lights behind, and the sun had set some time ago. It was snowing again, and it was cold. The frozen bones were still up there in their shallow, newly opened grave. There were people there, doing their jobs, but Woody couldn't help but feel he was abandoning someone. Even though he knew it wasn't Ken.

He tucked his pen and notebook back inside his jacket. What if that really had been Kendra? What if it was her spirit come to show me where to find her and help identify her kil—

He cut that thought off and followed Lois and the sheriff into the office.

Woody said, "I should get my car while we're in town."

The sheriff took him aside. "Don't go off on a wild goose chase. Remember, I need you to go to the doc's house with me."

Woody agreed, but it was only to appease the sheriff. He needed to be out searching. He could feel Kendra calling him. He could feel it in *his* bones.

CHAPTER FORTY-TWO
Dr. Death

Kendra came to wearing a frozen halo of pain.

Everything hurt, but at least she had her wits about her. She knew exactly where she was and why. Without waiting for the pity party to start, Kendra turned over on her belly and started to crawl. The shivering was so severe her chattering teeth caught the tip of her tongue, but she was so cold she didn't care.

She had managed to fall into the deepest part of the ravine. To make things worse, recent rains had softened the steep sides. Loose shale lay scattered all around her. It was the same area where Nicky Webb's pup had been found months earlier. Kendra had no idea how she would get back up the precipitous slope, but she knew she had no choice.

Here and there were tiny plants—saplings of some kind—that she used as handholds as she inched her way diagonally across the wall of the ravine. Twice she lost her grip and felt herself sliding backward, scraping more skin off her belly in the process. But she never slid all the way back. Each time she would simply dig in her toes and wait for friction to stop her. The handcuffs actually helped. What she couldn't grasp with her stiff, nearly useless fingers, she could nab with the chain or dig into using the iron plate.

Every few minutes she would have to rest and will the world to stop spinning. *Most likely a mild concussion. But nothing to do except keep going.* "Don't let them go to sleep." That's what she'd always been told when her children were playing high school sports. In case of head injury, "get to the doctor fast and keep them awake until you get there." *Ha-ha. Fooled you all. Got my nap already, and I'm not dead. Not even close.*

She licked up a mouthful of snow and let it melt on her tongue.

Thanks to her exertions the shivering had lessened somewhat and the snow soothed her thirst. Thanks to the cold, she barely felt the painful throbbing of her lips and face. As she realized the extent of her injuries, anger flooded back into her body. *Bastard*, she thought. *You'll pay for this.* She welcomed the red-hot emotion as if it were a warm, fuzzy blanket.

And then she stopped to rest again.

But she didn't stay still for long.

Her body began to ache where the snow had touched her exposed torso and hands. She bent her knees and pushed herself upward once again. From the air, one would have thought her a human crab scuttling across the side of the ravine in slow motion.

She tried to focus on something other than the pain. She imagined Woody talking to her. His face appeared in her mind's eye like a carrot in front of a horse. *I'm coming, Ken,* she imagined him saying. *You just tell me where you are, and I'll be there. We'll catch him together. But first, I've got to find you. Just tell me where you are.*

Kendra renewed her efforts.

Inch by torturous inch, she dragged herself sideways and upwards across the rough ground. Her fingernails were short. She was able to grasp the smallest plant and dig into the earth without bending the nails backward. She dug her toes in, too. And it was in this manner that, in less than an hour, she crested the lip of the ravine and lay like a dead thing, frozen feet hanging off in space behind her.

She cupped her hands in front of her mouth and breathed into them to warm the cold air and thaw her burning blue fingers. The steel cuffs were narrow bands of pain around her wrists, the frozen landscape a cruel lover tenderly soothing the pain of her injuries one moment, savagely inflicting more in the next.

I'm here, Woods. She conjured an image of the ravine in her mind and tried to send it with her message. She didn't believe or disbelieve in ESP or spiritual connections. She just knew he would find her if she showed him the way. *I'm here, Woody, right here.*

She curled her miserable body into a fetal position to conserve warmth around her core, and then she dozed.

***

He waited until she was all the way to the top of the ravine. He'd just crept away from watching the fun at his latest site when he spied her crabbing her way up the side. He was filthy from head to toe, blood mixed with grave dirt. He'd showered at home, but that had been several hours earlier. His darling Candy hadn't even been completely dry when he'd wrestled her into the shallow grave. Without realizing it, he'd wiped her blood across his face more than once.

Adding to his demented look was an expensive pair of infrared field glasses hanging around his neck. They certainly came in handy at night. *One more thing Candy won't be able to nag me about—expensive toys.*

Injuries no longer an issue due to the pain pills, the doctor hunkered down and waited until he was certain Kendra Dean was either asleep or unconscious inside her gray hoodie.

He raised the glasses to his eyes. Even with the expensive binoculars, she was little more than a wet lump curled up in the snow. *Perhaps I should simply leave her. She'll freeze to death soon enough, and the snow will cover her completely, possibly until spring. By then my car will be at the bottom of a cliff and I'll be in*

Mexico, maybe even farther south. Hope they appreciate me when I'm gone. I'm giving them everything but a map, just to make it interesting. But maybe I should have left them a map, too. I am The Killer Cartographer, after all. He chuckled at the thought, but he knew he wouldn't be able to simply leave her like that. She owed him something. And that something could only be paid in blood.

When he was certain she had stopped moving, he lowered the glasses and began to make his way toward her. He was amazed she'd made it out of the ravine at all, especially in that area. He was much farther along the top of the ravine, in a little crossover he'd used before. It was tucked away in a thick stand of trees and boulders right at the edge of his land. It was one of his favorite places. *His* woods.

Back at the house, he'd stuffed his winter hiking boots and socks into the passenger seat of his car. The trunk had been full. Candy may have been petite, but rolled up in their fat bedspread she had taken up a surprising amount of space.

There had also been quite a bit of blood and gore. He'd made an unholy mess with the chemicals, but it couldn't be helped, he'd been rushed.

He wasn't worried about that now, though. That chapter of his life had ended. Candy and her baby-fetish had put the quietus to that. Now, he had a new plan. A grand one. But first, there was the little matter of Detective Know-it-all.

As he crept along the edge of the ravine, he pulled another plastic-encased safety scalpel from his pocket. His lug-soled hikers gripped the bitter ground leaving deep imprints in the snow. Every few minutes he stopped and raised the field glasses again. The detective appeared to be unconscious or dead.

He continued toward her, the snow muffling his movements. He wasn't worried about the cops or searchers. Right now everyone was focused on his most recent girl, not this one. Besides, he'd seen the majority of the volunteers enjoying coffee and hot chocolate back at The Drugstore Café. He'd driven back in front of it only a few hours earlier with Candy packed securely in the trunk.

Soon he had crossed the boulder-strewn area separating the trail from the lip of the narrow ravine. This time, he didn't hesitate. *This time, I'll do what I should have done three days ago.*

She never stirred until he grabbed a fistful of hoodie along with a wad of her hair. With a grunt, he yanked her head back and raised the scalpel high.

Moonlight walked along the edge of the blade.

"Woods?"

The doctor cackled with glee. "Yes, you stupid cow. You're in the woods. My woods—Dr. Death." He didn't know where that had come from, but he wanted to be certain she knew exactly who had bested her. He wanted her to know who was ending her life. "Look at my face!" He crushed her head back exposing her throat to the cold night air. In his other hand, the scalpel was poised to slash. "Look what you did to me."

The snow had stopped falling; the clouds scudded away. Soft light illuminated his blood-streaked face.

Silence enveloped them.

He pulled her head back even farther. His moment of triumph was at hand, but his adversary was so weak it was like an anticlimax. She'd been so strong, so unpredictable; now she was nothing. Beaten by the elements, not by him.

Disgusted, he drove the blade toward her throat. He was ready to be done with her once and for all.

Kendra wrenched her head to the side.

A minute sound like ripping Velcro left him holding a loose wad of hoodie and a few strands of wavy gray hair.

Unable to stand, Kendra straightened her legs and rolled.

"Stupid *bitch*." The hoodie slipped from his grasp and he shook away the hair. "You can't get away from me. There's no place for you to go." He followed her, laughing, as she rolled up against a boulder. "And when they find my corpse in my burning car at the bottom of Jumper's Point, I'll be home free."

While he talked, the detective managed to get into a semi-sitting position, back shoved up against the solid rock.

Holding the surgical instrument like a tiny dagger, the doc stabbed at her arms and face with short thrusts, enjoying the way she cringed and jerked.

Just like in the hidey-hole, Kendra lashed out with her booted feet.

He sidestepped her easily. "No, no, no." He wagged the scalpel back and forth in front of her eyes like a shaming finger. "Fool me once, shame on you, fool me twice? Not in this lifetime." He lunged forward, slashing and stabbing with maniacal glee. *Guess there's a bit of life left in the old girl after all!*

Kendra held her cuffed hands in front of her face and continued to kick at his knees and ankles. Being wedged up against the large boulder turned out to be a blessing. He couldn't get behind her, and the solid rock gave her something to push against each time she kicked at him with her booted feet.

"No-o-o!" he shouted. He couldn't believe she was on the ground and he still couldn't get close enough to her jugular to end it. Moments earlier, he'd been certain she was on the verge of death.

He renewed his efforts, slashing at her feet and legs with abandon. The short blade drew blood several times, but she managed to kick it away more often than not.

Her hands were also gashed, and the thick sleeves of her sweatshirt were striped with blood. But she was still alive. And she seemed to be getting *stronger.*

In desperation, he fell on her, thrusting the scalpel toward her throat.

She held the square of metal between her hands like a small shield. It deflected the scalpel blade so that it skated harmlessly off into space beside her head.

The force of his thrust caused him to overbalance and fall forward.

Kendra pushed her face forward and sank her teeth into his nose.

The doctor bellowed, and she bit down even harder.

He yanked the scalpel up and would have plunged it into the side of her head, but his jerky movement tore the end of his nose clean off.

She had bitten right through the fleshy tip.

The scalpel fell to the ground as the madman collapsed back onto his haunches, blood spraying over his lips and chin.

Kendra spat the tiny mess into the snow and lashed out with both feet.

This time, she caught him directly in the solar plexus.

With a roar of surprise, the off-balance murderer flung out his arms and tried to stand. Instead, he tumbled backward over the edge of the ravine. For a split second, he resembled the famous statue of Jesus looking out over the city of Rio de Janeiro.

And then he was gone.

Kendra rolled to her hands and knees and started to crawl.

CHAPTER FORTY-THREE

Back to Clover

Woody got in the Mercury and followed the sheriff toward the doctor's house. He'd been amazed to learn how close the doc's house was to Ella Webb's. Later she would confess to him—over coffee at The Drugstore—how she'd found an ink pen from the doctor's clinic just outside her back door. She asked Woody if he thought the doc might have been the creeper that day. "I do," Woody had nodded. "In fact, I think you're lucky to be alive.

Today it appeared no one was home at the doctor's house.

They were sitting in the drive with lights flashing, but they were certain he was long gone. And they were nearly certain they knew the horrific whereabouts of Candy Stevens.

Nevertheless, good police work demanded they follow every precaution. In light of that, Woody kept watch over the front door, and Sheriff Puckett guarded the back.

The house was dark; windows blank.

Nothing stirred.

Just like at Kendra's lake house, the garage doors were solid—not even a window to peek through. *No doubt the chickens have flown the coop. I wish that were the only reason it felt so deserted.* But in his mind, Woody knew what they would find once they got inside.

He was right.

Once they'd determined no one was around, the sheriff broke the glass on the front door and reached inside to unlock it.

No alarm sounded. "Guess he didn't think of that," Sheriff Puckett muttered, flipping on the light switch as he spoke.

The two of them went in low, guns drawn.

The living room and dining room appeared normal, but the kitchen showed signs of a struggle. Smears of blood led them to the garage door.

Sheriff Puckett nodded at Woody, who flung it open and stepped aside.

The sheriff reached in and flicked that light on, too. The only vehicle in the two-car garage was a silver Subaru. The other side of the garage was empty, but they could easily follow the blood trail to the place where the vehicle had been.

With barely a glance between them, the two men made their way back through the kitchen and down the hall toward what they assumed would be the master bedroom.

Smears of blood stained the oyster colored carpet all the way. Shaking his head, the sheriff motioned for Woody to follow his lead.

Avoiding the fresh stains as much as possible, they made it to the bedroom door and found it had been kicked in. The bedroom walls were splashed with blood.

They crossed to the master bath. "He cleaned up in here. Bloody clothing on the floor and God only knows what in the bathtub." The sheriff was careful not to touch anything with his hands, and he seemed to follow the exact same path back across the bedroom floor. "Bedspread's missing. Don't touch anything until we get the crime scene techs out here."

Then he continued, "In light of the number of remains we're finding, and the fact that a detective is missing, I've requested assistance from the FBI in Albuquerque."

Woody didn't say anything he simply nodded. He knew it was the right thing to do; he just hoped they wouldn't come in and muddy the waters.

The sheriff called headquarters on his cell phone. "Find out what kind of car is registered to Dr. Edgar Stevens, and put out an Attempt to Locate. Mention that he's armed and extremely dangerous."

"Look at this." Woody bent over beside the tub and picked up something that looked like an empty bottle of bleach, only this one was marked Hydrochloric Acid. "Why would a doctor have industrial strength cleaning fluid? Could this melt someone?"

The sheriff nodded. "Not looking good for Mrs. Stevens, is it?"

Woody shook his head and set the container aside as evidence. That swatch of tweed fabric had pretty well convinced him it was her body in the shallow grave, but there was always a possibility the doc did that to throw them off.

The forensics van arrived, and the same techs got out and began pulling on paper booties over their shoes. They were becoming more experienced with each scene.

Woody told the sheriff he was going to the Antler's Motel to check in with Kendra's family. He was getting tired of playing catch up with this killer. It was time to go on the offensive. *I need to start my own search, but where to begin? What was that she'd said about a drowned tree? Wasn't that where she first felt as if she were being watched? And isn't that what led her to the girl in clover?* He thought of the tiny pink flowers in dream-Kendra's hair. *Is that what she was trying to tell me?*

He started toward the lake.

As he drove, he reminisced about the other case he'd worked in Stutter Creek. It had been Turk and John Stockton who had tracked the missing woman to Blue Cave. *So why haven't we given Turk something from Ken, something with her scent, to help track her?*

He pulled out his phone and called the sheriff to get John's number. "Already done," the sheriff replied. "John asked for an article of clothing as soon as we put him in charge of the search. We went back to her house and found a sweater in the hamper. John carries it with them each time they go out."

CHAPTER FORTY-FOUR
Red Flag

Kendra pulled the string from her hoodie and tied a large bow on a small plant at the edge of the ravine. Looking down, she could see the opposite side of the steep ravine— the place where she'd slid down to the bottom on the snow. She didn't look back, but she listened intently for any sounds that would indicate the doctor climbing back up.

Woods, she thought. Where are you? Can you see me now?

She curled her legs underneath her body and pulled herself up the side of the nearest boulder. *If he's coming back, I will not be lying down.* Determination coursed through her veins as a plan formed in her mind.

She turned toward the sound of the creek and began to hobble.

With the moon at her back, and the stuttering sound of the water on her right, Detective Kendra Dean walked. She was no longer cold; she was no longer hurting, she was angry, she was furious. And she was ready for revenge.

Going downhill was easier than going uphill had been, but going downhill was still hard. The snow illuminated the ground, but it also covered those treacherous tree roots and tangles. After a few minutes, she happened upon a stout branch sticking out of the snow beside the trunk of a stately pine. She unearthed the branch and found that it was just the right length for a walking stick.

Leading with the stick helped her ferret out roots. It also halted her headlong motion when she was on the verge of tumbling over on her numb and swollen face. But it required a curious amount of dexterity. The handcuffs caused her to hold it out in front of her body like a divining rod, a divining rod to follow the water home.

After a time, the clumsy gait became almost second nature. Take a step, poke the snow, take another step, and poke again. As the creek descended into a lower altitude, the snow cover grew thinner, and the dark ground became more difficult to see. That slowed her even more. Now when she poked the stick down, it often hit the earth before she was ready, jarring her hands and sending shock waves up her arms.

The creek empties into Copper Lake. It may take hours, but I will find my way home. All I have to do is follow the creek to its end.

Each time she stumbled or tripped, Kendra told herself there were only ten more steps to go. Then after those ten, she would go ten more. And then ten more.

By breaking the trek into ten-step chunks, Kendra managed to make her way down the rest of the mountain.

When she saw her house, she thought she was hallucinating. Her heart began to pound, and it was all she could do to keep from breaking into an excited sprint. The sky was before-dawn-gray peppered with faint stars. Down here, the snow had stopped completely.

Kendra didn't know how long she'd been out of the tree line and walking on level ground; she'd been so focused on her ten-step gait that she had almost lulled herself into oblivion.

And then she was home.

She wasn't surprised to see yellow tape across her front door.

How long has it been? Two days, three, even more? She couldn't recall for certain, but at this point she didn't care. She had a plan, and nothing was going to stop her from implementing it. But first she had to get in the house and get out of the handcuffs.

She tried the front door without disturbing the tape.

It was locked.

She wondered if the doctor had locked it after dragging her unconscious body out to his car, or whether the sheriff—or Woody—had locked it after discovering her missing.

Doesn't matter, she thought.

She peered in through the window to make certain no one was inside, waiting for her to come home—one of the kids perhaps—but it appeared the coast was clear. For a moment, she wondered *why* none of the kids were here. Did they not realize she was missing? But then she scrapped that thought knowing it would not help with her plan.

First things first.

Hobbling severely, her stiff leather hiking boots chafing worse with every step, Kendra edged her way around the house looking for the easiest entry point. She'd actually done this very same thing right after she'd first moved in. As a detective, she'd wanted to know any weak spots in her home's defense system. But it had all been safe. She hadn't even felt the need for a security system.

Turning her face away, Kendra jabbed the end of her stick through the lower pane on the bedroom window and knocked the hanging glass shards aside easily. *Who knew a walking stick could be so handy? Should have had this all along.*

It took some effort to get through the window with her hands still locked in front of her body, but once again the stout stick came to her aid in balancing.

Insides, she was struck by the stale silence, as if the house were on hold, awaiting her return. "I'm here now, by God," she said aloud.

She went straight to her bureau, got the key to her footlocker, and pulled it out of the closet. Inside were her cuffs, the universal key still attached. She recalled the day she'd packed everything away—the day after she'd been told to hand in her badge and her service weapon while the investigation was in progress.

The key popped the mechanism, and she twisted the cuffs off her wrists. The metal plate thunked to the floor and actually knocked a tiny triangular chip out of the old wood.

For the first time in days, Kendra could move her hands and arms independent of each other. She stretched her shoulders carefully. The freedom was magnificent and painful.

Bracelets of dried blood crusted each wrist where the skin had rubbed away. She untangled the cuffs from the metal plate, and tucked them in the back pocket of her jeans. She then pulled her Glock out of the storage locker. It was the same gun she'd carried the day she'd gone fishing and found the woman in clover.

This was her personal weapon. She wasn't a huge gun aficionado like many of the officers she'd worked with over the years, but she was proficient. She put in lots of time at the shooting range to make sure of that. In her line of work, a gun was a necessary tool.

She looked at the shoulder holster nestled in the bottom of the locker. It had been custom made for her frame. She'd worn it to work every day for the past dozen years—but she didn't pull it out. Her shoulders were so stiff and sore she knew it would be more of a hindrance than a help.

From the laundry room she retrieved a clean, dry tee shirt, her only other fleece hoodie—the first one was frozen stiff where it had been wet—and a pair of clean, dry socks. She located her multi-pocketed fishing vest and slipped it on, stashing the Glock in one pocket, shifting the cuffs to another.

In the kitchen, she gazed longingly at the cold black coffee still in the Mr. Coffee pot, grabbed a bottle of water out of the fridge instead, and tucked another in a third pocket. Then she rummaged through the pantry for portable food.

Blueberry bars and trail mix went into a front vest pocket.

She'd been home less than fifteen minutes.

In the living room, she saw where someone had dumped the contents of her purse out on the table but she didn't know if the doctor had done it, looking for something while she was unconscious, or if Woody or one of the deputies had done it. She wanted her phone, but it wasn't there.

For a moment, the cold ashes in the fireplace and the naked Christmas tree in the corner made her pause and think about giving in, building a new fire, and making a fresh pot of coffee while dialing Woody on the old landline.

But it was only a moment, and then she was out the front door and headed back toward the area where she'd found the girl in clover. She suspected his bunker was somewhere near there and if there was one thing she was sure of, it was that a wounded animal usually goes to ground.

Kendra felt certain the fall off the edge of the ravine hadn't killed him. After all, she had slid right down to the bottom and suffered only scrapes and bruises. Nope. She was going to have to take care of him herself. He'd made it personal. He was no longer just a criminal suspect to be found and hauled in for questioning—he'd crossed the line *and* proved his guilt when he'd kidnapped, drugged, and raped her.

Questioning time was over.

Now was the time for payback.

Pulling the first bottle of water from her pocket, Kendra popped three aspirins into her mouth and swallowed them with a deep drink. Her throat was so sore and scratchy it took the sheer force of will to keep from choking.

She followed the aspirin with half a blueberry bar, unwrapping it and shoving it into her mouth as she walked. Her strength seemed to be returning. Maybe it was psychological, or maybe the severe nausea and dizziness she'd suffered earlier had been due to the drugs he'd given her and not due to a head injury or giardia.

Whatever the reason, she was profoundly grateful.

Without a backward glance, she followed the edge of Copper Lake until she came to the beginning of Stutter Creek. It flowed into the lake over a series of falls. John Stockton had once told her it was a favorite spot for teenagers in the summer. Apparently they would often swim in the deep, clear, pool nearby. "I should know," he'd said. "I spent a whole summer there with Beth way back when we were teens."

Though intrigued, Kendra hadn't had time to thoroughly explore it yet. And it certainly wouldn't be today. Even though she'd just passed the falls on her way down the mountain, she'd been so intent on getting to the house, she hadn't given them a second thought.

Now, she looked for her own tracks in the thin snow and followed them straight back up the incline to where the base of the mountain began. *Can't believe I'm doing this. Probably should call Woods—but I'm off duty, I'd say that gives me carte blanche. And I owe that murdering doctor. He's going to wish he'd killed me when he had the chance.*

For a moment, a red flag went up. *Why didn't he kill me right away, like he did the others?* She knew he'd had both the capability and the opportunity. *What am I missing?*

She thought of the humiliation of the rape kit, and disease tests in her near future—the AIDS test alone would have to be repeated every three months for the next year—and she renewed her vow to make him pay.

She was amazed at how spry she felt, considering everything she'd been through. *Maybe I simply worked out all the frozen stiffness and soreness by continuing and not giving up. Didn't athletic trainers always say the best way to get rid of pain was to work through it?* As soon as she'd gotten rid of the cuffs and got her weapon—and donned new socks—she'd felt like a new woman. Except for the scrapes, bruises, blisters, and that God-awful stinging in the nether regions. But she wasn't about to dwell on that now. Time for that later.

The weak sun teased her as it rose above the mountains. The air down here was crisp, not cold. Her breath puffed out in front of her, and Kendra knew she hadn't felt this alive since handing in her badge.

Her legs were almost as weak as the winter dawn, but she stuffed a handful of trail mix in her mouth and ignored the trembling. Going uphill was much slower than coming down had been. She also had to be hyper vigilant. He was out there somewhere. No way he would still be in that ditch. *Nothing in life was that damn easy.*

As with most difficulties, Kendra found she'd been provided an equalizer. Even though the going-up was slower and more tiring, it was also now daylight, and she could easily follow her tracks.

On the other hand, that meant the doc could follow them, too. But so can Woody or the sheriff if they're out and about this morning.

So many possibilities. Best to put one foot in front of the other and not dwell on anything too much. She stepped off to the side and sat on a rock to catch her breath.

After a few moments, she felt exposed. She got to her feet and began to creep upward again. Her stick was in her hand, it had served her well coming down the mountain, maybe it would be of even more use going back up.

She recalled how she'd slept the sleep of the almost-dead on the frozen slab of rock after she'd escaped from the bunker—and that's when the question that had been nagging her finally came to the forefront—if she really had heard him cock a weapon while she was sitting at the top of the bunker's ladder, and if she'd really heard him shoot his way out of the bunker, then why hadn't he just shot her when he found her at the top of the ravine? Had he seen the searchers? Were they so near he was afraid of alerting them?

She turned the possibilities over in her mind as she climbed.

The sun never grew very strong, and the higher she got, the colder she felt. Staying in the shadows chilled her even more. However, beneath her clean, dry hoodie, a fine layer of perspiration begged her to strip off one of her layers—the fishing vest perhaps—and let the cool air do its job.

She had to take another break.

Going up was getting her down. She finished off the first bottle of water and rested in the black shade of a huge spruce. Her exhausted muscles cried out for relief. *I just need more water and protein. That's all.*

She opened her second bottle of water and ate some more trail mix.

Maybe this desire for revenge is making me stupid. I should've called in to let everyone know I'm all right. Never been a victim before. What was I thinking? Just so damn angry...

She thought back over the confrontation at the top of the ravine just before she'd kicked him over. Something else about that incident begged to be reexamined.

What am I not remembering? What have I overlooked?

Kendra pictured the scene in her mind. She had her head down, crawling toward the boulder on her hands and knees, cuffs impeding her forward motion painfully, fully expecting to hear the whine of a bullet pass by her head at any moment. But instead, he'd screamed at her, yelling something about Jumper's Point even as he followed after her, laughing and slashing.

What had he been yelling about Jumper's Point?

What was it?

Suddenly, it dawned on her.

He'd said he would be home free after they found his car at the bottom of the point. No, he said they'd find his corpse in his burning car at the bottom of the point.

Kendra could scarcely believe she'd almost blocked that out. Biting off his nose and kicking him over the edge of the ravine, that's what she remembered. His boasting had been little more than background noise.

It suddenly became apparent what she should do.

Get to Jumper's Point. Her truck key was hanging by the back door. If it's still there, I ride out to the Point. If it's gone, I call Woods to come get me.

Struggling to her feet, muscles creaking with age and misuse, she tucked the empty water bottle back into one of the vest pockets and glanced upward.

Going back felt like giving up, and that grated against every fiber of her detective's being, but she was pretty certain she'd find him at the Point—if he'd survived his bloody fall—and she was sure there was no time to waste. She could imagine him crawling along the bottom of the ravine all the way to the Gypsum Trailer Park—hitching a ride there, perhaps—coming all the way back for his car—wherever he had stashed it.

Walking stick in hand she headed back down the trail, careful not to tread on either set of her footprints. She had no idea where his car might be, but she figured it was somewhere near the bunker. *Find him first, and then worry about all that.* She made a mental note to tell Woody about the string from her hooded sweatshirt. She'd tied it on a bush right at the place she kicked the murderer over the edge.

She made it back to the house in record time. The key to the truck was right where she'd left it. She picked up the handset on the kitchen phone and dialed Woody's number.

CHAPTER FORTY-FIVE
She's Alive!

Woody figured a good place to start would be the campground store where Kendra had once mentioned buying bait. He wheeled the Mercury into the store parking lot. A cheerful older gentleman in a white butcher's apron greeted him as soon as he stepped inside.

"How's it going, my friend?" The man's voice had the booming quality of a Baptist preacher.

"Here on business," Woody replied, pulling out his ID. "Detective Woodrow James. I'm investigating the disappearance of my partner, Detective Kendra Dean." He let that sink in while he gave the place the once-over. It was empty of customers at the moment, but the smell of fresh bait permeated the air. It was not a bad smell, simply a bait-store smell.

Woody looked down at the dark floorboards beneath his feet. They'd held up well for a bait and fish store, considering how often they must have been wet. *The fish odor is probably ingrained into the wood by now. But the actual fish cleaning advertised on the sign out front undoubtedly takes place in the shack out back.* He glanced at the big man's apron—it was pristine—apparently he hadn't cleaned any fish yet this morning.

"William Mullens." The man wiped his palm on his apron and held out his hand. "Folks call me Bill. Sorry to hear about Detective Dean. She's been in here a time or two, though not recently. At least, not while I was here. My part-time clerk told one of the deputies earlier that she had come in a few days ago for a can of night crawlers. I must've been out in the shack at that time." He shook his head. "Super nice lady, everyone speaks highly of her. You, too, as a matter of fact." He nodded. "I never met the two of you when Allie went missing, but I know you were both a big help back then."

Woody acknowledged the man's gratitude with a hard squeeze of his hand. "Appreciate that," he said. "Can't believe it's Ken who's missing, now." He wanted to acknowledge the coincidence of the circumstances, but his need to move on with the hunt was too strong. "The owner of The Drugstore told me she mentioned a fishing hole she liked around here. Said it was a drowned tree—those were her exact words. Thought I might search that area again, on my own, since I know she felt as if someone was watching her that day. You know any place like that nearby?"

Bill Mullens nodded. "I do know that place. Best catfish hole on this end of the lake. That old oak fell in years ago— made a heck of a home for fish, snakes, all kinds of critters. Eats up fishing line, though. Easy to lose hook line *and* sinker out there."

Woody shifted position from one foot to the other. "Sounds like the place she described. She would like that sort of challenge." He hesitated while Bill turned and perused a wall size map of the lake.

"Right here." He pointed a thick forefinger at a spot on the map. "Drowned tree—you can't miss it. All the locals know that spot."

Woody studied the map a few moments then thanked him and turned for the door.

"Pardon me for saying so," Bill called out. "But I know for a fact that searchers have already combed that area..."

Woody stopped. "Thanks, I just like to be thorough." He raised one hand in a goodbye gesture and opened the door.

Bill touched the brim of an imaginary cap. "I understand that. I'm sure I'd feel the same way myself."

Woody let the door close behind him and hurried to the Mercury. He moved it around behind the store and made his way to the spot he'd seen on the map. It didn't take him long. Once he'd got the visual in his mind, he knew just how to get there.

The drowned tree was just as he'd imagined it. Eerie, otherworldly, mossy branches visible just below the surface, reaching up as a drowning person would reach up, in hope of rescue. But as Bill had warned him, there wasn't much hope of finding anything new. The movement of the searchers had tracked up the whole snowy, muddy area. All along the shoreline, boot and shoe prints overlapped the edge of the water, deeper in some spots, nearly invisible in others.

He backed away from the lake into the tree line and made himself a part of the landscape, watching, listening, feeling. There was nothing to see except a cottontail cropping nervously at some plant barely sticking out of the snow, nothing to hear save the wind washing the treetops, nothing to feel other than the certainty that Ken was still out there, somewhere.

Woody couldn't seem to make himself leave this spot. He was positive this was where Kendra had been when she was being watched. He felt some sort of connection here, something he was supposed to see, to figure out if he had the patience to be still and let it come. His phone vibrated in his pocket. He'd turned the ringer off to preserve the silence.

He checked the screen.

Sheriff Puckett.

Woody clicked ACCEPT CALL.

"Sheriff?"

The big man didn't pussyfoot around. "One of the searchers found a gun. We ran the serial, and it's registered to Doc Stevens. Been recently fired, but then it must have jammed. It was deep inside a tangle of blackberry bushes."

"As if someone threw it there to hide it?"

The sheriff snorted. "Yeah, or threw it in a fit of anger."

Woody thought that over. "Thanks, Sheriff. Can you send me the GPS location where it was found? I'd like to head that way."

"Will do. I feel like it's the first solid lead we've had."

When he received the coordinates, Woody mapped the route on his phone. The app he'd downloaded was surprisingly clear and accurate. There was only one problem. After a few minutes hiking, he lost the signal completely. At that moment, Woody became so frustrated he could easily imagine throwing his phone into a blackberry bush. *Should have taken the time to go by the station and pick up one of those handheld GPS units that work on satellites rather than cell towers. Idiot! Kendra would give me hell for that oversight. I hope it isn't one of those mistakes that come back to haunt me.*

Suddenly certain time was of the essence, he turned around and headed back down the trail at a run, thankful the scant snow showed him his footprints.

Fortunately, he hadn't got very far from his vehicle.

When he made it back to the camp store, he climbed into the Mercury and barreled out of the lot, tires throwing up a white veil behind. He pressed the sheriff's number on his keypad, glad to see he had a signal again. But before the call went out, his phone beeped to let him know he had a voice message.

Woody pressed the PLAY icon and almost drove into the camp store's dumpster when he heard the recorded voice coming from the tiny speaker. "Woods. I need your help. I'm calling from my old landline—"

He pictured her cell phone in his jacket pocket.

"—I pushed the doctor into the ravine. But I don't think he's dead. He may be headed to Jumper's Point with a hostage. He said something about staging his own death. I'm headed there now."

Woody immediately called the sheriff. *She's alive! Ken is alive!* His hand shook, and his gut felt as if the bottom had dropped out of the roller coaster he'd been on.

The sheriff answered his phone.

"Sheriff Puckett? I got a voice mail from Detective Dean." He held his phone up to check the time. "Call came in twelve minutes ago. She pushed the doc into a ravine, made it back to her house, got her truck, and now she's headed to Jumper's Point. Tell me where that is and I will meet you. She thinks the doc may be headed there, possibly with a hostage."

The sheriff didn't question anything Woody said. He simply told him the quickest way to get to the local lookout spot, and then reminded him to be cautious when approaching. "I'll meet you there," he said. "Thank God she's alive. Let's keep her that way."

CHAPTER FORTY-SIX
Fire & Rescue

Kendra had only been to Jumper's Point once when she first settled in Stutter Creek and spent her days looking the place over. It was a lovely spot west of town where a long, slow drive up a narrow, paved road led to a scenic lookout wide enough for a dozen cars. From the vantage point of the famous locale, one could gaze out upon the entire snow covered valley below the town.

A stout guardrail ran around the edge of the lookout. The intention was for cars to park and shine their lights out over the breathtaking view. Past the rail, the land fell away, straight down the mountain to the valley floor below. On the level of the lookout, the tops of the tallest pines and firs appeared as toy decorations in a child's mountain-forest diorama. Looping out the other side of the lookout area, the narrow road continued up the mountain toward the Alpine Ski Lodge.

Kendra turned on to the narrow road, plans forming and reforming in her mind.

It had taken only twenty minutes to get from the lake house to the lookout. The roads were clear. The morning was warming up nicely, and the snow had not returned. She had taken back roads to avoid a chance encounter with law enforcement, or one of the searchers whom she assumed would be in town. It wouldn't do to be delayed while the doctor carried out his last evil plan. She touched her Glock. It was on the seat beside her thigh. She was taking no chances this time.

The morning was still new, damp with dew, and saturated with possibility. *And if he isn't here? No problem. Simply sit and wait. Take a nap. Drink some more water. Let Woody take over*. Her mind coiled around and around as her truck followed the twisting road up and up and up.

In moments, she could see the end of the road. She had to either stop and get out, or drive straight into the entrance. She eased the truck off the road and killed the engine.

From here she could creep up to the scene and look it over, unobserved. At this elevation, the still fluffy snow carpeted the forest floor and muffled her movements.

She pressed the truck door open carefully, and then exited with the gun at her side, barrel pointed downward. It was obvious there had been other vehicles on the road. She had to be ready for action.

From behind a tree, she had a clear view of the entire parking area.

The doctor's champagne colored Toyota sat a few feet this side of the guardrail. Kendra had seen the car around town on more than one occasion. She could see a figure slumped over the steering wheel, but from this vantage point, she couldn't tell if it was the doctor or not. If so, what was he doing? Was he unconscious, or dead?

Taking a deep, steadying breath, Kendra carefully raised the Glock and stared down the barrel. Lining up the shot, she made certain the figure in the driver's seat was directly in her sight. From here, she had a definite kill shot through the driver's open window. *Just give me a reason. Just one false move.*

He'd said the car would be at the bottom of The Point. She watched, waiting for movement, one second, two, three, and then it happened. The doctor stood—he wasn't in the driver's seat at all. He was bent over on the opposite side of the car doing something out of sight.

So he did get a body double. How did he do that so quickly? She spared a glance at the form slumped over the steering wheel—was the man still alive? Her finger tightened on the trigger as she sighted not on the figure in the car, but on the doctor as he bobbed up and down on the opposite side of the car.

He appeared to be dousing the car with some kind of fuel. He'd said it would burn.

She wanted to wait for Woody. For the cavalry to ride in guns drawn and sirens blaring, but she wasn't positive they were coming. *Did Woody even get my message? I should have taken another moment and called the sheriff, but if I had, this creep might already be finished with his little game.*

As the doctor made his way around the rear of the car, Kendra caught the acrid odor of gasoline. In his hands, she saw a red and yellow can. He was splashing the fuel across the vehicle with short, jerky motions.

No time to wait.

"Put the gas down," she commanded.

The doctor's face showed his surprise.

He clutched the can in front of his body and rushed toward her.

"Stop or I'll shoot!"

He charged ahead as if she were waving a red flag.

Kendra set her sights on his feet and squeezed the trigger.

He stumbled and her bullet pierced the bottom of the metal can.

KA WHOMP!

The explosion blew the two of them in opposite directions.

It also ignited the doc's fuel-spattered clothing.

Kendra saw him fly through the air like a human firework, bright orange against the clear blue morning. In her mind, Jumper's Point became superimposed over an image of the ravine, and she couldn't remember where she was or how she was supposed to get out.

She heard someone screaming.

Kendra looked down at her hand, but her gun was not there. Her thoughts began to melt together as surely as the plastic aglets on the ends of her bootlaces.

Woods? Is that you?

Lying prone beneath a tree, Kendra struggled to wake up.

Some sound played upon her senses.

It whispered through the tops of the pines twenty, thirty, forty feet above her head. It was a lonely, rushing sound; a sound Mother Nature has made throughout time, even before anyone was around to hear it.

She tried to collect her thoughts. She felt as if she'd been wandering around in a fog since the day the doc had slapped her with the SAP and whisked her from her home.

She wanted to be up and moving, toward home, toward safety, toward her old life, but just like that day near the lake, she is suddenly certain she's no longer alone.

Woody is that you? Or is it that evil doctor?

Her instinct was to call out, but hesitation sealed her lips. *If it's the doc, will I be able to take him a third time? Third time's a charm, so they say. But still, could I?* For the first time in her life, Kendra wasn't sure she could defend herself.

She wanted an equalizer like she had before, down in the hole, but it was too late, the shape was headed her way.

Then it split into two shapes.

Kendra closed her eyes and willed herself to be invisible.

"Over here!" A voice yelled.

"Is it her?"

"Yes! Hurry!"

"Be careful, *please*. Bring the *something* (the word was lost to the wind)."

Kendra got the feeling she should recognize the voices. Definitely not the doctor, these two were obviously looking for someone. Were they looking for her? Was she still down in the hole? It seemed so dark all of a sudden. If it wasn't so dark she'd be able to see the trail—snow made it so easy to see the trail. But what was that rushing sound, had she found the creek after all?

She felt the searchers hovering. They didn't touch her, but they touched the thick hot air, moved it away from her somehow. What was that sound, that glow?

"No," one voice said. "Wait—"

Kendra tried to move, to let them know she was okay. But she couldn't even seem to open her eyes.

And then she could, and it wasn't foggy at all.

It appeared to be a bright, sunny morning. Everything was orange.

She gazed around.

She had a bird's eye view of a clearing at the edge of a steep drop overlooking a tree-choked, snow-dusted, valley. A burning car sat in the center of a scorched area of an otherwise snowy clearing. Flames bubbled the paint and licked at the inside of the vehicle, eating up the upholstery and carpeting.

Across the way, a twisted red and yellow gas can lay beside a blackened figure. The can sported a blown out hole faced with sharp petal-points of metal. It looked like something from a cartoon, something that might have held Wile E. Coyote's Acme fuel. Kendra knew she'd seen that can, or one just like it, but she couldn't remember where or when.

The figure on the ground was unrecognizable. Flames had stripped it of most of its clothing as well as large areas of its flesh. In several places, Kendra could see charred bone poking through the blackened skin. The sound of burning was as loud as rushing water—or wind through the treetops.

The detective side of her—*am I still a detective?* There seemed some question about that, but she couldn't recall exactly what it was—wanted to examine the remains closer, but her roving eye continued until it came upon a woman lying beneath a tree.

Kendra floated, looking down at the woman in her multi-pocketed fishing vest.

A veil of peace surrounded her. She was no longer angry, or afraid, or in pain. She thought about trying to get closer to the scene on the ground, but something pulled her onward.

She glanced back once, surprised to see a shape moving away from the area, moving off through the trees. *One of the searchers, perhaps, going for help. Help for the burning man.*

Onward, she thought. Onward.

Her bird's eye view widened to include a swath of flashing lights speeding toward the scene. *Ambulance? Or a fire truck for the burning car?*

She continued on. There was nothing to hold her back there. That world had become tenuous, transparent. Ahead she could see light and little else. Bright white light that seemed to illuminate a feeling she couldn't describe. Kendra wanted to know that feeling, to experience it, to crawl inside it and stay. She floated endlessly, content to allow time and place to slip away.

The light grew even brighter, all encompassing, warm as the womb. Everything else disappeared—and then a voice cut through the light like scissors cutting through an umbilical cord.

"Is she alive?"

Kendra heard the question, but the sound seemed to emanate from the bottom of a bottle of white Caro corn syrup. She could picture the thick clear liquid with words floating. Something about the young woman's voice was achingly familiar. But Kendra could no longer see that world. She could hear the words, but she couldn't find the visual.

"Of course she's alive. She's *tough.*" Kendra knew that voice, too, but the timbre was strained, anxious. "Be careful," the deep voice ordered. "Don't hurt her. She's been through enough."

Then the young woman's voice again, sobbing. "She's not *breathing.* Make her *breathe.* Give her oxygen or some*thing.*"

Suddenly Kendra sensed the young woman's pain, and it was so overwhelming she could no longer feel the warmth of the light. *If I can ease her pain, I will. I will do anything to ease her pain. Then I'll go back, back to that feeling in the light.*

The siren arrived, piercing the veil, pulsing in perfect time with the red and blue strobes.

Kendra felt the movement of something sliding beneath her, but try as she might, she could not see what was going on—everything remained black. *What if they're putting me in a body bag? What if they think I'm dead?* The thought struck her in the chest like a sledgehammer. It took her breath away. *Is that what this is? Am I dead?*

Nooo! She tried to yell. I'm in here! I'm not dead!

A silvery warmth enveloped her. She felt weightless again. A rocking motion, as if she were in the cradle Bill had built for the kids.

"Mom?" A gentle voice, gentle pressure on her arm.

"Stand back little lady." Another deep voice. "We've got to get her stable. She's in shock."

Stillness, no longer rocking. The rumble of an engine, smell of exhaust, the scent of burning hair, gasoline, burning flesh. Kendra couldn't make sense of all these things—These are a few of my favorite things—and yet it made as much sense as the gentle pressure on her arm.

The other deep voice. "Detective Dean, stay with us. Stay with us now. We're trying to start an IV. Can you feel that?"

No. Everything is warm. Thank you, one more thing to be thankful for. Like the lacy pattern of the gasoline tablecloth lying on the snow.

Kendra drifted away. She didn't want to "feel that." Whatever "that" might be. She wanted to go back to the white light or stay here in the silvery warmth with the gentle hands, and the person who called her Mom. *But where were the gentle hands? Where did that voice go?*

She started to gasp. The sledgehammer lay heavy across her chest, holding her down, strapping her down. She began to struggle. Weak memories surfaced like dead fish: the robbery suspect stepping in front of the UPS truck, Bill's suitcase by the front door, Carrie's hand rubbing her baby belly, Willa and Charlie arm in arm, singing, and Keith, blasting Lady Gaga as he drove away. And then there was Woody, his face, his kind face, and a mad doctor cackling, hurting her, chaining her to the cold, cold floor.

Where was that warmth, that light? That sweet voice?

Renewing her efforts, Kendra flailed her legs, twisting her body against the weight on her chest.

"Hold her arms," a voice commanded. "I've got the—*shit!* She ripped out the IV."

"Detective Dean, hold *still*. You're in the ambulance. We've got to stabilize you and get you to the hospital."

Someone moaned. Who is that? Who's in here with me? Maybe it was the other victim, the one who wore the sapphire ring. Or even the doctor, with the burned hair and melted snow skin.

"Why is she moaning like that? Is she in pain? Is she having a seizure?"

Ahh, the sweet voice was back.

Kendra relaxed.

"Mom? It's me; it's Willa."

Kendra felt the soft hands on her legs. But it couldn't be Willa; she was hundreds of miles away, having a baby. *Or was that Keith's wife? Or Charlie and Carrie? Who's Rory?*

The moaning stopped.

She gasped a few times as someone strapped an oxygen mask to her face.

The paramedic swiped a meaty hand across his forehead and sat back on his heels. "I thought we'd lost her there for a moment. Your touch brought her back."

Willa nodded. She was tucked into the corner of the ambulance near her mother's feet. "I'm going, too," she'd told the paramedic when she scrambled aboard at Jumper's Point. "I don't take up much space."

The guy appeared to be on the verge of ordering her out, but Woody had stepped up and closed the door from outside, and that was the end of that. The paramedic knocked on the wall of the ambulance to let the driver know it was okay to drive.

Willa patted her mother's leg again.

The silvery shock blanket crackled slightly.

CHAPTER FORTY-SEVEN

From The Stutter Creek Sentinel
Detective Dean's condition upgraded
Identity of second body still uncertain

Kendra wanted to say, "That's a hell of a headline," but she couldn't make her voice work. She tried to swallow, but the tissues in her throat seemed to be stuck together.

Woody's eyelids drooped, and the paper fell to his lap. His face was unshaven; his eyes circled with fatigue.

Kendra watched him sleep. Parts of the last few days were still with her, but the *reason* she was in the hospital eluded her. And then there was that horrific soreness in her throat. *What happened to me? I remember the bunker and the trek up and down the mountain. I remember the ravine and biting off the doctor's nose. Then a big blank spot.*

Her own eyes began to feel heavy, and she was halfway back to her drug-induced Nirvana when she recalled the explosion that had knocked her across the clearing. She jerked and flung out her arms. The bed rail rattled in protest.

Woody stirred. "Ken?"

She opened her eyes again and raised one hand in cautious greeting.

An IV trailed from her arm.

Woody crossed to the bed. "I thought I heard you move." His voice was rough. "Are you awake?"

Kendra looked at him, her expression unreadable.

"You okay?" he asked. "You were on a ventilator for the last couple of days, but they weaned you off this morning. The doc said your throat was very swollen and raw." He leaned down and pressed his lips to the top of her head. "Thank God you left me that message. I got there as soon as I could." He looked into her face, hoping she understood what he was saying. "Willa and the others are downstairs having a cup of coffee, wondering what to do with themselves." He grinned at last. "You scared us, boss. You really did."

She looked into his eyes. Confusion muddled her brain. She needed answers, but couldn't ask the questions. With her free hand, Kendra made writing motions, as if with a pen.

Woody understood immediately. "First, a sip of this." He held a plastic cup of water to her lips and held her head up so she could drink. Most of the water dribbled out the side of her mouth.

He pressed the CALL button and alerted the nurse that Kendra was awake. "They kept you sedated while you were on the ventilator," he explained. "That's why you may feel groggy." He took a small chip of ice from a Styrofoam pitcher on the bedside table. "Try this." He placed the chip on her tongue. "It might be easier to handle. Just let it melt."

She closed her eyes as the ice melted. For a moment, she was back in the forest, licking up snow.

Woody pulled his notebook and pen from his shirt pocket, opened to a blank page, and handed them to her.

Turning the small notebook sideways, Kendra thought for a moment, and then wrote, "The doctor?"

Woody smiled crookedly. "I assume you are not talking about kindly Dr. Strahan here in the hospital."

Kendra frowned.

"Don't worry, boss. You took care of Doc Stevens. Apparently it was your bullet that punctured the metal gas can and ignited a blowback. It puffed up and exploded just like a bomb. Blew you clear across the parking area. You were lying at the edge of the woods—unconscious—when Willa and I got there."

He stopped for a breath and then continued.

"It was a miracle. She and Charlie were just coming into town when I raced by, on my way to the Point. They fell in behind me. If they hadn't… well, I don't know. The paramedic said Willa's voice is what saved you."

He stopped talking again, to let her absorb everything he was saying, but Kendra tapped the paper impatiently, needing to hear it all.

Woody understood. "The doc must've spilled gasoline on himself as he was dousing the car with it. The explosion set his clothes on fire and burned him to a crisp."

Kendra tried to shake her head, but dizziness stopped her. The pain in her skull was back, but she didn't know if it was due to the explosion or the sedatives she'd been given. They always made her feel rotten.

She scribbled on the paper again. "How do u know it was him?"

"Why wouldn't it be him? Didn't you see him before you took that shot?" Woody sounded utterly perplexed by her question. "There were more remains found, you know. His wife, Candy, was the most recent."

Staring at the window, Kendra realized it was daytime outside. Sunlight illuminated the blind-covered window making it appear to be a work of art. *White light. What is it about warm white light?*

"Open blinds?" she wrote.

Woody complied.

Behind him, Ken scribbled furiously.

"His wife. He called her The Betrayer. Not surprised he killed her." She wrote some more. "He had a plan to get away. A body-double. In the car. Doc was going to fake his death, use someone else's body. Where's other man? And the ring?"

Woody took the pen away from her. "Slow down, boss lady. You're getting too worked up." He sat on the edge of the bed and took her hand in his. "We'll get it all sorted out, don't worry. The main thing is; you're safe. Right here. Right now." He squeezed her hand. "You're *safe* with me."

The nurse came in. "Look who's back." She smiled as she wrapped a blood pressure cuff around Kendra's free arm. "Sorry if that hurts." She indicated the myriad healing slash marks on Kendra's arm where the killer had slashed through her hoodie at the edge of the ravine.

Kendra just shrugged.

Woody stood and moved aside to get out of the way.

"Any other pain?" The nurse concentrated on checking her pulse.

Kendra pointed to her throat.

"Can't talk, huh?" The nurse slipped her another couple of ice chips. "It'll get better soon. I've got some numbing spray I can use if the doctor okays it. We've got a call in to let him know you're awake." She patted Kendra's arm. "Just rest quietly and don't try to talk. You had a collapsed lung. That's part of the problem. In fact, that's why you were on the vent." She started toward the door. "How about a cup of ice cream? That should help your throat."

Kendra nodded. All at once she was ravenous.

With a twinkle in her eye, the nurse asked, "Vanilla or chocolate?"

Kendra held up two fingers.

The woman laughed. "Both it is, then."

When she was gone, Woody sat back down on the edge of the bed. "You're going to be okay." He took her hand again. "And I've got some good news about your suicide perp."

Kendra waited for him to continue. She felt as if she should be more excited, more concerned to hear what he was about to say, but she still had so many questions about the doctor.

Woody continued. "Once our techs went through his computer we found out what he was afraid of."

Ken arched her brows.

"Child porn," Woody said. "His computer was full of it. In fact, remember the little girl we found in the trunk?"

Kendra nodded, the image of the murdered child immediately filling her mind. It had been one of the cases she could never let go of.

"He had images of her. And we were able to trace them directly back to her parents' computer. They were all part of the same child porn ring. That gives us even more ammunition in the case against her parents. If I have my way, they'll never get out of prison."

And if I had my way, Kendra thought, they'd never even breathe again. But she didn't say that. She didn't say anything at all. Instead, she reached toward his pocket for his pen and notebook.

Woody handed it over with an admonishment. "Only a couple more questions then you've got to rest. I texted the kids downstairs to let them know you're awake. They should be here any moment."

Kendra nodded, the pen scratching across the paper. "Am I reinstated?"

Woody shook his head. "Still have to go through the formal hearing and all that."

She tugged at the neck of the ill-fitting hospital gown and wrote some more. "Were there two bodies at Jumper's Point?"

Now it was Woody's turn to shake his head. "Just the doc. And you."

Kendra lay the pen down and closed her eyes. Then she picked it up again. "There <u>was</u> a man in the car—(she underlined the word *was)*—I saw his shape behind the wheel. Was the car completely burned?"

At that moment, Willa rushed through the door and fell on her mom with open arms. "I was so afraid," she whispered.

Tears pricked Ken's eyelids as she recalled Willa's touch in the ambulance. She wanted to ask where they were staying but, of course, she couldn't speak and the pen and notebook were crushed between their hugging bodies.

Willa didn't let go, but she did sit up and let Keith and Carrie come in for hugs. "So glad you're out of ICU," Carrie said. "I knew you'd be okay, but it was awful for a while."

Ken touched her belly and smiled.

Carrie looked at Woody with a question in her eyes.

"Sore throat," he explained, touching his own. "She'll be back to giving orders in no time."

The nurse popped in just then with the tiny cups of ice cream.

Keith took them from her and shooed everyone off the bed so he could bring his mom up to a sitting position. "This will help." He grinned and began to spoon-feed her as if she were an invalid.

The icy treat felt so good to Kendra's throat that she didn't even attempt to protest.

She ate both cups and took a few sips of water. Now and then she looked up to see Woody standing in the corner, watching. She smiled and lay back, drained.

Dr. Strahan walked in, white coat flapping. "Everyone out," he said. "You can return, two at a time, during visiting hours tonight. The patient needs her rest."

Woody stood back, waiting until all the kids had left among promises to hurry back as soon as possible. Then he stepped up to the bed and took her hand. "I'll be downstairs." He pulled her cell phone out of his pocket and placed it in her palm. "Text me when you want."

Ken was amazed at how the shape of the phone in her hand made her feel. It was like being given back the keys to her life. She squeezed his fingers, and he drew her hand up to his lips.

Dr. Strahan cleared his throat, obviously eager to get on with his examination.

Woody's lips lingered for a split second, his eyes never leaving hers.

Two weeks ago, the obvious affection would have made Kendra uncomfortable. Now, she didn't care. No one knew how close she'd come to leaving them forever. *Did I die?* She thought about texting Woody that question; instead, she allowed him to leave and then typed it into the phone and held it up for the doctor to see.

He frowned and took her hand. "You were in shock when they brought you in. But your heart never stopped. However, you did have a collapsed lung, and I've had other patients say they had NDEs—Near Death Experiences— without being clinically dead."

Kendra nodded. *So that's what it was, a near death experience.* She felt better. Just having a label for it made it tolerable.

For now at least.

CHAPTER FORTY-EIGHT
Home

After the doctor left, Kendra tried to sleep, but her mind swirled with so many questions she began texting Woody almost immediately. "Can you come back up?"

Woody sent her a smiley icon and appeared in the doorway. He hadn't made it past the small waiting area at the end of the hall.

"Hi," she mouthed.

He strode to the bed, leaned down, and kissed her lightly on the lips. "I thought I'd lost you."

Kendra wrinkled her forehead and texted. "You know you can't get rid of me that easily."

Woody laughed. "So what did the doc say?"

Kendra's fingers flew over the keypad. "Brain okay. Lungs healing. Throat will be fine in a day or two. No STDs." She stopped typing and looked at Woody to see if he understood.

All the color drained from his face. "Rape kit?"

She nodded and wiped away a tear. It wasn't a tear of pain or self-pity; it was a tear of anger. She was still furious at the things Edgar Stevens had done. Even though Woody said her bullet had caused the explosion and, as a result, his death, Ken felt cheated. She hadn't seen him die. Nor had she been given the satisfaction of hauling him to jail.

Instead, she'd been out cold while he burned. If it was really him. Her mind couldn't accept his death—not without seeing it for herself.

She wanted to be done with him, with his madness. She didn't want to have all these doubts. But I did see someone in the driver's seat while the doc was splashing the gasoline around. What about that guy? Was he alive, did he just get out and walk away while the car and the doc burned? Or is there another possibility? Something even more bizarre?

After a moment, she tapped out another message. "The doc's body was really burned. Did DNA confirm his ID?"

"I called the sheriff and told him what you said. It's the first we'd heard about the possibility of a third person there." He pulled a straight-backed chair to her bedside. "He's going to make certain the M.E. sends a sample out for testing. There's only one problem."

Kendra waited.

"We haven't been able to locate any living relatives. We'll need at least one blood relative to match the sample with."

Kendra lay back completely exhausted. "I never thought of that." She put the phone aside and closed her eyes, ready to give in and go back to sleep.

"Before you drift away," Woody said. "I need to ask you something."

Kendra opened her eyes.

"How did you know the doc's body was completely burned? You were unconscious when I got there. The paramedics said the blast knocked you out."

She looked down at the phone and tapped gently. "I saw everything." Then she let her hand rest on the crisp white sheet. She didn't expect him to understand, but she didn't think she could text that much information. Especially since she didn't really understand it herself.

Over the next two days, her health improved dramatically. Just having Woody and the kids there every day made it easy for her to get better. Bill came, but she told the kids she didn't want to see him. She texted him and told him to go on back to Vegas.

Kendra wanted to forgive and forget. She knew it would be healthier if she could. But just now, she wasn't ready. In fact, she was holding onto her grudge as if it were a lifeline.

The day after Bill came, Keith and Charlie stopped by on their way back to Albuquerque. Willa was also there. She was having a devil of a time convincing Charlie he didn't need to stay and drive her back to Tech.

They were all chattering when Woody came in with the sapphire ring.

Kendra took the ring and held it in her hand like a talisman. Then she told how she'd found it on the floor of the bunker. "He said we would never find the girl who wore this because he had changed the coordinates. Said he carved a D on it instead of a compass point."

Woody appeared stunned. "He told you that?"

Kendra nodded. "He loved to brag. To let me know how he was outsmarting everyone." She caressed the dainty ring, her eyes soft, faraway. "He said the D stands for Dawn. Seventeen steps toward Dawn. Maybe that was the girl's name, I'm not sure. Do you know?"

Woody scratched at the stubble on his chin. "Yeah, the missing girl is named Dawn. But what about this other thing he said, *toward* dawn? Maybe that means seventeen steps toward the East since the sun *rises* in the east." He hopped off the window ledge where he'd been sitting. "Dawn rises. Maybe he had planned to unearth her next." He shook his head. "I have to get this info to the sheriff." He held out his hand, and Ken placed the sapphire ring in it. "And I have to show this to Dawn's sister this afternoon. When I told her a ring had been found, she described it to me. I'm pretty sure it will link her sister to the doc. And with this new information, I think we may be able to find her."

He leaned over and kissed Kendra's forehead, something the kids had gotten used to seeing. "Since we've found three vics, we're seeing a pattern. It seems he buried them all in one area of the forest in the rough shape of a wheel. We just haven't located the hub, yet."

"That will be the bunker," Kendra said. "The bunker was his workshop, his hidey-hole, his playpen." She turned her face away and began to tell them what she'd been through and how she'd gotten loose. "Too bad he was so burned," she said, finally conceding—since the S.O. could never turn up any evidence to the contrary—that she must have imagined the other figure behind the wheel. "Otherwise you'd see where I bit off the tip of his nose."

Woody sat up with a sparkle in his eye. "Did you?" He laughed delightedly. "Where is it now? Could it still be there? Or did you swallow it?"

Kendra gagged and rolled her eyes. "Of course I didn't swallow it. But I did tie my hoodie string around a stunted juniper at the exact spot where it happened. Then I kicked his ass over the rim. If you find that bow-tied string, you might get lucky." Then she said, "Nah. That piece of nose wouldn't still be there. Animals would have taken it by now, besides, it was just the tip." She held up the end of her pinky finger. "No bigger than this."

Woody grinned. "If I bring you a map with your place and the ravine marked on it, do you think you could point me in the right direction? We've had a couple of miracles already. Why not one more?"

"Is it important?" Keith asked.

"Could be," Woody replied. "We could use it to match his DNA with the burned body. Then there would be no question it was him."

"Remind me not to piss off your mother," Charlie whispered to Willa.

Willa jabbed him with her elbow, but she had a look of admiration in her eyes when she did it.

Kendra shrugged. "I'll take a look, but I warn you, I was pretty loopy then." She thought Woody's idea was a needle in a haystack sort of operation, but since the snow had fallen continuously since that day—something the ski resorts were calling their personal miracle—if the piece of flesh hadn't been eaten, then there was the possibility it *had* been frozen and preserved.

She didn't have much time to worry about it, though, shortly after Woody and the boys left, Dr. Strahan came in and, without fanfare, released her to Willa's care.

Before she knew what was happening, Kendra was back at the lake house, installed on the sofa with the TV remote in her hand.

"As soon as Rory and Carrie come by, I'm going into town for groceries," Willa said. "But I'm not going to leave you alone just yet."

Kendra waved her concerns aside. "I'm not an invalid," she protested. "Besides, Dr. Strahan said I needed to get up and move around, remember?" She threw the blue afghan off her legs and prepared to stand.

Willa sat down in the wing chair. "It can wait until they get here."

Ken shook her head and went to the kitchen. When she opened the pantry door to see what they needed from the store, her insides froze.

When she recovered, she said, "I really wish you'd go ahead and get it over with—Carrie and Rory will need to get on the road. They're just stopping to say goodbye. Besides, I'm starving. That hospital food was nothing to write home about. Homemade tortilla soup sounds really good. Shoot, I could even go for some of your broccoli rice casserole." She stuck her head around the kitchen door. "If you hurry, you'll probably be back before they even arrive."

Willa gave up. "I swear I feel like you're trying to get rid of me. But if you *promise* to go back and lie down, then I will go for groceries."

Kendra exhaled shakily, a rush of worry burning in her frozen veins. "I'll be napping if you need me." She took one more glance into the pantry and then closed the door gently, but firmly. "By the way, I appreciate you coming out and cleaning up while I was in the hospital." She made her way to the living room as she spoke. "And bringing my truck back from the Point, of course."

"It was nothing," Willa said. "In fact there was really nothing to do. Charlie drove me out there and then followed me home. He's the sweetest guy, Mom. I'll be glad when you get to know him better."

Easing herself back down into the sofa cushions, she clicked on the TV and turned the sound down low. "I'll rest right here until you return."

Willa picked up the truck keys. "Everyone in town has been asking when they can come and visit, what shall I tell them?"

Kendra laughed. "Tell them to come on. Tell them I'm looking forward to company."

She waited until she felt the cold swash of air waft in from the garage followed by the sound of her F-150 starting up. Charlie had driven Keith's car to Texas Tech when he brought Willa to Stutter Creek—now he was on the way back to Albuquerque with Keith, so Willa was using the truck.

Kendra continued to wait until she heard the garage door rattle down, and then she got up and hurried toward the bedroom. As she passed the front window, she saw her truck making tracks in the fresh snow. Kendra could imagine Willa cranking up the CD player.

In the master bedroom, Kendra went straight to the nightstand. In the false bottom—made to look like a regular drawer—was a biometric lock box holding her old .38 revolver. She'd had the pair of nightstands custom made when the kids were little. They were the only pieces of furniture she'd brought to the rented house.

She placed her index finger on the access pad of the lock box, and it opened immediately. Without preamble, Kendra pulled out the gun and checked the load. It had been her first handgun. She clicked the cylinder closed.

Something was wrong in the kitchen.

Every can in the pantry was stacked according to size and facing the same way, label out. Only someone with severe OCD would go to those lengths in another person's pantry. And she knew only one person in Stutter Creek with that particular disorder.

Quietly, she made her way back to the kitchen and opened the fridge.

As she expected, it had also been reorganized.

What a psycho. At least he didn't leave a gory calling card.

She took a deep breath, gripped the pistol in her shooter's grip, and began a thorough search of the house.

CHAPTER FORTY-NINE
Lab Report

Woody was leaving The Drugstore Café when his phone rang.

Sheriff Puckett's name appeared in the INCOMING CALL bar.

Woody pushed ACCEPT and held the phone to his ear. He'd left the Sheriff's Office only a few minutes earlier. He hadn't needed the topographical map after all. He'd been out with John Stockton and Chet Boone ever since leaving the hospital that morning. They'd found the bunker and another set of remains. Turk had even located Kendra's bow-tied hoodie string, but there was no mention of a piece of random flesh.

"Detective James?"

Woody's blood pressure skyrocketed. Something in the sheriff's tone put him on high alert. "Sheriff Puckett? Something wrong?"

"Lois Campanelli just handed me the lab report on the body from Jumper's Point."

Woody sucked in a breath. "It isn't the doc?"

Sheriff Puckett cleared his throat.

Woody imagined him adjusting his reading glasses.

"Preliminary autopsy showed no smoke in the victim's lungs."

Disbelief flooded Woody's body. "What does that mean, exactly?" He thought he knew, but he wasn't making any assumptions.

The sheriff's voice remained even. "It means he didn't inhale any smoke. At all. The guy was dead *before* he burned."

Woody's pace quickened. "Ken was right. He must've had a body double. Doc may still be alive. Thank God Ken's in the hospital. I'm headed there now—"

"Detective Dean was released this morning," the sheriff interrupted. "She's probably already home, but there's no answer on either phone. I've sent a deputy that way, and I'm leaving the office now."

Woody executed a perfect U-turn and laid three hundred miles worth of rubber on the asphalt as he accelerated away from town and back toward Copper Lake.

Then he called Kendra's cell phone.

It didn't even ring.

Just went straight to voice mail.

CHAPTER FIFTY

Confrontation

He'd waited until the overhead door was almost down, then he simply rolled beneath it into the dark chill of the garage. The concrete was frigid, and his clothes were damp from the snow.

He'd been staying in her house since he'd found out she was still alive. Mexico would have to wait. Just before Willa brought her home from the hospital, he'd slipped outside to avoid detection.

It had been a nice hiding-in-plain-sight place to recover. He'd almost been caught on a couple of occasions, but now he knew what to listen for; the old garage door rattled like Jacob Marley's chains.

He had been injured in the blast, but not as badly as he could've been. Oddly enough, the fumes in the near-empty gas can had caused it to explode outward, away from him and toward her. He had been blown back a few feet, and his clothes had caught fire, but she had *flown* across the lot. She had appeared to be dead. He was a doctor, and even he hadn't been able to find a pulse.

Should've made certain. Should've bashed her skull in with a rock, or shot her with her own gun.

But he'd done neither of those things. He was a doctor. He'd been certain she was dead. His own hubris had caused him to make a mistake. So he'd decided to go with an abbreviated version of his original plan.

After rolling in the snow to put out his burning clothes, and checking Kendra for a pulse, Edgar had simply dragged the already-gas-soaked dead man from the front seat of the car and placed him behind the mutilated gas can.

He then used scraps of his own clothing to wick the fire from the car to the man. Before he scrambled down the mountain, he made sure the poor man's face and hands were burned away.

Then he hightailed it back to his bought-for-cash car where he'd had the presence of mind to stash his antique doctor's bag with its emergency money and clothing. He figured once they found the scene at Jumper's Point, he would have to get to Mexico any way he could. With his bitten nose and blistered skin, there was no way he could board a plane. Hire someone, he thought. *Hire someone to sneak me across the border. All it takes is cash. And that is one thing I've still got.*

But when he'd heard the ambulance racing away from the scene hot, with lights flashing and siren blaring, he knew they'd found someone alive after all.

Sure enough, it was that thorn in his side, Detective Kendra Dean.

And now she was home.

And her daughter was gone.

He softly turned the doorknob leading from the garage into the kitchen. It was open as always. *Where is she? How bad off is she?* He crept inside and listened carefully. He could hear her moving around in the bedroom.

Quiet as snowfall, he slipped into the living room. The coat closet was large. He slid in among the garments and waited.

***

Kendra moved from room to room, revolver at the ready. Vertigo, due to a fifty percent hearing loss in one ear, made her feel clumsy and unsteady. Not knowing if the knock in the head with the SAP had caused the hearing loss, or whether it was the gas can explosion, didn't bother her. She didn't worry about why; she only worried about getting better. But spending four days in bed after all she'd been through did not give her a feeling of super hero-ness. And she certainly hadn't expected to come home to this feeling that things were not as they should be.

But she wasn't going to let her Willa be in harm's way. That's why she'd insisted she go on to the grocery store. Time to call Woody and make sure he was on his way. At least she'd got her voice back. She picked up the landline receiver and propped it on her shoulder. There was no dial tone. It was as if she had pressed a conch shell to her ear. She dug into her purse on the counter. Her cell phone was not there.

Her hackles stood on end.

Something outside the kitchen window caught her eye. Fresh footprints in the snow disappeared around the side of the house toward the garage.

"I know you're here," she said. "What do you want?"

The closet door didn't squeak, but he must have touched an empty hanger because it set off a chain-reaction of *clink clink clink clink clinks* and then he was there, blocking the doorway between the living room and kitchen.

"We've got some unfinished business." His voice still held its edge of arrogance even though his face appeared to have been run through a trash masher.

Kendra smiled. "You look like shit, Doc. What happened? You tangle with a wildcat?"

Fury colored his wounded face. "Just one more thing I owe to you." He raised his hand to show her the scalpel.

"Seriously? You brought a scalpel to a gunfight?"

The doc's sadistic smirk faltered. "I've been through every inch of this dump. You don't have any more weapons."

Kendra raised the .38 and aimed it at his groin. "You're wrong about that, but you're right about the unfinished business. What did you do to me while I was unconscious? And where's the video, on your cell phone? You perverts always record your evil acts."

"C'mon, Detective. You know I can't use *my* cell phone." He held hers up so she could see it.

"I want *your* phone. I want that video. Give it to me."

The doctor threw his head back as if to laugh, and then he lunged at her, scalpel in hand.

Kendra pulled the trigger. The report was extremely loud in the confines of the kitchen.

The impact knocked the doctor to the floor.

At the last moment, Kendra had twitched her aim.

Blood gushed from his thigh. The scalpel hit the floor with a tiny *plonk*.

The doctor's hands scrambled to stop the bleeding. "You shot me!"

Kendra kicked the scalpel away and picked up her cell phone. It had fallen from the doctor's other hand. Watching him writhing on the floor, a cold stillness came over her. "That first shot was for me," she said. Then she cocked the hammer.

"The next one will be for the girl with the sapphire ring."

He didn't seem to hear her. "Give me something to stop this bleeding!"

Kendra ignored his demand. "I'm afraid I may have hit the femoral artery. But you're the expert. What do you think, *Doctor*?" She leaned back against the counter, turned on her phone, and pressed nine one one. "This is Detective Kendra Dean, and I've just shot Dr. Edgar Stevens in my kitchen. Please send an ambulance."

She knew her address would go out on the radio with the ten code for shots fired, so she immediately called Woody so he wouldn't freak out when he heard it. She'd seen the missed call and the voice mail.

"Don't rush," she said when he answered. "I've got Doc Stevens here in the kitchen." She looked down at the murderer bleeding all over the tile. "But he's not going anywhere."

Woody spewed forth a few colorful exclamations and then told her he was nearly there.

She pressed END and returned her focus to the doctor. "Now, about that video …"

"There's no video," he screamed. "My phone was ruined in the explosion. Now help me. I'm *dying*." His voice was that of a bully used to getting his own way.

"Oh, I'll help you all right." She took aim at his chest. "I'll help you the same way you helped all those other women."

Bad to the Bone began to play.

She punched the speaker icon.

"Don't kill him, Ken." Woody's voice sounded a little more normal. "Like you said, he's not going anyplace."

"But what if he beats the charges somehow?"

The Mercury slid into the driveway.

She pressed END and backed up to the door leading into the garage. Without taking her eyes off the doctor, she reached in and flipped the switch to open the overhead.

Woody burst inside, grabbed her face in his palms and looked her in the eye as if to prove to himself that she was truly all right.

"Don't worry." She lowered the hammer on her .38. "I've called the paramedics."

Woody leaned over the doctor and frisked him for weapons. He pulled something from the inside pocket of the doctor's fleece lined jacket. Then he began pulling open drawers until he found a stack of clean dishtowels. He slapped them down beside the doctor.

"These won't do, you idiot," the doc bellowed. "I need a tourniquet!" Woody handed Kendra the envelope he'd taken from the doctor's jacket, and then he took off his own belt and worked it under and around the doc's upper thigh. "Shot him in the femur, huh?"

Kendra shrugged. "Thought it was appropriate. His scalpel is on the floor. Be sure to bag it for evidence."

The doctor didn't say a word. He was too preoccupied with tightening the belt around his leg.

"Do you think he looks pale?" Kendra asked.

Woody nodded. "Definitely. Good thing you called the paramedics already. Hope he doesn't bleed out." He stood and looked down at the man who had caused so much pain and suffering.

"Attempted murder," the doc mumbled. "Sue you. Attempted murder." His voice trailed off.

Kendra looked into the envelope. "Airline tickets," she said. "From Mexico City to San Pedro Sula, Honduras."

Woody laughed. "You're kidding me, right?"

Shaking her head, Kendra held them up for him to see.

Woody stared at the man in disgust. "Murder capital of the entire world. That's pathetic. Honduras matched the coordinates he carved on his own wife's femur." He glanced at Kendra. "By the way, we found the bunker. Found the pictures on the wall, the door blown off its hinges, blood on the floor, everything just the way you described it."

He took the .38 from her hand. "Seventeen D was the clue we needed. It was seventeen steps toward dawn— toward the east—from the previous set of remains. We would have found it, eventually—Turk located your hoodie string, by the way—but the doc *telling* you just sped up the process. Can't believe he was that stupid."

Kendra removed the cylinder from her weapon and laid it on the counter. "He was so certain I'd be dead; he just couldn't resist telling me how he'd outsmarted everyone." She resisted the urge to do even more damage to the man on the floor. "Wonder how he was planning to get to Mexico City?"

"Good question. I'm sure he thought he had it all figured out." He stopped speaking when the doctor fell over on his side.

Sirens reached their ears.

"Wow," Kendra said. "They made good time."

Woody began documenting everything with his cell phone camera.

Kendra stepped around the doctor and started toward the living room to lie down. All the fight had gone out of her. "Hey, Woods…" She stopped in the doorway.

"Yeah, boss?"

"What about that sapphire ring?"

"You were right. It belonged to Dawn, the dog walker. The sis said it was the only thing they had left of their mother."

"I knew there was something special about that ring."

The doctor made a strangled sound, and his hands fell away from his shattered leg.

"Time for CPR?" Kendra asked.

Woody shook his head. "Still breathing. Believe me, if he stops, I'll start."

She sighed. "Do you think some people are born evil? Or does society make them that way?"

"The old nature versus nurture question?" Woody winked. "That's one we'll have to discuss over drinks when this is all over."

Kendra smiled an exhausted smile. "I know a little place in Kansas that makes a hell of a nice White Russian."

Woody raised one eyebrow. "There's a great Holiday Inn nearby, too. If I recall correctly." He picked up her revolver just as the paramedics rushed in through the still open garage. A sheriff's deputy was right behind them.

"I'm putting your .38 into an evidence bag, Ken."

"Don't forget the scalpel," she replied.

The paramedics immediately cut away the doctor's pant leg to see the extent of the wound. They were momentarily shocked at what they saw.

"Detective." The deputy stared down at the doctor's injured leg. "You might want to see this."

Woody leaned over the paramedics shoulder. "Are those tattoos?"

The deputy nodded. "They look very similar to the bone carvings, don't they?"

Woody whistled a single, long, note. "Sort of like a road map to burial sites. Wonder if he has any on the other leg?"

The EMT quickly cut away the other pant leg to reveal several more tats and a nest of twisted scars.

"Well, I'll be damned." Woody took out his cell phone and clicked several more pictures. "There are way more than the three we've found."

Kendra spoke up from the doorway. "Those plus the pictures from the bunker should help us find the rest of the victims." All at once she had to know if she was in any of those pictures. "Hey…"

He looked up.

"Am I in any of those bunker photos?"

He shook his head. "All skeletal."

Kendra breathed a sigh of relief.

The paramedics started an IV and loaded the doc onto the gurney. Woody made certain he was properly restrained—even though he was barely conscious—and in another minute they were out the door.

Sheriff Puckett arrived as they were loading him into the ambulance.

The sheriff stopped them so he could have a quick look. "I heard you took off the end of his nose." He glanced up at Kendra, who had joined Woody on the snowy drive nearby.

She nodded. "Do what you have to, right? Take a look at the self-tats on his upper thighs."

The sheriff's eyes grew wide as he leaned in closer. "Are those map coordinates?"

"Yep." Kendra leaned against Woody. "And he had airline tickets in his pocket—destination, San Pedro Sula, Honduras."

The sheriff took off his hat and mopped at his forehead with his handkerchief. "Now I've seen everything. Go ahead, boys. Load him up." He turned to his deputy. "Don't let him out of your sight for a minute."

"You can count on me," the deputy said.

And then they pulled out of the drive, the deputy leading the way.

In a moment, the ambulance turned on its lights and siren.

The three left standing in the drive were surprised to see Rory's Taurus coming toward them.

Sheriff Puckett stood aside as it whirled into the drive, and Carrie tumbled out and rushed toward her mother.

"Mom! Oh, thank God! I saw the ambulance leaving, and I thought..." She trailed off and wiped her eyes. "How am I going to go home when these things keep happening to you?"

Kendra hugged her. "Nothing to worry about. I promise nothing else will happen. It's all over now."

Woody patted her shoulder. "Trust me, I will be here to make certain of that. This is going to be my new home for a while. It's only a half-hour drive to Pine River. And I have a lot of unused vacation time."

Carrie broke down and allowed Kendra to usher her toward the porch. "I'm so glad you're okay. I thought it was starting all over."

"Nope, it's finally the end of this nightmare."

Carrie looked at her in confusion. "You mean the killer was still alive? He was here?"

Kendra nodded. "He was a crafty one all right. But he's definitely out of commission now."

Carrie grabbed her belly and sat down on the top step. "Oh, my." A look of amazement crossed her face.

"Honey?" Rory hurried over and sat down beside her. "Is it the baby? Are you having contractions?"

Carrie looked up at her husband. "Maybe, but it's too early."

Woody said, "We'll go in my car. Rory, the two of you get in the back seat. Ken, you can ride in front. We're going to the hospital just in case."

Kendra looked at Sheriff Puckett. "Is it all right if I leave?"

He nodded. "I'll wait here for Cranky Lois and then I'll meet you at the station later." He shook his head as if he dreaded seeing the M.E. again. "Detective James, I've got your cell number in case I need either of you."

Woody nodded.

Kendra laid a hand on the sheriff's arm. "He was already here when Willa brought me home. I think he'd been staying here—" she stopped in midsentence. "I forgot about Wills. She'll be back with the groceries any minute now."

"I'm calling her," Carrie said. "Go on with the story, Mom."

Kendra quickly told Sheriff Puckett everything that had happened, and Woody handed over the evidence bags and forwarded the crime scene pictures to the sheriff's phone.

"Good work, you two. I'm just glad he didn't add anyone else to his burial wheel." He glanced at Carrie. "Now, go on and take care of this one, I'll be in touch."

Woody stepped back inside and picked up Kendra's purse and jacket.

"Guess I'm going to have to start calling him boss, huh?" She indicated Woody with a nod of her head. "I'm gone for a few weeks, and he steps up and takes over."

The sheriff laid a broad hand on her back. "Sure glad you're all right," he said. "I was hoping you might think about coming to work for us full time."

Kendra gazed at the big man, astonishment lighting her face. "You know, I think I might like that." She let her gaze travel around the picturesque setting. "The people of Stutter Creek took me in when I needed it. And Copper Lake has been a real balm—except for that one minor incident, of course." She smiled to show she was being facetious, and then she glanced up at Woody. "Besides, there are rules against fraternization between coworkers at the Pine River S.O." She leaned into her old partner, and he pulled her close. "One of us was going to have to transfer anyway."

From the backseat of the Mercury, Carrie called out, "Mom? I think I'm having another contraction."

Kendra looked heavenward. "Please, let it be a false alarm. I'm not sure I'm ready to become a grandmother just yet."

Woody grinned and looped his arm around her shoulders. "Sure you are. I'm calling Keith right now, just in case. Maybe we can catch them before they get too far away."

Kendra hugged him tightly. "Thanks, Woods. You think of everything."

The End

ABOUT THE AUTHOR

 Ann lives in Texas with her husband and rescue pets. She loves libraries and book stores and owns two e-readers just for fun. Ann writes what she likes to read. This is not her first foray into horror – almost everything she writes has a kernel of darkness at its heart. Check out her short fiction, *Chems, Lips, Coldspot,* and *The Fee.* Those are a few of her short, speculative works.

Takers is her first novel length horror story for 5 Prince Books.

Her Romantic Suspense series (5 Prince Books) consists of: Book One, *Stutter Creek,* and Book Two, *Lilac Lane*. Book Three, *Copper Lake,* will be out soon. Her other book for 5 Prince Publishing is *All For Love*, a women's novel of heartache and hope. It, too, is built around a kernel of darkness.

Ann's paranormal book series centers around a couple of teenage ghost-magnets: *Stevie-girl and the Phantom Pilot, Stevie-girl and The Phantom Student,* and *Stevie-girl* and *The Phantom of Crybaby Bridge.*

Her most recent short story, *Sleepaway Pounds*, won first place in a short-story contest. It is included in the anthology, *Seasonal, Sweet, and Suspenseful*.

Public contact information of Author

Click STAY-UP-TO-DATE at Amazon Central to be notified when new books are released:
http://tinyurl.com/6wl3oe2

5 Prince Books:
http://www.5princebooks.com/annswann.html
Blog: www.annswann.blogspot.com
Facebook:
www.facebook.com/annswann.authorfanpage
Twitter: @ann_swann
Email: swannann76@yahoo.com
Goodreads: http://tinyurl.com/6vuw7vl

LILAC LANE (buy links) - Suspense ~ New Release

Ella and son escaped her ex's drunken wrath once.
Now he's out of jail. Can they survive another round?"

Here's a really brief snippet from *Lilac Lane:*

He shattered the old wooden door from the inside with
one well-placed kick from his size twelve boot.

The chair was still beneath the knob, but the top panel
of the door had splintered. In the moonlight coming
through the kitchen window, Ella could see his massive
silhouette.

With another kick, the entire door disintegrated. Shards
of wood flew in all directions. The red kitchen chair went
scooting across the floor until it hit a piece of debris and
flipped over on its side.

Amazon   **http://tinyurl.com/qf2makb**
iTunes   http://bit.ly/1z7ArgW
Barnes and Noble   http://bit.ly/WJt2H1
Smashwords   http://bit.ly/WJt8yf
http://www.5Princebooks.com

ARe http://bit.ly/1lzgV4S

Soul Gardener, was originally published in *Timeless,* an anthology of paranormal love stories. She has also published short fiction in *The Alfred Hitchcock Mystery Magazine, The Binnacle*, *The Rusty Nail*, and several local magazines and anthologies. She also has an apocalyptic horror novel coming out in 2015.

Books from 5 Prince Publishing

www.5princebooks.com

Grace After the Storm Sandy Sinnett

Abandoned Soul *Doug Simpson*

Throne of Jelzicar/Warriors of Gravenlea S.D. Galloway

Fatal Desire Christina OW

Unwrap the Romance Anthology

An Ill Wind James P. Hanley

Stargazing Bernadette Marie

The Grand Dissolute Joel Van Valin

Old Amarillo Sara Barnard

Nobody's Business M.J. Kane

Walker Pride Bernadette Marie

Reasons Box Set Lisa J. Hobman

A Secret to Keep Railyn Stone

The Three Wives of Adam Monroe Bernadette Marie

How to find Happiness Lindsay Harper

The Dacque Chronicles Doug Simpson

Redemption Series Melynda Price

An Everlasting Heart Series Sara Barnard

Fatal Obsession Christina OW

The Doom of Undal Katrina Sisowath

The Escape Clause Bernadette Marie

Permanent Spring Showers Scott Southard

Reasons to Stay Lisa Hobman

Wings Pete Abela

Reasons to Leave Lisa Hobman

Love Finds its Way Wilhelmina Stolen

The Paper Masque Jessica Dall

The Silver Unicorn Wayne Orr

The Merger Bernadette Marie

Lessons from a Two Year Old Pete Abela

Christmas Presence Lisa J Hobman

The Copper Rebellion Jessica Dall

The Christmas Tree Guy Railyn Stone

The Calling Jim Hanley